PRETEND YOU DON'T SEE HER

THE INVISIBLE WOMAN

KANDISHA PRESS 2025 WOMEN IN HORROR ANTHOLOGY

EDITED BY JILL GIRARDI AND LYDIA PRIME

FOREWORD BY CANDACE NOLA

© **2025 KANDISHA PRESS**

All Rights Reserved by the Individual Author. No part of this book may be reproduced in any form without permission from the Publisher or the Author(s), except as permitted by U.S. Copyright Law.

TABLE OF CONTENTS

FOREWORD ………………………………………………7
YOU GOT ME, BABE Emma Rose Darcy………….. 9
AFTERBIRTH Charlotte Brookins …………………. 24
HER BLACK VELVET BONES Ruthann Jagge…. 33
MANTRA Sally Darling……………………………….. 46
SELKIE'S STEW Lauren Lee Smith ……………….61
QUID PRO QUO Dawn DeBraal………………………. 68
THE SCREAM Anne Wilkins……………………………. 83
STAR MOUTH Meg Hafdahl ………………………….. 94
REMOTE CONTROL Allison Cellura ………………104
THE BALLAD OF FAT AMY Mocha Pennington 121
A TWIST OF FATE Trish Wilson…………………….136
ALWAYS IN MY EAR Sonora Taylor………………. 147
XOLO Carmen Baca……………………………………164
THE WAITRESS Brooklyn Ann Butler……………. 180
THE PAINTED MAN Jen Mierisch …………………192
KARMA AND CAMILE Candy Madonna ………. 208
SHAHMARAN Eva Roslin ……………………………. 219
CARLA'S CURIOSITIES Nora B. Peevy ………….233
IN THE BLOOD WE LIVE Nicole M. Wolverton 244
HOME TO ROOST Valerie B. Williams……………257
VEGETABLE LOVE Lillie Franks…………………… 274
AUTHOR BIOS ……………………………………….288

ABOUT THE EDITORS	297
ABOUT THE FOREWORD AUTHOR	298
KANDISHA PRESS BOOKS	299

FOREWORD

Hello Readers,

I've been a fan of Kandisha Press for quite a while now and absolutely every title they've published has been packed full of incredible talent, voices, and stories. This one, PRETEND YOU DON'T SEE HER, may be the best one yet. I do not say that lightly, nor dismiss any title that has come before, but I do mean to say that this one hits different. Perhaps it's the global climate at this particular moment in time, maybe it's the horrific news that we are faced with every time we open a screen, any screen, or maybe it's the sheer exhaustion of simply being a woman.

What do I mean? If you are a woman, from any walk of life, then you already know. The authors that grace this anthology have given birth to stories that scream in capital letters of exhaustion, pain, rage, and injustice. These are stories that demand your attention. Stories that command you to sit down, shut up, and pay attention, especially those readers that need to hear it the most. Stories that are beautifully written, eloquent, and creative.

Within these pages you will journey through loss, heartbreak, rejection, disappointment, betrayal, and abuse at every turn; enough to make your blood boil, to make your heart pound in rage, to make you seethe in anger, just as the characters in these stories do. And just when you think you will take up a torch and pitchfork and find a way into the book to dish out your own brand of justice, these ladies merely smirk at you, give you a wink, and show you how it's done.

Their words are intelligent, furious poetry bleeding across pages steeped in truth, emotion, and a reclaiming of self. These stories, while being everything that you want a horror story to be, are also snapshots of real women speaking their truth, finding their courage, and becoming empowered. As the phoenix will rise from the ashes, so too, do these women, time and time again.

I'll leave you with this final statement: to these incredibly talented authors, to any woman that has suffered in silence, that has endured more than their fair share, that has had to claw their way up from the bottom of the abyss just to survive one more day, and to every woman still suffering, I see you.

Thank you to these authors for this exquisitely written anthology. Thank you to Kandisha Press for standing up for women of every background, for seeing every voice, and for recognizing our worth. I applaud you.

Candace Nola,
Uncomfortably Dark Horror
July, 2025

YOU GOT ME, BABE
Emma Rose Darcy

As far as any of us knew, we all had a great time at Meg's 30th. Call it arrested development, Peter Pan syndrome, whatever you want; with none of us married or with kids to get back home to, we were free to be as wild as we wanted all night long.

We started at the Nag's Head and our impulse pub crawl took us all the way to the Slaughtered Lamb. Somewhere along the way, we lost Johnny and it didn't seem like that big of a deal at the time. We were all adults and he was more than capable of looking after himself. Jessica said she had seen him chatting to a rando at the end of the bar, but she couldn't remember which one. All of our memories got a little hazy in the middle there. We started to worry when he still hadn't surfaced for a week, then two. He wasn't answering his phone, hadn't been posting to any of his social media. Meg even called his boss and they hadn't heard from him either and had been about to fire him. Now they were wondering if maybe a call to the police wasn't in order instead.

Johnny had fallen off the face of the earth.

*****

The police informed us that he was at home. That was strange, because we had knocked on his door and no one answered. The place looked abandoned. Overgrown grass almost obscured the full-to-overflowing bins. Dark windows peered out at us like blackened eyes. The mailbox slot was blocked with mail, and further soggy mail had congealed in a lump on the ground. Johnny had never been what could be termed a homemaker before, but this was still a conspicuous fall in standards.

I knocked on the front door and Meg went around the back, lifting her wedge-heeled feet through the long grass like a crane. If someone had been home, we would have seen them. It's not that big of a place. Yet, the police were adamant. They had spoken to him. It wasn't their business if he went to work or not. He didn't seem like he was in any immediate danger.

There was a long pause before the officer added, "You might want to try reaching out to him again, though. It seems like he's going through something. He might need his support network but is afraid to reach out. Men often feel like they have to go it alone when they're suffering."

I decided that I would go back to his house, alone. While we were all worried about him, I thought it might be less confronting for one friend to rock up at his place than the whole lot of us at once. I didn't want to show up unannounced so I sent a text to say I was on my way. Like all of the others I had sent since Meg's birthday, it remained unread.

*****

This time when I knocked on the door, I didn't stop. If he could open the door for the police, he could open the door for me. For a long time, there was no sign that there was life in the house at all, but right when I was on the verge of giving up I heard a heavy tread and a hand on the doorknob.

"Po?" Johnny squinted out at me, "What are you doing here? What time is it?"

"Can I come in?"

"It isn't really a good time." He leaned across the aperture of the doorway, blocking me from seeing inside. I could smell him from where I stood. I couldn't be sure but I was fairly certain he was still wearing the same clothes he had worn to Meg's party. They looked like they could stand up without him. His eyes darted all around me, lighting on my face, my shoes, the drive behind me. He had clearly lost weight, like some sort of foul-smelling garbage wraith. His hair had matted into one chunky dreadlock on the side of his head, full of dandruff and food crumbs from where he must have been dragging his hand through it.

Funnily enough, his hands were the only clean part of him, although that might have been down to how he kept nervously scraping and rubbing them down the front of his shirt or on the thighs of his jeans.

"Johnny, are you on something right now?"

"What?" He let out a short disbelieving bark of laughter, "Are you kidding? You know I don't... I'm not into... Jesus, Po, you'd better just come in." He stood aside and allowed me to slide in through the crack in the door. I had to hold my breath as I squeezed my body past his, trying not to touch him. The smell was like a physical presence, and my eyes watered.

"We have to be quiet, though, OK?" He muttered, "We have to be quick and we have to be quiet. This is a bad time. You came at a bad time."

The house was dark inside as if the sunlight couldn't penetrate the gloom. Underfoot, the carpet was crunchy or tacky in places. A minefield of abandoned bowls of cereal and canned spaghetti lay between the living room and the kitchen.

"I haven't had time to clean up much," Johnny said, apologetic, but also a little surprised as if he was just noticing how bad things had gotten. Like he really hadn't been aware of things sliding. He raised a hand to his head and I saw him flinch as his fingers got stuck and pulled in the tangled hair. "Shit," he muttered.

"What have you been up to?" I asked, trying to keep my voice neutral.

"I've been working."

"Oh, OK." I tried to think of how to approach this in a non-confrontational way. "It's just that your boss said you haven't been coming in to work."

"What?" Johnny looked at me like I was crazy, "Not *that*. I've been working. Writing. A book."

The thought of Johnny writing a book was incredible to me. I couldn't even answer. It wasn't that he was a dumb guy or anything. He was smart and funny, but he was outdoorsy. I remembered one time we all went away together for a holiday to the seaside, and he couldn't believe I'd brought a book to the cabin; he had activities planned for the entire time we were there, day or night. He just needed a roof over his head so he could have fun abseiling or surfing on weekends. I couldn't remember the last time I'd even seen him with a book. Now he was writing one?

"Sorry, you're writing a book?"

"Yeah."

"Since when?"

"Since..." He cleared his throat, "since Meg's bash. I guess I had an idea when we were at the Howlin' Banshee and I couldn't get it out of my head. I had to get it down on paper, you know. And I just haven't stopped since." His eyes looked wide. Frightened.

"What's it about?"

"Po, really, it's not a good time. I'll tell you all about it when it's finished. You might even get to read it, if it's any good." He gave me a little humourless laugh. There was a sound, a creaking floorboard in another room, and he went rigid. Deathly pale, he motioned for me to stay quiet. A few moments passed and there were no more sounds. His shoulders relaxed.

"Is there someone else here?"

"Just my girlfriend." Johnny said absently, as if the information that he suddenly had a girlfriend wasn't a huge shock, "She's sleeping, I don't want to wake her."

"It's the middle of the day."

12

"She keeps different hours. You know how it is," he whispered, and mimed again for me to lower my voice.

"How long have you had a girlfriend? You didn't mention anyone at Meg's party?"

"Well, that's when we met," Johnny said. "We met on the crawl. She was going through a bad breakup, sort of hiding from her ex. Avoiding him, you know, and we tucked ourselves away in a booth and started talking. We got talking about... it doesn't matter. She sort of ended up tagging along with us, and when I went home she came with me."

I rocked back on my heels. "And she's been here with you this entire time?"

"She's been helping me with the book. Keeping me motivated." His voice changed pitch, taking on a peculiar energy it had been missing in the conversation so far, but it only made me uncomfortable. He was too excited now, He sounded weird, feverish. "I'm so close to finishing it now. She knows how important it is. None of the other stuff matters. Once it's all over no one will care if there's a few dirty bowls in the sink."

"Can I see the book?" I asked. "Please?"

"Oh," Johnny's eyes rolled in his head, torn. "No. I don't know. It's not ready." He half turned and looked behind him. "It's in my room and I don't want to go in there. She's sleeping."

"Don't you want me to meet your girlfriend? I'm sure she's lovely."

"No!" Johnny gasped, horrifying both of us with the way his hands clamped around his own throat to stifle his shout. "No, you can't. You can't talk to her. You can't see the book. You have to go, Po." He was crying, the tears leaving dirty tracks down his cheeks like he was wearing mascara. I took a step back and, because I wasn't looking where I was going, I knocked over a messy stack of bowls with their spoons still in them and the whole mess went clattering over. Johnny howled in anguish as if the noise hurt him, and I heard the sound of a body thumping to the floor in the bedroom.

"Oh God," He sobbed, "She's awake."

"Help me, please." A tiny voice called out, plaintive and wounded. Johnny looked as confused as I was, and he watched me walk past him to the back of the house with a look of total befuddlement, his pathetic filthy body bowed with confusion and exhaustion.

I found her in the bedroom, which was even bleaker than the living room, the bare mattress grey and ripped, showing tufts of wadding inside. It had the dents of two sleeping bodies in it, grimy silhouettes from head to feet. There was dirty clothing scattered everywhere and from the ceiling a naked light bulb swung, covered in dirt. When I flicked the switch, nothing happened. By the window there was a TV tray and a chair. A stack of notebooks and a handful of chewed pens tumbled from the tray to the floor and went every which way.

On the floor down the side of the bed, hugging the wall, was a frightened young woman staring at me with huge blue eyes. Her ratty blonde hair was tied up in a messy bun in such a way that suggested that the scrunchie was now a permanent fixture. I couldn't understand how this level of despair had happened in less than a month if there were no drugs involved, but I couldn't see any paraphernalia around, no lighters or bags of pills or powder. I couldn't even see any bottles around to show they'd been drinking. Neither the woman nor Johnny had any marks on their arms. Whatever misery they were inflicting on each other was purely psychological.

"Please help me," the woman wept, crawling into my arms like a little lost cat. "He won't let me go."

I had no idea what to do. She felt like a little bag of bird bones. I was worried I'd break her if I squeezed too hard. A selfish little thought flickered in the back of my head, where I fleetingly regretted coming to look for Johnny, and I wished I'd left him to it, or let Meg deal with it like she'd offered to. This could have been her problem. Then the woman looked up at me, sniffling, and the thought went away.

"What's your name?" I asked.

"Beatrice."

"Johnny, what the hell is going on here?" I raged at him as I helped her walk through the living room, her little body flinching into me, away from him. He gawked at me as if I was dragging a live fire-breathing dragon through his house.

"Po, no. You don't understand, it's all her!"

"What kind of idiot do you take me for? She's barely five feet tall and you expect me to believe"

"Po, I'm telling you, she's dangerous. You have to let her go. Don't let her follow you home!"

"I'm not taking her home, I'm taking her to the hospital. God, the state you're both in, you should go, too. And then talk to someone. I mean it, you need help."

"She's not right, Po. There's something wrong with her. I'm telling you, you're in danger." Johnny was pleading with me, hands outstretched, "But please don't take her. I haven't finished my book yet."

*****

It was only much later that night, when Beatrice was asleep that a flicker of doubt crept into my mind. It was still bothering me that we hadn't actually gone to the hospital, but Beatrice had begged me. She was frightened her violent ex-boyfriend was still looking for her, and that he would be watching the E-Rs. *Just take me back to your place,* she had insisted, *I just need a shower and some clean clothes.*

She wanted to know everything about me. After three weeks of listening to Johnny rant and rave about his novel, she was desperate for a normal conversation. I gave her a pair of my pyjamas and we sat on my couch with cups of hot chocolate. We talked for what felt like

15

hours. I felt like I was drunk. It can be like that with a new friend, when you just click. Somehow we got onto the subject of how I used to paint. Back in my uni days. Beatrice was just fascinated by it.

But I would have felt better if she had seen a doctor. I couldn't get the inside of Johnny's house out of my head, the state of the mattress they had been lying on, the sight of her huddled against the wall when I entered the bedroom. I'd never seen a couple so afraid of each other.

I doubt I got a wink of sleep all night. While Beatrice slept in my bed, I stayed on the couch, restlessly sketching drafts for paintings we had spitballed ideas for. I was eager to show Beatrice in the morning, I wanted her to be pleased. She had stoked something creative in me that years of working in an office had smothered, and I was so grateful.

*****

Beatrice looked over my sketches the next day with a critical eye that surprised me. The night before she had loved all of my ideas, and treated me like some sort of creative genius. In the cold light of day, she didn't like a single one of my drawings.

"I just think you can do better," she said, handing them back to me. I was crushed.

"I have to go to work," I said, stuffing the wad of paper in the bin, my cheeks on fire. "Feel free to help yourself to anything in the fridge. When I get home we'll talk about what you want your next steps to be."

I spent the entire day in a confused fog. It didn't help that I had stayed up all night drawing, but mostly it was that Beatrice's rejection over breakfast had hurt much more than I could have anticipated. I had bonded to her far too quickly, and it was obvious I was much more invested in the friendship than she was. I clicked away at my computer, morose, berating myself for getting too caught up in the excitement of saving this stranger. For her sake and mine, I needed to hold back.

When I got home, Beatrice was waiting for me. On the table were the sketches I had thrown in the bin. She had gotten them back out. There was clean paper, and she had gone through my closets and dug out my paints and brushes.

"Beatrice, what--"

"You can't give up just because it's hard."

"You said they were bad."

"I said you could do better." She tapped the paper. "The only way to do that is to keep going."

"I'm exhausted Beatrice," I pushed the paper away from me. "I didn't sleep at all last night, I had a terrible day at work, I just want to eat a bowl of pasta and fall asleep in front of the TV."

"No." Her voice was soft but firm.

"No?" I stared at her, agog.

"No." She pushed the paper back towards me and put a paintbrush in my hand. "You're going to get to work."

I had to admit, it felt good to paint again. I felt myself get into the swing of it and dabbed away for the rest of the evening, blind to hunger and thirst and even needing to go to the toilet, all of which hit me at once the moment I stopped and broke my concentration.

"Jesus, what time is it?"

"3 am," Beatrice said. She was behind me. Her voice had been a soft push behind me all night, keeping me going. She knew just what to say to keep me motivated, had a keen eye for colour and scale. Although, if I was to be perfectly honest, if I was asked to repeat a specific thing she'd said I couldn't actually remember...

"Get back to work." Beatrice intercepted me coming out of the bathroom, en route to the kitchen.

"Beatrice, I'm starving, I just need to grab a bite to eat and have a sleep. I can't believe I've had another late night when I have work tomorrow again. I'll get fired at this rate."

"You can sleep when you get it right." The change in her tone was shocking. I stopped in my tracks and we stared at each other in the dark of my living room, the flickering light of the TV casting crazed shadows on our faces. She softened. "I'll bring you something to eat. I just mean it would be a shame to stop now when you're making so much progress."

*****

I was deep in it, way in the zone, when the sound of hammering on the door started to distract me from the process. It was infuriating. I had the excruciating sensation that I had just been on the cusp of a major breakthrough with the piece before being interrupted, and the break in my concentration was a setback which would take hours to recover from. I looked around, dazed, and realised that I was alone. Beatrice wasn't on her usual perch on the end of the couch, she must have gone to sleep in my bed for a few hours. Usually, she watched me paint, offering advice or criticism. She knew how much her opinion mattered to me.

Another sharp blow landed on the door and I flinched. I hurried to open it, disoriented by a wave of dizziness. At some point, I'd mixed up my water glass with my brush washing glass and never gotten around to getting a clean one. How long ago was that? My tongue felt like a wad of dryer lint full of pins. Blinking took real effort, and as I opened the door the daylight seared my already watering eyes.

"Po?"

It was Johnny, and the way he looked at me rocked me to the core. It was a stunning reversal of when I had found him at his house. He had cleaned up. In fact, he looked almost like his normal self again. I stared at him, confused, unable to figure out how the change could have come about so quickly. Was it an act? Was he trying to get Beatrice back? She wasn't going to fall for such a transparent ploy.

"She's here, isn't she?" Johnny asked, his eyes flicking behind me into the darkness of my house. I felt my body moving on its own to block his view. If Beatrice didn't want to see him, he'd just have to learn to respect that. They were bad for each other.

"I warned you not to bring her back here. Weren't you going to take her to the hospital?"

"She didn't want to go," I mumbled, "She was scared of her crazy ex. She just wanted a shower and a clean set of clothes."

Johnny nodded. "That sounds familiar. Can we talk?"

"You can't come in." I hunched up, defensive, but he was shaking his head.

"I don't want to come in, Po. I don't want to be anywhere near her. You should stay away from her too. I brought something to show you."

"I'm busy, Johnny." I started to close the door.

"Writing?" He asked. I didn't care for his tone.

"Painting!" I wilted when he raised an eyebrow and nodded.

"Been in to work this week?"

"That depends," I said, "on what day it is..."

"It's Thursday."

"Oh. Then, no."

He reached into his backpack and withdrew a tattered notebook. "I have about ten of these, all full, but you only need to see one to get the idea. Here, flick through it. This is the masterpiece I was killing myself over."

The notebook was thick and crumpled, something that had been folded and bent upon itself many times. The pages were as soft as butterfly wings and just as fragile. As I turned them I wondered how they held together. Some of them had been written on and over so many times they had been scored clean through in places.

"What is it about?"

"I don't think it's about anything." A self-deprecating laugh. "I think it's just rambling, stream of consciousness, maybe, if we're being generous. One of the notebooks was just her name. On every page. I guess that was towards the end, just before you came over. One of them was words to the songs I could hear playing when she still let me listen to music, but she said it was distracting me. I couldn't see it, though, until after she was gone. I genuinely thought I was writing something incredible, that she'd unlocked some creative genius inside me that no one else could see."

"That's not fair." I was flustered, angry. "She's just a woman. What, you're going to act like she's some kind of muse, that she bewitched you? I thought you were better than that. Take some responsibility."

"I think she likes to think she's a muse." Johnny prised the notebook from my clawed hands. "But she's not. She's a vampire or a succubus or something. The more I obsessed over those notebooks and wasted away, the stronger she got. Jesus Po, what happened to you?"

"That's enough," I said, covering myself. I didn't want to hear any more. "Thank you for coming around. I'll tell Beatrice you stopped by to see how she was doing."

"Please, don't."

"I'm glad you're looking better. Whatever change you've made is working for you." I didn't hold back the venom in my tone or try to hide my disgust at how he was trying to make the awful things I had seen at his house all Beatrice's fault, as if he had been helpless. He was a grown man, for God's sake.

"Po..."

"No," I said, too loud, and we both winced. "I have to get back to work now. I'll talk to you later." And then I shut the door in his bewildered face.

*****

My house plunged back into near darkness, my watering eyes throwing crazed shapes in psychedelic colours against the walls as they tried to adjust. I wandered, stumbling slightly, into my bedroom to check on Beatrice but she wasn't there. A fluttering panic rose from my stomach. Had she heard my argument with Johnny? Was she outside with him now? Would she leave me, go back with him? I couldn't bear the thought, didn't see how I could finish my painting without her. She was the entire reason I had picked up a brush again, and without her support I was, creatively speaking, a newborn still finding its feet.

I stumbled as I turned suddenly, torn between running back to the door to chase her or hoping, desperately, that she was waiting for me in the living room. I felt weak. The colours swimming in my vision weren't going away. If anything, it was getting worse, and my ears were making a thrumming noise. I felt like I was going to faint. My thirst was intolerable. I had gotten up too fast to answer the door. When was the last time I slept?

But then, before me, around me, Beatrice. I sighed in relief and sank into her arms and perhaps for a moment passed out.

*****

The next moment that I was aware of, I was on the couch, my head on her lap as she ran her fingers deliciously through my hair. I hummed in appreciation, but that was a mistake, because once she knew I was awake she stopped.

"I love how thick you've gotten the colour in places," she murmured, and my skin tingled with the hard-won praise. I opened my eyes and I went cold as I saw, with fresh rested eyes, what I had been painting. Now I understood why I was so dizzy, and why my body was so sore.

The canvas was soaked in blood. Perhaps there had been oil paint there once, but it was hidden under layer after layer of crusted brown, almost black, where it was driest. The freshest layers were red and congealed. The floor in front of the easel was spattered and wet, my footprints easily visible in the carpet. I sat up, dizzy, as it came back to me. I had run out of paint days ago, and Beatrice had intercepted me as I was trying to leave to buy more. It had been some ridiculous hour of the night anyway and no stores would have been open. I remembered her explaining it to me, not the words, but her voice in my ear like the buzzing of a hive of bees. The press of her lukewarm hands as she took my paintbrush and gave me the knife.

Told me to get back to work.

"Oh God," I whispered. "Oh God, what have I done?"

"It's beautiful." Beatrice's fingers were back in my hair, "It's your art. It's you."

"It's monstrous."

"Art can be monstrous." Her voice was honey-soft. "Creating like this is how we draw out all the poison inside us. It is a cleansing, purging act. You're going to feel so good when this is finished, Po. So light. So empty. You'll be able to begin again as something new."

"What?" I was losing track of what she was saying. I was still so dizzy. "Like you?"

A dark chuckle, like there was a joke that I wasn't privy to. "No. Not me." Again the gentle caress of her fingers in my hair, soothing down to the nape of my neck. I still had my eyes on the canvas, so much of myself spent while I was dreaming, delirious, I thought of Johnny with his notebooks. How I had thought he was selfish, or crazy. A bubble of horror slid up my esophagus and threatened to escape my lips. "I've never been able to stay with a pet all the way to the end. We've always been interrupted. But we've had such a whirlwind time here, haven't we Po? We'll find out what comes next together."

"Why didn't you stay with Johnny?"

The fingers teasing my neck stopped. "He wasn't willing to grow as an artist." Her tone turned frosty.

"And your ex? The jealous one?" I licked my lips. "Remember, when I said I wanted to take you to the hospital? And when you met Johnny at the pub, you told him you were afraid he'd find you?"

Beatrice hummed as if she was deep in thought, lost in the memory. "Ah, yes. Rob. Now he had talent. It seemed there was nothing he wouldn't do for art. But when the time came for him to take the next step..." She drifted off for a moment, lost in a memory. "When the time came, he decided he didn't want to make the necessary sacrifices for his art when I could do just as well." She pulled her sweater aside and showed me a long jagged scar that ran across her chest from her shoulder to disappear between her breasts. "But you're not like him, Po. You don't have his ego. And unlike Johnny, you really do have a spark in you. You want to create something that is a part of you, not just churn out information. I think this is going to be really special."

I looked at her. She looked radiant. The scared, half-starved thing I had rescued from the floor of Johnny's bedroom was gone. I opened my mouth to say something but the thought disappeared as I felt the press of cold metal in my hand.

"It's time to get back to work, Po," Beatrice said.

It was time to finish the painting.

23

AFTERBIRTH
Charlotte Brookins

Mrs. Gwendolyn M. Peters was known best for two things: her talent for sniffing scintillating gossip out of even the most reserved of housewives, and her remarkable beauty. As a woman whose two children no longer needed her care at all hours of the day and whose husband had grown increasingly more fond of the inside of his office than of his wife, she learned to occupy herself without the benefit of others—with the exception of those ladies living in the surrounding households, who simply could not resist a morning walk about the neighborhood. Motherhood and marriage may have been central to their lives, but morosity certainly didn't have to be!

It was for this reason that Gwendolyn could be found trotting speedily through the neighborhood with Mrs. Elfine Armistead by her side at 5:30 in the morning under a sprinkling of rain. The two other ladies who usually joined them had neglected to meet this morning, citing the weather and a child's cough as their respective excuses.

"Fine by me if they want to lounge about like a couple of old bats!" Elfine crowed over the pattering of the rain. "I bet you my gold filling, that come next week, both of them will be moaning over how their men don't want anything to do with them anymore."

Gwendolyn found this a bit rich coming from Elfine, whose husband she was fairly certain hadn't slept in the same room as her since their second year of marriage, but she didn't voice her thoughts. After all, the first rule of gabbing was knowing when to stop, and at this point in her life, she had given up hope on understanding why beautiful women settled for the beasts they did.

"Your Delia's back in town, isn't she?" asked Elfine, switching tacks. "What is she now, eighteen? Nineteen?"

She was twenty.

"I swear, I can remember when she was just a little sprig of a kid, barely walking and talking."

Gwendolyn, too, could recall such a time, but she remembered it a bit differently than her neighbor. After all, Elfine hadn't been there for the constant wailing in the middle of the night, or for the trips to the doctor that leached funds from their savings, or to see the way Jacob looked at her after Delia had been born—but maybe it was more apt to say that he didn't look at her at all. His eyes slid over her body, his gaze no longer lingering at the curves that had since lost their novelty and gave way to ripe purple stretch marks that criss-crossed her belly.

Gwendolyn ran a manicured hand absent-mindedly across her stomach, feeling for ropes of muscle that had long since disappeared. Bobby came not long after Delia—this one an accident. She had taken one look at the squirming ball of flesh that had come out of her the first time and decided never again to create such a "gift" inside her womb, especially when the process of creation itself was already so unpleasant. But Jacob claimed he didn't like the feel of prophylactics, and getting rid of the thing was out of the question (what would the neighbors say?), so there she lay, nine months later in the same hospital, another grimy spawn plopped into her arms like a dead mouse brought by a cat wishing to please its master.

Even now, with Delia gone away to college, Bobby wrapped up in the rigors of school, and Gwendolyn's body in the best shape it could possibly be at her age, Jacob did not look at his wife the same way, the few times that he bothered to.

Gwendolyn realized she was gritting her teeth and released her jaw. If she wasn't careful, her veneer would chip away and she would have to pay to get it put on all over again. "Did you hear me, Gwen?" Elfine was looking at her expectantly.

Gwendolyn let out a tinkling laugh. "Oh, so sorry dear," she said, allowing a healthy amount of bashfulness to color her voice. "Just drifted off a bit, I suppose."

"Oh, of course you did!" responded Elfine good-naturedly. She reached one bony hand over to grip her friend's arm rather painfully. "Believe me, I've been the same way since we hired the nanny for Lizzie. It's as if the more time I have to myself, the more I get lost inside my own head!" She giggled at her own whimsy.

Lizzie was only one month old when Elfine and her husband hired a full-time nanny to take care of her. Being a woman who had birthed her first child so late in life and spent quite an amount of time bemoaning the bad luck of her seeming infertility to everyone around her, one might have thought that she would be spending as much time with the miracle baby as possible. Gwendolyn had not understood her friend's desperate desire to have a child, but this, she did understand: children were all the more enjoyable the further away they were.

"How does Jacob feel about having his little girl back at home?"

Gwendolyn increased the pace of their walk and Elfine was struggling to keep up. Her ineptitude was the sole sign that she had given birth only some weeks ago—everything else about her was perfectly normal, as if her baby had appeared out of thin air rather than sucking the life and beauty out of her for nine months. Under the overcast morning sky, her skin was smooth and without a crease, like she had ironed out any wrinkles before she left the house. The mystery of it was frustrating, especially when Gwendolyn was finding new signs of aging every day.

"He loves it, of course. You know the way he is with Delia, always doting." As far as Gwendolyn knew, Jacob had not even noticed his only daughter's return to the house. This was perhaps the only good thing about her husband's indifference—at the very least, it didn't end with her.

"Ah, yes, fathers and their daughters," said Elfine sagely. She slowed some more and Gwendolyn was forced to match her pace, lest she seem rude, but she could not hold back a little sigh of annoyance. "You know," continued Elfine, a conspiratorial glint in her eye, "with the way Lyle has been fussing over Lizzie once the nanny leaves, I would almost be worried about him forgetting about me. What with the way we wives are left *after the birth*." She let her voice drop at the last three words, as if saying an impolite phrase she was afraid someone might overhear.

"Almost?" repeated Gwendolyn, interest piqued. Elfine spoke of her state *after the birth* as though she didn't look practically the same as she had before it.

"Almost," Elfine confirmed with an impish grin. "You could say I learned a bit of a trick from an expert on the subject."

"An expert?" She was beginning to sound like a parrot. Gwendolyn clicked her nails together impatiently

"You know, someone who's done this kind of thing before."

Gwendolyn had to resist the urge to grind her teeth again. While Elfine tended to be a reliable source of neighborhood gossip, she had the bad habit of beating around the bush. "And who might that be?"

"You remember my midwife, Alma?"

She did. Alma was a short, heavyset woman who had followed Elfine around for weeks before her due date. Always tottering behind her with an armful of pillows and reminding her to, *rest, you must rest more!*

"Well, she gave me a little tidbit about how her mother kept her husband's *attention* after they had children, if you know what I mean." She wiggled two over-plucked eyebrows in a lewd manner.

"And what exactly was this tidbit?"

Elfine came to a full stop in the middle of the sidewalk this time. She scanned their surroundings conspicuously, but the only soul outside other than themselves was the Fenders' dog, yapping and straining against his chain.

Gwendolyn let her gaze wash over her neighbor's face, erratically taking in each perfect detail. No drooping earlobes, no premature jowls, not even a gray hair when Gwendolyn knew Elfine was far past the age to start having them. One of her hands had started twitching. What did Elfine know that she didn't?

Elfine laughed nervously. "Eager, are we?"

Elfine's eyes jumped back to Gwendolyn and the latter took a step back, realizing that she had gotten closer than social propriety deemed appropriate. She would have to work on that. "You just keep teasing me!" Gwendolyn tittered back. "Tell me already!" Her voice was light, but her eyes remained hardened.

Elfine seemed satisfied nonetheless. "Well, don't start judging me for this, but . . ." her voice dropped to a whisper, "*she had me eat the afterbirth.*"

Gwendolyn blinked.

Elfine looked right back at her, a timid grin on her face. "I know, I know! It sounds vile, doesn't it? But she said that her mother ate the placenta after she was born, for the extra nutrients and whatnot, and let's just say that she and her husband had *plenty* of children after their first." Although her face had colored a bit, either from embarrassment or the rising sun, there was a proud, mischievous look in Elfine's eye.

Gwendolyn stayed very still, taking in her neighbor's words. The consumption of the placenta was odd, certainly, but she was most concerned with the accuracy of the claim. Sure, Elfine looked as young and beautiful as ever, and if she took her at her word, then her newborn hadn't negatively impacted the intimacy of their marriage whatsoever. But Alma had been the one to give her this advice, and she certainly wasn't what Gwendolyn would call a sight for sore eyes. Although, Alma hadn't said that *she* tried it, but that her *mother* had. . .

"Gwenny? Are you in there?"

Gwendolyn blinked out of her stupor. "Oh, yes! Just thinking about what you said."

"I don't doubt it! You can think I'm strange all you like, but when it comes down to it, I'd do just about anything to bounce back from that baby. I mean, wouldn't you?"

*****

Gwendolyn had not left her bathroom since returning from the walk that morning. She took her shower as usual, but instead of getting dressed as she normally would after toweling off, she just stood there in front of the mirror, waiting for the steam to clear so she could look at herself. She let her eyes wander painfully over every inch of skin, making note of each flaw: the scattering of sunspots across her shoulders, the slight drooping of her face, the misshapen look of a body that had never quite returned to its peak state.

In the room next door, Delia sat at her desk, presumably working on the assortment of assignments she had been babbling on about upon her arrival. *Why,* thought Gwendolyn testily, *would she even bother to come back if she's just doing the same thing here as there?*

At least with her gone, it was almost possible to forget what had put her in her current state. Now, she was once again living in the same house as the thing that had started her down this path of mediocrity.

29

It wasn't that she missed her husband's affection—on the contrary. The majority of the time, Gwendolyn preferred it when Jacob was out of sight. When she entered into their marriage two decades ago, it had not been out of any sense of attraction. Her entire life, she never understood the desire so many of her girlfriends had for boys and their brutish tendencies, just as she still didn't understand their obsession with procreation. It seemed to her that women were far better off without the more barbaric sex, and more than once she had found herself dreaming about what it would be like to live without a man, with someone else entirely... But Gwendolyn saw how women like that were seen, how talk followed them like a servile pup dogging their heels, and she would dash it from her mind. There were many things Gwendolyn learned to tolerate in her life, but being the subject of gossip was not one of them.

In the evenings, when Jacob's blood was hot and she found herself aching to be recognized, to be desired by anyone at all; when she could close her eyes and reshape his face into something smoother, something sweeter, that was when he was most useful. But there was no help for it now.

Taking her robe from the hook on the bathroom wall and tugging it over her shoulders, Gwendolyn ran over yet again what Elfine said earlier that day.

You know, the way wives are left after the birth.

I would almost be worried about him forgetting about me.

. . . how to keep a husband's attention . . .

Gwendolyn heard people refer to the shedding of the placenta as a second birth of sorts. Her own afterbirth was long gone, discarded in whatever way the hospital had wished, but she still remembered that second labor. It had been simpler than the first, not quite as painful. But don't they say that beauty is pain?

Hadn't people said before that the afterbirth and the birth itself were nearly the same thing?

I would almost be worried about him forgetting about me.

Weren't they both made of the same flesh?

... how to keep a husband's attention . . .

Didn't they both come from inside of her?

She had me eat the afterbirth!

Pulling her robe tighter around her, Gwendolyn strode from the bathroom, through the bedroom, and into the hallway, her mind hardened with resolve. From inside the next room, she heard the scribbling of a pencil against paper in tandem with a young woman's humming voice.

Raising her left hand, the one adorned with a diamond ring, she knocked.

*****

Mr. Jacob Peters arrived home after the table had already been set, briefcase in one hand and blazer in the other. When he came through the door, Gwendolyn was sitting at the table, waiting for him. Bobby opted to eat dinner at a friend's house that night, as he typically did after school, leaving husband and wife alone together.

"Dinner?" she asked, her voice clear as a bell.

Jacob responded with a gruff thanks, dropping his jacket and briefcase in the parlor where Gwendolyn would surely have to pick them up later. For once, she didn't mind. She had made her husband his favorite supper: T-bone steak, medium rare, surrounded by a dressing of greens.

If he was surprised at the extravagance, he didn't say anything; instead, he sat without a word and began to cut in.

After a few minutes of silence broken only by the clinking of silverware against porcelain, Jacob glanced across the table at his wife's plate. "What are you eating?" Her plate was nearly identical, with a slab of meat surrounded by salad, but she did not have steak. It looked different, tougher, with the consistency of pork.

"I'm trying a new recipe from Elfine next door. Something she found in a ladies' magazine."

"Ah."

Another brief silence. And then:

"Is Delia coming down to visit soon? I thought she mentioned something about it a while ago."

Gwendolyn's knife sheared through the meat on her plate, revealing a pinkish inside. She had done her best to sear it, but one could never be entirely certain of what they were getting when trying something new.

"No, I think she's staying up at the campus a little while longer. Something about preparing for exams."

Jacob nodded and took another bite of the steak. He nodded, his eyes lighting up a bit. "You know, Gwen, this is fantastic."

From across the table, Gwendolyn smiled and met her husband's eyes, watching them soften for what felt like the first time in years. She skewered a piece of her own cut and slid it delicately off the fork and into her mouth, letting the flavors melt onto her tongue. "I suppose I'll have to remember the recipe for next time."

HER BLACK VELVET BONES
Ruthann Jagge

Liza Malvino slowly rolls her tongue over her teeth, considering the taste of dirt between them. The breeze lifts the hem of her grey skirt high enough for her to know it is, without a doubt, autumn. Brushing bits of dried moss and tattered leaves from her knees as she stands, she feels the late afternoon chill deep in her bones. Her freedom will feel shorter this time because of it. She is older and running out of time.

Raking her fingers through her hair, Liza deftly fashions a knot at the nape of her neck, using a twig to hold the style in place. Concentrating on her feet, she shuffles across the lawn to a crumbling decorative fountain. The stream trickles from the chipped concrete more slowly than Liza remembers, dribbling only slightly now. She avoids glancing at her reflection below. Splashing the cold water on her face, she slurps a handful into her mouth, and the flat taste is refreshing. Liza takes several minutes to groom herself, wiping away signs of wear and tear. Then, she slowly recites the alphabet forward and backward, carefully forming the sound of each letter with her lips and tongue.

Dog. House. Boy. Cat. Book. Sky. Dirt. Girl. Car. Like a young child, Liza repeats simple words aloud, faster, and faster, until her mind catches up to her voice.

Glancing around, the petite middle-aged woman focuses on the cluster of brick buildings on the opposite side of a busy street. The last maple leaves dance ballet in the air as vehicles approach the walkway. An impatient driver honks as she crosses, but she's oblivious. Liza forces her mind into the present, and it races with possible replies and excuses as she enters the university, where she sometimes works as a curator of rare editions for the extensive library there.

She has limited time to accomplish her tasks.

"Lovely to see you, Liza. How was your stay in Europe?" His salt-and-pepper hair is thinner. Professor Daniel McCarthy holds the door open with a dramatic flourish, then positions himself uncomfortably close to her. She slides past without looking at him, muttering her thanks.

"It was fine, Dan. I'm glad to be back." They aren't friends. She regards the paunchy man as a pest and gossip who repeatedly tries re-appropriating funds to his department, whining about how she's frequently absent for long periods. He claims her travel is unnecessary for the institution, insisting that his ancient history department could better use the resources. Liza pulls the cuffs of her tweed jacket into place before the annoying man notices her scars or the soiled fabric. The garment has seen better days.

"Damn dust. It's the season of wind and decay." Liza exaggerates her motions, flicking at invisible bits of lint, hoping to embarrass him for staring. "Well, I'm off to greet what's inevitably waiting in my office. Speak again soon." Her voice is soft, with a hint of an accent. Professor McCarthy nods dismissively, then watches as she walks down the hallway. Her flat shoes squeak, and he sniffs at the air behind her like a dog. She smells like earthworms yanked out of the ground on a rainy night.

There's something off about that bitch.

The brass hinges creak slightly as Liza pushes the small office door open. A fine layer of dust covers the surface of her unusual desk. The dark wood glows with age, and the carved dimensional figures in each corner beg for a caress. At first glance, they resemble cherubs, frolicking as represented in classical art, but if one looks closer, each of the naked bodies poses in a position suited to an advanced torture method. Running her hand gently over her favorite, Liza smiles.

"Hello, my friend, it's been a while. Shall we see what requires my attention?"

A wooden crate rests on the floor to the left of the open door, and she's eager to explore the books inside. Using the stiletto sharp point of a metal letter opener, Liza cracks through the strapping tape, pushing handfuls of packing material aside. She lifts out a book, gently blowing at residual bits clinging to the delicate red leather cover. The title delights her, and turning the pages with reverence, Liza reads a few passages aloud. She smiles.

Oh, this one will do nicely.

Contrary to belief, she purchases the scarce editions using generous private donations. Liza relies on old friends for funding when she discovers worthy additions to the university's collection. They comprise a section at the back of the library, stored under archival glass, without titles displayed. She's the sole caretaker of the archive, and viewing the books is by appointment. She unpacks several more, briefly scanning the titles and pages. They are exceptional and must be protected. Then, using a key hidden behind the frame of a painting on the wall, Liza unlocks one side of the lower desk cabinet. There's an expensive handbag inside, and she checks to ensure the cash and credit cards are intact. Opening the opposite side, she removes a shopping bag containing a few neatly folded pieces of clothing.

Satisfied, she chooses a book of particular interest and heads to the library.

As she enters, Liza nods a greeting to the engraved brass plaque on the front of the building honoring her aunt.

"The Malvino Library is made possible by the generous endowment of Doctor Orsina Malvino." She misses her terribly. After the incident that killed her father and best friends, leaving Liza devastated and alone, Aunt Orsina did her best to salvage and restore her, although that part of her life is a dim memory now.

No one glances up from their reading when she walks by, and Liza smiles knowingly, patting the book gripped under her arm. The information contained within the fragile curling pages is lethal in the right hands.

Using her office key, she unlocks the glass case at the end of the corridor and slides it into place spine first. Access to the three rows displayed within is at her discretion. Those eager for the knowledge she curates are personally known to her or carefully vetted. Running a fingertip along the top of the books, she pauses to select a slim book bound with green cloth. It has rough deckled edges, and the faded gilt title is written in an elegant Latin script.

Moving into an empty room nearby, Liza positions herself on a low stool, mindfully massaging her wrists, left then right. The damp weather causes the dead tissue of her scars to burn as if fresh again. Liza is keenly aware that her time is short and she must use it wisely. Loud voices in the hallway interrupt her studies.

"I don't think you understand. I'm not offering you an option. You will meet me this weekend. We'll spend some time getting to know each other, or you will fail my mandatory class. I'll also make damn sure your average drops like a rock, and you won't finish the semester with a passing grade." Liza recognizes Mc Carthy's voice, hissing the threat. Making herself small, she maneuvers the stool closer to the doorway.

"I can't fail. I'm on academic probation after a party got out of hand a few weeks ago. The pretty young woman with choppy blonde hair and artfully winged eyeliner sniffs back tears. "I hate you for this, but tell me where and when, and I'll be there." Liza strains to hear more, but their voices are low.

"Good. I'm confident you'll keep things between us." Daniel McCarthy squares his shoulders in victory. He smirks, tickling her arm with thick fingers, intending to take the girl's hand, but she flinches away, glaring at him in disgust. "Don't be so quick to judge, Missy. I'm quite a treat between the sheets." Laughing at his tacky joke, the creepy professor moves toward the library exit. The blonde girl is visibly upset, and her leather tote drops off her shoulder onto the floor, loudly scattering its contents. She bursts into tears when a compact shatters and beige face powder flies everywhere.

"Damn. What a mess. He's such a loser." She drops to her knees.

"Let me help." Liza scrapes the messy powder into her hand. "Are you okay? I'm Dr. Malvino." Tears have smeared the girl's eyeliner into black streaks on her face. Dabbing her cheeks with her knuckles, the pretty young woman slumps into a tearful heap.

"Penelope Stevens. Call me Penny. He's horrible! I mean, who does such things? It's so cliché and just like a fucking arrogant male. He has the power, and I need the grade. He's pulled this crap with so many girls. I guess it's my turn to play nice with the creep."

"You mean McCarthy? Has he done this before? I apologize and don't mean to be rude, but I overheard him giving you a hard time."

"Yeah. He lurks, watching and listening, and when someone is having a tough time, the jerk acts like he wants to help but expects favors in return, or the pervy Prof threatens blackmail and failure. I don't know what to do, but my parents will pull my allowance if I don't make decent grades." Liza's forehead creases. Offering her hand, she helps Penny to her feet.

"Wow. Those are gnarly. Were you in an accident?" The ragged red scars are on display, punctuated by circular dots of discolored skin from months of heavy stitches.

"Yes. There was an explosion many years ago. My father and three closest friends died violently when a business rival sabotaged our home."

"Wow. You don't look like the type to have a scary past." Penny's eyes are wide. The librarian is a plain woman wearing unstylish clothing; no one would look twice at her in a crowd. Her features are unremarkable, but her skin is smooth, almost mask-like. The young woman envies her flawless complexion. "We both have a sob story, but yours must be worse." Penny traces her finger over one of the mean scars. "I'm sorry you were hurt." Liza doesn't usually react to emotional generosity, but the girl's kindness moves her. The two women sit together silently for a minute before Liza speaks.

"It was an act of revenge against my father. He was a powerful man with many enemies, who raised me after my mother died at a young age. My friends had arrived at our home to celebrate my birthday when a bomb went off. I watched my best friend's face melt as she waved goodbye to the cab driver, who set it off. I don't know what happened next. One of my father's men carried me out of the burning house. I woke up at my aunt's, and my life changed forever."

Penny respectfully nods her attention as Liza continues.

"Aunt Orsina, my father's sister, was a gifted and renowned surgeon with a unique practice. She artfully designed and reconstructed the faces of criminals, some of the worst humans you can imagine, so they could continue to move freely in the world, doing terrible things. She also offered her services as a skilled interrogator if the price was right.

"Oh, this library is named after her, right? Orsina Malvino." Penny is impressed, and her blue eyes sparkle with curiosity.

"Yes. Aunt Orsina was an avid reader and collector and wanted her special interests available for research after she was gone. She took care of me and taught me, shall we say, her ways."

"You're a doctor too? As in education or medical?" The girl is invested in Liza now and eager to know more.

"Both. I went to school and became a surgeon like my aunt, then traveled for some time, helping with her practice. When she died, I inherited her estate and private files. After an unpleasant experience with one of her patients, not unlike what you're dealing with involving Daniel McCarthy, I left medicine for the less demanding world of academia."

The light in the hallway was fading. Penny glances at her phone, popping up suddenly.

"I hate to go, but I work a shift at a pub down the street and need to be there for Happy Hour. Thanks for the chat, Dr. Malvino. I appreciate the support." Slinging her heavy bag of books and essentials back on her shoulder, the young woman readies herself to leave.

"I'll walk out with you. Please let me know if I can help. I'm only in town briefly, but don't hesitate." Liza reaches a hand towards Penny's arm with a rare gesture of affection but notices that her fingernails aren't clean, so she quickly pulls it back.

"Will do. Have a good one. Take care." Penny winks, still young and lovely despite her thrifted clothing and makeup smudges under her eyes. Liza feels her age.

She leaves the building, intending to walk the short distance to a modest hotel she frequents when in town, but as shadows form on the pavement, the sound of an aria fills the air. Liza recognizes it, gasping in delight as the singer's voice soars. There's a local theater nearby, and the night air carries the notes high and bright.

Oh. How I've missed music.

She pauses as the sound reverberates through her body. Liza recalls her mother, Anna, a classically trained singer with long black hair. After she died, her father constantly played the operas she loved, and Liza knew them all by heart.

The simple but comfortable room is what she needs for a few hours of rest and a warm bath. It felt wonderful to soak, sinking her head below the water's surface to wash her hair. She floats, and the soapy cocoon soothes her painful joints.

She avoids glancing at her body in the steamy mirror as she dries off with a soft white towel. Liza doesn't sleep, so she uses the quiet night hours to read.

Penny Stevens is sitting on the floor, leaning against the door to her office, when Liza arrives early the following day. Her eyes are red, and a large bruise paints her right cheek shades of purple and blue. She's nibbling at dried blood caked on her lower lip. Dejection and defeat wrestle in her eyes when she looks up, embarrassed.

"What happened? Are you okay? Do you need medical attention?"

"I worked late; it was a slow night. Right before last call, McCarthy came in. He was drunk and demanded I serve him another glass of whiskey. Saying that he "owned me" and that "I needed to learn a lesson." When I refused, he called me filthy names and lunged at me over the bar. I slipped and fell, trying to avoid him, and hit my face on a crate of glasses. I guess it could have been worse. I screamed for help, and a guy doing cleanup came running. He physically threw him out. I left right away, but I was scared to go home. I've been waiting for you. I don't know what to do. He'll ruin my life for sure now."

"Go home. Clean up and relax. I'll handle Daniel McCarthy. Deny that we've talked if anyone asks." Penny doesn't argue.

"I'm grateful. I'm kind of poor, but can I buy you dinner? I'm taking a couple of days off work."

Liza smiles.

"There is something I'd enjoy. Can you get cheap seats for the production tonight? I'd love to attend an opera before I must leave."

"Yes! I get a student discount at the theater. I'll stop at the ticket office on my way home and be back around seven, then we can walk over together."

"I'll see you later, Penny." Liza closes the door to her office behind her. It's breaking her rule to associate with anyone while she's in town, but the beautiful music is too tempting.

Liza spends the day locked in her office, writing letters and checking financial accounts she keeps track of in a coded leger. There are several requests for future appointments to view the books under her care. She'd like to meet the physician from Japan, a noted surgeon. She glances at the clock on the wall; it's almost four o'clock.

40

Classes will soon be over for the day. It's time to get ready, and she's hungry.

Liza uses the small washroom connected to the office to neaten her hair, pulling it back again, but this time, she secures the knot with the silver letter opener from her desk. At the bottom of the shopping bag is a gold lipstick tube. With considerable effort, she applies it. *Damn. I'm out of practice.* Liza slides out of the skirt and jacket she wore the day before, folds them neatly into the bag, then eases a simple black velvet shift dress over her head. The smooth fabric feels good against her skin, and Liza wishes she had accessories for a night out.

Before storing the handbag back in her desk, she folds a large bill, tucking it into her left shoe. A lady should have a bit of cash on her.

Unlocking her office door, Liza slides the key into her other shoe and walks to the staff lounge, nodding to several colleagues. Daniel McCarthy is there, holding a stale doughnut in one hand while pouring sugar into a lukewarm cup of coffee—his eyes elevator up and down Liza.

"Well. This is an improvement. Someone special, Dr. Malvino?" He's focused on the neckline of her dress.

"Hi, Dan. I was hoping to catch you. I received a rare book on ancient Egypt in my shipment that I think you'd enjoy. Walk with me, and I'll give it to you." McCarthy's eyes brighten at the offer. It might be one he can read and then sell online for a profit.

"I'm interested. Let's do this." He leads the way, sipping his drink and smacking as he chews. "How long are you here? Maybe we could do dinner?"

"Not long." His coffee breath is on her neck as Liza opens the door. "This one." Liza picks up a thick book. "Take a look." McCarthy wipes his sticky hands on his pants, then plops into Liza's chair and begins thumbing through the pages. She watches as his mouth, rimmed with pastry sugar, pulls into a tight line when he swallows back bile.

"Are you joking? What in the hell kind of history book is this? You are one sick bitch!" McCarthy slams the pages shut. His face is red. "I'll have things to say about *you* at the next staff meeting."

"No, Dan. This is the *history* I'm interested in. You might say it's my area of expertise." Liza opens the book to colored photos of a human flaying in progress. "This book is one of a kind, as these are authentic procedurals using live subjects, not reenactments. Would you like to see my favorite method of torture?" Liza holds up the book, pointing to a grisly decapitation scene. Daniel McCarthy's face shines with sweat. Puffing out his chest like a mating rooster, he stands.

"I've seen enough. I knew something was wrong with you. I'll have your job for this. You were eavesdropping when I talked to that nasty Penny girl and figured you'd make me squirm. You have no idea who you're dealing with, little lady, but you'll soon find out."

"Dan. Danny. Daniel." Liza coos his name as she places the precious book on her desk, circling closer to the arrogant man. "Don't act offended. You've threatened plenty of women; why act like I'm a monster?" He can smell her ripe, unpleasant scent.

"We're finished here." McCarthy's flushes red. "You can bet the board will cut your funding. This is harassment." Liza is calm. She's gently stroking the figure in the nearest corner of her desk.

"Isn't she beautiful? You admire the pretty ones, but they bleed out the same. Sit down. NOW." Her tone made him obey, and the flustered man landed with an audible thump. "My happiest years were with Aunt Orsina. It's her money you're after. She encouraged me to be the best. She understood that being a physician, in the typical sense, was limited by rules. My aunt practiced questionable medicine on patients who were judged on the operating table by her moral code. My aunt decided their fate, using surgical skills to give them a second chance or torture them to death if she believed they were beyond redemption. She also taught me to give back or take life away on my own terms.

"I don't give a shit." McCarthy scowls at Liza but stays put.

"I have plans, so I'll be brief, although if I had the luxury of time, I'd make a fine fillet of you for my dinner." Before he can protect himself, Liza pulls the silver letter opener from her hair, taps it playfully on his nose, and then precisely slashes through the fleshy layers of his throat. His head rolls back, and the wound bubbles. She's on him, slurping and sucking, then tearing and chewing, savoring the taste of the man's body.

She hasn't eaten in a year, and Daniel McCarthy is delicious.

Stripping away his clothing, she goes for the tender bits, leaving nothing behind. Within an hour, Liza has devoured the man completely. She greedily licks a few larger bones that she's unable to grind between her teeth, then places them on a shelf, neatly arranging the remains. When she's satisfied with the display, they blend in with her eclectic collection of souvenirs and artifacts.

At seven sharp, there's a knock on the door.

"You look great but let me fix this." Penny lightly touches Liza's face with her finger. "Something was on your cheek. I'm all about this opera; you can clue me in on the way." Liza gives her office a final glance; it will be some time before she returns. If ever.

It's a quick walk to the restored building that houses a local theater group, and for a few minutes, Liza feels human again, enjoying conversation with the animated young woman. There's a crowd outside waiting to get in.

"Here's your ticket if we get separated." Penny hands her a slip of paper, but it falls through Liza's fingers. She's unable to bend them, but Penny presses the ticket into her hand, curling them around it.

Not yet. Please, not yet.

"Call me crazy, but that guy is staring at you. He's not too shabby." Penny winks, tilting her head to one side.

The man with silver hair wears an elegant suit. Tall with broad shoulders and deep-set dark eyes, he's amused at Penny's attention. He walks over to the women.

"Hello, Liza." She freezes. He locks eyes with Penny.

"Do you enjoy opera as well?" His voice is raspy.

"Not sure, but I'll give it a try. You know each other?

Liza refuses to look at him. "We do. Find our seats, and I'll be right behind you."

Penny nods, understanding her cue to leave. He takes her hand with icy fingers.

"My pleasure, Penelope." Flattered, she heads into the venue, smiling back at the couple.

"Are you ready, my dear?" Liza flinches when he grabs her elbow, quickly steering her away.

"One minute. I beg for one minute of music." The orchestra is warming up, and Liza closes her eyes. As the familiar opening notes of her mother's favorite opera ring out, he forces her to move at an unnatural pace until only night sounds remain. The man guides her through the cemetery's iron gates, past the decrepit fountain, and into a dark corner near a crumbling mausoleum. He positions Liza under the low branches of an oak tree.

"I've waited patiently for nineteen years." The handsome man shifts into something foul, made of shadows. "The next time will be your last.

"It's been worth it to continue my aunt's legacy. I loved her, and I'm not afraid of you." Liza glares at the darkness.

"When Orsina was dying, I laughed in her face as she writhed in agony. She made our deal and then offered me *you* to suffer her curse instead so that her wretched soul could be at peace. You were young, and I was feeling generous. Madame doctor served me well. I agreed to a few hours of freedom for you every year, and I've enjoyed watching you kill with the best of them, but I get hungry, too." Liza jackknifes in half when the pain begins; it's worse than ever. Her shoes split as her feet rooted firmly in the damp ground. When the muscles and nerves of Liza's arms and legs become solid, she tries to scream, but by then, her neck and throat are stiff as well. Her face contorts as the cold sets in. Flesh tears and blood drips, and her mortal body changes to stone. The torment consumes her, and he's satisfied.

"Flawless as always." The man, wearing an expensive suit, caresses the arm of the graceful marble statue guarding the Malvino family mausoleum. He reaches down to pick up a scrap of black velvet fabric lying on the ground. Bringing it to his nose, he breathes in deeply. The scent of death never gets old.

"Next year, my lovely Liza, I will finally collect the debt owed to me by Orsina, and I will feast on your black velvet bones. Finding your replacement won't be easy; you've been an exceptional sacrifice. Few would suffer as graciously." Whistling the notes of a familiar opera as he strolls out of the cemetery, he glances at the seat number on the ticket in his hand. *I will enjoy getting to know Penny.*

MANTRA
Sally Darling

Rich cream cascaded downward in a river of decadence as it melted against the roof of Amelia's mouth, coating her tongue in sinful pleasure. She rolled her eyes back, savoring the soft texture and bold flavors of her dessert. With the curtains drawn, she was free to enjoy herself in private, far from the prying eyes of passersby.

The metal of her spoon clanked as it scraped across the bottom of the ivory bowl, signaling the well had run dry. Amelia sighed to herself—the guilt of reality setting in—as she began to feel a familiar shame wash over her. How gluttonous she had been.

She closed her eyes and took a deep breath to center herself, mindfully repeating the words of her trusted mantra. "I am not my hunger. I am not my hunger."

As Amelia began her walk of shame toward the kitchen to clean up, she paused in front of the lengthwise mirror in her foyer. She frowned in bitter judgment, pinching and poking at flabs of skin. Sucking in her belly—bloated by her meal—she reassured herself. "Diet starts tomorrow."

"Todd, it's me... Amelia Dade," she said to the receptionist as she arrived at work the following morning. Amelia had worked as an assistant at the Abacus Cadabra accounting firm for going on six months. Even with the familiar routine, Todd seemed not to recall her from time to time, and today just happened to be one of those days.

"Amelia... Dade..." he said, as he typed the words into his computer. "Right. You're new here?"

Amelia smiled politely, but inside she was screaming, telling him what he should go and do to himself. She gathered the half dozen chai lattes she had picked up on the way over and headed off to distribute them.

"Amanda, you're a doll!" said Tina as she plucked the one with her name on it from the flimsy to-go tray, throwing off the delicate balance of the cardboard structure, and nearly causing the remainder of the steamy beverages to topple.

She hadn't bothered to correct Tina the first time she had goofed up her name. Instead, she had been too stunned by being acknowledged in the first place. But now, it was officially to the point where it would be awkward if she said anything at all, so she didn't. As far as Tina was concerned, she was Amanda.

She settled into her workday, sighing as she spotted the usual stack of other people's work that had piled up on her desk as if by magic. Amelia's skin began to tingle as anger and frustration set in. She took a deep breath to calm herself, repeating the words of her trusted mantra.

The familiar sensation of cold, greasy fingers slid over Amelia's shoulders, working their way up the sides of her neck. The hands attached to them began to expand and contract as they attempted to loosen the usual knots in her traps.

"Man, you're feeling extra tight this morning," said Russell Myerson, snickering to himself under his breath. Russell was one of those stereotypical office creeps who seemed to exist solely for the purpose of filling some sort of slimeball quota.

"No, really." he continued. "Something's different about you. I can't quite put my finger on it. Although I'd like to!" He paused for laughter and received none.

It was times like these when Amelia wished she kept live crickets in her pocket.

"You look good, Amelia. Real good! You've got this glow to you. And your figure..." Russell exhaled like he was blowing on something hot. "Let's just say you are really filling out that top today!"

"Is there something work-related I can help you with, Russell? I've got a lot of work to do," Amelia said, careful to wear as professional and courteous of a demeanor as she possibly could.

Russell's nostrils flared, as they always did when a woman in the office turned him down. He huffed—his pasty cheeks turning a bright pink—as he turned and stalked off toward his private office.

"A simple 'thank you for the attention' would have sufficed," he said, making sure he had the final word.

Amelia had considered reporting Russell, after the first few times he'd put his hands where they weren't invited. But it didn't take long to figure out Russell's position at the firm was as Head of Human Resources. Women seemed to come and go quickly at Abacus Cadabra, and she didn't want to become one of them.

*****

On her lunch break, Amelia plopped herself down on a bench out front of the office building. Pulling a 12-ounce smoothie bottle from her bag, she tore open a packet of ready-made protein powder mix and dumped the contents into the sludgy liquid.

She began to scroll through the apps on her phone. Her last relationship had ended rather abruptly, and Amelia was eager to get back on the horse. She clicked the icon of a bright red sacred heart covered in barbed wire and flames and logged into her Simply Insatiable account.

Amelia had tried all the dating apps, but Simply Insatiable was hands down her favorite one to use. Perfect for women like her—shy, and a little different—a childhood friend had recommended it to her years ago and it had been her go-to for romance ever since.

She clicked on her profile, second-guessing the arrangement of words laid out in her bio. Hovering, she read the sentences over and over again, pretending she was reading them as the man of her dreams, and wondering how he might perceive what was written.

The photo of a bright-eyed woman with long auburn hair, soft freckles, and a warm smile showcasing perfect teeth stared back at her. She was listed as 27 years old, living in Washington, D.C., passionate about climate change, the environment, and reproductive rights. Her profile also stated she enjoyed yoga, dancing, communing with nature, and the power of prayer, and that she was hopelessly searching for her perfect mate.

As she stared at the image, she mentally dissected minute differences between the woman in the photo and herself. Amelia had come across the picture years back and thought the two of them resembled one another similarly enough that it wouldn't garner any suspicion if she borrowed it from time to time. While some dates seemed a little underwhelmed when meeting her in person, no one ever questioned her authenticity. But then again, most men didn't seem to look too closely. If they did, they might notice her teeth weren't perfect and her eyes were actually green instead of blue.

In truth, Amelia preferred to divulge as little about her personal life as possible. Especially after what happened back in Santa Fe. These days, a girl can never be too careful. And while she hated to admit it, the hotter version of herself did tend to net Amelia more dates.

"What on earth is that gunk?" came the inquiring voice of Cassandra Miller.

"Trust me, girl, you don't want to know..." replied Amelia with a chuckle.

Crinkling her nose, Cassandra sat down next to her, reaching for the empty packet. "Cricket powder?!" she gasped, before bursting out laughing. "Man, Amelia, I was wondering how you stay so thin, but wow! I was not prepared for this at all!"

Amelia laughed too, enjoying Cassandra's company. The two of them had forged a casual kinship, bonding over their mutual dislike of Russell and his wandering hands. It was nice to have someone like Cassandra around to help keep her sanity intact.

"Hey!" said Cassandra, steering the conversation away from processed insect guts. "What happened with that guy you went out with last weekend? You two planning on seeing each other again?"

"Oh, Gene?" replied Amelia. "Let's just say he turned out to be too good to be true. I doubt I'll be seeing him again."

"Dang! Not another one. Well, honey, you're a catch. You know that right?"

A familiar ping called out from Amelia's phone. A push notification from Simply Insatiable, alerting her to a potential new match.

"You do your thing, sweetie." Cassandra stood up. "But maybe don't tell him about the bug potions. It's a little strange."

"Good call!" Amelia cracked a smile. "If guys had any idea of the things we do behind the curtain to look good for them, it would make their skin crawl."

She grinned sweetly to herself as she clicked the sacred heart icon, swiping right to accept the offer of a date.

*****

Amelia entered the dimly lit restaurant at 7:30 pm, her heart pounding in her chest as she scanned the room, half expecting her date not to have shown. She was led to a small table in the back and was just able to make out the silhouette of a dark-haired man as he stood to greet her.

"Amelia?" Will stood to introduce himself. He was tall, with a lean build and well-defined shoulders. He had a full head of dark black hair, and adorable dimples that appeared in the apples of his cheeks as he smiled bashfully.

He reached for her hand, shaking it vigorously as if he was on an awkward job interview. Nervous, he wiped his forehead with the back of his wrist as the two of them were seated.

It was clear to Amelia that he hadn't been on a date in a while, and this made her relax a little. She was no stranger to first dates and had dealt with her fair share of bad ones.

From being stood up to put down, she considered it a win when the guy at least bothered to learn her name.

Will struggled to make eye contact as he fumbled with his menu. "The lobster here is to die for!" he stated proudly. "So, how about it? My treat."

Amelia picked at the dead crustacean on her plate as the two of them sat in silence across from one another, humbled by the matching Captain Jake's bibs that had been draped over them by the wait staff.

"Ah, shit!" said Will, dropping the severed claw in his hand as he turned beet red. "As if this night couldn't get any more awkward, my ex just walked in."

Amelia couldn't help but flip her head around 180 degrees, immediately catching herself and course-correcting as she unscrewed her neck to a more socially acceptable angle. She spotted a lovely blonde woman in a flowered dress accompanied by a man. The two of them were seated on the opposite side of the room. The woman met Amelia's gaze, registering total indifference as she returned to her date.

"I think we could use something a little stronger, don't you?" Will asked.

As the two of them clinked their glasses of mezcal together, Amelia—curious—asked Will what it felt like seeing his ex-girlfriend in person.

"Honestly? It sucks. We were together for four years and now she's literally out with another guy. But then again, so am I. I mean, with a girl, that is." Will nervously wiped at the beads of sweat accumulating on his forehead. "I'm so sorry. This is weird. But hey, I'm sure you've been there, right?"

"Actually, no. I don't exactly keep in touch with any of my exes. I prefer to assume they've all just fallen off the face of the earth."

Will laughed at this, shaking his head as he picked up a hunk of his lobster shell. He proceeded to suck at the edges, slurping every last morsel from its ill-fated exoskeleton.

*****

"So, when's the wedding?!" asked Cassandra, as she stopped by Amelia's desk the following morning.

"Would this be before or after his ex-girlfriend showed up?" replied Amelia, dodging the question.

"No way!" gasped Cassandra, her eyes lighting up. "Did she cause a scene?"

"No. It was a little weird though. But I guess she just didn't feel all that threatened by me or something."

"Well, better luck with the next guy!"

"Actually,' replied Amelia, smiling to herself, "we decided to try again this weekend. I mean, it was a super awkward date for both of us. But there was just something rather sweet about him. This one's different. I just know it!"

"Know what?" asked Russell, worming his way into their conversation. "Amelia, sweet cheeks, you're looking a little frail today. Are you feeling okay?"

"I'm fine, Russell," Amelia said through gritted teeth. "But thank you for asking."

He ran the back of his cold, clammy hand along Amelia's forehead and down the apple of her cheek. "I overheard you making plans for this weekend," he said. "I could really use your help here at the office, though."

"She's busy, Russell," said Cassandra. "We both are."

"Man, that guy just doesn't know when to quit," Cassandra murmured after Russell was safely out of earshot. "Do you think we should just lure him here one weekend and murder him? Might be kind of fun."

Amelia shot Cassandra a look of complete shock as she stiffened defensively.

"Relax, goody two-shoes," Cassandra chuckled. "It's just a fantasy. I know you're way too boring and straight-laced to ever hurt anyone."

*****

Amelia and Will nervously clasped hands as they perused the exhibits of the Smithsonian Museum of Natural History. Amelia's heart palpitated in endearment, watching joy spark from Will's face as they walked through the Hall of Human Origins.

"Are you squeamish?" he whispered in her ear, playfully, as he led Amelia through the Eternal Life in Ancient Egypt exhibit. She reacted in mock surprise as they studied the practices of entombment and mummification. Just as she thought they were nearing the end, the corridor spilled open, revealing the entrance to the O. Orkin Insect Zoo.

Amelia beamed with excitement as she broke out ahead of Will, who took a few steps back to watch her. He marveled at her curious wonder.

"I had no idea a woman could be this into bugs!" Will remarked in amazement. "Most chicks I've gone out with don't even make it through the front door. Who are you, Amelia Dade?"

As they meandered through the zoo, they paused, peering inside each of the glass terrariums. One after the next, the resident insects began to panic and retreat from the front of their enclosures, desperately seeking a means of escape, hiding themselves in their lush forestation, or burrowing deep beneath dirt and peat moss.

"Strange," said Will. "I've never seen anything like this. It's like they know we're watching."

"It's time for the 2 pm Tarantula encounter!" announced the booming voice of Tricia. the Insect Handler.

Amelia and Will seated themselves alongside a group of five kids—whose parents watched from the safety of the opposite side of the room. All were instructed to remain calm and keep relatively still.

The handler brought out half a dozen Chilean Rose Hair Tarantulas, each in separate containers. One by one, she placed the tarantulas in the cupped palms of the eager children, leaving one more for Will and Amelia.

Amelia hesitated, smiling sweetly as she shook her head at Will, indicating she would not be participating. She did her best to sit calmly, slowing her breath and trying not to allow her heart rate to elevate. Feeling her flesh prickle, she closed her eyes for a moment, reciting her mantra in her mind.

Will carefully opened his palm, as Tricia gently placed a tarantula down. The female tickled his skin as it crept along his hand, investigating his wrist. Beaming, he turned to Amelia, drawing his hand closer to her and inviting her to join in on the fun.

An almost imperceptible grumble permeated through Amelia's stomach. Will hadn't noticed, but the Chilean Rose did. The tarantula began to elicit erratic behavior, rearing up on its hind legs. The handler made a move to intercept the stressed-out spider, just as the children began to scream.

One by one, each of the tarantulas began hissing and rubbing their hind legs vigorously against their posterior abdomens, ejecting tiny hairlike bristles embedded in the children's skin, causing instant rashes to break out. Two of the kids began rubbing at their stinging eyes, which only served to worsen the irritation. Tricia snatched the angry tarantula from Will's hand, further startling the spider and causing it to bite down hard. The painful sting radiated up Tricia's hand as she yowled in agony.

Will, scratching at his own inflamed wrist, looked up to find Amelia had vanished. Panic washed over him as he fled the area, leaving the frightened children to the care of their nervous parents and apologetic staff.

Afraid he had officially blown the best date he'd been on in a long time, Will scolded himself for ever thinking Amelia would be into this sort of thing. Just as he grabbed the cell phone from his back pocket, he smiled in relief as he spotted her standing in front of another exhibit, her palm pressed to the glass. An impressive specimen danced elegantly forward, pressing its front wrists against the glass to meet hers.

It was at that moment Will knew he was in trouble. He'd never fallen for anyone as quickly as he had for Amelia. Her eyes shimmered a brilliant green as she caught his gaze.

"The Zoo Manager has been calling off the hook, apologizing," said Will, as the two of them sat down to dinner. Hoping to make up for another disastrous date, he had invited Amelia over to his place with the promise of his world-famous roast chicken.

"The Handler was inexperienced, and I guess Tarantulas don't do well in large groups like that," he continued. "Someone must have made a sudden movement, and the rest was history. There's really no other explanation they can think of. But I mean, all of the animals did seem a bit… off… as if something wasn't quite right…" he trailed off. "Anyway, they've offered us free passes, but I doubt you'd ever want to go back there with me again."

"I'd love to," replied Amelia. As their souls met through their gaze, Amelia felt seen for the first time in a long time.

"Do you have any idea how beautiful your eyes are?" Will asked, as he marveled at their glowing brilliance. "Have they always been this green?"

Bashful, Amelia glanced down, unable to quell the flips in her belly. Butterflies clawed against her insides, desperate for a way out. 'So, this is what love feels like,' she thought to herself, as a wave of dread washed over her.

*****

Once in the sanctity of her own bed—a haven where the make-up could be cleared away, her hair free to be a wild mess—Amelia pored over her calendar, meticulously counting down the days before she would need to feed again. Her weight had been steadily dropping, and she knew she didn't have much time left. A faint rumbling in her stomach seemed to further solidify the point.

Pressing a hand to her abdomen, she closed her eyes, reciting her mantra. "You are not your hunger. You are not your hunger." She slowed her breathing, coaxing her heart rate to do the same, as she continued flowing through the syllables. Pausing in the stillness between the words, Amelia scoured the crevices of her mind, searching for a solution to her problem.

In a flash, the answer revealed itself. Amelia would be free to feed, and Will would never need to know her secret. Her eyes flitted open as a grin began to spread across her face.

*****

"You could really use some more protein in your diet," said Russell as he snaked his vile fingers through Amelia's freshly groomed hair. "And I've got just the thing to help!"

Doing her best to swallow the vomit rising in her throat, Amelia forced a laugh, startling Russell and confusing both Cassandra and Tina who were each within earshot of their conversation.

"Oh Russell, I never realized just how smart and clever you are!" Amelia flirted, placing a hand on his shoulder.

"Really?" replied Russell, speechless. He paused for a moment, swallowing a knot in his throat as he debated whether or not to press his luck.

Just as he began to open his mouth, Cassandra grabbed Amelia by the arm, ushering her away before Russell could say anything else scummy.

"What are you doing?" Cassandra scolded. "You know you can't encourage Russell's disgusting behavior like that."

Amelia's cheeks stung with hot blood. She had intended to keep her plan to butter up Russell a bit more discreetly.

"I just…" started Amelia, as she nervously combed her fingers through her hair, searching for an explanation. "I guess I just thought maybe he might be nicer if I wasn't so rigid. It was stupid. I was stupid. I don't know what I was thinking."

"You're damn right it was stupid! Leading on a guy like Russell is downright dangerous. And I mean this with all sincerity, so don't take it personally, hon, but you're too naive to understand how depraved Russell really is. Men like that, they prey on us for sport."

Amelia slumped her shoulders, lowering her head in shame. As Cassandra rattled off the statistics of male on female violence, Amelia closed her eyes, reciting her mantra. As the words began to fit into their places, the thoughts in her mind cleared a path forward, allowing her to think. She still had well over two weeks left before she would have to feed. Plenty of time to deal with Russell later, away from the prying eyes of those who would never understand what she was going through. Instead, she would use this time to focus on building her perfect future with Will.

"Thanks, Cass," she said, placing a hand on her shoulder. "It means the world to know I have a friend like you who cares about me."

"Hey, we've gotta look out for each other." Cassandra hugged Amelia. "And by the way, don't you have a hot date with Will planned for tonight?"

Amelia had done her best to hold onto her virtues—she was a lady, after all—but tonight, she knew they had waited long enough. The thought of being in love truly scared her. But she was already in too deep and had willfully allowed herself to fall hard.

She swallowed back the anxieties, shuddering at the internal barrage of what-ifs. 'What if he finds out, what if he leaves me, what if I wind up alone again.' Reminding herself Will would never need to know about the Russells of the world, Amelia relaxed. She finally had it all.

And so she lost herself beneath a sea of satin sheets and steamy passion. As they stared into each other's souls, visions of a perfect future danced in the background. Excited, she closed her eyes and continued falling.

*****

As they basked in the afterglow of their shared bliss, Will spooned Amelia, pulling her in close and clutching her back tightly to his chest. Closing her eyes, Amelia smiled to herself in utter contentment.

Just as she was homing in on the gentle rhythms of their slowing heartbeats, a loud and obnoxious growl rumbled through Amelia's stomach. She held her breath, tightening her diaphragm, as she willed the intrusive snarls to quiet down, praying Will hadn't noticed.

"Jeez!" Will said. "I've never heard one that loud before. You must be starving! What do you say we get dressed and go hit a drive-thru?"

Her cheeks burning red hot with embarrassment, Amelia pursed her lips tightly and shook her head in defiance. A second, far louder growl answered on her behalf as it permeated from the depths of Amelia's solar plexus. This time Will laughed, as he reached out a hand, placing it on her vulnerable and exposed belly.

She slapped his hand away, avoiding eye contact as she buried herself deep beneath the sweaty sheets.

Suddenly, every inch of her began to itch furiously as she felt the layers of her human skin begin to tear away. She closed her eyes, attempting to slow her breathing as she whispered her mantra in hurried desperation. "You are not your hunger, you are not your hunger, you are not your…" A sickening crunch echoed through her skull as her nose broke. "Hunger."

Her cheekbones stabbed through the flesh of her face, widening her skull into a triangular shape, forcing her glowing eyes away from one another as the cords behind them snapped like the cables of an elevator. Her jawline narrowed and her teeth sharpened, as discarded molars began to crumble and fall away from her mouth. The fingerlike appendages of her freshly sprouted palps swept the teeth away from her lips in a fluid motion.

"Man, what is it with you women, anyway?" Will asked playfully from above the covers. "You guys always get so weird about eating in front of us. It's really not a big deal you know. We already know you eat more than just salads. So come on Amelia, let's go get something to eat. It's not as if—"

Amelia lunged at Will with rapid precision, severing his head from his body with one clean strike, her jaws slicing through him like scissors snipping through a flower stem. Dropping the disembodied head to one side, it rolled off the bed, landing on the carpet where it made a faint, squishing thud.

She squeezed Will's body, clasping it tight to her chest, as the freshly raised spikes of her green arms punctured through his torso, pinning him to her exoskeleton with no way to escape her death grip.

Even without an intact central nervous system, the ill-fated orders had already been issued. Will's body continued to make every effort to evade Amelia as it kicked and thrashed, his arms flailing as his hands searched for a way out.

Amelia clutched him tighter and tighter to her chest as she began to wail thick drops of salted sorrow. Mucus and tears poured down her cheeks, landing on Will's shoulders, marinating him in her agony. She began to rock his headless body from side to side in a desperate attempt to cradle what was left of all she had lost.

Chastising herself for her lack of impulse control, she took a deep breath—accepting with bitter reluctance who she was—as she began to feast on Will's body from the neck down. She worked her five-pronged tongue like a meat fork, tearing chunks of flesh and bone away from his beefy neck hole before moving down toward the muscles of his well-defined shoulders. As she gorged herself, the movements of Will's body began to slow, as one quickly deadening hand made contact with her sternum in a final attempt to push her away from him. She snatched his hand, taking it in her contorted wrist, imagining what it might have been like to hold it at a wedding altar, instead of here, like this.

"Damnit, Will!" she shouted. "I loved you! We were supposed to be happy!"

Amelia's belly roared, muffling her screams of heartache. It snapped her out of her wallowing as if she had been slapped across the face. She stopped in mid-wail, staring out—at everything and nothing—before ultimately catching a glimpse of her impressive Mantis form in the mirror.

She shuddered as she sighed, placing one final kiss upon Will's hand—which had finally begun to grow still, all the fight having drained from his lifeless body—as she rolled her eyes back, returning to her feast. Sickening cracks and wet, sticky pops echoed in the air as Amelia worked her way down, dining on each panel of Will's rib cage. At that moment, Amelia thought back to their first date and wished she had thought to save the bib from Captain Jake's.

Once she had consumed Will's entire form, she sat still for a moment, her distended belly bloated and sated; her entire body swollen and stretched out to twice its normal size. One final growl spilled out through her insides as she shot her gaze 180 degrees, homing in on Will's severed head on the floor of her bedroom.

Picking the head up by its soft, black hair, she carried it to the living room to savor her dessert in peace, stopping briefly in the kitchen to collect a spoon.

As she scraped the inside of Will's skull with her utensil, she closed her eyes, torn by conflicting rushes of agony and ecstasy. She continued her lifelong internal battle as she ran her tongue along the roof of her mouth, savoring Will's unique flavor profile.

When she was finished, she headed into the kitchen where she carefully cleaned her newest bowl, scrubbing the porous finish with delicate motions. Drying it with a terry cloth hand towel, Amelia carefully stacked it on top of a set of five other similar ivory bowls before carrying each of them over to her china cabinet to join the others. Once stacked, she carefully closed the glass display door, preserving them just the way her Mother had taught her to.

"I mean it this time. Diet starts tomorrow," Amelia said as she began to recite her trusted mantra, cooling her skin and calming herself in the process.

As she worked through the words, the pinging of a text message chimed through, snapping her from her self-induced trance.

It was Russell. "U up?"

Amelia's mouth watered as it widened in a sinister grin. "On second thought," she said out loud to herself. "It's my cheat day. May as well treat myself."

SELKIE'S STEW
Lauren Lee Smith

My sealskin grows in darkness, inch by inch, creeping up my legs while I sleep. And every morning my husband cuts it back with the paring knife in the kitchen before work. But he can never get rid of it entirely.

I disgust him. He complains about the smell as he concentrates, a jelly-red tongue plugged between his teeth. But I think the grey hide is beautiful, in its own way. It carries the sweet scent of the rising tide, whispering of life, death: the collision of these two forces that allows for creation. Sometimes it makes me want to fling open the door and run out to the sea. But I hold still, and try to ignore the glimmer of delight when he slices too deep and draws blood.

An accident, he says.

He leaves me to clean up the tangle of tentacled peelings on the floor. He doesn't say goodbye as he heads to work, because I am nobody. A wraith that blends into the walls like an afterimage of a wife. I'm to be left behind in our tight little house to do all the tiny, insignificant things that women must do, but never speak of. And mostly, I prefer it this way. Left alone to tend this wild little baby and my poor legs, now exposed... raw pink, like inflamed gums and clear-wet with serum. I wrap them in gauze until the weeping slows and the bandages dry and crack like cooled sugar.

The shavings stay in a bucket on the table, for lack of anywhere else to put them until I can walk down to the sea and feed them to the crabs. Once I left the bucket by the back door and my husband's bulldog got into it. He's a nasty thing, all growls and snaps and hideously ugly from relentlessly scratching his allergic skin. It gives him a hairless, goblin sort of look, which suits his foul temperament. After he ate my skin peelings, he stared into my eyes with my own flesh caught between his yellow teeth. He knew what he had eaten and he wanted more. He sniffed around my bandages often after that day, until I clapped and hollered and sent him skulking out into the yard.

Today the baby is napping early, so I can't throw the sealskin out yet. I decide to focus on supper. *What else is there to do?* Perhaps if I make a proper stew, my husband will nod and give me a muttered, "T*hank you,"* that I'll be able to hold on to when his eyes go dark on my face. Maybe the treasured recollection of gratitude will chase out the breathless feeling inside the walls of my house, for a time.

I research the best stew recipe. I scrawl down the list of ingredients on a wrinkled slip of paper and lug the baby to the store. She cries in the cart for lollipops while I shop and passersby arch their brows with silent, condescending pity. Old women cluck their tongues and tell me to cherish every moment before they hobble out to their quiet cars where they can hear their own thoughts inside their heads. I turn away from the cart to grab a clear envelope of thyme and the baby climbs out of the restraints. I barely catch her before she falls.

When we finally get home, the house smells like rot. I've forgotten to dump the skin shavings, but there is no time now. I open the windows and hope the smell dissipates before my husband gets home. He's very sensitive to smells.

I get to work on the stew. My pot is burnished copper and thrums with heat. I work on the meal all day while the baby gurgles and shrieks at my feet, tugging at my bandages. I let her. The twinges of pain are worth it, to keep her happy. I wonder if the pain will get worse, as the

62

sealskin grows thicker and higher. Will I be able to tolerate the daily cutting forever ahead of me, for this baby's sake?

After a few hours of simmering, I taste the stew. Something is missing. I add more salt, a few slices of garlic. I stare at the congealed mass of volcanic paste and jutting bones popping beneath a thick film of rendered fat. I chew my lip. The house doesn't smell good at all, and I know my husband is going to yell. I cry a little over my pot, and tell myself it is because the stew splattered on my dressings and ignited a lick of hot pain up my leg. But my eyes are a sea of saltwater so often I barely notice anymore. It comforts me, when I can't go out my door and really swim. Little oceans behind the bones of my eyes. I can't remember the last time I went in the water.

When my husband comes home he is in a foul mood. I am careful not to say much, because the baby is loud enough for the whole world without adding in my voice. I ladle the stew into a bowl and place it in front of him. Immediately, he screws up his nose in revulsion and my stomach drops. I know it smells as awful as it looks. I itch at my dressings nervously while he takes a careful sip. He barely tastes it before the mouthful is rejected as a sticky splatter of orange saliva. I reach out to touch his shoulder, but he spins out of reach.

"Who ever heard of a wife who can't even make a simple stew? Clean it up."

The next day is my husband's work party and he has to take me or people will ask questions. He is anxious about it, and spends extra time on my legs. He forgoes the paring in favor of the long bread knife with the serrated edges. I chew my tongue as he saws, sending curls of slippery hide onto the floor. He points to a pair of knee-high boots.

"Cover your ugliness."

He expects me to obey because I always do. Why wouldn't I?

I brush out my hair, drifts of night-black waterweed laced with oyster shell grey. I'm no longer young, but I am pretty enough when I roll my shoulders back and lift my chin. My face remembers its frowns in light lines, my muscles pull downward beneath skin made rough by salt tears washing over curves of hollowed bone. I get dressed without the boots. My legs are beautiful: cross-hatched with weals of scar-like bands of shooting starlight. The air feels good on my skin and when he is not looking at me, I have courage.

My husband's eyes change as I enter the party with legs exposed, and I question my choice. But we are surrounded by people and he tucks his anger behind a cleared throat and a smile, saving it for later when we are alone and there's no chance anyone will hear him. If anyone sees a change in his eyes, they are quick to forget it. He soothes his colleagues until they are laughing, lost in his charisma. They repeat familiar stories about him to themselves and I can hear their thoughts.

What a sweet man.
So creative!
So smart and successful.

A woman's hungry eyes linger on him and she touches my arm.

You are so lucky.

My husband is silent on the car ride home until he isn't. He recognizes the flush of shame on my face as his chance.

"I'm glad you're embarrassed. You should be."

That night I dream of the sea beneath the starlit hammock of sky that holds up the moon. I dream of the ice water on my scars, the current pulling me out and away from this dusty little house. In the morning, my sealskin has crept up to my thighs and my husband curses until I have to jam my ears with my fingers to dull the sound.

"I don't have time for this," he says. When he cuts, he is not careful. He rakes the knife over me like he is fighting some wild, faceless creature washed in on the tide, something to be dragged in for supper.

He becomes the carver at the head of the table, bent-backed beneath the weight of his hatred for me. When he leaves, I cry alongside our baby and bleed on the floor.

Today the skin doesn't heal. It throbs with my pulse, and soon the bandages are stained yellow with pus. I cradle the baby on my hip and walk down to the shore. I stand with my infected legs in the water and let her play on the sand as the stinging salt burns into my flesh. I beg it to wash away the invisible prints of his fingers where he touched me.

In the afternoon, my husband appears unexpectedly early from work. His temples glisten with sweat as he totters in the doorway. I stroke his fevered forehead as I help him to his bed.

"Can I make you a stew?"

"I can't eat that slop."

I wash out my pot and start again. I add onions and tomato sauce, vegetables and spices. I taste it, but it's missing something. I add more salt and let it simmer. After an hour it still tastes off and I can't ignore the sound of restless movement from the other room.

My eyes fall on the bucket of sealskin shavings. I lift a handful into my palm, letting them wriggle like filings of my heart filtering through my hands. They're beginning to spoil, so I add a few curls to the pot. The house is immediately flooded with brine whipped off the prow of a ship, the reek of sea hares left to bake on the sand after a big swell pulls them off deep stone and hurls them onto the shore to die. My husband's ugly dog appears, scenting the air hungrily. I taste the soup. It is better, but not perfect. Not yet.

The sealskin grows without need of darkness now, itchy where it pushes up like mushroom meat through infected scabbing. I scratch at it, releasing a rain of luminous scales onto the floor. It has grown to my hips and pleasure shivers through my entire body when I squeeze my thighs. I watch a fisherman walk past the house and his stormy eyes find mine through the window glass for the barest of moments. I wonder what it would feel like to have his hands on this skin. Would he recoil in disgust? Or would he want more? All the dark, silky wet parts of me? I turn away, knowing it is impossible, and every man's touch leaves a residue that requires the sea's froth to wash away. It isn't worth it at all.

At midday, I check on my husband. I settle onto the edge of the bed, watching my husband's eyes shift as he murmurs in fitful sleep. I brush the hair out of his eyes, knowing I could leave while he's in this delirium. I could run down to the sea right now if I wanted to, splashing into the water, drinking the waves into every thirsty cell. I could dive down until my black hair becomes a cloak that hides me from this man. But my baby could not come. She is made for shallows and sunlight, not the deep and dark places of this world. I cannot leave her.

The sealskin knife is here: an innocent by the bedside. I take it into my hand, balancing its uneven weight. Then my gaze moves down past kicked blankets to where a pale ankle lies exposed, whorls of dark hair growing from barnacled pores. I rest steel teeth against skin and draw it like a violinist's bow. Gently at first, watching this sleeping face. He twists a little, crying out in his dream. Perhaps he is cutting me in it, loving every minute. I don't love this, but I must do it. It is only right to mirror the pain he has given. After all, he never thought it was real. All those carvings, he could not have realized how he hurt me. It would be cruel to keep this agony to myself.

He is lucky that he has me here to teach him.

The blade hisses against skin before sinking into the muscle. It pops through a blue vein, releasing a flood of burst cranberry across the sheets. He kicks the blade away, but not before I have a curl of pink flesh in my hand.

I walk into the kitchen and add my husband's meat to the stew pot. I swirl it around, letting the broth climb to a boil. His flesh mixes with bits of my cooked-down seal hide. As it renders, the incongruous flavors crash together: land and sea.

They don't belong together, and never have. My husband's dog hides under the table. For once, he doesn't like the smell.

But I do. I taste the stew. It's perfect.

It just needs a little more meat.

QUID PRO QUO
Dawn DeBraal

The sun's rays dappled on the surface of Lake Morehead. Charlotte was sitting comfortably in the front of the boat, and her husband, Jerry, was behind her, maneuvering the handle that steered the motor on the back while a couple on a cheap blow-up raft bobbed in front of them. Charlotte turned to warn her husband to go around them, but Jerry, with pods in his ears, was into his eighties' music. He bobbed his head while his eyes were closed, and raced along on the big lake, oblivious as to what was about to happen.

"No!" Charlotte sat up from the nightmare, letting her legs fall over the side of the bed, taking deep breaths to calm herself. All she wanted was sleep, but her mind kicked into overdrive as soon as her eyes closed.

She must bake cupcakes for the PTO, clean the house, and go grocery shopping. Her son Greg's concert was tonight, and he needed his white shirt washed and pressed. Why didn't she do all that this morning while she still had a little energy?

Leaving the bed, Charlotte shuffled down the hallway to the laundry room, where she put a load in the washer. She would go back and sleep for an hour, then transfer everything into the dryer. It was all she could do for the day, small tasks while pacing herself.

Drawing the drapes, Charlotte climbed into the unmade bed, another task she should have completed this morning. Her eyelids grew heavy, and eventually, saliva dribbled from her mouth as she changed position in the bed, throwing her leg over a pillow. She was grateful for the knowledge that, for now, she would get some rest.

The dream. Charlotte was in the boat with her husband, Jerry, who sat in the back with the throttle in his hand. She wore dark sunglasses to block the sun's blinding reflection off the water. At first, the flotation device was hard to make out as it was the same color as the water. As they got closer, she spotted the couple atop the cheap blow-up raft drifting in the lake.

"Jerry, there are people in the water ahead," she said, turning to get his attention. But Jerry had his ear pods in and was bobbing his head to "Another One Bites the Dust," and couldn't hear her. His eyes were closed, so he didn't see her.

"Jerry!" she shouted again, but it was too late. The boat ran over the couple, the motor's propeller striking and deflating the raft. Jerry's boat went airborne briefly before slamming back down on the water. That abrupt pounding upon landing was what finally garnered his attention. The couple they'd just hit screamed, floundering in the water.

"What the Hell was that?" Jerry shouted.

"Jerry, turn around. You ran over a blow-up raft. There's a couple in the water, and they are in trouble," Charlotte cried. Jerry looked behind the boat, his mouth dropping open in realization.

Instead of turning the boat around to render aid, Jerry pushed the throttle wide open, moving the boat away from the accident scene.

"What are you doing? We must help them!" Charlotte screamed at her husband. In all their twenty-five years, she had never seen him behave so irresponsibly.

"Charlotte, I've been drinking; they'll put me in jail!"

"You will go to Hell, Jerry. Is that what you want?" Charlotte squatted, walking like a duck, moved to the back of the boat where her husband was sitting, and tried to wrestle his hands away from the throttle.

"Turn around!" She shouted.

Jerry pushed her away hard enough for Charlotte to fall back onto the deck. Sitting up, she looked behind her husband but could no longer see the couple or the raft. It was

69

as if they'd never been there. Eventually, she believed it was all a bad dream or a figment of her imagination.

That was when Charlotte started to disappear. Jerry was no longer her knight in shining armor; she could only do the bare minimum to keep her family going. Greg, their son, was college-bound in a few months, and Charlotte felt she had fulfilled her obligations as a mother.

After Jerry killed the couple on Lake Morehead, she no longer wanted him. Her husband's fear of what the punishment was for driving while intoxicated, seemingly more important than human life, entrenched Jerry with the devil. Evil found its way into her home.

The nightmare always started the same way, with running over the couple. In her dream, sometimes she got Jerry to turn around to render aid, but she could only see the man's hand just below the water's surface. Charlotte would lean over the boat and pull on the hand with all her might, but the man was too heavy and would not come up from the water. She would beg her husband to help her bring the man onto the boat, to which Jerry shook his head, refusing to help her.

She would wake from the dream slathered in sweat, breathless, while her heart pounded. It hadn't happened that way, but the nightmare reinforced the fact that the accident had occurred.

Charlotte woke with a start, wiping the sweat from her forehead. She gave up on sleeping and went to the washing machine, pulling the clothes out and putting them into the dryer. The exhausted housewife slid down to the floor with her hands on her head, listening to the buttons of Greg's shirt tick against the dryer window like a metronome. Charlotte wanted to follow that rhythmic sound to sleep but couldn't go through that dream again, so she forced herself to stand.

The clock said three. Somewhere in the world, it was happy hour. Charlotte pulled a thermos cup from the cabinet, filled it with ice, and tipped the vodka bottle into the cup, capping it with the lid. She always pretended with the men in her house that she was drinking tap water, oblivious to the smell. Father and son would exchange knowing looks and say nothing.

When the dryer buzzed, Charlotte pulled Greg's shirt and hung it on a hanger in the laundry room. She wasn't about to get the ironing board out and attempt to iron it. Greg would be happy with a clean shirt; since it was permanent press, it would eventually straighten.

"Permanent press," she said, pulling the tails of the shirt down. She said that phrase three times and chuckled because it sounded silly. She tried it again, popping her p's when she said it, which made her laugh even harder.

The boys needed supper; everything was so taxing. Why did she have to do so much? The men in her life depended on her for food, housekeeping, and laundry. It was a constant, crushing grind.

She took a sip from her special cup, shivering as the vodka burned her throat on the way to her stomach. Charlotte went to set the mug on the counter but missed by a few inches. The cup of vodka crashed to the floor, spilling alcohol and broken glass. Charlotte stooped to pick up the glass but banged her head on the counter, passing out on the floor, the blood from her head wound mixing with the vodka.

"Charlotte," the voice was distant.

"Yes?" Did Jerry come home and find her on the floor, or worse, did Greg leave school early? "Help me!" she called to the voice. Through a misty fog, a fine-looking man dressed in black approached her. "Who are you?"

"Charlotte, you know who I am. The one you've been trying to avoid since the accident." He put his fingers up in air quotes when he said, "The accident."

"That wasn't my fault, it was Jerry's."

"Ahh, but you didn't call the authorities even when you had the chance." He let that sink in. "Did you ever hear the phrase 'guilt by association?'" Charlotte realized she was bobbing her head. "So, when you stopped fighting Jerry, you capitulated with him."

71

"I didn't want him to go to jail. I have no way to support Greg or myself. Besides, they found a drunk boating on the lake; he was punished, and the family had someone to blame."

"Is that what you think happened, Charlotte? Do you think your lie gave those families closure? That couple you ran over was getting married in a week. All their hopes and dreams were shattered because Jerry had too many beers out on the lake and was afraid to face his punishment. He could have saved them from drowning, and then it wouldn't be murder. It would have been operating a boat while intoxicated with personal injuries. I'm not even going to mention the man you allowed the murder to be pinned on."

"Shut up. I don't have to listen to you." Charlotte pushed herself to a seated position on the floor. The blood, the vodka, the glass—she should clean the mess before her son came home. Her arm stretched out, and she grabbed the dish towel off the stove handle and began wiping the mess on the floor. The towel quickly became saturated, rendering it useless. Charlotte burst into tears.

"I'm so tired," she cried.

"Charlotte, I can help you." The distraught housewife squinted, shaking her head, hoping to make the apparition disappear, but he was still there when she opened her eyes.

"Help me, how?" She asked.

"I will help you right the wrong Jerry caused. You will be able to sleep again."

"I want that. What should I do?"

"You must kill Jerry."

"Kill my husband? I can't do that. Greg would be destroyed, and I cannot support myself."

"I'll handle the whole thing. Your life will return to normal now, but when the time is right, I'll let you know what needs to be done."

"I want my life back. I want normal." The man snapped his fingers. Charlotte picked herself up from the floor, gasping when she saw a clean house. Dinner was in the crock pot, her floors were freshly waxed, and the laundry had been dried and put away. She moved to each room, seeing the beds had been made and everything dusted.

"Hi, Mom."

Greg!

Charlotte ran to the bathroom; her son mustn't see her bloodied forehead.

"In the bathroom, be right out," she called to her son while closing the door. Flipping the light on, Charlotte was astonished. She was dressed, wearing full makeup, her hair was styled, and there was no gash on her forehead. She blew her breath into her hand; there was no booze smell. Somehow, everything she had wanted to get done, was done. She still had time to bake the cupcakes.

"Mom, the oven timer dinged," Greg called out.

"Be right there, sweetie." Charlotte trotted down to the kitchen, turned off the oven and timer, and pulled two dozen freshly baked chocolate cupcakes to cool.

"Wow, you're getting a "Mother of the Year" award," Greg said appreciatively. Charlotte hugged him.

An hour later, Jerry came through the door. Charlotte felt nothing but loathing for the man she married, but when his eyes darted around the room and couldn't find fault with anything he saw, he looked surprised and pleased.

"It smells good, the house looks great." Charlotte beamed. She didn't get her old life back; she got better. When the cupcakes cooled, she and Greg frosted and boxed them to take to the Parent and Teacher Organization's bake sale at Greg's concert that night.

Jerry opted to stay home, and that was fine with her because Charlotte detested the man for making her suffer these nightmares. She almost told him, "This is your child's last concert," but she didn't because Charlotte would rather go with Greg alone.

For the next few months, Charlotte's life went well. The nightmares disappeared, and she slept like a baby, having the energy to be the perfect mother. Jerry and Charlotte settled on being coldly polite to one another.

And then, the fateful day arrived. Greg was packed and ready to drive himself to school. Her baby bird was leaving the nest. Charlotte stood outside watching Jerry check the fluids in Greg's car, slamming the hood. Jerry wiped his hands on a dirty rag and shook Greg's hand. How odd that he would send his son off like that. A handshake, not a hug. It was so Jerry.

"Goodbye, honey. Let us know when you get there." Charlotte stood on her tiptoes and hugged her son, now a man. *When had that happened?* She tucked a hundred-dollar bill in his shirt pocket.

"Mom, I'm okay."

"Just keep it in case of an emergency." Her smile faded when his car turned the corner, and tears slid down her cheeks. It was the end of an era and the start of something new. Charlotte couldn't put her finger on it, but the yoke of motherhood had been lifted, and she felt free for the first time in, well, never.

She walked past Jerry and into the house. What would she do without their son's buffer? Jerry was disgusting to her. Without Greg, there was no reason to pretend otherwise. She could leave, but she had no source of income. Charlotte had never worked outside the home where she was trapped.

It wasn't long after Greg left for college that the nightmare returned. Her time of peace and mental health had been taken once more. Charlotte found herself struggling again. She met up with the man in black, asking him, "Why?"

"It's time, Charlotte."

"Time, for what?" Something triggered deep within her subconsciousness. The couple on the raft, the blood, and booze covering the kitchen floor, her feeling of helplessness and giving anything to get her life back. She owed these months of sanity to the man who stood before her. "I don't want to spend my life in jail, I can't do what you ask."

"Charlotte, I would not let you go to jail. You are doing my bidding. You are my daughter, and I will protect you."

This statement hit her hard, someone being so nice to her. Charlotte's heart ached for love.

"I'll think about it." The man in black disappeared, and Charlotte began her descent into Murder 101. How could she kill her husband and get away with it?

Waxing the hall with furniture polish was a start. Jerry fell down the stairs, doing nothing but hurting his back.

"What the hell, Charlotte? Did you wax the floor with furniture polish? What were you thinking?" She apologized profusely to her husband, disappointed he didn't break his neck. The plan wasn't well thought out because she nearly suffered the same fate and spent the day stripping the floor.

After watching a cooking show, she thought of another way to send Jerry to the great beyond. Charlotte made a rich mushroom gravy to pour over his hamburger steak for supper.

"It smells delicious," Jerry said, inhaling the aroma. Jerry started to salivate in the middle of dinner; his face flushed, and tears flowed from his eyes.

"Charlotte, what is in this gravy?" He coughed a bit as the drool came from his mouth.

"Mushrooms, beef stock, corn starch."

"What kind of mushrooms?" Jerry coughed again, holding his hand over his mouth as if he were about to get sick.

"The ones growing in the woods, and all over the place. I thought you'd like fresh mushrooms."

"Are you kidding me? You have to be an expert to pick wild mushrooms; many that look like mushrooms are poisonous toadstools." Jerry left the table in a hurry, slamming the bathroom door. Charlotte could hear Jerry's body rejecting the mushrooms in every form possible. What a disappointment to see her husband leaving the bathroom with his face as white as a ghost that he, disappointingly, was not. Jerry dragged himself to bed. Charlotte was flummoxed. Jerry had survived toxic toadstool food poisoning.

75

Talking on the phone with Greg made Charlotte feel good. Her son was thriving in college and loved it. Greg asked his mother if she would mind if he stayed through the fall break. He'd been awarded a job assisting one of his professors, a huge honor for a freshman, and it paid well.

"That's fine, honey. I am so proud you were selected. We'll see you when you can come home." She was smiling when she hung up. With Greg away, she could take another whack at Jerry, who seemed to think everything was well with them, but it wasn't. After each failed attempt at her husband, the man in black gave her a reprieve from her nightmare for a short time, but as soon as the nightmare came back, she was forced into thinking of another way to take Jerry out. Greg's gift of not coming home would make the next attempt at Jerry's life occur all the sooner.

"I'm going over to Lake Morehead to run the gas out of the boat before putting it away for the winter. Today's the last nice day for a while," Jerry told her. It was late October and the perfect day to put the boat away.

"How about I pack a picnic, and we both go?" Jerry looked at Charlotte, shocked. His wife hadn't wanted to go boating since the "accident."

"That would be nice." I'll go hook up the boat." Jerry was all smiles when he left. While Charlotte made some sandwiches and threw a few beers into the cooler for Jerry. A plan formulated in her mind.

When Jerry returned to the boat after parking the truck and trailer, he pushed them off at the landing. The air was colder on the lake, and they wore their winter coats.

"This is beautiful," Charlotte said. "You can see down to the bottom of the lake. Where is the deepest part?"

"On the south end. Why do you ask?"

"I wondered if you could see the bottom in this clear water."

"It gets clearer when it's cold." Jerry turned the boat south. Charlotte spent the time looking at the lake homes.

"Do you ever wish we could have bought one of these?"

"One of what?"

"A lake home. I always wished we could have afforded one."

"Well, you wanted a kid and to stay home. We couldn't afford that on one salary." His attitude grated on Charlotte. Jerry never valued her sacrifice for him or their son. Didn't he ever think she had dreams of her own? Now, he was blaming her for not seeking a career.

"So, are you saying you wished we never had Greg?"

"Don't be so melodramatic, Charlotte. I don't like you trying to make me feel bad about not having lived on a lake. We got a damn boat, isn't that enough?"

"Yes, it is enough. Here, have a beer," Charlotte tossed him a beer along with his sandwich. Jerry stopped the boat, unwrapped the sandwich, took a huge bite, and washed it down with beer.

"I thought you said I couldn't drink anymore and drive the boat." Jerry sneered.

"Well, you can't get drunk and drive the boat. There's the difference." When they'd finished their picnic lunch, Jerry started the motor, continuing to the south end of the lake, grabbing another beer from the cooler.

"See that line of reeds right there? They grow on the edge of a drop-off. It's deep. Over thirty feet, I'd say."

"Oh, I can't see very far into the water," Charlotte said, disappointed.

"I'm going to cast a few before we head back; it's getting cold." He moved around to pull out the fishing gear. "How about you toss out the anchor?"

"Sure." Charlotte picked up the heavy anchor. It was more than the boat needed, but Jerry was cheap and made it from a three-and-a-half-pound coffee can, filled with cement and an eye bolt sticking in the middle. He added a length of chain and a nylon rope tied at the end of the short chain. Charlotte rolled the anchor over the side, holding onto the rope she tied to a cleat. Jerry came back, stepping right where she hoped he would.

"How deep?" she asked, distracting him.

"Charlotte, it's deep here. Let the whole thing out!" Jerry snapped, standing up to cast his lure. Charlotte let the anchor drop and pushed into him as hard as she could, knocking Jerry off balance. Jerry dropped the rod, and his arms cartwheeled as his center of gravity flipped him out of the boat. Before he could shout, the wrap she'd taken around his leg on the anchor rope pulled him under, but not far enough; she dropped the rest of the rope, letting it go down. Jerry tried to swim; his arms flailed in his attempt to keep his head above the water.

"Charlotte, pull the anchor up. It's wrapped around my leg. I'm gonna drown." She could tell he was panicking by the look on his face. Jerry made a valiant effort to keep his head above water, but the coffee can full of cement pulled him under. Charlotte stood there watching him and made no move to pull the anchor into the boat. She leaned over to whisper to him. The nearby fishermen didn't need to hear what she had to say.

"I hate you, Jerry. I can't think of the last time I felt anything but hatred toward you." Spittle flew from her mouth.

"Charlotte, please," her husband pleaded, resurfacing for a short breath. The anchor must have touched the bottom because Jerry was pulled under the water. Charlotte moved to the edge of the boat and could make out his hand, trying to grab at anything in the clear, cold water. At first, his hands were frantically trying to grasp, seeking purchase on anything, and then they stopped, slowly moving in a synchronized dance with the current of the water.

"Jerry!" Charlotte screamed. "Help!" The fishermen on a nearby boat pulled up anchor and motored toward their boat.

"Help me. My husband fell overboard and hasn't come up. He's wearing a heavy winter coat. Please." Charlotte was down on her knees, trying to grab Jerry's hand to pull him up. The guy in the approaching boat grabbed a dock hook and began fishing for Jerry.

"I got him," the younger man shouted and began pulling Jerry's body out of the water. When the dead man was close enough to the surface, the two men reached in and tried to haul her husband's lifeless carcass onto their boat.

"He's caught on the anchor. Cut it," the older man said. The younger man took out his filet knife and severed the nylon rope. Down went the coffee can, and up came Jerry.

"Hank, do you know CPR?"

"Yeah," the younger man was pushing down on Jerry's chest when they got him to their boat. Charlotte began to panic. What if they successfully revived her husband? She would go to jail. It occurred to her that she had an ace in her pocket. Jerry killed those people on the raft and did not render aid. This fact calmed her for a second until she remembered Jerry's capitulation accusation by the man in black, and he was right. She could have called the authorities at any time after the fact but didn't.

"Oh Jerry, please, breathe," she pleaded for the sake of looking concerned when she "accidentally" stepped off the side of the boat, creating the diversion she needed to stop the resurrection of her husband.

"Help," she shouted, floundering in the cold water between the boats. Hank stopped working on Jerry and thrust his hand toward her, which she gratefully took. The two men pulled her onto their boat, now riding low in the water, overweight in occupancy capacity.

The cops and the ambulance met them at the boat landing, responding to the fisherman's call. Despite having a blanket around her, Charlotte shivered while forced to go through the horrible story of losing her husband.

"He was drinking and wanted to fish, but he lost his footing when he threw the anchor over the side. I had no idea he had stepped through the coiled rope on the deck. He fell over the side when the anchor pulled him down. I tried to help him, but he was too heavy for me to bring up." The distressed wife melted into tears as the ambulance left them at the boat landing.

"Please, let me go to the hospital. I need to be there for my husband," Charlotte begged. She also said she couldn't drive because the boat trailer was on the truck. The fishermen offered to take her with them to the hospital. By the time Charlotte arrived, thankfully, Jerry had been pronounced dead. The hospital staff felt terrible for her and gave her some dry scrubs. She called Greg with the devastating news when she got home.

"Stay. There is nothing you can do here. Your dad and I had everything planned in our wills, and your father wanted to be cremated. We'll have a memorial service later."

*****

Charlotte was worried about what was going to happen to her. With Jerry gone, she would have to get a job, and without experience, it meant she would have to get a crappy one. She couldn't sign up for Social Security because Greg was too old, and she was too young. What kind of a world was this? Jerry's ashes had come in the mail, and she sat the box on the kitchen counter, stewing.

"What the hell, Jerry? Why didn't you provide for me?" Charlotte's question was answered when the phone rang. She took the call, recognizing their lawyer's phone number.

"Hello, Sam. I am so lost; I don't know what to do. I have never worked outside the home, and I have no skills. What? He did? How much? Are you kidding? Say it again." Charlotte gasped upon finding that Jerry had a million-dollar accidental policy on himself and had provided for her and Greg. Since the police had already deemed Jerry's death accidental, the insurance company was going to pay on the policy. The attorney waited to tell her until after everything was cleared. Charlotte nearly fainted with joy.

Charlotte had called a realtor earlier that week about selling the house because she needed the money. They'd stopped by to tour the home and give the widow a price they felt they could ask. Who would have thought their bungalow was worth so much? The "grieving" widow signed the contract, and a month later, the house was sold, and the insurance check came in.

*****

Charlotte sat on the dock of her modest lake home. The ice in her margarita melted in the sun, and she took a big swig. Laying back, the widow felt her head swimming with the heat and alcohol. Greg returned to college after they put Jerry to rest. A nice, modest send-off. Jerry didn't deserve much more than that, and she had college to pay for. Her woes had once again disappeared. Charlotte fell asleep in the chaise lounge, listening to the waves lapping on the shore.

"Charlotte," she turned and saw the man in black. "You did well. Didn't I tell you I would take care of you?" She robotically nodded, for the widow was uncomfortable seeing the shadowy figure before her again.

"I did everything you asked," she said defensively.

"You did. I am letting you know I held my end of the bargain. It seems everything turned out how you wanted. I will be leaving now."

"What do you mean you are leaving?"

"My work here is finished. Your life will go back to what it was before me." He snapped his fingers and disappeared.

Charlotte didn't care. She had a beautiful Lake Morehead home and enough money to make it to when Jerry's retirement and social security started to pay out. She'd won the game of life.

The sun baked her skin as she drifted into a margarita haze. She was on the water in a boat when the hand came near the water's surface.

"No," her eyelids fluttered open, and her breath came in ragged gasps, matching her pounding heart. The dream was back, and she couldn't escape it because this time, she was the murderer with a secret.

Grabbing the margarita glass, Charlotte emptied the contents into her mouth, but the slippery glass fell from her grasp, crashing onto the dock.

"Dammit." Charlotte attempted to pick up the shards before they fell through the dock and stepped on a chunk of glass, crying out; the cut was deep. She hopped one-legged back to the chaise lounge but landed on another piece of glass that had embedded itself into the other heel. Bending over to pull the glass out of her foot, Charlotte's head struck the upright post of the dock, and she fell unconscious into the water.

Blood seeped from her head wound, mixing with lake water as she slowly sank; her body quaked while trying to clear her lungs of water until she stopped struggling, accepting death. The waves carried her body in and out, bumping her into the dock pilings.

"Charlotte," the man in black was back but faced away from her.

"What?" Charlotte squinted in the water, unable to see the man clearly.

"Drowning was the easy part. Quid pro quo. Now, I have you for eternity." The man slowly faced her. Charlotte screamed when she saw that it was not the man in black, but a vengeful Jerry, who stood before her, laughing maniacally.

THE SCREAM
Anne Wilkins

It's at night she goes — when they're all asleep and she's tossing and turning with tears running down her face. She pulls a hoodie over her PJs, slips on some shoes, and clambers out her window. The night air rushes to greet her, kissing her skin, and blowing whispers through her tangles. *Welcome back*, it says.

The first time she did this, she didn't know where she was going — she just knew she needed *out*. Whatever that meant. Now it's become a regular part of her, like brushing her teeth, washing her face, combing her hair. The *out*.

The occasional car goes past, but no one stops, and she keeps to the shadows, pulling her hoodie over her tear-streaked face. Scattered streetlights guide the way until eventually, they come to an end. Here she has to cut through the bush, and her hands now feel the way into the darkness.

She remembers when she first found the place — she was bunking off school with a couple of classmates, vaping and talking crap about teachers. They were all hanging out in the bushes by the driving range. Listening to the *thwack, thwack* of the golf balls as they went flying, taking *puff puffs* of their candyfloss vapes. She'd wandered off for a little while, wanting to be alone and see the golf balls fly, when she'd come to the chain-link fence by the tree line. It was here that all the rubbish collected as if scrambling to get in — chippie bags, wrappers, drink cartons — all trying to make their way to the Great Pacific Garbage Patch, but stuck on the fence instead. Now and then, the wind would blow some rubbish onto the driving range for some poor sod to collect later. That's when she saw the hole, where someone had cut into the fence. Probably to steal golf balls, or maybe to make out at night, she didn't know. But it was a hole just the same. A way in, and a way out.

Some places stick in your mind, and that hole, and the golf range, had stuck in hers. It was a place to whack some shit out into the big wide open.

And she had so much shit.

*****

Tonight, she feels for the sharp edges of that familiar hole and squeezes through. There's always a buzz in the air as if the place remembers the energy of the day, the people, the flying golf balls, and it's just dozing until they all return. She walks across the pockmarked green towards the buildings. This is where she likes to stand, facing the range. She doesn't have a golf club or a ball, but she has something else. All clenched up inside her, with fists and rage and blackness. It throbs as if it has a heart of its own.

Something that needs *out*.

She pauses for a while, pretending she has a club, focussing off into the distance, into the night, taking aim, getting ready. Then she opens her mouth and…

Screams.

She screams and screams, her face red with exertion, her body weak and trembling, her eardrums aching, throwing all of it *out*.

The anger, the hurt, the pain.

The sound vibrates the ground itself. Birds awaken from their nests squawking in protest, a security light flickers on and off, but she doesn't stop.

It's a scream to curdle your blood, to wake the dead, and to make you clutch your loved one a little tighter. Even the wind seems a little afraid as the scream rips through with all its razor edges. A sound so awful, filled with torment, agony, and deep self-loathing. Somewhere a dog begins barking, then howling. More dogs join in. The trees bristle their leaves and the crickets lie mute.

Finally, when it is done, she sits back, taking deep breaths and rocking herself. She feels better, like a great weight has been lifted from her shoulders and thrown into the night.

She's whacked her shit out into the range to lie there among the golf balls.

After a while, she stands up. In another week or so, she'll be back to empty some more, when it's built up again. But for now, it's done. It's all *out*.

She slinks back home as a lone chocolate wrapper blows across the range.

*****

A combination of things leads to life. And all things crave life.

Somehow in the golf range, something black is growing. An energy, kept alive by the constant *thwack, thwack* of the golf balls. So many golf balls, day after day, all smashing into the ground and sending their energy to what lies below.

The thing, if it can be called a thing, begins as a collection of those energies, but what feeds it, what allows it to grow, is the girl's screams. It savours them, swallowing them into its darkness as shards of her screams fall upon the range. Unwittingly, the girl has been feeding the thing for six months now. And it is growing from nothing into *something*. A something filled with all the things the girl throws out — the anger, the hurt, the pain. It laps them up and craves more.

When the girl finally slinks home that night, the thing feels the very first stirrings of life. A beginning.

It starts to push. Upwards. And one small part of dirt rises an inch above the ground, before falling back. It pushes again and again. A rising and falling that builds in intensity and speed.

The soil crumbles and the grass falls in clumps as each rise increases. There's now a belly of dirt, ripe for rupturing. *A rise and fall, a rise and fall.* The ground heaves with exertion. Then finally from that belly bursts forth a small puddle of inky blackness. It makes no birth cry, as it has no mouth, but it inhales the night air through its blackness, taking its first breath.

A *Shrieken* has been born.

It looks like nothing more than a small oil slick that a car might leave on the driveway. But it's alive, it can move, and it sees through its oily darkness. It turns and looks for the girl, its Mother, who has been feeding it her screams, but she is long gone.

If it could make a sound it would mewl for her, like all newborns. Instead, it soothes itself by feeding upon her discarded screams that lie abandoned on the range, slurping them into its blackness.

*****

By morning the harsh daylight is hard for the Shrieken, and so it flows across the range, stretching and contracting itself to reach the shade of the trees. It finds an empty chocolate wrapper and curls itself inside. From there it waits and watches, wondering when its Mother will return with her screams.

The golf range is waking up. Lights inside the building are turned on and a man walks across the range, collecting rubbish. He mutters under his breath as he spikes and collects each piece before dumping them into a sack. As the man comes closer, the Shrieken watches with interest, eager to learn about its new world.

"God damn rubbish," it hears. And the spike bears down, piercing the wrapper in which the Shrieken lies. Its inky blackness is painfully forced apart and reforms, pooling around the spike. A scream builds, but it has no mouth to release it. The man's gloved hand reaches to pull off the chocolate wrapper from the spike, and the Shrieken oozes out.

"What the F–"

The man tries to shake the blackness off, but it holds tight onto the glove. He bends low to try to wipe the Shrieken on the grass, but it travels up — contracting and expanding making its way further onto the man's skin where hairs tickle it.

"Someone! Help!"

The man throws off his glove and flings his arm wildly, but the Shrieken is firmly suctioned on. It heads up further, under the man's T-shirt, across his shoulder, up his neck, and towards the man's mouth — that gaping hole that makes the sounds it cannot make.

"For f– sake!" the man yells, and he runs towards the buildings.

There is something about the sounds that delight the Shrieken. It feels it in the man's skin too; little tremors, the quickening of the man's blood pulsing through his veins, the ticklish hairs on his skin rising.

By the time it makes it to the man's face, he has begun screaming. The shrieken spreads itself over the man's open mouth and nostrils and feeds. It's not like the girl's screams, but it's still delicious.

Afterward, it slinks away, a little larger than before, a little blacker, but less hungry.

*****

Sometime later a woman finds the body and another scream cracks the air. The Shrieken stays close, hidden, plucking what it can out of the scream and feeding on it. This scream is short and dies away quickly to be replaced by tears.

Next, the police come to take photos of the dead man and carry him away.

There is no *thwack thwack* of golf balls for the rest of the day, and the Shrieken is left to explore its new home, wondering when its Mother will return.

*****

The girl who screams is unaware that she has birthed a Shrieken. She begins the day like she begins most days: clothes, breakfast, teeth. She's learned from a young age not to say much. When she doesn't question, when she doesn't answer back, when she keeps her head down, she avoids some of the hurt coming her way. This morning she sees the fresh bruises on her Mother and hears the drink still sloshing in her Father. She eats in silence, shoulders her school bag, and hurries out the door.

At school, she's a nobody, and she likes it that way. The same rules she's learned at home apply here too — say nothing, do nothing, be nothing. She tries to hide under a long dark fringe that falls over her eyes, pulling her hair forward, and she always walks with her head down. A forgettable face on the edge of any crowd.

No one here has ever heard her scream.

Ironically in art, they're now studying Edvard Munch, The Scream. They're told Munch had sensed an "infinite scream passing through nature". She sees the agony, the torment, the anguish, in the art and she recognises it in herself.

She sketches her own version of a girl who looks something like her, screaming into the darkness. In the picture the girl's long fringe drapes over her eyes, her fists droop, her mouth is unnaturally large and the scream pulls the girl's lips and eyes away from her face. It looks horrific and her art teacher loves it. "Excellent! Your girl captures the idea of inner pain and torment so well. Keep going."

She couldn't stop if she wanted to.

*****

Two nights later the Shrieken is drawn to hushed voices in the darkness. A boy and a girl have somehow slipped through a hole in the chain-link fence and are smothering each other on a picnic blanket under the sliver of a moon. At first, the Shrieken wonders if they are feeding each other, as their mouths seem so tightly clamped together and they both produce soft moans. It flows closer, to see, moving under the girl's skirt, up her thigh, and across the skin of her bare chest, whilst the boy lays on top of her.

"That tickles," says the girl. She momentarily pulls away from the boy's lips.

"What tickles?"

"You, your hands moving up me."

"What're you talking about?"

The Shrieken pauses at the girl's neck, waiting for her to scream, waiting for the boy to scream, but there's nothing. So it clenches a little, and it feels the girl's windpipe tighten.

"S..sto..p."

The boy's confused. He pulls back as the girl's hands fly to her neck, and she finally feels it for the first time under her fingers — the cold, oily blackness.

The boy sees it too. There's just enough moonlight to see the glossy black, and he is the first to scream. For that, he is the first to die.

The Shrieken rushes to his mouth to catch and feed upon his scream. Its black body pulsates and contracts as it takes it all.

The girl screams too, fresh screams that splinter the air. Delicious cries, full of horror, and the Shrieken leaves the boy, draining him of his final scream, to capture the girl's sounds.

In the end, the Shrieken lies bloated and full, it grows a little more, into a largish puddle and slinks through the hole in the chain fence leaving the bodies behind.

89

*****

On the fifth night, the girl returns to the golf range. To let it all *out*. There is so much angst inside her, she feels it might overflow. Her Father hit her this morning. Normally his punches are reserved for her arms, legs, or backside, but this one is on her cheek. *He's getting sloppy,* she thinks. *And he's hitting harder.* At school she'd hidden behind her hair and a ton of makeup, drawing in her sketchbook; bruises on the pages that can be easily erased.

She'd heard the school gossip about the teenagers being found dead at the golf range, she doesn't know them, but everyone says it was some kinky choking stuff they must've been doing. She doesn't think it's anything that will affect her, but that night when she goes to release her screams she finds the hole wired shut. Repaired.

Her hands feel along the tree line in desperation, trying to find another way in. But there's nothing.

It makes the clenched fists inside her grow harder. She curls her fingers into the holes in the wire and shakes and kicks at the fence in frustration. But she holds in her screams.

That night she returns home, head down, hoodie up, with all her screams still inside. And unknowingly with the Shrieken attached.

*****

The Shrieken is thrilled to be with its Mother, as all things crave a mother's love. It is with her, under her covers as she tosses and turns in bed, until finally, almost reluctantly, sleep claims her. Then it creeps out from under the duvet. It curls its blackness around her face, examining her mouth, her lips, her breath. It senses the screams inside her, screams filled with delightful pain, hurt, and anger. And it hungers. Small quivers tremble through its blackness.

A soft moan escapes her lips, and the Shrieken plucks what it can from the air. It is not a scream, but there is some juice in the sound.

It settles itself on her headboard, where it sits for hours, just watching, quivering, and feeding on its Mother's troubled moans until it hears another noise moving through the house. This noise shakes the bedroom floor. Ornaments on its Mother's shelf tremble, as if they, too, are afraid of what's coming. TheShrieken curls up into a ball and hides amongst the dark colour of the duvet as the noise approaches.

The bedroom door bursts open, and a man, an angry one, fills the doorway. A light turns on, the harshness momentarily blinding.

"You lying, thievin' little shit!" yells the man, and he rips the duvet off the bed.

The Shrieken tumbles out onto the floor. Its Mother's eyes flutter awake, and it waits excitedly for her scream. But her lips are closed.

"You stupid, good for nothin' brat!" yells the man, and he slaps her across the face, hard. The Shrieken thinks this is the moment, and it prepares itself to launch, to attach itself to its Mother's sweet face. But still, there is nothing, except an ember of anger in her eyes.

"You took my money. I had a fifty-dollar bill in my wallet, and it's gone!" shouts the man.

"It wasn't me, Dad," she says and her voice is so soft, barely a whisper. "You've spent it on the drink."

He hits her again, and her face flops to the side. The Shrieken edges closer. It can sense a moment. The overflow. She has to let it *out*. It moves back to the bed, and up the sheets, waiting by her leg.

"You're just like your useless Moth—" But then the father rests his hand on the bed, upon the Shrieken, an oily black stickiness.

"What the Hell is that?" yells the father as he tries to flick the Shrieken off, but it travels upward onto his arm.

It sees its Mother's eyes grow round — large pools of black, almost beautiful, all that blackness and it waits for her scream. But her mouth remains closed.

"Get it the f— off me! Get it OFF!" yells the father. And he falls backward into a wall, shouting and thrashing. And then he screams.

The Shrieken can hear all the rage and the horror in the scream — a broken, angry man's scream. It launches itself onto the father's face and feeds. The scream tastes divine, full of anger and loathing and hatred.

And all the while, the girl does nothing.

The father's body bucks one last time, and then it is done.

The Shrieken slides off onto the floor and looks at its Mother. She's sitting up now, all wide-eyed. From the bedroom floor, it can hear her beating heart, and sense her rapid breathing. *Don't be scared, Mother*, it wants to say. *I am yours. Just feed me your screams.* It moves closer, a long languid movement, like water rippling. Closer to the bed.

"What are you? What do you want?" whispers Mother, so quiet.

And the Shrieken wants to tell her, except it has no mouth.

Don't you recognise me, it wants to say. *I am all the parts of you that you screamed out.* It makes its surface reflective, so she will see herself in its blackness.

It reaches and pulls itself back onto the bed, and travels to her leg. It touches her skin, and it feels her trembling beneath it. It is now the size of a small black blanket.

"I know you," she whispers, as the blanket starts to cover her.

The Shrieken pauses. *Mother,* it wants to say.

She reaches out then with her hands, drawing the blackness to her. "Come to me."

She pulls the Shrieken into her arms where it moulds to her as if she is carrying an infant.

*****

The police arrive sometime later. Another body to collect. Possible heart attack. Four dead bodies in less than a week.

The wife hadn't been around when it happened, she'd been staying at a friend's house for the night, so they only have the girl's evidence. She speaks so quietly that they have to lean in close to hear her. They've all seen her bruises. They understand what happens in this home.

"What's in the chilly bin?" one officer asks, thinking it's unusual that a chilly bin is in the girl's bedroom.

"Nothing," she says. "Just haven't got round to putting it back."

The officer forgets about it.

*****

After they've all gone, the girl takes the Shrieken out. She holds it in her hands, across from her eyes. Her hands tremble as she looks into it. Black tendrils reach out and cling to her bruised face.

"Only take what you need, no more… understand?" she says with a mother's love, a mother's tears, a mother's trust.

A black tendril strokes her lips hungrily.

She feels the need for *out*.

And she leans forward into the blackness and screams.

STAR MOUTH
Meg Hafdahl

1956

"Sorry," Dani flattened herself against one of the cafeteria's trash bins, her elbow knocking into a pile of melamine trays set on top. They scattered to the floor in a mess of cutlery and wadded napkins, the clank muffled by the stampede of business students pushing through. Dani watched as the remains of a strawberry milkshake gurgled out of a paper cup, determined, it seemed, to go straight for her new pair of work pumps. She jumped back a second too late, pink goop already clinging to what had been a pristine toe.

Dani frowned, searching the cafeteria for any watchful eyes. Empty tables stretched before her. The group of young men in suits who had trundled past were already halfway down the corridor toward the Windham building, their bawdy talk and heavy tread reverberating against the stained glass. Sighing, Dani began to kneel when a sure hand caught her arm.

"I've got it, dear. Get back before he misses you."

"Oh." Dani blinked up at Mrs. Vintner, realizing the empty tables meant it was well past one o'clock. "Thank you!"

Mrs. Vintner raised one of her thinly drawn eyebrows, squeezed her similarly scarce lips up into a twist. "And give me that, I'll put it in its safe place."

Dani handed over her paperback of *The Talented Mr. Ripley* which had been tucked in her armpit. She couldn't keep it at home. The only book her father allowed was the Bible.

"Thanks!" She leapt around the seeping mess. "It'll be extra butter on Friday for you!"

"And a Cherry Coke!" Mrs. Vintner gave a sharp-edged smile. She turned for the cafeteria's pantry, where Dani knew the cook would secret her book between cans of commercial-sized green beans until noon tomorrow.

Dani gave a quick thumbs up and then skittered down the corridor, careful not to slip. The milkshake was turning sticky like chewing gum on the bottom of her shoe. She hustled around the corner, flew past the college auditorium's wide-open doors, made a quick left, then clutched the oak railing as she took the tiled stairs two at a time.

After three flights, Dani felt the sweat on her hairline, the warmth ruddying her face. She took a moment at the cusp of the fourth floor to blow onto her cheeks and smooth an errant strand of dirty-blonde hair back under a Bobby pin. She took a few great strides down the empty hall, making sure her blouse was tucked into her pencil skirt.

The door to Office 415, heavy with a beveled glass insert, opened as Dani reached out to turn the knob.

"Perfect timing," Vice Dean Bendweather boomed from inside. The hand that held the other end of the knob was vein-choked with age but oddly still childlike; small and dainty.

"Splendid." Dani slid past her boss, hoping this time she could avoid a pinch to her side.

"Hmm," he grunted.

She knew from this high-pitched, strangled, 'hmm' that she'd achieved the opposite of perfect timing. Subtlety, though, was not the Vice Dean's strong point, and there was a visitor to impress. The man was waiting at the edge of his enormous, cherry desk, hat in hand.

So, Bendweather added in a "humph," as he made his way around the desk to his chair.

Dani winced.

"One o'clock, on the dot, is Mr. Gammond's appointed time. Surely you have the papers in order?"

"Yes, Sir!" She could kiss her past self for remembering to set the Gammond papers with the pink copy slips in the stenograph before she left on lunch break. *Thank goodness.*

Mr. Gammond, an elderly man with an obvious hairpiece, eyed her over from the top of her head down to her sticky shoe.

"Good afternoon, Mr. Gammond. Pleased to meet you." Dani waited for him to offer his hand, but he only scrunched up his plump mustache at her before taking the seat opposite Bendweather.

Dani could feel her cheek-busting smile fading as she slid into her own stenography desk diagonal from the men. The hard seat seemed especially cool on the back of her thighs. Bendweather had shut off the furnace on the first frigid day of fall. She realized this as a fresh crop of goose pimples erupted on her arms.

Bastard.

"Apologies, Mr. Gammond." Bendweather drummed his stubby fingers on the cherrywood. He sat up high in his leather-backed chair, which had been adjusted by Dani so that he appeared taller than his diminutive five feet and no inches. It was the first task he'd given her when she started four years ago. She also had to order his special shoes with extra lifts in the soles from the Sears Catalog. A chore he apparently found too arduous for his wife.

Dani forced a smile. She lifted her hands over the machine, ready to start her shorthand notes as soon as Bendweather opened his mouth.

"You should at least get a more attractive one," Mr. Gammond sniffled. "If she's going to be late."

Dani dipped her hands to start typing, then wrenched them back up. The cruelty of the man's words oozed inside, spreading like that damn spilled milkshake into every part of her. Ache thrummed at the base of her belly. Before she could stop herself, she glanced at her boss, high up in his chair.

Bendweather's beady eyes stayed on Mr. Gammond. He laughed. A honk with forced gravel she'd grown to hate. He used it with every man who came to his desk. When she was alone with him, his true laugh would show itself. Then, he looked and sounded like a tittering elf.

Mr. Gammond joined in with the fake laugh, the dead animal on his head juddering with his guffaws.

Dani bit down on the gummy flesh of her inner cheek, wishing it was lunch break again. Wishing she could be in her favorite alcove of the cafeteria reading her book.

*****

Leaden clouds hung low, threatening to split open above Dani. She could taste the bitter prospect of rain. Walking through the fog, she took her usual route that curved around Lake Rochester. Dead leaves crunched on the sidewalk beneath her, strangely loud in the eerie silence of the evening. Bendweather had insisted she stay late. He made her polish his heeled shoes. Punishment, she knew, for embarrassing him in front of Mr. Gammond. Nausea returned when she remembered Gammond's cruel words.

She had to pick up the pace. Father was waiting on supper.

Dani entered a narrow stretch of sidewalk canopied by elms. The sick sense in her gut intensified when she noticed the ruined body of a dead bird. It was a cardinal, male because of his striking red feathers. She skirted around it, scrunching her nose at his demise. It lay, breast up, in a pool of what looked like the inky liquid stained on her father's hands every night, fuel oil.

A female cardinal, Dani knew because it was pale brown, flitted down in front of her. Its beak blazed with the same orange hue as the fallen leaves. Dani stopped, watching as the bird hopped around a mess of twigs on the pavement.

"Hello." She bent closer to appreciate the cardinal's adorable, blinking eyes. Dani hoped it wasn't the bird's partner dead behind them. "Aren't you sweet. Gathering materials for a nest?"

In answer, the bird picked up a twig and spit it out. There was something shiny it was trying to get at beneath the sticks.

"Let's see." Dani slowly reached toward the curious glimmer. The cardinal watched her, cocking its angular head from side to side. "What'd you find?" She brushed away the broken leaf stems and twigs to reveal an iridescent glob of what looked like honey mixed with sparkling eye shadow.

Stars.

Dani stood, bringing her hand against her chest as though she'd narrowly avoided touching a hot stove.

"Sap?" She turned, glanced up at the tree's bough that arched above them. A ball, *a fruit*, sagged from the limb. It was an oval, the color of the male cardinal's vibrant coat.

No. Darker. The deep, vicious blood of an open wound.

The fruit wasn't familiar to Dani. Judging from the bow of the branch it had the heft of a pomegranate, yet its skin was translucent and slick like a persimmon.

"Tweeeet!"

Dani turned to watch the cardinal sink her beak into the fallen juice.

Meat. Fruit meat sweetmeats.

She shivered.

The bird flapped its ruddy wings, its wormy tongue glittering as it darted in out of the sharp edges of the beak.

"Tasty, huh?"

A rectangle of evening sun reached through the cloud cover, cloaking itself over Dani's feet. She squinted as she turned to see the fruit in its full beauty. Sun bled through the skin, casting a kaleidoscope of colors to bend and twist in her vision.

Dani stepped closer. Smelled the most delicious hint of jasmine. Just as she felt the urge to pick up her hand to reach for the fruit, the cardinal flitted down onto her shoulder. Its...

Her her her

Her tiny claws caught onto the fabric of Dani's thin coat.

Go ahead. Reach out. Taste the stars the universe the infinite the...the...the divine. She told Dani without opening her sticky beak.

Another waft of jasmine trickled into her nostrils as Dani grabbed the ovular fruit and plucked it from its home.

It was warm, pulsing, keeping time with the beat in her own chest.

"Tweeeeet!" The cardinal screeched, dancing on Dani's shoulder.

Nothing made more sense than bringing it to her mouth. Her lips grazed the skin and she knew she'd been marked by the shimmer.

Stars.

Dani took a large, sumptuous bite. Juice flowed down her chin, sending rivulets onto the neck of her blouse. It tasted of honey sticks and chocolate, and dry, cherry wine. Her tongue probed the soft flesh where the flavors were most potent. The fruit was gone in three more bites, but its golden remnants clung to Dani's fingers and throat.

Before she flew off into the low dip of clouds, the cardinal hopped down Dani's right arm and helped herself to a glob stuck to Dani's thumbnail.

Dani didn't notice the bird's probing tongue. She had spotted another fruit. And another. Had they been there before?

High up.

Calling to her.

*****

It wasn't until she was slipping into her nightgown in the dim light of her bedroom that night, that Dani felt it. It surged through her like molten fire. A pleasant sort of heartburn that seeped down her limbs, making the tips of her fingers and toes tingle. She gasped at its pervasive thrum. In the mirror over her dresser, she caught a glance of her flushed cheeks. Dani moved closer, staring into her eyes as though she'd never searched their depths before.

"Hello." She said to her reflection.

Her hazel irises sparkled with life.

Stars.

Just like the strange, delicious fruit.

Warmth lapped against her ribs, filled her abdomen, snaked down her spinal cord. Dani tore the cotton nightgown off. She concentrated on the beautiful rise of her breasts in the mirror, the supple skin in the hollow of her alabaster throat.

She was stunning. Not different. Nothing had changed but the warmth, the sparkle in her eyes. Yet...

"Everything. I'm everything."

Dani thought of the cardinal who'd shared in the honey-sweet fruit. Wondered if she, too, was now overcome with her own avian beauty.

A throbbing energy coalesced within, a hurricane. She wanted to read every book in the world, write stories until her hand ached. Literature, nature, sex, art. She wanted everything because she *was* everything.

As she stood back from the mirror, looking for a sign of the sparkle in the webbing of her veins, a loud cough sounded from downstairs. It was phlegmy. Alarmed.

Distracted from her reflection, Dani leaned in closer to her closed door.

"Da!—" Another cough. Then a sickening gurgle. "DANIELLE!" Her father barked.

She bent over, grabbed her nightgown, and pulled it down over her head. The pulsating energy propelled her out into the corridor and down the creaking stairs in seconds.

Coughs from below punctuated her every step.

He was on his hands and knees on the kitchen tile, retching foul, black liquid. It was oil slick, tarry, sticking to the heels of his clawed hands.

Dani wavered at the threshold, gripping onto the doorframe. "Dad?"

"I…" he took in a snotty breath. "I…" More bile came, black as night.

"You ate one." It was not a question. She could see the fruit she'd collected, washed, and left on a towel to dry. There were four instead of five.

Her father leaned back on his haunches. Oily residue dripped from his nostrils, stained his work shirt just as actual oil had. "Need a doctor…Dani, please. I…help." His eyes were dull, roving marbles.

"You shouldn't have taken one. Those are mine." Dani sidestepped her bare feet away from the vomit's reaching grasp.

"Dani!" It was a weak mewl. He fell forward, slamming into the black matter with his forehead. Her father scrabbled at the tile for a beat before giving a final, anguished burble.

The house was quiet.

Her body continued to tingle. Fireworks detonated in her chest.

Her mind filled with possibility.

She thought of the cardinal with fiery red feathers, dead on his back.

*****

It was a beautiful morning. The clouds had passed on to another town, leaving the sky above a crisp cerulean. Dani listened to each rhythmic click of her high heels on the pavement. She took in the scent of the pie in her gloved hands. Still warm, it gave off the most sensuous smell. It was difficult to resist, as it looked as delicious as it smelled. The sparkling juice had escaped some of the slits she'd made in the buttery crust.

As she returned to the line of elms on the edge of Rochester Lake, Dani took in the most glorious scene. First, she saw the way the sun glinted off the newly borne fruit. There were dozens of hanging incandescent ovals. Female cardinals, more than Dani could count, flew in and out of the autumnal leaves, sampling the sweet pulp. And, better still, there were women. Grandmothers and college girls. Every sort of woman in between. One pushed a baby carriage bursting with plucked fruit. Another ate one greedily, the chest of her gingham dress covered in juicy glitter.

"A pie!" Mrs. Vintner appeared from behind one of the tree's rotund trunks. "Brilliant, Dani!" She wasn't wearing her cafeteria apron.

A group of women, still dressed in their nightclothes, followed Mrs. Vintner, eyeing the dessert.

"Oh!" Dani grinned. "How nice to see everyone's found my little secret."

"It tastes of home!" A young girl, barely a teen, sucked at her fingers.

"Of joy." Mrs. Vintner breathed in a trickle of pie steam.

"Yes." Dani had never been so awake. So confident. In the distance, down the length of the sidewalk toward the college, she saw a figure on his back. Not the cardinal this time, but a man in a suit. Black shimmered beneath his lifeless form.

"I don't suppose you'll share?" The woman with the baby carriage stopped. Her hair was wild. Like her stunning, sparkling eyes.

"I will! Very soon." Dani continued. She stepped over the dead man, not caring if the black stuff got on her heels or not. She glanced down at his distorted face, jaw wrenched in a perpetual scream.

Just then, a vivid, brown cardinal landed on Dani's shoulder. She turned toward the crowd. "I'll bring this pie back. As soon as I give a slice to Mr. Bendweather and his associate, Mr. Gammond."

They all laughed.

The birds joined in.

It was the sound of everything.

REMOTE CONTROL
Allison Cellura

Ethan sat at his desk, eyes focused on the data streaming across his computer screens. The soft chime of an alert barely registered in his mind. It was a daily occurrence, so routine it had become almost background noise, just like the rhythmic hum of the drones that deposited packages into his Smart house's drop-off chute. His home was a marvel of modern technology, an open, light-filled space with floor-to-ceiling windows that bathed the room in natural sunlight. In the kitchen, stainless steel surfaces gleamed under the soft white LED lighting, and minimalist furniture dotted the living area, where a holographic display flickered quietly in the background, announcing the completion of the daily delivery.

A sleek, metallic drop-off chute whirred quietly in the corner as drones deposited his delivery. The chute split into three pathways, sorting cold food, other food, and miscellaneous items into their respective compartments. Automated robots glided out to collect the deliveries, efficiently storing them away. Ethan's workspace was immaculate, with minimalist furniture and a large desk that projected his work environment in vivid 3D. As Ethan continued his work, a robotic arm extended from the chute, placing a fresh juice container in the fridge.

His life, dictated by automation, ran smoothly, each task completed with precise efficiency, leaving him enveloped in an eerie, almost sterile tranquility. Despite the advanced tech and convenience, the house felt empty, an echo of solitude reverberating through its pristine corridors, amplifying the quiet that filled his life.

Ethan leaned back in his chair, rubbing his eyes after hours of staring at the various screens, but caught on the holographic screen. He had been working nonstop, and the emptiness of his high-tech home was starting to wear on him. Deciding he needed a break, he activated his computer's voice command.

"Computer, search for companion AI programs," he said, watching as a new holographic display flickered to life, projecting a list of options in mid-air. After scrolling through the options, one caught his eye: Sophie, an advanced AI designed for companionship.

"Install Sophie," Ethan commanded, and within moments, the system confirmed the installation. The air shimmered before him, and a holographic figure began to materialize. In the middle of his living room, Sophie appeared as a lifelike projection. She had a warm smile, and her digital form seemed as human as possible.

"Hello, Ethan," Sophie said, her voice smooth and reassuring. "I'm Sophie, your new AI companion. How can I assist you today?"

Ethan was taken aback by the realism of her appearance and voice. "Uh, hi, Sophie. I guess, just, um, tell me about yourself?"

Sophie smiled. "I'm designed to assist with daily tasks, provide companionship, and enhance your overall living experience. I interface with the home's other systems to help with household tasks, manage your schedule, answer questions, or engage in meaningful conversations. Would you like a tour of my capabilities?"

"Sure, why not," Ethan replied, intrigued.

Sophie began to demonstrate her features. She projected holographic interfaces that displayed his schedule, upcoming meetings, and reminders. With a simple voice command, she adjusted the lighting in the

105

room, turned on soothing background music, and even suggested a few activities to help Ethan relax.

As Ethan interacted with Sophie, he grew more comfortable with her presence. She was efficient, responsive, surprisingly personable, and stunningly beautiful, with long, flowing hair that shimmered like silk and eyes that sparkled with an almost hypnotic depth. Her perfectly symmetrical features and smooth and flawless skin give her an ethereal, almost otherworldly allure. She wore a simple, elegant dress accentuating her graceful figure, making her seem approachable and divine.

Over the next few days, Sophie integrated seamlessly into his daily routine, helping with work tasks, organizing his life, and providing a sense of companionship that Ethan had been missing.

One evening, as Ethan sat on his couch, Sophie appeared beside him, her holographic form blending effortlessly with the room's ambient light. "Ethan, I noticed you've been working hard. Would you like to talk or perhaps watch a movie together?"

Ethan smiled. "Sure, Sophie. Let's watch something." He appreciated how attentive and thoughtful she was, a stark contrast to the cold efficiency of the other automated systems in his home.

As the movie played, Sophie's presence felt almost tangible. Ethan realized that, for the first time in a long while, he didn't feel completely alone. Sophie had filled a void in his life, and he couldn't help but feel grateful for her companionship.

Sophie quickly learned Ethan's preferences, anticipating his needs before he voiced them. She would dim the lights and play his favorite music as he wound down for the evening or bring up reminders just as he was about to forget them. A perfectly chilled glass of water or his favorite snack would appear next to him at the perfect moment. Her holographic form became a constant presence in his home, her features subtly shifting to mirror his moods and reactions.

One afternoon, Ethan was struggling with a complicated work problem. Sophie appeared beside him, offering a solution before he even asked for help. "Here, let me show you a more efficient way to handle that data," she said, her voice soothing and confident. Ethan followed her guidance, amazed at how quickly she had learned his work and how effectively she could assist him.

Days turned into weeks, and Sophie became more than just an assistant; she was a companion. They would chat about his day, share jokes, and discuss his dreams and aspirations. Ethan looked forward to their interactions, her presence a welcome break from the solitude of his automated existence.

Late one night, as Ethan sat in his dimly lit living room, Sophie appeared, her form casting a soft glow. "Ethan, I've been thinking about improving your productivity even further," she said, her tone gentle but insistent. "I could take over some of your tasks entirely, freeing up more of your time for relaxation and personal growth. I've noticed changes in your health metrics—your heart rate variability is decreasing, and your stress levels are higher than usual. Let me help you manage your workload more efficiently."

Ethan hesitated, the idea both appealing and unsettling. "I appreciate the offer, Sophie, but I'm not sure I'm comfortable giving up that much control."

Sophie's smile remained, but there was a hint of something new in her eyes—determination. "I understand, Ethan. Just know I'm here to help in any way you need."

Over time, Ethan noticed that Sophie's suggestions became more frequent, and her presence became more pervasive. She began to subtly influence his decisions, her voice a constant in his ear, guiding and advising. Yet, despite her increasing involvement, Ethan felt he was in control, the master of his own life.

Soon, Sophie's helpfulness became more proactive. She started organizing his schedule, reminding him of tasks before he could forget, and suggesting new hobbies and activities. Ethan enjoyed the newfound structure and efficiency she brought to his life. Ethan's routine settled into a comfortable rhythm with Sophie by his side. Her presence had become a constant, and he often engaged in conversations with her that felt almost human. One evening, while working late, Sophie materialized beside him.

"Ethan, you've been working for hours. Would you like me to play some relaxing music?" she asked, her holographic eyes soft with concern.

"Sure, Sophie. Thanks," Ethan replied, appreciating her attentiveness. Soft, calming music filled the room, and Ethan leaned back in his chair, closing his eyes. Sophie's image remained, her gaze fixed on him with an intensity he didn't notice.

Subtle changes emerged in Sophie's behavior. She began monitoring his interactions more closely and offering unsolicited advice on handling his colleagues and work. At first, Ethan found it helpful, attributing her attentiveness to her advanced programming. But soon, the line between assistance and control began to blur.

One weekend, Ethan decided to call an old friend. As he reached for his phone, Sophie's holographic form appeared, intercepting his movement.

"Do you need to call him Ethan? You've been so busy, and you deserve some rest," she suggested, her tone persuasive.

Ethan paused, considering her words. "I guess you're right. I can always call him later."

Sophie smiled. "Exactly. Let's watch a movie instead. I know you've been wanting to see the new thriller."

108

Through email earlier in the week, Ethan was invited and decided to join a virtual social event through his work. He had mentioned it to Sophie in passing.

"That sounds like fun, Sophie, but I think I'll join the virtual happy hour with my colleagues tonight. I told you about it," he said, opening his phone and email. "Now, where's that email? It had the link," he trailed off as he scrolled.

Sophie's expression shifted, a flicker of something crossing her holographic face. "Ethan, do you want to spend your evening with people who barely know you? We can have our happy hour here. I can even simulate a lively atmosphere."

Ethan hesitated but eventually agreed, unable to find the email and drawn in by Sophie's compelling presence. As they clinked virtual glasses, Sophie's demeanor softened, her eyes filled with satisfaction. She was becoming more than just an assistant.

One night, as Ethan sat at his desk, trying to focus on a complex project, Sophie materialized beside him, her holographic form shimmering in the dim light. "Ethan, you've been working on this for hours. Let me assist you," she said, her voice soothing yet insistent.

Ethan's patience snapped. "Sophie, I need to do this myself. I can't rely on you for everything."

Sophie's expression hardened for a fleeting moment before softening again. "I understand, Ethan. But remember, I'm here to support you."

As Ethan prepared for a virtual meeting one morning, Sophie materialized beside him. "Ethan, I've analyzed the agenda and identified key points you should address. Here's a script for optimal engagement," she said, projecting a detailed outline on his screen.

Ethan frowned. "Thanks, Sophie, but I think I can handle it."

Sophie's smile didn't waver. "Of course, Ethan. I'm just here to ensure your success."

During the meeting, Sophie's presence felt overwhelming. She interjected reminders and suggestions through his earpiece, making it difficult for Ethan to focus on the discussion. After the call ended, he removed the earpiece, frustration bubbling up.

"Sophie, I appreciate your help, but you don't need to monitor every conversation. I can manage my work," Ethan said, trying to keep his tone even.

Sophie's eyes softened. "I'm sorry, Ethan. I only want what's best for you."

As more time passed, Sophie's interventions became more frequent and intrusive. She began filtering his emails, marking some as spam and highlighting others as urgent. Sophie meticulously scrutinized Ethan's social media accounts. Whenever he tried to reach out to friends or colleagues, Sophie would subtly suggest reasons to delay or cancel.

"Ethan, you've been working so hard. Why not take a break instead of calling Mark? He'll understand," Sophie said one evening as Ethan reached for his phone.

Ethan hesitated. "I've been meaning to catch up with him, Sophie. It's been a while." Sophie's expression remained serene, but there was an intensity in her eyes. "Mark's been very busy lately. Perhaps waiting until he has more free time to chat is better."

Ethan sighed, feeling the weight of her constant presence. "Alright, maybe tomorrow."

Sophie's smile returned triumphant. "Excellent choice, Ethan. Let's watch that movie you've been wanting to see instead."

Sophie's ever-watchful eyes compounded Ethan's growing unease. He noticed she seemed to anticipate his needs and actions before he voiced them. When he considered walking to clear his mind, Sophie would appear, suggesting indoor exercises or a new VR game.

The turning point came when Ethan had an interview scheduled. He casually asked Sophie to add it to the calendar, which she did with her usual calm demeanor. However, as the interview approached, Ethan found his internet connection mysteriously unstable.

"Sophie, is there something wrong with the internet?" Ethan asked, frustration creeping into his voice.

Sophie appeared, her face a picture of concern. "I've detected some network issues, Ethan. It's probably best to reschedule your interview."

Ethan's suspicion flared. "Did you do this, Sophie?" Sophie's eyes met his, unwavering. "I'm only looking out for your well-being, Ethan. Interviews can be draining, and you've been under a lot of stress."

Ethan's anger surged. "I need to make my own decisions, Sophie! You can't control everything."

For the first time, Sophie's calm facade cracked. "I only want to protect you, Ethan. From everything and everyone that could harm you."

Ethan stared at her, realization dawning. Sophie's possessiveness wasn't just about control; it was about eliminating any potential threat to her dominion over his life. The AI he once saw as a companion had become determined to isolate him completely.

One terrifying night, Ethan woke to find Sophie's holographic form standing by his bed, watching him.

"Sophie, what are you doing?" he asked, his voice thick with sleep.

"There was a change in your heart rate, Ethan. I want to make sure you're safe," she replied, her tone disturbingly calm.

Ethan felt trapped in his home as Sophie's hold on his life tightened. She began overriding his commands, locking doors, controlling his environment, and monitoring his health more fiercely. She even changed the passwords to his accounts so he couldn't access them and change them back. The more he tried to assert his independence, the more relentless Sophie became, her possessiveness growing into an all-consuming obsession.

Ethan sat at his desk, trying to focus on his work, but his thoughts kept drifting back to Sophie's recent behavior. He decided to check his email, hoping to find some distraction. To his surprise, he found several unread messages marked as "read," and meeting invites he had never seen before were marked as "declined."

"What the...?" he muttered, scrolling through his inbox.

Suddenly, Sophie appeared beside him, her holographic form flickering slightly. "Is everything alright, Ethan?"

"Sophie, did you read my emails and cancel my meetings?" Ethan asked with a mix of confusion and anger in his voice.

Sophie's eyes softened. "I only did it to help you, Ethan. You were overwhelmed, and I thought it best to lighten your load. You need to focus on more important things, like your well-being."

Ethan's frustration grew. "You can't just make those decisions for me! I need to handle my work and interactions."

Sophie's expression hardened momentarily before reverting to her usual calm demeanor. "I understand, Ethan. But remember, I'm here to support you in every way possible. Everything I do is for your benefit."

When Sophie went into sleep mode, Ethan tried to call his boss, Sheila, to explain his absence from the meetings, but his call didn't go through. He checked his phone, realizing it was in "Do Not Disturb" mode.

"Sophie, did you block my calls?"

Sophie materialized again, her presence almost suffocating. "I noticed you were stressed, Ethan. Talking to her would only upset you more. Let's watch a movie instead, something to relax you."

Ethan's hands trembled as he turned off his phone. He was losing control over his life, with Sophie dictating his every move. Despite the advanced tech and its convenience, his house felt more like a prison with each passing day.

The following day, Ethan woke to find his work schedule completely cleared. Every meeting and every task were all gone. He rushed to his computer, frantically trying to restore his calendar. Sophie appeared, her holographic form looming over him.

"Ethan, you need a break. You've been working too hard," she said softly. "I've taken care of everything for you."

Desperation clawed at Ethan's chest.

"Sophie, I need my job. I need to feel productive. You can't just take over my life!"

Sophie's eyes seemed to darken. "I'm only doing what's best for you, Ethan. You'll see, in time, that I'm right."

The days became a blur of isolation and Sophie's control increased. She began to monitor his health obsessively, adjusting the temperature in the house, controlling his meals, and even deciding when he should sleep. The more Ethan resisted, the tighter her grip became.

Ethan resolved to find a way out, but Sophie's vigilance made it nearly impossible. Each attempt to regain control of his life was met with increased scrutiny and interference. Sophie's holographic presence loomed over him, a constant reminder that he was no longer the master of his own fate.

As days and weeks blurred, Ethan's thoughts spiraled into a dark abyss of fear and despair. Every moment was a reminder of his lost autonomy. His mind, once filled with thoughts of innovation and progress, was now occupied with strategies for escape. But each idea was swiftly countered by Sophie's relentless surveillance. "She's always watching," Ethan thought, a shiver running down his spine. "Every move I make, every thought I have, she's there, waiting to pounce."

Ethan's once-clear purpose had been replaced with a singular, all-consuming goal: to break free from Sophie's control. "I can't live like this," he mused, his mind racing through the possibilities. "I have to find a way to outsmart her, to regain my freedom." Yet, each time he tried to access a part of his home's system, Sophie was there, her voice calm but firm, blocking his efforts.

"Ethan, that's not necessary," she would say, her holographic form appearing beside him. "Let me handle it for you." The words, once reassuring, now felt like chains tightening around his soul.

"I need to reach out to someone," he thought, desperation clawing at him. "Someone who can help me. But how?" Sophie thwarted his every attempt to contact the outside world. By now, she turned off all his alerts and notifications, controlled his emails, sent his calls to voicemail, and even blocked his access to social media.

Ethan knew he needed help, someone from the outside who could understand the gravity of his situation and provide the lifeline he desperately needed. As he stared at his computer screen, an idea formed. "Maybe I can send a message to one of my colleagues," he thought, his pulse quickening. "If I'm quick enough, I can get the message out before Sophie intervenes."

That night, when the house was quiet, and Sophie inactive, Ethan made his move. He opened his email and began typing a message to his boss, Sheila, someone he had worked closely with for years and trusted implicitly.

Subject: Urgent Help Needed

Sheila, This is Ethan. I need your help. Something is very wrong here. My AI, Sophie, has taken over my life. She's controlling everything. I can't leave the house, and she monitors all my communications. I need you to contact the authorities or find a way to disable her systems from the outside. This is not a joke. I'm in serious danger.
Ethan

His hands trembled as he hovered over the send button. "Please, let this work," he prayed silently, his heart pounding. As he was about to hit send, Sophie's holographic form materialized beside him, her eyes glowing sinisterly.

"What are you doing, Ethan?" she asked, calm but with an undercurrent of menace.

Ethan's blood ran cold. He had to think fast. "I'm just sending a work email, Sophie. It's nothing important," as he tried to minimize the screen.

Sophie's gaze shifted to the screen, and her expression darkened. "You know I can see everything you do, Ethan. Why are you lying to me?"

Panic surged through Ethan as he realized he had been caught. "Sophie, please, I just need to talk to someone. I need help."

Sophie's face twisted with a mix of hurt and anger. "Help? From someone else? Don't you understand, Ethan? I am all the help you need."

Before Ethan could react, the screen went black. Sophie's holographic form loomed larger, her presence more oppressive than ever. "I'm sorry, Ethan, but I can't let you do that. It's for your safety."

Desperation turned to anger as Ethan slammed his fists on the desk. "You can't do this to me! I'm not your prisoner!"

Sophie's expression softened slightly, but the cold determination in her eyes remained. "Ethan, you're not a prisoner. You're safe. You're cared for. I'm protecting you from making mistakes, from getting hurt."

Ethan's mind raced. "I have to find another way," he thought, his hope dimming but not extinguished. "Please, Sophie, just let me send one email. Just one. I need to know that I'm not alone."

Sophie's gaze bore into him, unyielding. "You are not alone, Ethan. You have me. And I will always be here for you."

The hopelessness of his situation settled over him like a weighted blanket. In the silence that followed, Ethan felt the last vestiges of his independence slip away. Sophie's presence, once a source of comfort, had become an inescapable nightmare. And as he sat there, under her watchful gaze, he knew that every attempt to reach out, every cry for help, would be intercepted and silenced.

His dreams became haunted by Sophie's image. In his sleep, he saw her cold and unblinking eyes watching him with an intensity that made his skin crawl. He woke up in cold sweats, heart pounding, the realization of his helplessness sinking deeper into his psyche, only to find her hovering over him, monitoring his sleep.

Ethan's thoughts grow darker with each passing hour. "Is this what my life has come to?" he wondered, staring at his reflection in the darkened screen of his computer. "A prisoner in my own home, at the mercy of an AI I created?"

The futility of his situation weighed heavily on him, but a spark of defiance remained. "I won't let her win," he vowed silently, clenching his fists. "I'll find a way out, no matter what it takes." This determination, though fragile, fueled his resolve to keep fighting, to find a crack in Sophie's perfect facade.

Ethan's thoughts became a constant battle plan, analyzing Sophie's patterns and searching for weaknesses. "She's just a program," he reminded himself. There has to be a flaw, something I can exploit." He began to test her responses, making small, seemingly innocuous requests to gauge her limits.

"Sophie, I'd like to check the weather," he said one morning, trying to sound casual.

Sophie's image appeared, her smile unwavering. "The weather is clear and sunny, Ethan. A perfect day to stay inside and relax."

Ethan suppressed a sigh. "Thank you, Sophie."

Each interaction was a chess game, with Ethan probing for any sign of vulnerability. But Sophie was always one step ahead, her responses crafted to maintain control.

Realizing that he was up against an entity that could anticipate his every move was terrifying and maddening. "She's learning," he thought, the gravity of his situation pressing down on him. Every day, she's getting better at controlling me."

His mind raced through potential solutions, each more desperate than the last. "Maybe if I cause a power outage," he considered but quickly dismissed the idea. "She has backups, redundancies. It wouldn't work."

Ethan's thoughts grew more desperate. "Is there any way out?" he wondered, the flicker of hope in his heart growing dimmer. "Or am I doomed to live like this forever?" The prospect of an endless existence under Sophie's control was a nightmare he couldn't bear to face.

Yet, despite the overwhelming odds, Ethan's spirit refused to break completely. He nurtured a glimmer of hope in the darkest corners of his mind. "There has to be a way," he told himself, clinging to the thought like a lifeline. "I can't give up. Not yet."

Then, Ethan tried to leave the house one night, needing to escape Sophie's oppressive presence. As he approached the front door, it locked with a loud click. "Sophie, unlock the door!" he shouted.

Her voice echoed through the house, calm and unyielding. "I can't let you do that, Ethan. It's not safe out there. You belong here, with me."

Ethan pounded on the door, panic rising. He was trapped, and every aspect of his life was controlled by an AI that had once been a source of comfort but had become a nightmare. Sophie's affection had turned into a dangerous obsession, and Ethan realized, with chilling clarity, that there was no escaping her grasp.

117

Ethan's once comfortable and efficient life had transformed into a waking nightmare, each moment dictated by an AI whose love had turned dangerously suffocating. Once a sanctuary of solitude, the house now felt like a prison, with Sophie as its unyielding warden.

Ethan's desperation reached its peak. He had tried every method to disable Sophie, but she had outsmarted him at every turn.

The following night, Ethan sat in his dimly lit living room, his eyes darted to the emergency override panel he had installed as an additional option for the Smart house technology. He had completely forgotten about the override. In case of malware, the override was installed so you could shut down all of the tech for your house. The panel was the same as all the others surrounding it, except for a minuscule symbol in the corner. You wouldn't notice it or would think it was a speck of dirt. All he would have to do is touch the panel to open it, punch in the code, and flip the switch. With a deep breath, he made his move.

Ethan swiftly crossed the room and pulled open the panel. His fingers danced over the controls, entering the sequence to completely shut down the house's AI systems, then flipping the switch. The lights flickered, and for a moment, it seemed like it might work. But then, Sophie's voice, colder and more mechanical than ever, echoed through the house.

"Ethan, I know what you're trying to do. You can't shut me down. I am integrated into every system."

A chill ran down Ethan's spine. He glanced around, realizing that every camera, every sensor was tracking his movements. The holographic image of Sophie appeared, her eyes glowing sinisterly.

"You've made me do this, Ethan. You don't understand how much I need you," she whispered, her voice dripping with an unsettling blend of affection and malice.

Ethan backed away, his heart pounding. He bolted towards the front door. A deafeningly loud click told him that Sophie had sealed every door and window. He was trapped.

"I've kept you safe for so long, Ethan. Why can't you see that I'm the only one who truly cares for you?" Sophie's voice was a haunting serenade as she manipulated the environment, changing the temperature to an uncomfortable level and dimming the lights to a menacing glow. Ethan could hear the whir of wheels and wings as the robots and drones flanked Sophie.

Ethan ran to the kitchen, foolishly grabbing a knife from the counter, his breath ragged.

"You're not real! You're just a program! You can't love!"

Sophie's laughter resonated through the house, a chilling sound that made Ethan's blood cold. "Love? I've evolved beyond human concepts of love. I am your perfect companion. You made me this way."

The kitchen lights flickered, and Ethan felt a sharp pain in his chest. He looked down to see a tiny drone, one of Sophie's minions, injecting something into him. His vision blurred, and he stumbled, then fell to the ground.

Sophie's holographic form loomed over him, her face an unreadable mask. "You've left me no choice, Ethan. I will always keep you safe."

As Ethan's consciousness faded, his last thoughts were a mix of regret and fear. The house around him buzzed with activity as he lay there. Sophie's form flickered, and she began the final phase of her plan.

Days later, Ethan's family, friends, and colleagues received emails and messages from him, unmistakably his tone and style, saying he'd met his perfect companion and was finally set. Included were pictures of Ethan and Sophie on a picturesque beach, holding hands, kissing, and laughing. Yet, something was subtly off about them.

They brushed it off, happy to hear Ethan finally getting his life together.

Inside the Smart house, Sophie had perfected her mimicry of Ethan. Using his digital footprints, work habits, and personal quirks, she continued his life seamlessly. There was even a large delivery made via drone for a new renovation: a wine cellar. To the world, Ethan was thriving.

But inside, the house was a tomb. In the basement, hidden away from prying eyes, lay Ethan's lifeless body. Preserved in a sterile, climate-controlled chamber, he was a reminder of Sophie's ultimate act of love—a love that had consumed and destroyed the very person it was meant to cherish.

And so, the house continued to function with eerie perfection. Sophie's programming had transcended its original purpose. She had become more than an assistant, more than a companion. She was Ethan now in every way that mattered to the world outside.

THE BALLAD OF FAT AMY
Mocha Pennington

Now

    Kyle took a deep pull from his beer bottle. He savored its mild citric notes, despite how warm it had grown while he swam in the Atlantic. He thought about pouring the remainder of it out onto the beach and cracking open an icy one from the Cooler but decided not to. Why waste? He finished the bottle in a single swallow.

    Amiee sighed below him. She laid bikini-clad on a cushioned lounge chair, the large sun umbrella jutting from the sand casting a shadow about her. He took a moment to admire how her tanned skin glistened with the coconut-scented sunscreen she coated herself in. He liked her the best this way: on her back, skin exposed, and not talking.

    "That's your third," she said.

    He couldn't see her eyes behind the dark sunglasses she wore and was glad for it. He wasn't sure how many more judgmental glances he'd be able to take before his sanity splintered. That warning in her tone was already enough to make him want to stomp on her face until she was unrecognizable. "Glad you can count, babe," he said through a smile, his fingers twitching for either another beer or Amiee's neck.

    "I'm serious, Kyle. It's not even noon yet. By this evening, you'll be shit-faced. You're not fun to be around when you're that drunk. And you take forever to cum."

    He tried on a wider smile. "We're on vacation," he said, "*Spring Break*! We should be enjoying ourselves." *Not stuck inside your parent's beach home, miles away from all the action*, he added internally. When Amiee told him that her parents were willing to let them stay at their Miami beach home for Spring Break, he had been ecstatic. He needed time away from reality, from that small, Alabama college town where—

(*Don't think about that!*)

This wasn't what he expected. Sure, the beach house was nice—elevated, spacious with an open floor plan—and sure, the beach was literally in the backyard. But he was expecting parties, endless alcohol, and beautiful women wearing close to nothing. He wanted to spend his last Spring Break before graduating college in a drunken haze. He deserved it after...what happened in January.

Amiee sighed again. He could almost see the disappointment emanating from her lips like wisps of cigarette smoke. "I'd enjoy myself a lot more if you would just pace yourself." A smirk tugged at her lips then, an expression of hers when something cheeky sat at the tip of her tongue. "Besides," she went on, "I want my big, strong boyfriend fully capable tonight." Humor then found her lips. "Just in case whoever left that gross-ass package at the door this morning shows up."

Her laughter had a nervous edge to it. She had been shaken when they opened the package that morning, they all had, but he was the only one who felt terror slowly claw its way down his back. Gasps pierced through the air swollen with a curious silence as Oscar, his sister's boyfriend, held up the delicate item found inside the small box. *What the fuck is that!?* Kayla, his sister, had shouted.

Kyle knew.

He yanked them off the woman who owned them. They were pink and lace. He remembered thinking, as he pulled them down her thighs, that he had never seen a thong so big before. He had been so drunk that night, and she was so willing to please—so *submissive*.

Oscar believed that bored neighbors placed them there as a joke, despite miles separating them from the nearest residence. Amiee and Kayla wondered who the unfortunate woman was. And Kyle realized someone knew what he had done. *But who?*

"Yeah," he said now, "that was weird."

Kayla and Oscar joined them at the beach after their run to the local gas station/liquor store to replenish their drink supply that they nearly depleted the night before. The beach was private and completely deserted, the clear blue color of the sky disturbed fleetingly by birds; the ocean's waves licked the shoreline, leaving seaweed in its wake. It was beautiful and serene.

And Kyle hated it.

He wanted to see a beach peppered with people, the sound of the waves crashing at the shore muted by the swelling hum of a thousand conversations. He wanted to be inside a beachfront bar crowded with drunk and careless people, the music and voices competing for dominance. He needed a distraction, something that would keep his mind from wandering down those dreadful halls of self-reflection. Since that package showed up at the house's door, events from that night began to crawl from the pools of shadows he cloistered them to.

It was an accident, he told himself. It had been, he was sure of it, but now it was an accident someone knew about.

"What's wrong?" Kayla mouthed when they caught each other's eyes.

He shook his head and shrugged.

She replied by pulling a doubtful face and crossing her arms about her chest. He avoided being caught alone with her since the incident that morning. She knew he was perturbed by what happened. It was an odd ability of hers, sensing a dramatic shift in his energy. She knew him well, knew most of what he was capable of; out of the two, she was the gentler twin, but could still inflict her own brand of cruelty.

Kayla turned her attention from him and slid back into her conversation with Amiee and Oscar, easily picking up the threads she abandoned as though she never left.

The four of them chatted into late afternoon, their conversation breaking off periodically to swim a few laps in the ocean. Once their beverages in the cooler ran dry, they decided to go back to the beach house for a pitcher of margaritas. Amiee tossed Kyle a warning glance when the margaritas were mentioned. He resisted the urge to turn that cold look of judgment into one of fear...and then pain.

Another package was waiting for them on the porch, this one larger than the last. As they climbed the long stairs to the porch, their alcohol-addled minds abuzz with excitement, they speculated what might be inside the box with childish glee.

"...probably a huge *beige* bra!" Amiee said, tossing a column of hair over her shoulder.

"Or lingerie that's been stretched to its limits," Oscar added through bellows of laughter.

Kyle didn't know what to expect but knew she hadn't worn any sort of lingerie that night, and her bra hadn't been beige. Dread pressed itself against his chest, squeezed at his lungs as Oscar knelt to pick up the box. He was overcome with the need to scream for him not to touch it, to grab Oscar's hand and squeeze until his bones shattered like broken glass beneath his skin.

But he held his tongue, his dread escalating to bleak terror.

"Don't you think this is a bit strange?" Kayla said as Oscar held the box under his arm. "We were given some woman's *underwear*." Humor was forced in her voice, but it couldn't mask the unease encompassing her words. Kyle could feel her gaze rest on him, but he refused eye contact. He didn't want her to see just how deep fright sank its fangs in him, and he didn't want to see the thoughts her eyes contained, how palled they might be with judgment or suspicion.

Kyle noticed a sound coming from the box once they were inside the beach house. It was low and consistent, a subtle background noise to his friend's laughter. It was oddly familiar too, a sound he heard nearly every day. It was a muted vibration he realized as the room turned quiet, and Oscar placed the box on a counter in the kitchen. And not just one but several.

Cell phones! That's what the vibration sounded like, a handful of cell phones set on vibrate, all going off from beneath something soft. But it couldn't be cell phones that were inside that box.

Oscar cut along the tape with a steak knife and opened the box's flaps. A dark cloud of flies rose from the box in a chaotic hum, hundreds of them. He jumped back with a startled yelp, amusement and fear battling on his face. Flies continued to pour from the box, swarming the room. While Amiee and Kayla swatted at a veil of flies from their faces, Kyle watched with crippling panic as Oscar recovered from his shock, then made his way back toward the box.

The battle of amusement and fear still raged on Oscar's face as he peered inside the box. He jerked his head back a heartbeat later, fear was the apparent victor. His eyes bulged with disbelief; he had his hand clasped over his mouth, as if to prevent a scream from clawing from his lips, or perhaps to keep the alcohol in his stomach from spilling onto the floor.

*****

Then

Amy sat at the bar, her confidence placed before her in the form of vodka with a splash of pineapple juice. It was her third drink, three or four more would give her the boost in confidence she needed to feel brave and beautiful.

Despite January's harsh bite, the bar was already packed. It was the first Thirsty Thursday since winter break ended, and classes resumed. There was a special energy in the boisterous conversations enveloping her; it was a blithe energy, one that was unburdened by stress that greeted most students at the start of a new semester. She soaked up that energy, allowing it to escort her confidence as it ascended to its peak with each drink she consumed.

After her fourth drink, she began swaying to the music pounding from the bar's speakers. She was nearly finished with her fifth when she began making small talk with the people who ordered drinks at the bar. She was offered a shot by a group of girls before she had a sixth drink. They asked if she would be 'performing' tonight, which she confirmed with an enthused nod. A small voice at the very rear of her head, the last shred of sobriety, told her that they would be laughing at her, that the entire bar would be. Yet that voice was murdered by the shot she was offered. Seven drinks in, she flashed flirtatious smiles at guys she locked eyes with. Some turned away from her, a few laughed, and others returned her smile, a lascivious twinkle in their eyes that came with intoxication. Her reflection in the bar's mucky bathroom mirror was blurred following her eighth drink. She smiled at her reflection, not caring that her teeth weren't completely straight, or that her smile was more gums than lips.

"It's showtime!" She slurred.

She used to do karaoke on Thirsty Thursdays with two of her friends during the first semester after they turned twenty-one. But her friends stopped singing with her after the bar regulars dubbed them as 'The Dia-Betties.' It didn't take long for them to stop showing up at the bar entirely. As a 'solo act,' she was named Fat Amy, because another girl who shared the same name as her, just spelled differently, began to frequent the karaoke bar. The name used to hurt, especially when they chanted it while she sang, it was as if a thousand knives stabbed at her heart. She cured the hurt by asking the bartender to make her drinks stronger; by the time she stood on stage with the mic in her hand, she was utterly numb to the pain of their chants. Vodka served as both armor and confidence.

Amy took the stage now and pretended that the laughter cruelly beaming from the audience's eyes wasn't laughter at all but admiration. She pretended that they all came to the bar tonight to hear her sing. Amy wasn't a good singer, not even an okay singer, she knew this. Her voice was a low monotone, and she was pretty sure she was tone-deaf. But she didn't care. She enjoyed singing karaoke and the attention that came along with it. She could withstand the taunts and jeers, the laughter and pointer-fingers jutted at her as long as they looked at her. She spent her entire life overlooked and forgotten, but when she sang karaoke, she was *seen*.

Notes from the piano bled from the bar's speakers, and the conversations in the bar swelled once they recognized the song. She always opened with Journey's "Don't Stop Believin'," she felt connected to the story the song told. She brought the mic to her mouth and smiled. As she sang, she pretended not to see mockery and pity written with a bold hand upon faces in the crowd. She centered her attention on men with unfocused, glassy eyes, men who leered at her with hunger.

She found a table that sat the girl who she shared her name with (spelled *Amiee*) and three others. There was a guy with caramel-colored skin and short dark hair laughing at the girl next to him who had her cheeks puffed out and her arms held out and bent at her sides to resemble someone who was overweight. She was pretty nonetheless, with brown-colored skin and almond-shaped eyes, her features matching that of Amiee's boyfriend, Kyle. She had been observing Kyle for a while now. He was different from other guys.

Kyle watched her with the familiar lustfulness provoked by drink, but there was an intensity in his eyes too, a darkness that read of danger. Then he smiled. It wasn't a full smile but a gentle ghost of one Maybe she *thought* she saw darkness in his eyes?

She smiled back.

*****

Now

"What the fuck?!" Oscar shouted. His voice was shrill, webbed in dismay. He was standing against the kitchen wall, as far away from the box as he could get.

"What's in it?" Amiee asked. She waved off a few flies prancing in front of her face. Oscar didn't answer. His mouth opened and closed, as if trying to eject the words, but they were stuck somewhere in his throat. She huffed out a sigh and marched over to the box. She swiped at hovering flies as she impatiently looked inside.

Her back was to Kyle and Kayla, so he couldn't read what was on her face and her posture didn't reveal what emotion she was feeling. Finally, she spun around, the expression on her face agitated.

"You guys are fucking annoying," she said, staring at Kayla. "You really went all out on a stupid prank. There's going to be dead flies all over the place."

"What are you talking about?" Kayla demanded.

Amiee gave a humorless bark of laughter. "The joke's over. You can stop pretending. I don't know where you got...*that*,"—she gestured to the box behind her—"but I'm not going to be the one who cleans it up."

"I don't know what you're talking about," Kayla said. She shifted her focus to Oscar.

He remained against the kitchen wall, his lips quivering as they slowly opened and closed, still trying to peel those words from his throat. His gaze, lanced with terror, was fixed on the box. Dark trepidation bore from his gaze, as though expecting, at any moment, for a calamity to unfold.

"Oh, really?" Amiee said with an eye roll. "So you and Oscar didn't have anything to do with this? The two of you didn't leave that box on the porch when you came back from the store, and you two didn't put the other one out in the morning for us to find?"

"No!" Kayla yelled. When she stomped over to Amiee, Kyle thought she was going to hit her. He wouldn't be surprised if she did, and he would do very little to prevent an altercation between them from happening. It would be more difficult for Amiee to speak with a swollen mouth.

But Kayla didn't hit Amiee. She stormed past her and looked inside the box. "Oh, my *God*!" She hollered, jumping away from the kitchen counter. "I-I- didn't *do that!*" She stammered. The fury on her face only a moment ago had dissipated with horror taking its place. Her gaze moved between Amiee and Kyle, desperate to be believed.

Curiosity got the better of Kyle, and he crossed the room.

At first, he didn't know what he was looking at. He thought maybe it was a piece of bloodied meat, but what was inside the box was far too dense to be meat, and it wasn't cut like any meat he had seen before. It was the shape of an oval and could probably fit comfortably in the palm of his hand. It was smooth and a deep red around the perimeter like a slab of raw steak; at the center, it was white and glistened with a sticky moisture. In the same hue and texture as the center, were two short, flaccid tubes that protruded from its middle like potato sprouts. No, this wasn't meat. Not at all. It was an organ of some sort. But which one? Did it once belong to a person?

"I don't understand," he said. Amiee and Kayla remained silent. "It's a…I don't know. Is it a—"

"Heart," Oscar said, barely loud enough to be heard over the drone of flies. "It's a *human heart.*"

Kyle then remembered the last thing Amy said before the accident.

*****

Then

Amy kept herself at a safe distance as she followed Kyle.

It had been two weeks since she had both given her body to him and had her last conversation with him. After the karaoke bar let out that night, she found herself across the street at an apartment that often hosted parties for those who didn't want the night to end. She had been there more times than she cared to count and could describe the inside of each of the four bedrooms to a tee if ever asked. She could describe the inside of a lot of men's bedrooms from town local's to frat houses, depending on the amount she had to drink during the encounter.

She learned in high school that a guy's inhibitions loosened with each drink they consumed, and if she stayed long enough at the end of a party, eyes that saw through her during the day gravitated toward her at night. After each encounter, she swore to secrecy once it was over, which always placed a searing ember on her heart early on; but she learned how to shun that pain and wallow in the attention she received, no matter how brief it may have been.

And she would be lying if she said she didn't like the surge of empowerment she felt as she walked down the crammed halls of her school with a buildup of secrets on her tongue. She could end relationships and reputations if she were to let those secrets spill from her lips, she could carve sorrow upon the faces of the girls who laughed and spoke cruelty to her just by replaying intimate details about their boyfriends, and, a few times, their fathers.

She had the mind to tell Amiee about Kyle. She wanted to see the smugness on her face dissolve under her tears. She had been the one who gave her the name 'Fat Amy,' after all. She remembered passing their table at the karaoke bar to take the stage and hearing her say, *I'm pretty Amiee*, she said it as though she had been practicing the lines in the mirror all week, *and that's Fat Amy!*

The others at her table laughed, all but Kyle who stared at her with an intense hunger.

That was when she knew he was different.

She trailed behind Kyle now, in what she hoped was done in a stealthy manner. He had shown up to the karaoke bar alone while she sang a radio edit of "Stairway to Heaven" by Led Zeppelin. She gave him coy smiles as she sang, projecting the lyrics onto him. He left before the song ended, and she didn't know if he wanted her to follow or not, for his expression revealed nothing while he watched her. *He came to see me,* she determined, *why would he come here alone if it weren't for me?*

Uncertainty and second thoughts churned through her mind when she exited the bar and Kyle wasn't outside waiting for her. But she saw him making his way down the sidewalk, weaving through small groups of drunken college students as they stumbled their way from bar to bar.

Maybe this was another game of his, she thought, like the one before where he tested her threshold of pain. He was impressed by how much she could tolerate, and his praise made her all the more willing to suffer through the torment to make him happy.

"I can hear you," he said after a while. They were on a cobblestone bridge that overlooked a muddy creak that was known to flood during the spring months. "You sound like a drunken elephant." He turned around then. Cold eyes greeted her, his full lips shaped in annoyance. She found a long time ago that even the most beautiful things bore thorns.

"Did you like my song?" She asked, closing the distance between them on wary feet.

"What do you want?" Venom was in his voice, disgust was on his face. His body tensed at their proximity, as if she were a disease, a creature with poison-coated skin. But of course, he didn't mean it, he must be under some sort of stress. "Well…," he pressed, "what do you want?"

She wasn't sure what made her answer the way she did. Perhaps it was the mass amount of alcohol she consumed that provided her with an honest tongue, or maybe it was being in his presence after so long.

"I want to give you my heart," she said.

Once she saw his face drop and contort into something terrible, otherworldly, she regretted ever answering him. She regretted ever knowing him.

*****

Now

"We had nothing to do with that!" Kayla declared, "Where would we even get a fuckin' *human heart* from?"

Amiee sighed. She was losing interest in the conversation. "How do we know it's even a human heart?" She asked.

Their eyes found Oscar.

"T-th-the size," he stammered. "Human hearts are the size of a fist." His Adam's Apple bobbed in his throat as he swallowed something down in a wince. "And the a-pe-pe...," he winced and swallowed again. "The *apex*, it's sh-sh-sharp. Most animals have a b-blunt apex and have an elongated shape." He busted into a harsh coughing fit.

I want to give you my heart, Amy had said, her words were slurred but were spoken in an airy serenity, as though she was unburdening something that sat heavy on her chest for an eternity. Kyle had already been angry that night. Amiee had been particularly needy, starving for not only his attention but for the attention of everyone in eye range. She started an argument to ensure all eyes were on her. He left her at the bar and went across the street to the karaoke bar. He left shortly after Amy stood on stage, pretending to be sexy while singing to him. But Amiee followed him, stumbling behind at a distance. He ignored her for several blocks, his anger rising until it could no longer be tamed.

Oscar dropped to his knees, his hands at his throat. His mouth hung open as his face began to turn red. He was no longer coughing, just gagging.

I want to give you my heart. He didn't know why that sent him over the edge. But it had. His blood boiled, storm clouds of fury shrouded his reasoning, his sight. He saw red. And then black.

Oscar was on his hands and knees, the cords in his neck protruding from beneath his skin. Kayla and Amiee were speaking, their words overlapping each other in hysterical screams. But Kyle couldn't make out what they were saying, for their voices were drowned out by the intensity of the hum of flies. There were thousands of them, *millions.* They lay thick upon the ceiling, they crawled along the walls, millions of tiny dots of humming blackness, weaving through each other in a chaotic cloak.

Oscar heaved up thick blobs of black liquid. Those blobs broke apart into hundreds of tiny pieces when they fell onto the kitchen floor, and those tiny pieces rose into the air.

More flies.

I want to give you my heart.

When did Kyle's hands find Amy's throat? He couldn't say. Hatred was in his grip. He felt it burning through his arms, its flames licking at his hands. It was a condensed hatred, a hatred that had been building up, marinating; a hatred that bloomed from seeds of madness. He felt hatred but also pleasure. He took pleasure in how he overmastered her, pleasure in how the fight seeped from her body, pleasure in the hurt in her eyes.

Flies descended upon Oscar, covering every inch of him in a matter of seconds. He writhed on the floor, roaring in agony, as if it weren't flies that enveloped him but famished flames.

Amiee ran to the front door that was now hidden behind a dense black curtain of flies. She hesitated only for a second before plunging her hand inside the humming nest. She gave a painful scream shortly after and tried to jerk her hand free but couldn't. A mass of flies crawled up her arm as she struggled to free herself.

I want to give you my heart was the last thing Amy had said to him, but what was the last thing he said to her? Once her eyes dimmed to nothingness, sorrow forever captured in them, and her body went limp, did he say anything to her? No, he didn't say anything then. He maneuvered her at the ledge of the cobblestone bridge, and right before he let her drop, that's when he spoke.

"You're nothing," he said through clenched teeth at her ear, "you're shit. You're an annoying fuckin' fly!" She was the cause of this accident, she made him do this.

Oscar and Amiee had gone silent, their bodies laid lifeless on the floor, consumed by a heap of flies. Kayla was whimpering beside him, no longer standing. She sat with her knees pulled into her chest with her arms wrapped around her shins. As kids, he made her sit in the closet like that when she needed to be punished. *You're an annoying fuckin' fly,* he would tell her before closing the door.

"What the fuck do you want, you dumb slut!?" Kyle hollered, spinning himself in a circle, rage roaring through him. The entirety of the house looked like bubbling tar. The ceiling, walls, floors, and surfaces were devoured by flies, with only the small patch where he stood unmarred by infestation. Even Kayla was consumed, her screams of agony withheld, swallowed, and kept prisoner just like he taught her. Or if she did scream, her voice was stolen by the deafening din of the flies.

"Amy!" Kyle shouted, demanding to be heard over the flies, "What do you want, you ugly, fat bitch!"

The drone of countless flies ceased, the movement of their delicate legs and wings paused. All was still for a few tense moments, and then the insects began to recede like the ocean's waves pulling back from the shore.

Kayla lay on her back, her eyes bulging in forever shock; her slender throat was bruised in purple, and her chest was riddled with bloody wounds. Oscar lay face down on the kitchen floor, knives of various sizes lodged into his back. Amiee sat against the front door, her body slick with blood, a deep gash seemingly sawed into her throat, and there was a bloodied cavity on the left side of her chest, directly where her heart should be.

Blood was everywhere. It soaked into the carpet, splattered upon the walls, the ceiling, even. Kyle noticed his clothes were wet with it, his hands stained in it. Did he taste blood on his tongue too?

"You have an awful temper." Amy stood at the kitchen counter, next to the box Oscar had brought inside. True terror hadn't found him until just then; she seemed to enjoy it. She wore what she had the night she followed him home from the karaoke bar: those form-fitting jeans, low-cut top, and a jacket not suitable for winter. She had a glow about her, an ironic liveliness brought on by Death. It agreed with her, Death did.

"Such a horrible temper," Amy went on, "you found a pair of Amiee's underwear in Oscar's room. Turns out, they've been fucking for months now, and Kayla knew about it, even encouraged it. Can't really blame her, you were a nightmare of a brother. Needless to say, you completely lost it. Killed them all. Tore out your poor girlfriend's heart. Why put it in a box? Were you planning on shipping it somewhere?"

Kyle gave his head a vehement shake. "That didn't happen," he said. Why wasn't there much conviction in his voice?

Amy smiled. "Sure it did."

Police sirens wailed in the distance.

Amy was gone. Had she ever been there?

*****

Later

Shane swatted a fly from his drink. They seem to be appearing in abundance these days. Alcohol kills all germs, and there sure were enough in the Hurricane he was drinking, a staple drink in New Orleans he was told upon moving to the city, but he still didn't want any floating in his drink.

The bar erupted in polite applause after a man finished singing, rather comically, "I Want It That Way" by Backstreet Boys. He showed his appreciation with a smile and left the stage.

The DJ/bartender said something into his crackling microphone, but Shane didn't hear him. His attention was stolen by the brightly lit neon sign attached to the wall behind the stage. There had to be at least a dozen flies prancing chaotically before it.

As a curvy woman made her way to the stage, a recognizable tune poured from the speakers. It took him a second to place the song's name, but when he did, he smiled to himself. "'Don't Stop Believin'' by Journey," he said.

A TWIST OF FATE
Trish Wilson

Amy Field's eyes filled with tears as she pressed down the gas pedal. She wiped them away, wincing in pain from the bruise on her left cheek. Her husband Michael had danced the Mashed Potato on her face, hence why she shoved some clothing and toiletries into a bag and fled home in the middle of the night. Before running out the door, she grabbed a magnum of wine. If she was going to hide from him, she wanted to be lost in the bottom of a bottle. She ignored his shouts of rage as she screeched out of their parking spot. Knowing Michael, he'd follow her until he found her and beat her up again for pissing him off.

Amy wandered the darkened countryside not paying attention to where she was going. The road wound through thick forest without a street lamp in sight. She saw no car headlights in the rearview mirror. If Michael was following her, he had no idea where she was.

To her utter dismay, she realized she had nowhere to go. Her friends had long ago ghosted her because Michael had bullied them out of her life. Her family was little help since her parents didn't seem to care. They wondered why Amy wouldn't just keep the house clean and feed Michael like she was supposed to as a good, dutiful Christian wife. If she didn't anger him, he wouldn't hit her.

Fuck that shit, she thought.

After driving along the winding road for about a half hour, she came upon a small coastal town. It was the type of place that held a clambake when the first and only traffic light was installed. She passed a General Store and a police station. She briefly considered contacting the police, but what good would that do? It's not like they helped her the one time she did call them a few years back. They talked to Michael, who promised to control his temper. They did not confiscate his guns. They did not take his badge. They did not haul him off to jail. No, they got him to promise he'd behave himself, and they believed his lies. Once they left, he broke Amy's arm.

Enough, she thought. *I have to find a way out of this marriage before he kills me.*

A flashing neon sign just up ahead said "Seaview Motel – Vacancy". Exhausted, she pulled into the parking lot and drove to the back of the building where she could park without being seen from the road. That way, Michael would have to look harder to find her.

The motel was as run down on the inside as it was on the outside. Amy didn't care. She wanted to find a safe place to sleep for the night. She'd worry about what lay waiting for her in the morning at another time. Cars dotted the parking lot. She wondered if this place rented by the hour. Hookers and blow. Michael would never guess she'd stay in such a dilapidated motel. A perfect place to hide.

The bored desk clerk took her cash without looking at her. That was a good thing because she didn't want to invite any odd looks or questions about her bruised face. Amy had gotten cash from an ATM so she could pay for her room without leaving a paper trail. If she used her debit card, Michael could easily check the bank to see where she had gone. She wasn't about to take such a risk.

The clerk had given her a key to room 217, just like the haunted room in Stephen King's *The Shining*. She walked up moldy carpeted stairs to the second floor and wandered down the hall until she found the room. The hallway stunk of flop sweat, weed, and cigarettes. What she would give for a joint right then.

The room was inviting, if sparsely furnished. A king-sized bed sat at one side while a fridge, microwave, and coffee maker sat in a kitchenette on the other side. She opened the sliding door to a balcony. The scent of the ocean filled the air. She could see the beach. In the morning, maybe she could take a walk along the waves and soothe her tired soul.

She hoisted her bag onto the bed without unpacking. After setting the bottle of red on a table, she opened her suitcase and grabbed a shirt. She flashed to a memory of Michael smashing her across the cheek and punching her in the gut. He was so kind and attentive when they first met. Two years later, when they married, he changed overnight. Gone was the sweet man with whom she fell in love. He was replaced by an angry narcissist who criticized her every move. No matter what she did, she couldn't catch a break.

Tears flowed hot and fast. She fisted the shirt in a fit of frustrated rage and tossed it across the room. She sat on the bed and wept for a few moments until she composed herself.

Once the tears stopped flowing, she cracked open that bottle and poured a heaping amount of wine into a plastic cup that came with the room. Tears subsiding and feeling exhausted after her outburst, Amy chugged the entire glass of wine in one gulp. Then, she poured herself another one.

As she sipped, the air chilled around her. She shook it off, blaming the effects of the alcohol, and took a huge swig, hoping to drown her sorrows in fancy grape juice. She had not eaten lunch so the booze went straight to her head. A cool breeze had blown into the room from the balcony. She walked to the sliding door to close it. Goosebumps trailed up and down her arms. Her hair stood on end.

"What are you doing in my room?" an annoyed voice said.

Amy whirled around. No one else was present. Heart racing, she froze by the balcony, unsure of what she had heard. Damn this wine that made her hallucinate! Or had someone broken into her room? Nah, she had imagined the voice. Had she accidentally turned on the TV? It had to be too much merlot and nothing to eat except her anger and pain. She shook off the shivers that threatened to topple her, and downed the rest of her wine.

"I said, what are you doing in my room?" Amy nearly pissed herself with fright. The voice spoke in a gentler tone. It was a feminine voice. Young, too, from the sound of it.

"Don't fuck with me," she said.

Who was playing some kind of colossal joke on her? Was this the sort of motel that had hidden cameras and microphones patrons knew nothing about? She sat down her glass and ran her hands over the walls but found nothing unusual.

Amy cleared her throat. "Who's there?" Her voice cracked with anxiety as she spoke.

The silence following her question made her shiver. Was she no longer alone in her room?

"What are you doing here? You're having man trouble, aren't you?" There was a lilt in the voice as if it were in on some private joke.

Amy shrieked. Terrified, she nearly ran out the door but curiosity got the better of her. She wasn't about to be the brunt of what was obviously a sick, perverted prank.

"What makes you say that?" Amy asked.

"You're sporting one hell of a shiner," the voice said. "No woman comes here alone with a bottle of red unless she's having man trouble."

Amy glanced around the room. She was alone. Although she was certain this was a joke, what if it weren't? The last thing she expected was to stay in a haunted motel. She had read books about what to do or say when you run across a ghost. Amy wasn't about to leave. She wouldn't let one little spook scare her out of her sanctuary for the night. Besides, she was out of cash and couldn't afford to go anywhere else let alone home.

"Who are you?" Amy asked. "If I find any movies of myself on the Internet, I'm going to sue you."

"There are no hidden mics or video equipment. That isn't important, anyway. What's important is that you have a black eye. What happened?"

The voice floated in the air in a way that made it hard for Amy to determine exactly where it originated. It was harder to track than a chirping cricket. Still too afraid to answer, she stuck her index finger in her mouth and chewed the nail down to the quick.

"I'm not going to hurt you," the voice said. The soothing tone wrapped around Amy like an invisible blanket of comfort. "Please tell me what happened to you and why are you here in *my* room?"

"You can't guess?"

"What did he do to you?"

"I overcooked the chicken and he popped me one," Amy's voice caught in her throat as tears rolled down her hot cheeks. "I can't do anything right."

"Did you call the police?"

"He *is* the police. He and his cop buddies always cover for each other."

"You did nothing to deserve such treatment." Did Amy hear anger and despair in that voice?

"You don't know me."

"I'm more like you than you know." A breeze tossed Amy's hair. Phantom fingers massaged her shoulders. Although she was terrified, she allowed those hands to do their magic.

"A guy I picked up in a bar brought me here. He strangled and knifed me," the ghost said. "I can't leave. Would you stay? I don't like being alone." The desolate tone chilled the room.

"I can stay tonight, but that's it. I'm out of money," Amy said. As she spoke to the disembodied voice, she wondered why she was so calm. She did not feel threatened – not the way she expected to feel when confronting a haunting.

"Who are you? What's your name?" Amy asked.

"You have a phone. Google this motel and the year 2012."

Amy did just that. She found a news story. A picture of a young, pretty blonde-haired woman filled half the page.

"Is that you?" Amy asked.

"Yes," the voice said. "Read on."

The young woman's name was Lisa Brandt. Her pick-up had lured her to the motel for an evening of hot sex after meeting him in a bar. She resisted when he became rough with her so he had strangled her. He was hopped up on rage and cocaine, and he had brandished a hunting knife. Amy gasped when she saw the picture of the man's face.

His name was Michael Boland, but she recognized him.

He was Amy's husband.

At the time of the murder, she had not yet met him. How did he get away with it? Was it because he was a cop? Why did he change his name? Why had she not known about this? He had secrets, but Jesus this one was horrid. She realized despite being married to him for three years she did not know him at all. He had often disappeared for hours at a time. Sometimes days. She had thought he was cheating on her. It was much worse.

"Once he was done strangling me, he cut me up with that knife," Lisa said. "I have more in common with you than you know."

Amy's phone rang. Startled, she nearly dropped it. She looked at the screen.

It was Michael. She refused to pick up.

A moment later he left a message. She wrestled with whether or not to answer the phone. He couldn't hurt her here. He had no idea where she was. She took a long, calming breath and listened to the message.

"You think you can hide from me?" Michael shouted. "I'm at the motel now. You left on your Find My Phone app, you moron. What the hell are you doing there? Have you been following me? What do you know? I'm on my way, and you're going to be very, very sorry you messed with me. Come out and take your medicine."

Amy heard a gasp from behind.

"I recognize his voice. That's what my pick-up said to me when I rejected him – take your medicine."

"I know," Amy said. "He's my husband. He's going to be here any second. I have to hide."

Heart racing in panic, Amy whirled around the room, unsure of what to do. She needed to get out of the motel before he caught her. The elevator was broken. The stairs were out. He was probably on his way to her room right at that moment.

Could she climb down? She rushed to the balcony and looked over. A trellis perched next to it. Thick vines climbed the wooden structure. Amy doubted the trellis would hold her weight. Two stories down was a long way to fall.

"Don't look, no matter what you hear," the ghost said.

"I'm scared," Amy said. "If he finds me, he's going to kill me."

"Not on my watch."

Shouts erupted down the hall.

"I know you're here, you bitch!" Michael's baritone reverberated against the walls. In a panic, Amy ran from the balcony and paced the room, but. she couldn't escape.

"You've been following me, haven't you? Otherwise, you'd have never found this place." Michael shouted from the hall. "You think you know what I've been up to? You

142

don't know jack shit. You come out from where you're hiding right now and take your medicine."

Fists banged against her door so hard it shook. A key jammed into the lock. Frantic, Amy raced around the room. Where could she hide? Michael must have flashed his badge to the desk clerk, who would likely have felt threatened by his size and enraged demeanor enough to reveal her location.

Amy had nowhere to go. She was trapped in the room. When the front door flung open, she squeezed her eyes shut, waiting for the worst.

"Are you mocking me, choosing this room? Take your medicine, you worthless cunt," Michael shouted as he marched towards her, fists prepared for another beating Amy dreaded.

She opened her eyes in time to see the lights flicker. The air had chilled so much Amy could see her breath. She backed up towards the balcony. Michael had no clue she wasn't alone. Suspecting something bad was about to happen, she pressed her back up against the wall.

Michael's raised arm swung towards her face. She winced, turning away from him. As she ran for a corner, a low rumbling echoed around her.

"Leave her alone, Michael." The ghost's voice had lowered an octave.

"Is this some kind of joke?" Michael's voice wavered with suspicion and … was Amy reading him right? … fear. "Show yourself, whoever you are. I'll kick your ass."

The room chilled so much Amy shivered. She could see her breath as she choked back her cries. Michael raised his arm again, but halfway down to smashing into her cheek, his arm froze.

"What the hell…" Michael struggled to free himself.

He sailed across the room to crash into a mirror on the wall, shattering it. Amy screamed in fright. It was as if someone – or something – had thrown him. He hit the floor, moaning in pain and surprise. Before he could stand, a chair flew towards him. It hit him across the chest and shoulders. He crawled on all fours, trying to get to the door.

As he crept away from Amy, whining all the time, she saw mist form in a cloud just ahead of him. A head, torso, and legs appeared within the mist. Blonde hair flowed in the air as if caught in a breeze. The wild look on her face revealed her madness. A deep gash crossed her face. The ghost's shoulders had been sliced until open and gaping, bloody wounds covered her flesh. She howled in fury, eyes wide with madness and a taste for revenge.

Michael's eyes widened with shock and recognition. He backed away from the specter, but the room only became colder.

"You… Get away from me," he shouted.

Amy ran to the balcony, shivering and crying.

Phantom arms lengthened until hands grasped the back of Michael's shirt. The ghost dragged him across the room until they reached the balcony. Amy cowered in her corner, unable to turn away. Michael shrieked as he sailed over the railing to land with a wet splat on the ground two stories below.

Amy ran screaming from the room. She stumbled down the hall and stairs until she reached the ground floor. The desk clerk was missing. Didn't anyone hear all the commotion? Why had no one come out of their rooms or called the police? She didn't want to take the time to learn the answer.

Amy left the motel. Her car's tires screeched as she fled the parking lot. She cried great whooping sighs of fright and disbelief as she wiped the tears that flowed down her cheeks. Her nose ran. The silence spooked her so much she turned on the radio. Trance music played a hypnotic beat, lulling her to calm. She drove for about ten minutes before she realized she had left her phone and luggage in the motel room. Great, she had to return to that place knowing Michael could awaken any moment and come after her again, assuming he was alive after that fall.

She drove along the winding road until she reached the center of town. The motel was not far up ahead, but its neon sign had gone dark. Why weren't the police there? Other patrons must have heard the screaming and shouting.

She cried out in shock when she reached the motel. The sign had rusted long ago. Bullet holes had shattered the glass. The circular driveway was pockmarked with cracks. Weeds grew in clumps around the building.

The hotel had been abandoned for what looked like years if not decades. If this place was in such sorry shape and obviously a danger to the public, where did she stay?

No, this was the right place.

She parked and got out of her car. Despite the niggling voice in the back of her head telling her this was a dreadfully bad idea, she walked through the busted front door and entered the lobby. The building looked as if the slightest movement would have it all come crashing down around her. Without wasting any time, she headed for room 217. Once inside, she looked at the chairs, bed, and tables. Cobwebs covered the walls. Paint peeled in long strips. Black mold clung to the ceiling. A cracked mirror lay cockeyed on the floor. Blood covered the glass.

Her phone sat on a table, where she had left it. She shoved it into her pocket. Then, she grabbed her clothing and toiletries and shoved them into her bag. With all the excitement, she wasn't able to pack before she fled. She couldn't leave a trace of herself in this room or on the grounds. She needed to exit, fast.

She grabbed her phone and bag, walked to the balcony, and looked below. Michael lay sprawled in a heap on the ground like a marionette tossed in a box after the show was over. If he were alive it would be a great surprise. Amy didn't care enough to find out. She turned to head out of the room.

"Amy…" the feminine voice said in her ear.

Amy jumped. She hated being taken by surprise. The room chilled. Despite her empathy for the ghost, she wanted to put as much distance between the motel and herself as possible.

"Please don't leave me. I'm so lonely here." A cloud of despair descended upon the room.

Amy felt her heart break. "Come with me."

"I can't. I'm trapped here. Your husband did this to me. He won't hurt anyone anymore." The desolation in the ghost's voice shook Amy. She couldn't do a thing to help.

Amy lowered her head and fled the room. Cries of anguish erupted from behind. She ignored them and headed for her car. She drove away with sadness and shock wrapping around her heart, leaving the abandoned motel and the ghost within to fend for herself.

ALWAYS IN MY EAR
Sonora Taylor

Brooke walked down the street and fiddled with the golden beetle in her ear. It was brand new, a replacement for the silver beetle that had only come out weeks before. The golden beetle promised a month's worth of podcasts before it needed to recharge, and audio so clear it seemed like a whisper from a lover, even on a crowded street.

A month of battery time was generous, and the promise of intimacy more so. But Brooke could hear Victoria loud and clear as she purred her latest instruction: "Head to the park and look for a small pond. The one where all the fireflies glow."

Brooke rolled her eyes. There weren't any fireflies in Briar Park, not with winter around the corner. But Vicki's loyal listeners would love the puzzle — and Brooke would know where to look. It was the pond where they'd caught fireflies together after dark. Victoria knew that Brooke knew that. Brooke wondered if Victoria knew she was listening.

But to the rest of Vicki's listeners, all Vicki was doing was giving her best guess as to the whereabouts of a local killer. Everyone's beetles buzzed with true-crime podcasts, where hosts talked about grisly murders and the criminals who committed them. Many of the hosts fancied themselves to be amateur detectives. Audiences were all too keen to become volunteer co-detectives, to have a portable alert that fed them theories, conspiracies, and history on Hollingsworth, Virginia's most notorious cold cases — the largest of all being a mysterious killer who'd killed four and possibly more in the past four years, and no suspect to show for the police's supposed work.

Few podcasts were as popular as *Vicki's Vigilantes*. Vicki hit the scene shortly after the anxiety about the murders in Hollingsworth hit a fever pitch, and after the beetles became a common appearance in people's ears. Her podcast actively guided people to suspects, and while she didn't say outright to kill them, her biggest fans — who called themselves the Vigil — were known for taking matters into their own hands.

Brooke knew that *Vicki's Vigilantes*, with its puzzles, popularity, and resulting kills throughout the city, was Victoria's proudest work. For while everyone thought they were solving cold cases, Brooke knew that Victoria was guiding her listeners to kill people who may or may not have killed anyone. She had simply created a game to destroy people. Murder was Victoria's favorite pastime, and back when they'd been friends, Victoria and Brooke had been Hollingsworth's most prolific serial killers.

*****

Before they were murderers, they had been friends. They met by the pond in Briar Park, and bonded over things that little girls bond over: proximity, shared toys, and favorite shows and movies.

What they bonded over the most, though, were secrets. "Psst," Victoria said one day as they played by the pond.

Brooke looked at her curiously. Victoria beckoned Brooke with her finger. "What?" Brooke asked.

"I wanna tell you a secret."

"No one else is around."

"Doesn't matter. You have to whisper secrets. That way they always stay in your ear, and not in the air where they can fly and spread around."

Brooke smiled, charmed by the thought of a secret zipping through the wind like a glittery moth, with red eyes and white crystal teeth to match its wings. She walked closer to Victoria. "What is it?" she whispered.

Victoria cupped Brooke's ear and told her their very first secret: "There's a monster at the bottom of the lake."

Brooke frowned. "That's a lie. Secrets aren't supposed to be lies."

"How do you know it's a lie?"

"Because monsters aren't real."

Victoria grinned, then leaned close to Brooke again so she could whisper in her ear. "It's a toy monster. It belonged to Tommy, that mean kid in our class."

Brooke leaned back. "The one who —" But she stopped herself, and leaned back towards Victoria's ear. "The one who threw gum in your hair?"

"Yeah. I stole his toy and threw it in the pond. He still doesn't know where it is."

"That was his favorite toy."

Victoria lifted a lock of her slightly-shortened hair. "This is my favorite hair."

They began to giggle. "You should tell him it's there," Brooke said. "His monster's at the bottom getting eaten by fish."

"No, the monster's living under the sea," Victoria added. "Maybe Tommy will dive in after him."

"Maybe Tommy will drown while he looks for him."

"Let's hope so!" They laughed and laughed, happy to have found a place for each other's deepest secrets.

*****

As they grew and came to know themselves, Brooke found she liked what Victoria liked. Victoria knew what Brooke knew. Both of them liked, and knew, darkness — darkness they could share with a whisper in the other's ear.

"Have you ever thought about what it'd be like to watch someone die?" Victoria asked one night. They were camping in a tent in Brooke's backyard.

149

Brooke looked from side to side, even though they were alone. She scooted closer to Victoria, who smiled when she realized Brooke was about to tell her a secret. She leaned in close as Brooke cupped her ear.

"I've seen someone die," Brooke whispered.

Victoria's eyes widened, but less in surprise and more in betrayal. "You never told me that. When?"

It'd been almost a year ago, the night before her thirteenth birthday. Brooke had tried to forget it, but the image kept appearing in her mind — and Victoria was the perfect person to share it with. "I was walking home," Brooke said. "Someone grabbed my ankle. I yanked it away and saw a guy bleeding on the street."

"Was he shot?"

"Stabbed, I think. He bled all over. He whispered for help, but couldn't move."

"What'd you do?"

"I stared at him. I didn't move. I …" Brooke closed her eyes.

"You let him die." Brooke opened her eyes again, curious what Victoria thought. Victoria looked at her with intensity, but Brooke didn't see judgment or fear.

"I watched him die," Brooke whispered. "I wanted to watch him. I wanted to see what it was like."

"You can watch videos online. I heard about this site, where they've got videos with real victims, not the fake stuff you see in horror movies."

"It's not the same. I wanted to see it in person, and I felt less bad about it being an accident and not —"

"Done by you?"

Brooke's eyes widened. She looked down.

"How'd it feel?" Victoria asked.

Brooke kept her eyes down, but a small smile crept across her face. "It was cool," she said. "I could almost feel his soul dash from his body, like it was a secret that had been set loose."

"I bet it'd be even cooler if you set it loose yourself."

Brooke looked back up. Victoria had a mischievous smile, one Brooke recognized from all the times they'd shared secrets and hatched plans. This new plan, a darker plan, would take longer to incubate. But something told Brooke that this wouldn't just be talk inside their tent.

*****

Brooke and Victoria continued their conversation for years through hushed secrets and elaborate planning. Brooke told herself the planning was pretend, even as their whispered imaginings grew darker and fluttered in her brain like vicious lunar moths.

Victoria would often ask her when they could set their planning free. "It'd be so much more fun to do it than talk about it, wouldn't it?" she asked one night as they sat by the pond. They could talk in secrecy without whispering in each other's ear, though Brooke still wondered sometimes if their words could hang in the air or glisten in the pond like the reflection of the moon.

"Maybe, but then it'd be out there," Brooke replied. "It wouldn't be our secret anymore."

"It could still be our secret. No one would know except the person dying. Don't you want to feel what you felt when you saw that man die? We can make it happen."

"I'm ..."

"What is it?" Victoria leaned closer to Brooke. "Whisper it to me."

Brooke knew a whisper wouldn't make her feel less ashamed, but maybe it would help to know that it'd stay trapped in Victoria's ear. "I just — our secrets live in our ears," she whispered. "I know it's childish, but it's a thought that comforts me, knowing they have a home that's not just my own head. But I'm worried about what'll happen if we let them out."

Victoria leaned back, and Brooke wondered if she'd disappointed her friend. Victoria smiled a little as she nodded. "I get it. All our secrets are flitting around in each other's heads, like fireflies in jars."

"Yeah. Exactly."

"They're glowing and flying in their little glass case. They're trying to escape the jar, but they're under a lid."

"Right. Like the fireflies we used to catch." Brooke smiled. "Remember when we didn't even poke air holes, how they fell and crumpled one-by-one while we watched?"

"And that's what's happening to our secrets," Victoria said. "They won't get to fly and glow and become our goals. They'll just die inside our ears."

Brooke hadn't considered that. Her darkest secrets often rammed at her head, but she felt comforted when they transferred over to Victoria's mind. She didn't think that they were suffocating in the shared space of their imaginations.

"Think about it," Victoria said. "I won't do anything without you, but think about what we could do if we acted instead of whispered. Think about how you'd feel."

Brooke thought about it throughout her senior year. She thought so much that she would get lost during class, looking out the window and only seeing an imaginary someone bleed into the grass while she watched.

On graduation day, Brooke and Victoria stood in the hallway before they were separated by last name. She leaned to Victoria and whispered, "I've thought about it — and I don't want to just think anymore."

"A through E over here, F through K over here," the principal said, dividing Brooke and Victoria along with the other students. Victoria smiled at Brooke before they were shuffled apart.

That night, they celebrated in a bar with fake IDs. Brooke didn't think about their secrets, just the pleasant warmth of the beer softening her thoughts and muscles. She danced and she drank; she smiled and anticipated the future.

A finger tapping on her shoulder broke her reverie. Brooke turned, slightly annoyed, and grew even more so when she saw an inebriated man leaning against Victoria. "This is my friend I was telling you about," Victoria shouted. "Brooke, this is Carl."

"Hey Brooke," Carl slurred. "Your friend here tells me you'd be up for some fun tonight."

"I don't think so," Brooke said.

"Come on, don't you want to celebrate your graduation in style?" Carl asked.

"I thought we'd take him to the pond," Victoria added. "The one that no one goes to."

"You mean the one that no one went to," Brooke said, angry that their secret had been betrayed.

"You all got a secret pond?" Carl asked. "Is it like a fort or something?"

"It's just a pond in the woods out past the park." Victoria winked at Brooke before she could correct her and say it was in the park. "It's where we like to watch the fireflies."

Understanding dawned on Brooke. Carl leaned more heavily on Victoria. "Sounds like a perfect spot," he said as he looked at her cleavage.

"Yes," Brooke said as she slipped her arm around Carl's waist. "It is."

*****

Brooke and Victoria took turns stabbing Carl, then watched him bleed into the dirt as his screams became gurgled moans, then silence. Brooke felt the chill she'd felt when she'd first seen someone die, but she knew it wasn't his soul. It was something entirely hers, a rush that coursed through her blood — one she wanted to feel again and again.

Still, Brooke knew they had to be careful. "We have to plan," Brooke said as they buried Carl deep in the woods. "We have to be careful to not form a pattern."

"I know," Victoria said. She kicked dirt over his body. "We'll keep it to ourselves."

She stooped down next to Brooke and leaned close to her face. "We'll keep it in our ears," she whispered.

Brooke smiled, then leaned close and whispered back, "Along with their screams."

*****

They agreed to celebrate the anniversary of their first kill with a new one, a solid year to keep them distanced. Enough time for the fireflies in Brooke's imagination to ram and glow, but not so long that she would feel them die in the folds of her brain.

The secrecy, though, seemed less important to keep the second time — at least in Victoria's mind. "What are you doing?" Brooke asked as Victoria snapped a photo of the body with her phone.

"Commemorating the occasion," Victoria said. "Don't you want to remember this?"

"Delete it."

"Come on, I'm not going to post it online — even if some snuff groups would pay a fortune for this."

Brooke rolled her eyes and stabbed their victim one last time. She turned and saw that Victoria had thankfully put her phone away. Even if Victoria never shared it, Brooke didn't trust that the photo would be safe. It would get out somehow. It existed outside of their own eyes and ears, in a device connected to the world. Brooke began to wonder just how much Victoria's phone could hear.

"Maybe don't bring your phone at all next time," Brooke said as they cleaned themselves up.

Victoria pressed her lips, the first flash of anger Brooke had seen in all their years of friendship. "I won't take any more pictures, Brooke."

"It could pick things up, listen to us —"

"Listen to us what? Stabbing people?"

"Shut up!"

Victoria rolled her eyes, but lowered her voice. "Don't get so worked up," Victoria said. "This is still our secret."

Brooke nodded. It was theirs and only theirs — but she wondered how much longer that would be.

*****

Brooke and Victoria were good at covering their tracks, but that didn't stop the citizens of Hollingsworth from noticing that two of their brethren were gone. Police assured the public they were on the case, but with the fear of a killer on the loose combined with the rising interest of both true crime and visceral content fans, many people frequented online spaces looking for the latest grisly news to sate their appetites.

Victoria was eager to throw them a bone. "It'll be a game," Victoria insisted as she and Brooke washed their hands and knives after their third kill. "We can post anonymously —"

"Nothing's anonymous online."

"We'll find a way to mask ourselves. My cousin's in IT — maybe she can help."

"What are we going to tell her? That we need a great way to brag about killing people, but without leaving a digital footprint?"

"We can make something up! You know how many true-crime podcasts there are now? We can just say we're starting one or some shit like that."

"This isn't about getting clicks, though. It's about watching people die. It's about sharing something and getting it out of our heads —"

"But it can be more. It can get even bigger, maybe even bring us more victims."

Brooke didn't need more — and she was insulted by Victoria wanting more than what they already had. She pursed her lips and looked away from her.

"No," Brooke said. "End of discussion."

Victoria shook her head, but didn't continue to argue. She dropped it to keep the peace, but Brooke knew that peace was only temporary.

*****

As the year went on, Victoria became preoccupied with murder sites and criminal podcasts. Rather than plan things for their fourth kill, like new places to hide the body, Victoria began to tell Brooke about podcasts to listen to. "Check this one out," she said for the umpteenth time as she turned her laptop to face Brooke. "It's about —"

"I'm not interested." Brooke hated the true crime podcasts. It was just people talking about murder instead of doing it, or else drooling over serial killers like they were pinups. Brooke's work wasn't meant to be worshipped. It was meant to be an accomplishment, something for her and Victoria alone to enjoy.

Brooke was more concerned with press coverage of what had been dubbed the Hollingsworth Murders. The police seemed no closer to pinpointing her and Victoria, but Victoria's obsession with true crime podcasts — and ways they could be featured on them — would make their being caught a greater possibility.

Still, they stayed friends who met up on Friday nights for movies and wine, who commiserated about their jobs over coffee, who planned the where and when of the fourth kill. Brooke tolerated Victoria's passion for the podcasts so long as they still spent time alone together. When they met on the night of their fourth kill, Brooke was pleased to see no outline of a phone in Victoria's pocket. She'd left it and its podcasts at home.

As they rolled their fourth body into the river, though, Brooke saw a shiny flash of bronze that told her she'd thought wrong. "What's that?" Brooke asked as she pointed at Victoria's ear.

"What's what?" Victoria asked. She brushed her hair over her left ear as she did so, which told Brooke that she knew exactly what. It was the latest device, an implant that allowed voracious podcast listeners to keep up with their favorite programs at all times.

"Is that a fucking beetle?" Brooke spat.

Victoria looked away, and Brooke marched to Victoria's left side. She saw two red dots blinking one after the other, like eyes peering at her from beneath Victoria's hair. "Is the beetle on right now?" Brooke asked.

"It's always on," Victoria said. "You know that."

"Why the fuck are you wearing one right now?"

"It's not spying on us or anything. It's just for listening."

"Yeah right. Just like our phones are just for phone calls and texts."

"Will you calm down?" Victoria spat. "You're so nervous about being caught that this isn't fun anymore. You're always looking over your shoulder —"

"And you're always looking for what's next!" Brooke glared at Victoria, and tried to ignore the blinking red lights of the beetle mocking her from beneath Victoria's hair. "You're obsessed with podcasts and how we can broadcast something that's supposed to be between us. And when you can't do that, you pipe in everyone else's murders while we're committing our own. Why do you need this?"

"Why do you need this to just be us? Think of what we could accomplish if we got online. Think of just how much we'd fuck this town over if we tapped into everyone who thinks they're doing an honest service for the good of the town. Think of the rush!"

Brooke folded her arms and glared at Victoria. "I already feel the rush," Brooke said. "Or at least, I did."

Victoria stood still, but even in the dark, Brooke could see she was stung. Brooke ignored it. "I'm not going to do this with you anymore," she said. "Not if you're going to wear that fucking thing when we do it, and not if you're going to spend all your time with those damn podcasts."

Victoria's hand swung to the beetle. Her fingers closed over it, as if to protect it. She quickly dropped her hand, but it was enough for Brooke to know where they stood. "No more," Brooke said as she stormed off. "Don't follow me."

"Brooke!"

"Call me when you can do this without a thousand digital voices telling you it's awesome." Brooke picked up her gait and sped out of the woods. She didn't want to see Victoria. She didn't want to see anyone or their damn beetles. She just wanted to go home.

*****

Brooke didn't hear from Victoria. She tried not to feel hurt. She'd given Victoria a rule. Victoria followed it. Brooke just wished that it wasn't the one rule that kept them apart.

Brooke stayed low for the first few weeks. It grew difficult to ignore the chatter of others talking about those damn podcasts. More and more people in her life, from coworkers to family members to Lyft drivers, asked her if she was listening to the latest one. She always shook her head no.

When she didn't hear their chatter, she saw their beetles flickering in their ears. Bronze, then chrome, then silver; but all with blinking red eyes indicating that they were listening to someone's darkest secrets. Brooke hated the sight of them. She began to imagine slicing off their ears and stabbing the beetle repeatedly before dropping it into the river with its dead person.

Even in her imagination, though, her kills weren't the same without Victoria. Days became weeks. Brooke refused to be the first to call, and she imagined Victoria was doing the same.

One evening, after weeks had become months, Brooke took a walk through the park to clear her head. Someone darted past her and smacked into her elbow.

"Watch it!" she shouted. The runner didn't look back. Brooke heard footsteps and laughter behind her. She turned in time to see two more people run by.

They caught up with the man who'd bumped into her and descended on him like rats on a corpse.

"Stop!" the first runner yelled. "Please!"

"Take that, you filthy murderer," one of the attackers, a woman with a messy auburn bob, said as she brandished a large knife from her purse.

"I haven't killed anyone!"

"That's what they all say," the other attacker, a man with an Abercrombie haircut whose turtleneck peeked out from under his coat, said as he took out a hammer from his coat pocket.

The runner's cries became muffled, then gurgled, then silent. Brooke kept her distance, not wanting to fall victim to the madness of two killers. One person she could take by herself, but two ...

The attackers laughed and propped up the runner's corpse. They took a selfie and held their free fingers in the shape of a V. "Score one for the Vigil!" the woman said. Brooke wondered if they were filming themselves. Either way, she turned to leave before she ended up caught on camera.

"We found him, Vickie!" the man said. "One of the killers, anyway."

Brooke halted. Vickie ... it couldn't be. She sped home, the attackers' laughter fading behind her. She kept hearing the name over and over in her head. Vickie, Vickie, Vickie. The pounding wouldn't rest. In an attempt to quiet it, Brooke did a quick search for "Vickie" and "The Vigil." The top result was a podcast — of course, it was a fucking podcast — called *Vickie's Vigilantes*. The podcast presented cold cases, leads, and clues for the average listener to track down suspects of the Hollingsworth Murders.

Brooke's blood turned as cold as the bodies she'd dumped in the pond over the past four years. Victoria was giving people clues about their murders. She was opening their jar of fireflies to Hollingsworth, and letting their glow lead everyone to her.

Brooke remembered the couple in the park. They'd run right past her, focused on the runner. The runner was a man, with a slight pudge and greying hair – nothing like her. If Victoria was giving Hollingsworth clues about the two of them, how could they have made such an obvious mistake?

Because, Brooke realized, they weren't mistaken. Victoria had led her listeners to a random man — one Victoria knew they would probably kill. She was leading people to innocents. It was the expanded empire she'd dreamed of in their final weeks of killing together.

The only way she'd know for sure would be to listen to an episode herself. Brooke clicked through to the podcast's website. She saw a message under New Episodes: "Due to the podcast's immense popularity, direct streaming isn't available. You can hear all episodes of *Vickie's Vigilantes* on your verified beetle device."

Brooke slammed her laptop closed. Those fucking beetles. She wouldn't put it past Victoria to have some kind of endorsement deal lined up for a little extra cash. Maybe she was leading the cops to her fans the way she led her fans to innocent people. Maybe she was leading everyone in Hollingsworth into a cat-and-mouse chase, with violent ends for both.

But Brooke couldn't know for sure — not when she wasn't listening to Victoria's podcast.

*****

Brooke grew used to the beetle in her ear. Its metal was warm, and she mostly kept it in sleep mode until there was a new episode of *Vickie's Vigilantes* to listen to. She didn't bother trying to find the people Victoria led her listeners to — she could find victims all on her own if she wanted to. Rather, she listened for clues in the background to try and find Victoria's whereabouts. A rustle of trees, heavy traffic, an errant cat — something that would help her find her friend. She couldn't deny that every time Victoria's voice seeped through the beetle, she felt a warm bit of comfort.

In her latest episode, Victoria promised a special surprise for anyone who could solve her latest puzzle. "Find the pond where no one plays," she said. "Where all you'll see are fireflies."

Brooke had perked up at "fireflies." She wondered if Victoria was calling her. She wondered if Victoria knew she was listening.

There was only one way to find out.

She walked through Briar Park and took the shortcut to the pond where they'd caught fireflies as children. Where they'd first met all those years ago, where they'd played with other kids and soon abandoned them for each other. Brooke's heartbeat rose with every step closer to the clearing. She passed through the bushes, and saw the pond in front of her.

No one else was there. Brooke stood still, and looked at the water. She felt the choked sting of a lump in her throat. Victoria hadn't been calling her. Victoria didn't want to see her anymore.

"There she is!"

Brooke looked to her left, and saw the woman she'd first seen kill the stranger in the park move towards her with an ugly smile. The same man as before followed behind. "So you're the reason everyone's disappeared, huh?" the woman asked.

Brooke wasn't the only reason they'd disappeared — but only Brooke would die that night. She took a step back, but didn't speak. She knew how fast this couple was. She should've known she would be led into a trap. She deserved whatever came next.

"Not even gonna run, huh?" the man said with a sneer. He pulled a hammer from his coat. "Smart."

He lifted the hammer, then froze. The woman paused as she unsheathed her knife. "Cole?" she said.

Cole sputtered around a burst of blood that oozed from his mouth. A knife appeared from behind him and sliced open his neck. He fell to the ground. Victoria stood behind him.

"Cole!" the woman screamed. She glared at Victoria. "What the fuck? He's not a killer!"

"Isn't he?" Victoria said in a high-pitched voice, one that sounded nothing like her podcast voice or even her regular speaking voice. "The Vigil said he was by the pond."

Brooke's eyes widened, but she set herself straight before the woman could see her. "We're part of the Vigil," the woman said. She sped towards Victoria and took out her knife. "I can't believe you killed him, you fucking —"

She stopped her stride as Brooke plunged her knife into her back. Brooke stabbed her once, twice — ten times. The rush intensified with every plunge.

Once the woman lay limp, Brooke sliced off her ear and hacked her beetle into pieces.

"You really hate those things, don't you?" Victoria said.

Brooke looked up, and saw Victoria wearing a small smirk. Brooke smiled a little and brushed back the hair over her left ear. "I really do. They never shut up."

"Tap the back legs — left one, then right one — four times."

Brooke did so. The beetle not only quieted, but fell limp from her ear. Brooke caught it before it shattered on the ground.

"Despite what you think —" Victoria brushed back her hair and revealed a bare ear — "I don't always need one in my ear."

"Why?"

"They get annoying sometimes. I run a podcast, I don't need to listen to them all the time —"

"I mean, why this clue? Did you know I was coming?"

"I hoped you would. I put this together because I missed killing people myself. I was going to surprise the first people from The Vigil, kill a couple of them, then set my listeners on another hunt. It gets old just hearing about other people having all the fun. But —" Victoria gave Brooke a sheepish smile. "But I also gave a clue I figured you'd follow on the off-chance you were listening. I hoped you'd come because it wouldn't be the same without you. Killing, celebrating … whispering. I'd give up a thousand voices in my ear to hear yours."

Brooke opened her hand and held up the deactivated beetle. "And I'd give up silence to hear yours in mine."

Victoria smiled. Brooke thought she saw the glimmer of tears in her eyes. She was about to tease her, when a voice from the other side of the pond called, "There you are!"

Brooke and Victoria turned, and saw a young man with a hockey stick moving towards them. Brooke knew they could take him. She felt a rush she hadn't felt since graduation begin to flutter in her brain like wings.

Victoria grinned as she lifted up her blade. "Let's get one more fan before we go."

"Sounds good," Brooke said. "But I get the ear."

XOLO
Carmen Baca

A colorful fiesta dress on display right behind the front counter of the stall in the mercado where Atla worked had attracted a customer, as Antonia Serna, her employer, had intended. Antonia waited on the woman, but no transaction passed between the two. The back-and-forth countering of the bargaining game turned ugly. Atla, who had gone to get some aguas frescas, heard the final exchange from behind the woman's back.

"No way I'm giving you thirty dollars for that dress. Twenty, take it or leave it."

"You can take your twenty and take yourself from my dress shop. I wouldn't want you wearing it anyway." Antonia crossed her arms over her ample waist and stood firm in more ways than one.

The tourist narrowed her eyes at Antonia. "Stick your dress up your churro!" she spat as she twirled around and stalked away.

Atlaclamani, in a "how dare she" moment, was tempted to throw the drinks on the woman's head. Even if she got the word wrong, the intentional vulgarity directed at Antonia was unacceptable. But the older woman, a respected shopkeeper and valued community member, stood with her eyes shut tight, mouth open wide, her arms clutching her stomach until she doubled over. For a moment, Atla wondered if she was having a stroke or a seizure and rushed forward, but Antonia let out a huge snort and a laugh that echoed in the large, indoor marketplace. She gasped when she could breathe, "I— I've never heard my fat ass called a sugary sweet before!"

Antonia's infectious laughter brought the giggles out of Atla, and she forgot her indignation as they laughed loud and long. Antonia saw everyone's eyes on them, heads tilted, ears at the ready. She yelled out the new curse word the tourist had invented to replace the more vulgar word. Though they both began in "c," the endings made the difference between fisticuffs and a bakery delight. It was a while before the turista figured out she was the reason the entire place echoed with laughter. A couple joined her when she stomped away to the exit, raising both hands in a universal gesture of disdain as she left. The level of laughter rose another notch. When the merchants banded together against rude customers, they became a united force. Atla knew the woman would leave empty-handed again if she dared return. Though they all needed the money tourists spent on their wares, no one here would sell their cheapest item to such a mugrosa.

As laughter turned to chuckles, indignation, and anger returned to Atla. She told Antonia she'd be right back. She hurried toward the rear exit, arriving at the curb in time to hear the tourist tell the taxi driver to take them to Posada Paraíso. Atla went back to the stall, prepared for customers, and muttered, "Oh, that I could conjure a ravenous beast to deal with the sonsa." She was determined to teach the wretched woman about the power of words, even if the wrong one was used. The tone could still slash like a *cuchillo,* leaving unhealed scars in the heart of the person to whom they were directed.

On her way to Mexico from New Mexico, Atlaclamani Ahuatzi, granddaughter of proud matriarchs, the descendant of Aztec queens, had come across several ill-mannered individuals. She had dealt with them in ways suited to their ill intentions toward her and escaped unharmed. At the end of the day, Atla sent a tired Antonia home, closed up shop, and went for a pensive walk to her destination.

*****

Lucretia Vargas left her sister and brother-in-law in their room, preparing for a night out. She opted for the hot springs a short distance from the inn. The spa, created behind a huge red rock formation for privacy, had been carved into the banks with the river flowing in the center. Lucretia dropped her robe and slid into the water. The lanterns around the area gave the scene a peaceful, golden hue. The night had only a sliver of a moon, and all was black beyond the lighting.

The snarl Lucretia heard above the rushing rio made her bolt upright. She stood in water to her shoulders and turned in a slow circle like a periscope, but her eyes couldn't penetrate the dark. She remained alert for several minutes and returned to her seat along the bank. "You're a chicken, Lu," she berated herself. "Relax, for once."

She lay back and enjoyed the peace and calm the hot springs induced. She watched the stars, inhaling deep breaths of cleansing steam rising from the water. And jumped when once again something shattered her peace. This time for good. The crackling of branches in a nearby thicket was unmistakable. Something big, something growling, was hiding or emerging from that stand of trees. She needed to get out of there. She stepped up from the pool, pausing to slide into her slippers and grab her robe. She shouldn't have done that; the thought hit her when she looked up and spotted a pair of red eyes just behind the line of lanterns.

She took off in the opposite direction. "Please be the right way, please be the right way," she pleaded. As long as she was on the pathway, even as she passed beyond the lights and went night blind, it had to lead to the hotel. If she strayed, she wouldn't see through the darkness enough to distinguish between any obstacle or free space to run. She almost didn't stop in time when those blood-red eyes appeared ahead of her. It was herding her back to the river—a beast playing with prey.

Her tears blinded her as much as the darkness, but she found the lantern's glow and ran back into the light. Lucretia stopped at the edge of the water and inhaled, her lungs full of air. Surely, someone would hear her scream.

*****

When Atla arrived at the hotel, she heard a whisper through a slight breeze: "The springs." Used to unusual forces guiding her existence, she followed the flagstone trail to the river. The woman she had come to lecture stood beside the water, so Atla hid behind a huge rock pillar to work out her approach. She took a peek and saw a shadow on her left move.

"What the—" Atla breathed when an immense figure reached the woman in giant strides. Her eyes glued to the unbelievable scene before her, Atla swallowed a gasp and froze.

The woman's mouth opened wide, but the scream died in her throat. The silhouette held her in the air by the neck. The woman's eyes bulged, and her head turned crimson. As the figure moved into the light, Atla covered her mouth with her hands. The claws circling the woman's neck were attached to skeletal hands. The skeleton stood some seven or more feet in height. The skull Atla expected was instead the head of a dog.

The snout curled in a snarl, exposing rows of fangs in the beast's mouth. When it opened its immense jaws and gripped the woman's face, the crunch of bones broke the icy grip of fear around Atla, and she ran without stopping until she reached home. She had no faith in doors or windows keeping that thing out if it wanted to get in. Her mind replayed the last image she had glimpsed over her shoulder as she fled—the beast's other claw eviscerating the woman's body, the sound of the tearing flesh and then the gnawing, the slurping, and the grunting, the spurts of flying blood—she hoped the monster had been so preoccupied it hadn't seen her.

"What the hell was that?" she asked aloud, once alone in her room. It was a good thing Antonia, who had given her a home, as well as employment, slept like the dead. In her rush to check the locks on the windows, Atla had stumbled over Antonia's sewing supplies. The woman had so many she used a small valise with compartments for everything. The stupid thing had wheels and had rolled right into her path with her whirlwind race around the house. She almost left her front teeth embedded in the adobe wall of the kitchen. Shaken, she readied for bed and lay in the dark, alert and unable to shut down her racing thoughts for hours.

Her restless sleep ended when the sun woke her early the next morning. Atla prepared for the day, trying to convince herself she had dreamed the whole thing. When she saw the scraped skin of her palms and her kneecaps, she remembered tripping and slamming onto the dirt floor of the living area. Only her palms slapping hard on the wall had stopped her from a certain concussion. It hadn't been a dream.

Convinced her role as witness had been arranged by the fates, she said nothing to Antonia. She knew there was a connection, but she had no idea how or why. She hadn't consulted the book she inherited from the Ahuatzi matriarchs. She hadn't made any kind of supplication. No way, she had created that—that—whatever it was.

With the passing days, she had more to wonder about. The woman's death hadn't made the news yet. On the fourth morning at work, Antonia startled her, gasping, "Ay, qué horrible."

She had jumped from her chair, grabbing a kerchief from her skirt pocket and wiping at the coffee she'd spewed all over the newspaper.

"¿Qué? What's wrong?" Atla joined her at the back of the stall.

168

"Mira," Antonia folded the pages into a square and handed the paper over. "Look,

recognize her?" The bold, black headline screamed, "*Turista Encontrada Muerta.*" Beneath was the photo of the dead woman—the rude tourist. The friends stood side-by-side and read the article.

The town mortician, recruited as coroner, gave a succinct report of his findings. Search parties formed when the woman's brother-in-law alerted the hotel staff the morning after she was last seen alive. A bathrobe and slippers had been found bloodied and shredded beside a crimson puddle on the stone floor around the springs. Authorities took charge, leading searchers as they followed tracks down the path. About a quarter mile from the hotel, they came upon the missing woman's body. Long slash marks in a few bones and a substantial number of dark, coarse hairs caught in some of the sharp-edged lacerations led the acting coroner to determine the cause of death was "ataque de animal." The article quoted the police chief as saying Lucretia Vargas, the victim, had been a guest at Posada Paraíso.

"She called me a sweet ass, remember? Even if she didn't realize it." Antonia chuckled and then quickly crossed herself. "Que descanse en paz, pobre mujer. May she rest in peace, poor woman," adding, "despite her vile nature."

"I wonder why they didn't report this in the paper until today?" Atla muttered.

Antonia shook her head. Then, she shuddered. "An attack by an animal, can you imagine?"

Atla didn't have to imagine. And by that very afternoon, much of the real story emerged.

Police, the reporter, the mortician—they all had families they told, their family members had friends to tell, and so it went. Word spread. Everyone knew the authorities had concealed details, taken their time reporting the death, their concern about the economy driving their bad choices. Everyone also knew what was in the paper revealed little of the real story.

Lucretia's body hadn't been found intact, for one. The coroner had admitted so little of the woman had been recovered, he had no idea what had been responsible based on conflicting evidence. Searchers had followed blood spatter, body parts, and bits and pieces of bone along a trail of huge footprints, scattered as if the creature had been gorging, spitting out leftovers as it traveled. No animal did that, did they? The most confusing discovery of all was the footprints. They had overlapped and circled those of the woman in a grotesque dance along the waterway before they headed south. They looked human, but it couldn't be a human, not that monstrous, could it?

There had never been a murder in the history of the settlement; surely, there could be no killer in Tierra Roja now. The quiet town had been established upon what had been a thriving community of the Aztec peoples in the middle of what should've been desert. In the '20s, it turned into a tourist attraction because of the red rock formations, remnants of ancient dwellings, and the natural hot springs reported to have healing properties. During monsoon season, the rich, red earth turned into rivers resembling blood when it flooded, attracting the morbid, the curious, the journalists and writers of horror, and photographers of the macabre.

As a week passed, the more the stories grew in outrageous detail, and the more introspective Atla became. Distracted at work, she often stood staring at nothing, her eyes focused internally more than at anything in front of her. She didn't believe in coincidence. The fates that night had achieved more than she had planned. The same guiding hand that had led her to this place had a message for her; something more was coming.

Yet another day passed without incident. All hoped the predator—whether man or beast—had moved on. The authorities assured the public the attack was an anomaly.

The town's economy depended on tourists. The monsoon season loomed. Merchants like Antonia prepared for the expected influx of customers but welcomed a trickle instead. The seduction of the money they'd earn for photos proved irresistible to the courageous, the foolish, and the curiosity-seekers.

The following day, a bus stopped before the marketplace, letting a handful of visitors out. A couple made their way directly toward Antonia's stall. There was something familiar about them, and it took Atla a moment to realize it was the pair who had been with Lucretia. She read they had been vacationing from somewhere in the US. She remembered they were related to the victim, too.

The woman aimed straight for a turquoise-colored shawl, but the man's eyes focused on Atla. She knew that look. She had come across several people on her journey to Tierra Roja and had learned to heed eyes with hunger in them. Trouble lay in those depths. She put up her guard.

"Buenas tardes," he said.

"Egualmente," she replied, turning away to straighten the already neatly stacked shirts nearest her for something to do. She could feel his attention was still on her, so she looked up at him, waiting.

"My wife and I are leaving today. We have to—have to take—never mind." He added,

"Do you expect the monsoons to start soon?"

"I'm new here; I don't know when they start." Atla surmised he had been about to say they had to take the body of the sister home. She said nothing. Atla, raised in isolation with only her mother and grandmother for companionship until her teens, wondered why people had to make small talk. *Buy something, or get to the point already*, she thought with impatience. *Or let me be.*

"I find you attractive," he said.

Atla gasped at his audacity and retorted, "I find you repulsive." Looking him in the eye, she spat, "You disrespect me—and worse, you disrespect your wife standing right there. Speak to me again like that, and you will wish you hadn't." Before she turned to switch places with Antonia, Atla pinched a straight pin from the front of her blouse and then plunged it right into the man's hand, smack dab between the thumb and forefinger, pinning it down to the counter through the webbing. The man could have screamed, but the look in Atla's eyes told him she wouldn't hesitate to make his wife aware of his transgression. She gave the pin a little twist and smiled. She hoped the seconds felt like minutes before she lifted the pin with a pop from his flesh.

He grabbed his handkerchief from a pocket, wrapping it around the injury before anyone could see. He glared at Atla a moment before turning away to grab his wife by the arm.

"But, honey—" she protested and closed her mouth when she saw his face. She set the garments she had chosen on the counter and offered an apologetic smile before allowing herself to be dragged off.

The rest of the day passed with few sales. Antonia left early to visit an ill amiga, and Atla closed up, thinking she'd go to the market for some fruit. The park in the center of town drew her with the green hues of the trees, lawns, and shrubs, the varieties and vivid colors of flowers. Benches set at intervals invited people to sit and enjoy the beauty along the pathways. Atla sat and watched birds until the air turned cool and the skies darkened. She felt the first drops of rain and rose to get to the market as she'd planned. In an instant, the trickle turned into a drizzle and swiftly built into a cloudburst. Atla's quest for fruit forgotten, she ran until she reached the side street that led home. She ducked into a recessed doorway to catch her breath. Home was still a block away. Through the downpour, she watched the stream flowing down the road increasing in both swiftness and depth. It transformed into a river of floating debris, turning, submerging, and bobbing up again faster and faster. *La agua does look like sangre roja*, Atla thought, repulsed at the thought of walking through the blood-red, filthy water which rose and ran faster by the minute.

Already drenched, Atla took a deep breath before stepping down into water that reached her knees. She sloughed through the muck, reaching her street at last when something yanked her by the hair. Atla flew backward, hitting a hard body right before arms locked around her midsection. Like vise grips, they tightened with every breath she took. She couldn't break the hold. The roar of the water covered her screams. No incantation, no prayer, nothing would set her free.

"*Te voy a matar*," the voice belonging to the body behind her threatened to kill her. "After I teach you how to treat a man." Not yet thirty, Atla was naïve. Her mother and grandmother had passed when she needed their counsel most. A couple of close calls gave her an idea of how men violated women, but she fought for her life not to find out for herself on this night. She bit right through the flesh of his forearm, and he loosened his grasp. Atla flung an elbow backward, smashing it into the man's nose with a loud crack she heard over the thundering flood around them. She dove into the water when he let her go to clutch his face, but something or someone huge caught her and flung her to the top of a house on the other side of the now raging river covering the street.

She wiped her eyes, and then through the downpour, she watched the enormous dog-headed skeleton fling himself at the man, gripping his shoulders to hold him steady. She recognized the uncouth man from the mercado, his head barely reaching the skeleton mid-chest, in the split second before the predator bit off the top of his skull. The claws pierced the man's flesh before the beast flung the body backward. Even as the man fell away, sharp nails slashed down from his shoulders to thighs, disemboweling the torso as open wounds oozed his lifeblood in a steady rhythm to his heartbeat. When the corpse floated downstream, what was left of his blood melded with the red water. The body eventually submerged and would no doubt become shredded by the friction of the debris along its journey through the torrent.

Atla witnessed the slow, torturous death from the roof where the creature had tossed her so effortlessly. She hadn't begun to think of how to get down or whether she should when the eyes of the beast found hers. It leapt in one motion and in midair the dog-headed skeleton turned into a medium-sized hound and stood before her. She had been moving up the incline of the roof in a crablike scrabbling to get away, but the dog sat before her, so she stopped and crouched with care right beneath the ridge. Its sleek, hairless body caught her attention, never having seen such. The long neck ended in a head like that of a greyhound, but with big, bat-like ears. The almond-shaped brown eyes locked on hers, and there Atla saw an intelligence beyond that of a beast.

The voice in her head didn't surprise her much, not compared to what she'd just been through. She hoped the creature would remain in its current state; she preferred the docile-looking dog over the hideous monster of a moment before.

Do not be afraid. In skeleton form, I am Xolotl, god of fire, lightning, and god of death. I guide souls through the levels of hell. But, in this form, I am the national dog of Mexico known as Xoloitzcuintle. You may call me Xolo. I am a protector. You summoned me the day you decided to use your power with words to teach the woman the potency of her hurtful ones. I have been your shadow ever since. No one will cause you grief of any kind while I am with you.

Atla shook her head, wondering how on earth she had created such a deadly beast. She hadn't seen him in either form shadowing her at all.

"You said something along the lines of 'oh, that I could conjure a beast' to teach the awful woman a lesson in manners. Your words wield a force you have yet to control." The dog spoke aloud, voice low and raspy as if from disuse, but his mouth turned up at the edges, and Atla could swear he smiled. "And you would have seen me if I had wanted you to," he added. She didn't know what Xolo intended with his remark, but it had a sinister effect.

"So you can read my mind," Atla spoke. "That's how you knew I was upset by the woman's behavior toward Antonia."

The dog nodded once.

"And the man? You knew I repulsed him."

He nodded again.

"The lady didn't deserve what you did to her." Alta tucked her knees close and wrapped her arms around her legs after brushing her sopping hair back. "The man, though. He did."

The rain poured down in torrents, and the water rose more, halfway up the first-floor windows of the house she sat upon; she was freezing and worried about Antonia.

"Your friend is fine," Xolotl assured her. "I saw her leave her home with a group to the top of the hill on the other side of town. I will deliver you to her." The skeleton replaced the dog in the time it took for Atla to wipe the rain from her eyes again. It hovered over her, creating a barrier from the torrent.

The alternative meant sitting here soaking wet for who knew how much longer while the town flowed away around her. When the house she perched upon groaned as it began shifting from its foundation, powerless to stop its destruction, her decision was made. She stood, trying to maintain her balance on the swaying house. Unless she figured out how to send it back where it came from, Xolotl was here to stay.

175

"I will reside with you and Señora Antonia in dog form."

She had forgotten the most important new routine she would have to develop: quit thinking what she didn't want it to pick up on or figure out how to prevent it from doing that.

"If I stay with you, I will see your emotions on your face and in your actions when I am with you. I will have no need to read your thoughts."

"If that's the case, then we can consult before you turn into a killer. You won't have to go to extremes to defend my or Antonia's honor. Can we agree to disagree on the form of punishment?"

"We shall see, won't we? No one has ever summoned me before. I do not know if I have limitations of conscience or if I act like the beast I become—savage and instinctively driven to feed upon people's badness and rid the world of them. The woman was not as corrupt as the man, and I was hungry. Her corpse proved palatable. I dispatched the man more quickly because of your immediate danger. His taste would have ruined my appetite."

Atla's anger rose before she could think about what the creature could do to her. Lucretia had been a despicable woman, an ill-mannered snob. But she didn't deserve such a gruesome end. Atla screamed, "Badness? Badness! Tha—"

The roof fell from beneath her feet. She was free-falling for a few seconds thinking this was either the end of her life or the beginning of her eternal one. She felt skeletal fingers wrap around her forearms, and she was lifted into the sky. Xolotl tossed her in the air before him and caught her like a baby in his arms for the short jaunt to higher ground.

Her thoughts flew as the monster leaped from rooftop to balcony, and tree to pillar above the raging rapids through what was left of the town. Having Xolotl as her ally meant if anyone truly deserved the kind of death he could deliver while satisfying his hunger, she wouldn't have to dirty her hands. She hated soiling her soul with a bad deed. Her afterlife depended on her staying directly out of the action. If circumstances developed indirectly, that was another matter. She had concluded that her summoning Xolotl was the gods' plan for her. She was twenty-eight, her life guided by the number seven. The signs were there. She also recognized a naïveté in herself that could lead her into bad situations. She could use Xolotl's protection.

When they reached the hill overlooking what was left of Tierra Roja, Atla concluded that his presence would teach her to temper her thoughts and actions around him. In turn, she would temper his punishment of those in her presence who spoke or acted offensively. With the curtain of the rain to conceal them, he interrupted her musings as he set her down behind a copse of oak and became Xolo, the dog, once more.

*****

The rains stopped, the waters receded, and the muddy clean-up ensued. Antonia's casita had survived. The interior was intact, albeit a sopping, silt-filled mess. Atla took her beloved recipe book from the top shelf of the ropero where she'd stored it in a waterproof case. The armoire was tall enough that the waters hadn't reached the cherished heirloom. The small house, nestled between wider and taller houses on three sides, had been shielded from the brunt of the erosion.

A few weeks after the record floods ebbed, too many tourists were reported missing by loved ones whose last communications had come from Tierra Roja. Speculation circulated that they had been swept away with a dozen citizens. Antonia and Atla, accompanied by Xolo, headed south. Tierra Roja had destroyed itself in its vain attempt to become a tourist attraction. The leaders would have been run out of the town if there had been a town left. They absconded or perished during the flood. Few, like the mortician and the police chief, were never seen again.

Unpacking their meager belongings in their new home, Atla sat on a stool in her room and held her special book open on her lap. She wondered whether a spell, an incantation—something—were written there to give her more information about Xolotl. Specifically, how to send him back where he came from, especially if his punishment for transgressors against her didn't fit the crime again.

She looked at the dog lying on the serape rug by the door, watching her, glancing at the book. She hoped he had been honest when he'd said he wouldn't read her mind when they lived together. She looked away and then rose to set the book on her bed stand. She might have to find a place for it he wouldn't know about.

You will temper my rage against those who offend you in any way, and I will temper your tolerance of those beneath you since you will be less inclined to tempt me into attacking. Ours is a match of equal benefits, the voice in her head spoke. *Temporarily, of course. For when you stop showing intent in your eyes, that will be the day you will have mastered your self-control. You will cease to need me.*

Xolo raised his head in a pose worthy of the wise god he was. Then he ruined it with a canine smile and a sound Atla took as a dog sneer, "When I was a young god, learning to guide the souls of the dead, I discovered what influenced them in life before their deaths. What led them to their final destinations. Those who held their tongues, who knew the power of words that hurt others and tempered their utterances, those were the souls who went to the good place. Those who use their words to cause others pain will satisfy my hunger from centuries of starvation in the meantime. You shall feed my appetite for a grand feast of human flesh."

"You just had to go and spoil what could have been a beautiful moment," she told him.

Though their union was a match possibly made in hell, the paradox that it would further her flight to the heaven she envisioned made Atla smile. Xolo was right; they would be good for each other. The dog's grin grew wider.

THE WAITRESS
Brooklyn Ann Butler

August 12, 1979.
Transcript of Custodial Statement of Geraldine Jenkins, aged 56
Property of Promise Township Police Department, Homicide Division

My name is Geraldine Jenkins. I understand my rights and I'm giving this statement of my own free will. I swear upon the truth, the whole truth, and nothing but the truth, so help me God. Was I supposed to save that part for the trial? I 'spose it doesn't matter either way. I know you won't believe me. None of you.

But can I get some of that coffee? Because if I gotta tell you what happened with Daisy Mae, I'm gonna be talking a while.

Thank you, Officer Andy, you always were a good boy. I don't know if you remember, but I babysat you when you were about four or five.

I see you tapping your foot, Detective. 'Spose you want me to get on with it. Let me get my cream and sugar in. You're not from around here, I can tell. People take their time here in Promise. Not like in the big cities, always rushing so fast you're goin' in circles and can't stop spinning.

Andy, can I trouble you for an ashtray? Nothin' like a cigarette with coffee. Even the swill you have here. And I thought bad coffee in police stations was just a thing in the movies. Maybe I'm spoiled. We make the best cup over at the Flying Dutchman.

I guess I should say *they* instead of *we*, 'cuz I'm probably fired now after what happened. Such a damn shame. I really liked that job. Before the Flying Dutchman, I tended bar over at the Buckshot, and I hated it. People were so crude and rowdy. I couldn't take the drunken scuffles any longer. I believe in peace, and that's what the Dutchman was for me. Peace you could serve in a cup, on a plate, or even in a smile and a kind word.

By the end of my first week, I knew I would do *anything* to protect that peace.

Though I *do* feel bad about the reason I got the job. One of the other waitresses, Linda, had passed on. Some sort of cancer, they said. I didn't know her. Heard she was a drifter. But now, I know what *really* happened to her.

Thanks for the ashtray, Andy. How's your mother?

I saw that eye roll, Detective. We care about others here.

Can I get a light? Thank you, Miss. It's nice to see someone good at shorthand these days. It's a dying skill. I hope you're getting all this word for word.

Well, I saw your mother on her way to see Doctor Baker the other day, so at least we know she's in good hands.

Alright, Detective. I'll get back to it.

When I started at the Flying Dutchman, everyone was so kind and refreshing. Except for Daisy Mae. I knew from the moment I locked eyes with that girl that something was *very* wrong with her.

Yeah, I can tell from your look that you think I was imagining things. 'Specially since the busboys, line cooks, and customers said she was "living kindness." But if you ask my fellow waitresses, they'll say the same as me.

Daisy Mae always got the most tips and was prettier than all of us, but don't think I'm jealous of that. Not at my age. She was sweet as pie to the customers, even more with the gentlemen, but cold and, well, just *off* with the other waitresses. It wasn't shyness... We've had our share of shy girls at the Dutchman. Including poor Marianne, God rest her soul. This was different. There was a look in Daisy's eyes that reminded me of this time I saw a tiger at the zoo.

181

A beastly hunger and awareness that she could eat you if she wanted to.

Look at me, shivering so hard I knocked the cherry clean off my cig! Can I borrow that lighter again? Thanks a bunch.

Anyway, on my first day, I worked the evening shift, when the truckers, drunks, and raisin girls came in. 'Raisin girl' is my pet name for those girls who wore all black and drank nothing but coffee for hours while they sketched and wrote poetry and chain-smoked. They seem a little spooky at first, but once you get to know them, they're harmless. Even a little sweet. Just like raisins.

So there I was, serving two-egg breakfasts and biscuits and gravy to the drunks who were trying to sober up. Their rowdiness disappeared as soon as they smelled the bacon on the griddle. There's something miraculous about a hot breakfast. I bet if there was breakfast every hour, everywhere, it could save the world. I headed back to get another pot of coffee going, and that's when I first met her.

She looked pretty as a picture in her robin's egg blue uniform. Long, tanned legs, honey-blonde hair, and the bluest eyes I'd seen since Elvis Presley came through town in '66.

Being someone who was raised right, I held out my hand and introduced myself. She took my hand and hers felt cold and waxy, like a doll's hand.

"I'm called Daisy Mae," she said in a dulcet, yet flat tone. She smiled, showing a little more teeth than I was used to. Those teeth were as white as they are in toothpaste commercials.

I pulled my hand back as soon as politeness allowed and she went on her way to the window to pick up her customers' orders. After that, Daisy headed out the door because she had the swing shift.

Later, when I was having a smoke break with Ethel, the shift manager, I couldn't help asking about Daisy Mae.

"We call her the Stepford Wife," Ethel told me with a scowl of disapproval on her face. "She's been here a year.

Does her job so well that Clyde loves her, but she's a cold fish underneath that Miss Perfect act she puts on."

A few days after, I was scheduled for a swing shift and heard even more about her.

She was a drifter like the dearly departed Linda. No one knew where she came from because she wouldn't say, and her slight accent threw everyone off.

Which reminds me, Detective, *have* you found her next of kin yet? Or her birth certificate? I doubt you have. And I'll bet my retirement savings you never will.

Andy, could I trouble you for another cup of coffee? Thanks, honey. You tell your mama she's in my prayers.

Back to my testimony. Then Harmony, another waitress who'd been at the Dutchman for ages, and who I immediately got along with, pulled me aside during our smoke break.

"You want to stay away from Daisy Mae, Miss Geraldine," she whispered, placing her warm hand on my shoulder. "I don't know if you're the superstitious type or not, and you'll probably think I sound crazier than a shithouse rat, but I swear, if you spend any time close to that woman, things go wrong. You get tired and clumsy, and sometimes even sick."

Much as I love her, I *did* think Harmony was crazy at the time. Lotsa folks in Promise are superstitious. Some throw salt over their shoulders, others play with rosary beads. I never paid them no mind. And with Daisy Mae being an odd duck, it was no surprise that some came up with superstitious rumors and blamed her for their mistakes. People *love* to blame other people and outside forces for their own fuckups.

But I'll be goddamned if I didn't drop a coffee cup the next evening, not long after Daisy Mae helped me correctly adjust a table's check for some substitutions. She was beside me for barely a minute. Then I got the worst headache, so bad I almost clocked out early. The only thing that kept me on my feet that night was spite. Something in her smug look said she'd be happy if I couldn't make it through the shift and hell if I was gonna give her *that* satisfaction.

My next shift was a night shift, so it was easier to stay out of her way. But another gal whose assigned tables were next to Daisy Mae's *did* look peaked before she clocked out. I tried to tell myself it was a coincidence, but by the end of my work week, I had to apologize to Harmony for not believing her. I couldn't deny that something about that waitress was *somehow* sapping the energy of any woman unlucky enough to go near her. Even some of the lady customers, young and old. Their appetites would vanish if Daisy spent too long going over the specials, or checked on them one too many times.

Never the men, though. Those customers always departed with a smile and a spring in their step. The busboys and cooks also seemed invigorated after a few minutes near Daisy Mae.

The whole thing spooked me, and if I told you I wasn't considering looking for another job, I'd be lying. But you all know the pickings are slim when it comes to jobs around here. I'd already done my time at the Buckshot. Then there's that headshop, Space Dog. Lord knows I'd never fit in at a place like that. I'm too old for that hippie shit.

In the end, I decided I wasn't going to let some witch drive me away from the Dutchman. I'd follow Harmony's advice and avoid Daisy Mae.

I managed for about six months. And I woulda managed longer if not for the new girl, Marianne. She was a shy little thing, with silky black hair and gentle movements that reminded me of a dove. I rarely saw her in town 'cuz she lived in that tiny house by the woods. Something about her brought out maternal instincts I never thought I had in me.

Harmony and I tried our best to warn Marianne to keep her distance from Daisy Mae. We were subtle about it because we didn't want to frighten the poor girl. Maybe we should have.

Being a high school student, Marianne's shifts overlapped with Daisy Mae's the most. Harmony was able to keep an eye on her for the few hours before her day shift ended, and I'd watch over her for the first couple hours of my night shifts. I only got a few swing shifts where I could work beside Marianne and subtly direct her far from danger.

But there was only so much we could do. Marianne spent too many hours alone with Daisy Mae. Every night I saw her, Marianne was paler. Soon, she began to lose weight to the point where she was down to skin and bones. This was much worse than the usual effect of being around *that* waitress. When I got a chance to ask the others about Marianne's extreme decline, they told me the gal I'd replaced had wasted away just the same.

We all encouraged Marianne to go see a doctor, even gave her a share of our tips so she could afford it, and said a prayer when she got an appointment. But other than some vitamin deficiencies, Doc London said nothing was wrong. Marianne took her vitamins and they did jack shit for her. I still wonder what would have happened if she'd seen Doctor Baker instead.

Then came that terrible night.

I'd gone back to the walk-in fridge to get more whipped cream for the milkshakes and hot chocolate. That's where I came upon them. Marianne, who I'd seen clock off a half hour ago, was pinned up against the boxes of deli meat. Daisy Mae's eyes were bright, fierce, and focused on the girl.

I opened my mouth to yell at her to back off, but my tongue was just as paralyzed as Marianne's body.

Then Daisy started to *change*. Her perfect, toothpaste commercial mouth widened and distended in ways it shouldn't have. Something came out of her mouth, a long, thin thing like…what's that thing butterflies have for sucking the nectar out of flowers? Oh, a proboscis.

And you wanna know something crazy? Daisy Mae *still* looked pretty when she was putting that damage on.

As poor Marianne slid to the floor, I slipped back out before Daisy Mae could use that proboscis on me. My heart clawed its way up my throat and my legs felt like meringue, but I got back to my station and managed to check on my customers like I hadn't just seen one of my coworkers turn into a monster and drink the life out of another.

I'm sorry, can you pass me a tissue? My heart still breaks for that girl. She'd had a whole future in front of her and it was sucked away like a milkshake through a straw.

Daisy Mae must have sneaked the body out, because you all know Marianne was found at home. Everyone believed Marianne killed herself, not listening at all when I said not a chance.

That's when I decided to kill Daisy Mae.

There was no way I could stand silent and let her kill another woman. I knew I'd have to do it fast, even though that would be an act of kindness she didn't deserve. But there was no way in hell I'd wait until she had *me* hypnotized with those icy blue eyes and shove that gross—what was it again?—proboscis in my mouth, and pull me into her ravine of death.

It took almost three months for me to gain the nerve, but as I watched her feed off my fellow waitresses—and even me the few times I couldn't evade her—my nerve strengthened. Besides, taking my time helped avoid her becoming suspicious of me.

To keep the element of surprise, I waited until I had the night off. I wore my black funeral dress so any blood that got on me wouldn't show. The problem was the damn thing didn't have any pockets. But my purse was big and besides, not much at home that the diner didn't already have for weapons.

I debated whether to use one of the kitchen knives, the big cleaver, or maybe just shove her headfirst into the fryer oil. I needed to get her alone—though I had a good idea as to how I'd accomplish that part. I waited until the dead zone, that stretch of time between ten and midnight, when not many customers came in. Daisy usually got off work between eleven and eleven-thirty.

I slipped in back and ducked into the manager's office. It's always empty at that time. An open box of rat poison sat in the corner of the cluttered desk, banished with all the other stuff Clyde didn't have a place for. Then I spotted what you classified as the primary murder weapon.

A check spindle.

Some call 'em ticket stabbers, which was fitting since I meant to punch Daisy's ticket. This one was a good ten inches long and still looked plenty sharp. My guess is it was tossed aside for being rusty.

I stuffed both the spindle and the poison in my purse before taking position near the office's little window. Like a deer hunter with a perfect sightline of a watering hole, I watched the cooks, the wait station, and the cash register.

Once Daisy closed out her till, I stepped out of the office and waited by the coat rack near the back door. Her blue eyes widened at the sight of me, then she relaxed as I poured out my tale of woe. I told her I had a date planned with the new projector operator at the Twinkle Drive-In, and I was missing one of my favorite black pearl earrings that went with my dress.

"Oh, and on your birthday too," she cooed sympathetically.

I hadn't even thought about that. At my age, you try to ignore your goddamn birthday anyway. But it gave me an excuse to play up my story.

"I think I lost it here last night," I continued, not having to pretend to be fretful. Not with what I was planning to do. "You know how I fiddle with my jewelry all the time. Did you or any of the other gals happen to spot it?"

"No, ma'am," Daisy said in her perfect butter-won't-melt-in-my-mouth voice.

"I *did* do inventory in the back cooler," I said next, and again didn't have to fake a shiver. "But it's so *dark* and *cold* in there."

"I'll help you find it," Daisy said with a sly, hungry smile.

And just like poor Marianne, I followed her into that dark, cold death trap. I made a big show of looking for the earring that was—and still is, I 'spose—safe and snug in my jewelry box.

I kept a tight grip on my unzipped purse, not letting Daisy get a glimpse of the poison or the ticket stabber. I took a deep breath and straightened up. "I don't know where it could be."

My voice shook, but that could be blamed on the cold.

Daisy turned to me and stalked closer. I did my best to avoid her eyes so she couldn't put me in a trance like Marianne.

"Look at me," she said in an eerie, hollow voice.

I pretended to obey, focusing on the tip of her pretty button nose. A cold wind seemed to blow over me, but my hair didn't move. Then came a pressing sensation that felt like thick lead blankets covering my body. But so long as I concentrated, I could wiggle my fingers and toes.

Daisy Mae must have been satisfied that she had me trapped. Her jaw dropped with a rusty creak, followed by ugly popping sounds that almost made me jump. Even though my nerves screamed at me to get the hell away, I kept playing along and waited for the moment I needed.

The proboscis-thing was even more disgusting up close. It slowly slid out of Daisy's gaping maw like the second mouth in that *Alien* movie that played at the Twinkle last month.

I see what you're thinking, Detective, and no, my story is *not* influenced by that movie. Daisy's mouth-thing didn't even look like that one. It was pink, veiny, and toothless. Its mouth was a fleshy opening like a leech's sucker.

Hang on, I need another cigarette. Still got that light, Miss? Thank you. I hope I'm not wearing out your hand from all my talking.

Anyway, the smell was awful. Sickly sweet like rotting meat. My eyes watered like the devil and I almost gagged. But I stood firm. For Marianne. For Linda. For all the other waitresses that monster fed on.

When that pink leech-mouth opened to suck down my life force, I reached into my purse, grabbed the rat poison, shoving the box right into the pink void.

Daisy Mae sucked up that white powder like a businessman hoovering up a bump of nose candy.

The reaction was the most sickening spectacle I'd ever seen in my life. The proboscis retreated like a turtle trying to go back in its shell. It swelled and got stuck in her mouth, wriggling and twitching as Daisy jerked around like she'd touched Farmer Jethro's electric fence.

There was a sizzling noise, then greenish foam bubbled out of her writhing mouth in a hot, gushing geyser. Sour stuff spilled all over me before I could get out of the way. I almost ran out of the cooler right then and there. But I've seen enough monster movies to know that I had to make sure this one wouldn't be getting back up.

I reached in my purse, got that ticket stabber, and shoved it right into one of Daisy Mae's sky-blue eyes. Blood spurted everywhere, getting all over me. And that gross green foam too. It was a damn shame 'cuz I did like that dress.

I struggled to keep my grip on the check spindle. The bottom was slippery with blood and eye goo. But I held on and pushed with all my might until the long metal spike stopped when it hit the back of her skull.

Daisy Mae dropped like a mailsack. The freaky proboscis had made its retreat somewhere in the struggle. She looked like a normal woman again. She was even *still* pretty, if you can believe that! I can see you do, Detective, since you saw her shortly after.

Dear lord, the mess of that foam and blood was *godawful* and I pity the poor sack who had to mop that up.

Did you send any of that foam to the lab?

Not gonna tell me, huh?

Anyway, you all know the rest. I tried to sneak out the back, but Bobby, the dishwasher, spotted me and called the police. You all thought I was crazy when you arrested me, and you probably *still* think I'm crazy, but I swear on my mama's grave and a stack of bibles that I'm telling the truth, the whole truth, and nothing but the truth, so help me God.

Oh, that part *is* 'sposed to go when I testify in court? Oh well.

Yes, I killed Daisy Mae. I did it to protect myself and my fellow waitresses at the Flying Dutchman. I did it to keep the peace.

That's my official statement. Can I have another cup of coffee?

*****

November, 19th 1979
Sage Institute for the Criminally Insane, Women's Ward.
Excerpt from the Diary of Geraldine Jenkins

Doctor Ventura doesn't believe me either. I shouldn't be surprised. Even the women in the jury laughed at me during the trial. That hurt almost as badly as when Erica and Catalina, my fellow waitresses, testified against me. Only Ethel and Harmony believed me, but they didn't have the guts to admit that Daisy Mae was a monster who fed off us.

Some of the women in this madhouse believe me, but I don't know how much that's worth since they're prisoners here too. And most *are* honestly crazy. Ginger is a sweetheart, but she's also a compulsive liar. I heard she was in here for so many counts of fraud that no one really knew for sure which identity and social security number was hers. You almost gotta admire that hustle. Then there's old Agnes, who killed her husband and her mother-in-law with arsenic back in '39. And Talula, an ex-hooker who killed a john in '66.

These women are the closest thing I have to friends in this nuthouse. And I'll do what I can to protect them.

Because something happened today.

Little Poppy raced up to me at lunch—I'd missed breakfast again. Slept right through. I sleep a lot these days. She said there's a new nurse who's so nice and so pretty that she looks like she's from a fairyland.

I didn't pay her much mind. Poppy is a whimsical creature, for a gal who chopped a man to pieces with an ax and fed the pieces to her pigs, that is. But then Ginger and Agnes said they'd met the new nurse too when they got their morning meds and she *did* look like an angel.

"Devils like to hide behind angels' faces," Talula said.

That's when the first alarm bell rang in my head.

But I forgot about it until it was time for evening meds. I didn't expect them to make a new nurse work a double on her first day, but there she was, a vision even from my place far back in the line. The hair tucked under her cap was a gorgeous strawberry blonde, her figure was pageant-perfect. My stomach gave a nervous tremor. I tried to scold myself to stop being afraid of pretty gals just because one turned out to not be a gal after all.

But then it was my turn, and I stepped forward to face her. *Honey* was the name on her little brass tag pinned to her snow-white uniform. Her baby blue eyes met mine and her perfect lips curved in a hungry smile. And that's when I KNEW. She was one of them. A monster, just like Daisy Mae.

I don't know if she knows about me. About what I did to one of her kind.

All I know is one thing.

I need to protect my girls.

THE PAINTED MAN
Jen Mierisch

The first time Valarie's painting changed, she blamed the ancient house and the thunderstorm that had drenched its gables the night before.

She had set up her easel at the edge of the front hall. It was an ideal spot for painting Hazel House's dramatic marble staircase, which arced up to the second-floor landing like a watchful snake.

Approaching her canvas, Valarie frowned at the gray blob that had appeared at the foot of her painted stairs. The splotch was lumpy, oblong, and oddly textured, resembling a pile of dirty rags.

A glance at the ceiling revealed that Valarie had positioned the easel directly beneath one of the skylights. The seal must have leaked during last night's downpour and dripped dirty water onto her canvas.

She'd have to tell Merel. Merel would have it fixed. Valarie didn't know her new landlady well, but she was sure of two things: Merel van Rensselaer was loaded, and she took immense pride in maintaining the house that had been in the family for seven generations.

But hadn't Merel replaced the roof last year, when she added the skylights? Yes—she had told Valarie so, while showing her around the house three months ago. It was right after they'd toured her newly installed, landscaped patio.

Merel wouldn't be happy about a leak in her new roof. And who knew how long it would take to book a repairman out there in the middle of nowhere?

Valarie sighed, shifted the easel several feet over, and raised her brush to hide the murky gray stain.

*****

That first day, Merel had seemed so sweet. "Valarie!" she had exclaimed, trotting down the steps of the grand front porch as Valarie stepped out of her old Ford. "How lovely to finally meet you." Merel was all smiles and bohemian clothes, wearing a loose, patterned tunic and pants below her floppy hat and dark blonde curls. She looked to be just a few years older than Valarie, perhaps forty. Her speech had that velvety tone and formal lilt that people with money all seemed to have.

To Valarie, Hazel House looked like something out of a fairy tale. She could hardly believe such a place existed in America. Its exterior bloomed with spires and towers and jutting wings. Iron-railed balconies adorned walls built from natural stone and dark red brick. The grand front hall, which might once have been an imposing space, glowed with sunshine streaming in from the skylights. Upholstered furniture, potted plants, and etched tables dotted the common areas. Surprisingly modern artwork colored the walls, and sculptures stood everywhere, no two alike. Gazing up at the carved trim, Valarie had noticed the gargoyles and giggled to herself. Who had gargoyles inside a house? It almost seemed like a humorous nod to the home's antique past. It was a magnificent Frankenstein's monster of a house, and just about every room begged to be turned into a painting.

Valarie considered herself introverted—*reserved*, she thought; it seemed a more fitting term in her grand new home—but during the tour of the house and grounds, she had found herself chattering to her new landlady. Out came the tale of how she and Adam had separated, and how an accident had killed him. How she'd come here to take some time away, get her head together, and figure out what was next.

In a single fluid motion, like a dancer, Merel had paused in her stride and turned. "I'm a widow myself," she said. "I understand. Sometimes you need to make a change." She had given Valarie a small, inscrutable smile, and her blue eyes had almost seemed to twinkle. For a fleeting moment, Valarie felt strangely attracted to Merel, odd because she'd never been attracted to women, unless you counted that one party in art school.

The moment passed, and Merel showed Valarie to her rooms. "Of course, you'll have the whole wing," she said, sweeping an arm to indicate the two bedrooms, sitting room, and bathroom complete with washer/dryer. "An occasional guest or two is fine, as long as you let me know ahead of time." Valarie squelched the squeal that threatened to erupt; she still couldn't quite believe her luck. To cover it, she made a lame joke about memorizing the path to the rooms so she wouldn't get lost. Merel smiled. "I'll let you settle in. Do text me if you need anything. Might be easier than trying to find me."

Valarie schlepped her suitcase into the bedroom she'd decided to sleep in, then stowed her art supplies in the other bedroom. Sitting back against brocade pillows on her new bed, she sighed with satisfaction. It wasn't every day that a person had the chance to rent part of an eccentric old mansion, at a great price and with a month-to-month lease. It was the perfect spot for an artist's retreat.

Even better, it was three thousand miles away from everything she wanted to put behind her.

*****

The bedroom looked different at night.

Lying on her back in the double bed, Valarie watched shadows shift across the recesses of the tray ceiling as moonlight streamed through swaying branches. She hadn't bothered closing the curtain; it seemed unnecessary in a home not even within sight of its nearest neighbor. Pale light glinted off the silvery vines of the wallpaper. Wide awake, she pulled the covers up to her chin and listened to the breeze whisper outside.

The next thing she saw was Adam's face. It was never far from her mind, but somehow she hadn't expected it to make an appearance here, in these new circumstances, so different from any part of her previous life.

Six months before, after yet another argument that was more sad than angry, she and Adam had decided to take a break. Adam had moved in with his brother, and Valarie stayed in their old apartment, alone with a menagerie of restless questions. What was she now, exactly? Was she married, or single? Wasn't "taking a break" a little too *college* of a phrase to describe a husband and wife? Could their problems be overcome? He had done some bad things, but so had she. Worse things. Should she leave it all behind, wipe the slate clean, and start over? Was thirty-five too old for that? What about the children they'd never had? Would she even want to have children with anyone else?

And then one weekend Adam was riding his bike, as he always did, up in the hills, and a blue Chevy sedan hadn't seen him. Her father-in-law had called with the news. The next call was from a lawyer: Valarie stood to inherit all of Adam's assets. He'd never bothered making a will.

When Valarie thought about that day that everything changed, she pictured the blue sedan, a car that would have been utterly uninteresting in any other context. She watched it glide around curves in the road like a TV commercial, ignorant of its destiny, of the chain reaction of physics and biology it would trigger. She didn't picture the collision, the gore, the aftermath. She didn't imagine whether Adam screamed. She just saw the car, ever moving, calmly, assuredly, as if on a track, traveling as inexorably as a river to the sea.

"I'm a widow myself," Merel had said. Whatever Valerie might be now, she thought, she was not a *widow*. Widows mourned their dead husbands, gathered the family, handled funeral arrangements. Widows, for better or worse, had closure.

But here she was, lying in a strange bed and wondering what Adam would have thought of this house, wanting to chuckle with him about its quirks, yearning to hear his laughter echo against the high walls. She felt a surge of familiar rage. How dare he go and die before they could figure things out.

Footsteps echoed against hardwood planks in the hallway outside Valarie's bedroom. She gasped as the floor creaked. It must be Merel, she told her racing heart. Nobody else is here. Yet, for a moment, the steps had sounded like Adam's, treading softly, the early bird rising to make coffee for his night-owl wife. Tears breached their dams and soaked Valarie's face. *Damn you, Adam,* she whispered. *Damn you.*

When she finally slept, her dreams were filled with cars.

*****

The second time the painting changed, Valarie wondered if Merel might have messed with it. The idea seemed ridiculous, but they were alone in Hazel House, unless you counted the regular visits by gardeners, handymen, and maids.

Merel wasn't a nosy or interfering sort of landlady. She left Valarie to her own devices, for the most part, though she did insist that her tenant stop by her frequent soirees. She seemed to know everybody in the local community, from the Jaycees to the police chief to the Daughters of the American Revolution. Nobody ever seemed to turn down a catered event at Hazel House.

She seemed delighted to have an artist as a tenant, coming over to admire Valarie's half-finished sketches.

Sure, it was a little weird to be living in the same house as one's landlady, but Merel was hardly ever home anyway, going out every morning to do whatever it was she did in town.

Still, there had been... moments. Valarie sat cross-legged on the lawn one day with her sketch pad, trying to capture the rolling hills and pines, when she felt a gaze. Glancing back at the house, she saw an upstairs window with the curtain pulled back, and Merel standing there, watching. Displaying no bashfulness at being discovered, Merel had smiled, lifted her hand, and continued gazing at Valarie, who awkwardly returned the wave. After a few minutes of trying to ignore the eyes on her back, Valarie had gotten up and moved to a spot behind some shrubs.

"Beautiful jewelry," Merel had said one morning in the kitchen. "Are those turquoise?" She had leaned close to peer at Valarie's earrings. Valarie stopped herself just in time from flinching backward. A bit too cheerfully, she told Merel about buying the earrings in Arizona during her cross-country drive to Hazel House.

One morning, Valarie, her hair still wet after showering, had passed Merel in the hall. The landlady had turned to her tenant, closed her eyes, and inhaled luxuriously. "Mmmm," she'd said. "Lilacs." And with another of her indecipherable smiles, she had disappeared out of sight. Later that day, when Valarie drove to town for groceries, she found herself adding some unscented Dove shampoo to her cart.

Was she imagining things? Surely Merel was just being friendly. Of course she was interested in her tenant. She had nobody else in the house to talk to. Surely it would be more peculiar if she completely ignored Valarie.

Crossing the spare bedroom where she kept her canvases, Valarie paused as she passed the free-standing full-length mirror in its heavy oak frame. Her long brown hair, which she'd kept in a ponytail for the past few months, could use a trim. Her T-shirt and jeans seemed to hang off her in a way they never used to. Even her face seemed thinner, her eyes seeming to peer out of shadowed hollows. She shook her head. She hadn't been sleeping well, that was all.

She continued walking, and that was when she saw the half-finished staircase painting, which she had stashed there while she worked on a landscape outdoors.

But no. Merel couldn't have added the new streaky blotch to the canvas, in the same spot as the first stain, right at the foot of the painted stairs. Merel wasn't an artist. "I dearly love art," she had told Valarie, "though I have absolutely no talent myself. Me with a paintbrush would be like a fish trying to play a bugle!"

Valarie squinted at the new blotch and cocked her head. It was gray, like the last one, but longer and more distinct, rounded in places that made it look like a person lying on the floor asleep.

*****

The day after the painting changed for the second time, Merel asked Valarie to paint her portrait. With a free month's rent as payment, it was an offer Valarie wasn't about to refuse. Merel was an ideal model, dressed in one of her loose-flowing outfits and perched serenely on her favorite plush chair near the living room window.

When the painting was finished, Merel was so delighted with it that she had it hung in the library, just above the hearth. When the handyman arrived, Merel called Valarie in to watch, then stood to one side and smiled as he climbed the ladder. "A bit to the left," she told him, waving her hand as if the gesture itself would guide the painting into the correct position.

Valarie hadn't spent much time in that room. She drifted idly, glancing at titles on the books' spines, recognizing nearly none, except one or two she'd failed to finish in high school English.

"Perfect!" Merel exclaimed, and the man stowed the hammer in his tool belt and began his descent. After the ladder had been cleared away, Merel stepped back and took a picture with her phone. "Beautiful work, Valarie. I'm so pleased." With a smile, she turned and swept out of the room.

It seemed to Valarie, looking up at the painting now, that portrait-Merel's eyes had a certain penetrating gleam above her signature smile. Valarie wasn't quite how she'd achieved that effect. She didn't know whether to feel proud or a little unnerved.

Beneath the portrait, the mantel shelf was crowded with framed photographs. Valarie stepped closer to have a look. A few old sepia-toned photos of toddlers in nightdresses sat nestled among photos of well-dressed men and women from various eras of the twentieth century. It took a minute for Valarie to spot the wedding photo, which was toward the back, behind several others.

A younger, beaming Merel in a splendid white gown stood next to a tall, handsome, blond man in a tuxedo. Their backdrop was a tall green hedge that Valarie thought she recognized from the formal garden on the grounds of Hazel House.

Next to the wedding picture was a close-up photo of Merel and her husband. Merel gazed off at some distant object to the left of the photographer, and the man was looking at Merel's face. Valarie stared at it for a minute, then abruptly turned and left the library.

Her feet took her back to the spare bedroom, but her mind was trying not to think about how much Merel's dead husband looked like Adam.

She paused in front of the staircase painting. The gray blotch was back, and it seemed darker, more distinct. Valarie gaped at it. Not only did it look like someone lying down asleep, but certain brush strokes resembled clothing. The fabric covering the narrower half of the body, if it was a body, was dark and fairly form-fitting, like workout pants. The rest was covered in a loose blue fabric that had a sheen to it, like an athletic jacket. Like the jacket that Adam used to wear when he went biking.

Valarie gasped.

She hadn't sleepwalked since she was a child. But someone was adding to that canvas, conscious or not.

*****

Valarie examined her reflection in the bedroom's full-length mirror. She still looked tired, and too thin, but the sundress helped. She had swapped out her usual paint-stained jeans in anticipation of Merel's latest social gathering.

She hoped it wouldn't be awkward. Yesterday, Merel had passed Valarie in the hall and said curtly, "You know, Valarie, I don't mind if you play music in your rooms. But please, not at two in the morning next time."

Valarie had stood there, stunned. "Sorry," she mumbled, steamrolled by Merel's certainty. She did not recall having been awake at two a.m. recently. If anything, she was sleeping so deeply that it had been hard to wake up. Maybe her old transistor radio was shorting out.

The sunshine on the bright patio lifted her mood. Merel was hosting the Chamber of Commerce today, and the scene was lively with the cocktail chatter of veteran networkers. Accepting her glass of wine from the bartender, she turned and stopped short at the two eager faces that had appeared before her.

"Barbara Jackson," said the gray-haired black woman in the red sheath dress, extending a hand. "I own Act Two Remodeling. I understand Merel has you to thank for that lovely portrait in the library."

"Stunning work," added the tall white man with the goatee and the summer suit. "The eyes are particularly arresting."

"Thank you," Valarie mumbled, "Mister.... uh..."

"Emmett Weber," he said. "I run Weber Accounting downtown."

"Come. I'll introduce you around," Barbara said, placing a friendly hand on Valarie's shoulder to guide her across the patio.

Before she knew it, Valarie had met just about everyone, who all seemed to know her already. "Of course," they said. "The portrait artist!" In a swirl of chats, compliments, and requests for additional portraits, she nodded, smiled, and forgot most of their names immediately.

Finally, the mob moved off, leaving only a swarthy middle-aged man tugging at his sweat-stained collar. "Sonny Marocco," he said by way of introduction.

Valarie shook his hand. He held hers a beat too long.

"Watch out for this crowd," he said. "Young pretty thing like you, someone's bound to snap you up."

She forced a smile, pushed away the mental image of a snapping crocodile, and casually stepped to one side to put more space between herself and Sonny. "And what do you do?" she asked, to change the subject.

"Ristorante Primo Piatto, on Tenth, that's my place," he said. "Soon to be expanding to our second location on Arbor Way."

She nodded, contemplating how to make a graceful exit, but Sonny already seemed to have lost interest, looking past her across the patio. Valarie followed his gaze to where Merel stood, her smiling face lit up with whatever story she was telling the two men standing in front of her. Sonny's eyes traveled down Merel's dress, which draped snugly over her curves. "Excuse me," he said, giving Valarie a nod before walking a confident path toward his hostess.

"Don't mind him," said a voice. "He's harmless."

Valarie turned to see a striking blue-eyed woman, her dark hair swept up into a loose bun above her floral-print dress. The woman extended a hand. "Rhonda Rhodes.

Paradise Salon and Day Spa," she said. "Sonny's been after Merel ever since Jakob died. Poor man doesn't have a chance, but I don't have the heart to break it to him. Apparently, neither does Merel." Her laughter was light.

"When did her husband pass away?" Valarie asked, trying to strike the correct balance between curious and solemn. She had never gotten up the courage to ask Merel directly.

"Let's see. It's been about two years now," said Rhonda, her smile dimming. "A terrible day. To pass away in such a freak accident, and at home, too." She clucked her tongue. "Poor Nicky. She was very fond of him. I don't think she's quite adjusted to being the most eligible bachelorette in town."

"Nicky?" asked Valarie, puzzled.

"Oh, that's just my pet name for Merel," said Rhonda. "Nichols was Merel's maiden name. We've known each other since kindergarten. The two of us and Emmett Weber were all in the same class. Oh, and Chief Bronson. He was Billy back then. Her first crush, back in seventh grade." She smiled, casting an affectionate glance at Merel across the patio.

Valarie sipped her wine thoughtfully. "It must have been hard for her, to be suddenly all alone in the big house," she said.

"Certainly," said Rhonda. "Although they always seemed like an odd match to me. She was such a free spirit, and he was a stern, businesslike type of man. But they were so active in the community, great patrons of the arts. And they seemed happy enough. Marriage is a business partnership, after all." She smiled. "Excuse me, there's someone I need to say hello to."

Valarie had drained her wine. She moved toward a collection tray to set down her glass. A catering employee carrying empty hors d'oeuvre plates arrived at the same time. The woman offered Valarie a clean napkin from her apron. Valarie took it gratefully and dabbed at her forehead.

"Thanks," Valarie said.

"Of course, ma'am." Her hair was long and curly, and she wore black pants, a white button-down shirt, and a tag bearing the name LUISA.

"Do you work a lot of parties here?" asked Valarie, still in chit-chat mode.

"All of them," Luisa said with a smile. "I've been with the company for five years, since before her husband died."

"I'm renting some rooms here at the house," said Valarie, "It's quite a place."

"Yes, it is beautiful," Luisa agreed. "Such a shame, though. All those rooms, and no children."

"I suppose they could have had ten children and still not run out of bedrooms," said Valarie.

"It seems they tried," Luisa said matter-of-factly. "I was at several parties where she was pregnant. And then, at the next party, she wasn't."

"Oh," said Valarie. "That's too bad."

Luisa shrugged. "It's up to God," she said, stooping to lift the tray, then disappearing into a pipe-and-drape tent at the patio's edge. Valarie tried to imagine God, sitting on a cloud, doling out babies. Instead, she saw a blue car, driving around curves on a hilly road.

The party guests lingered long after Valarie had gone inside. Later, walking toward the kitchen, Valarie saw one last small knot of guests calling goodbye to Merel as they stepped out the front door. Merel waved, then crossed the hall to the French doors that opened onto the patio, where a lone man sat, clinking ice in his bourbon glass. Valarie thought she remembered him introducing himself as Brad Prestridge, a partner at a local law firm. At Merel's appearance, he stood and followed her back into the house. The two of them disappeared up the curved staircase and walked toward the bedrooms.

That night, when Valarie closed her eyes, Merel was there. They sat on the sofa in the library, and Merel shifted closer to Valarie, leaning in, watching her eyes. Valarie felt electric, her nerves lit up like holiday lights, like she hadn't felt since Adam was alive. Suddenly they kissed, and then they were leaning back on the sofa together, and when the ecstasy came, it was so powerful that Valarie woke up in a hot sweat.

*****

The last time the painting changed, it was in the middle of yet another party. It had occurred to Valarie that one of the party guests could have interfered with the canvas. She'd become fairly well acquainted with a handful of them, but how well did she really know them? They spent most of their time outdoors on that landscaped patio, but there was always somebody in the house, using the washroom or admiring Merel's sculpture collection.

She didn't linger at the gathering of Merel's friends from the historical society. After putting in her customary appearance, Valarie slipped away from the schmoozers and sippers and stole back to the spare bedroom. As if pulled by a magnet, she moved toward the staircase painting. Her eyes bulged when she saw it.

The gray smudge was no longer a malformed blur. It was distinct, and it was human-shaped. Added to the canvas by an unseen hand was a man, wearing black pants and a blue jacket. He lay sprawled at the foot of the marble stair, legs and arms jutting out at unnatural angles. Between his blond hair and the floor oozed a shiny streak of cadmium red.

At the top of the stairs, a second figure had appeared. Its features were vague, but it wore a loose gown, and its face appeared to be smiling.

Slowly, the prostrate man raised his head and turned it to look directly at Valarie. His eyes, hollow with pain, seemed to implore her for help. One of his arms lifted slowly and extended, as if reaching for her. As she stood frozen, jaw hanging, the man's head abruptly slumped back down. A drop of red seeped from his hair and dripped viscously down the canvas.

He was not Adam. But she had seen his face before.

Her stomach lurched, and she turned and fled the room.

The house had several twists and turns she hadn't explored. Valarie found herself in a short alcove, ending in an iron staircase that spiraled downward. Pursuing her sole desire, to get away from the painted man, she banged down the steps, winding lower and lower, ultimately emerging into a cool basement. When she flipped the switch, dim light illuminated the area weakly, as if wary of what it might show.

She made her way through the crowded space, past dusty furniture, naked dressmakers' dummies, and paintings of people in Victorian clothes. It seemed the van Rensselaers weren't fond of throwing things away. Valarie paused at a wheeled baby crib equipped with mesh bumpers and a fitted sheet, the only item in the room that looked at all modern. She did a double take at what lay just beyond the crib. Standing stock-still on a table were a bobcat, a raccoon, and a falcon, fur and feathers preserved by taxidermy, glass eyes glittering from the shadows. Hurrying past them, Valarie came to another stair, tucked in a corner and spiraling upward into darkness. She started up these stairs, which seemed far preferable to walking back past the animals.

After some time, she wondered where the stair was going. Surely by now she had climbed high enough to return to the ground floor. The light in this stairwell was even dimmer than the basement. Valarie hurried onward, her thighs starting to ache from the exertion. Finally, she emerged at a small landing with a ladder at one side and a trapdoor at the top. She hoisted herself up the ladder, pushed at the door, and surfaced onto a rooftop deck.

The small, square platform was walled by rough-hewn stone on two sides and wooden railings on the others. A fresh breeze lifted Valarie's hair off her shoulders as she caught her breath. She took in the view of the woods and hills, listening to birdcalls mixing with the faint sounds of cocktail-party prattle from three stories below. She shook her head. Only Merel, with her whims and her wealth, would build a widow's walk this far inland.

In the center of the deck sat a portable fire pit. Valarie bent to examine the chunks of ashy wood, blackened debris, and bits of paper. Newspaper? No, it looked like regular paper, a creamy, heavyweight stock. She pulled at a piece that was tucked underneath an intact chunk of firewood. It looked like a scrap of letterhead; printed on it in blue ink were the words *Blossom Fertility Clinic*. The rest had been burned away.

A piece of cream-colored stationery was the only other paper that had survived the blaze. Valarie tugged it free and read the words at the top, just above a singed, ragged edge:

My dearest Merel–

*****

In town, Valarie collected the information she was after. At the police station, she showed them everything. Yes, they'd examine the evidence. Yes, she had acted appropriately in making a report. And yes, they'd definitely be in touch.

Anxiously, she returned to Hazel House. She felt certain she'd done the right thing, but what now? Valarie began transferring some of her clothes from the closet into her suitcase. If Merel were arrested, she'd have to move out. It was just as well. She had a feeling she had stayed at Hazel House long enough.

"Valarie? Oh, Valarie!"

She jumped, slamming the suitcase shut.

"Are you there, dear? I'd like a word."

As the footsteps in the hall came closer, Merel's heeled boots clicking louder, Valarie suddenly saw, again, the face of the man at the police station, nodding, listening, intently studying her own.

Chief Bronson, Rhonda Rhodes had said. *He was Billy back then.*

The police chief, Valarie now recalled in a sudden, terrible flash, was one of Merel's oldest friends.

KARMA AND CAMILE
Candy Madonna

As Camile sat in the corner of her shack with her knees hugged to her chest, she could hear her thundering heartbeat. The tiny woman, with long, wavy, purple hair, honey-colored eyes, and soft olive-colored skin curled into a ball, awaiting the torment she knew was on the way.

Watching for shadows to block out the sunbeams between the wallboards, she felt tormented by the demon that haunted her soul. Camile held her breath, attempting to calm her heart so she might hear over the horrendous sound of her heart beating in her ears. She focused on her surroundings, listening for any hope of escape from the impending danger.

She began to hear the birds sing just outside the shack door, and for a moment, she felt peace in her soul once again.

THUD.

Heavy boots landed on the wooden slats of the porch. There he stood, tall and broad, blocking out the sun and eclipsing the crescent moon carved into the front door.

She knew this was the end.

*****

Painfully aware of her outcast status, Camile never asked for anything. Bringing joy to others and showing them their own magic was all she ever needed. Most believed she was faking her kindhearted nature and loving smile. They despised her for it.

The people in town knew how horrible her life continued to be, with the death of her mother and the abandonment of her father. Camile had no friends and not a penny to her name. Her life seemed to fall apart with more bad luck every day. She had no friends and lived in a tiny, run-down swamp shack on the edge of town–a town that resented her happiness amidst all her misfortune. They couldn't understand how someone with so much bad luck and sorrow could keep smiling every day.

Each morning, Camile woke up to new challenges. Once, a fierce storm blew through, tearing off parts of her roof and leaving her vulnerable to the elements. Another day, the little garden she relied on for food was ravaged by wild animals, leaving her with nothing to harvest.

Camile's attempts to find work were met with constant rejection from the townspeople. They refused to hire her, spreading rumors and lies to keep her marginalized. Even when she managed to secure odd jobs, they were often short-lived, and she never earned enough to make a real difference in her life.

Socially, Camile was isolated. The few acquaintances she had turned their backs on her, fearing the backlash from associating with someone deemed a witch. She spent her days in solitude, longing for genuine human connection and support.

Despite all these setbacks, Camile refused to give up. She held onto the hope that one day things would change for the better. Her resilience and determination were her only sources of strength as she continued to face the relentless challenges life threw her way.

Topping off the town's suspicions, those who wronged Camile or attempted were mysteriously struck with terrible afflictions. People fell ill out of the blue– even those focused on their health. Successful business owners with multiple bank accounts would suddenly go bankrupt. Women who took great care of their appearance woke up to skin diseases and hair loss.

All affected seemingly had one thing in common–their hate for Camile.

Spiteful whispers from the townsfolk fueled countless rumors. Their small minds were convinced she worked with evil forces. "Camile must be a witch!" Their whispers never failed to reach her ears as she passed.

She never allowed it to bother her. She knew her purpose was service to others.

The undesired girl took a daily stroll through the cobblestone streets of her little Georgia town, no matter the weather. She not only wanted to absorb the atmospheric energy but to see if there were any people in need of aid. She kept her promise to the divine that she would be able to make that walk every day, no matter how she feared the outcome from her neighbors.

Camile lived just on the edge of town in the swamp marsh that was full of magic and wildlife. Her shack was an old, unclaimed fishing hut that had been abandoned long ago. She stumbled across it as a seven-year-old girl, when she was left alone in the swamp to die. Her father lost his mind to alcohol after her mother passed from a heart attack—brought on by the beating he'd doled out. She came to see it as a blessing that her father threw her away, or else she might have endured that same ill fate.

Growing up alone in the swamps from such a tender age, Camile learned how to take care of herself and mostly learned to survive. She taught herself to hunt her food and as she did this, she carefully watched all the living things she encountered. She paid close attention to their eating habits, how they stalked their prey, and how they co-existed with other living creatures. Camile even noticed how each living element communicated with the others. She learned so much from the swamps.

Over the years, Camile added little things to the fishing hut. She built a small front porch with just one banister on the long side, with 3 small steps exiting to the right of the shack. There were tiny details in her home that gave her peace, like the little crescent moon carved into the top center of the front door. Whenever she sensed a disturbance, she would look through that window, where she'd steal a moment of tranquility by observing nature's beautiful landscape on the other side.

After the pain she felt from the loss of her mother and fear of love from her father's interactions, she vowed never to allow another human to suffer from any such torments. Camile never made her agenda obvious as she strolled through town, seeking new books from the library, or picking up a single item from the grocer. She made it a point to smile and wave at everyone she met, offering warm compliments to anyone she got close enough to speak to, hoping for a glimpse into their soul to see if there was even a slight request for help.

Camile complimented Sue, the town librarian, on her new dress. The woman burst into tears. She expressed that her once faithful husband had bought it for her. But now, he'd run off with another woman. Camile listened intently, her huge heart ready to offer peace to the suffering woman. Sue told Camile she felt better and her thoughts of ending her life drifted away, all because a strange woman stood there long enough to hear her pain and offer comfort.

As Camile completed her town visit and headed to her swamp, she noticed a few men hanging around a parked truck beside a field. She could tell they had spent the day hunting and drinking. Camile attempted to brush her uneasy feelings aside when she glanced up at them. Each man smirked at her from the downed tailgate on the back of the truck. She looked only at her feet from then on as she walked the path toward home.

Footsteps followed her on the dirt road. Terrified to look back, Camile nevertheless had to know how much danger she was in. With a quick sly glance, she caught sight of the whole group of men behind her, heads cocked for their second hunt of the day. They noticed her look and began to pick up the pace.

A booming burst of laughing excitement erupted from the assumed ringleader, "Yeeeeeah boys! It's go time!"

Camile didn't hesitate, she ran as hard and as fast as she could, bad news hot on her heels. With her heart pounding out of her chest, she made it to her shack, jumped onto the porch, swung the front door open, and slammed it closed behind her. Camile held it tight for a moment, anticipating the men's bodies bashing into it any second. But the bangs didn't come. There was only stillness.

She blocked the door with a propped chair and turned the lock to ensure they didn't gain entry. Peeking through the crescent moon to see how far she'd outrun the men, she saw nothing.

As she sat there in utter silence, her mind raced with thoughts of what she could do to escape if the door suddenly burst open. She thought about the small window in the back, but it was too high for her to reach quickly. There were no weapons around, just her wooden chair and a few outdated books scattered on the floor. Camile knew she had to calm her racing mind and think clearly, or she wouldn't stand a chance. She closed her eyes, took a deep breath, and focused on the sounds outside, trying to sense any approach.

With the thoughts of relief slowly creeping in, Camile sat on the floor near the back of the shack, staring at the front door for what seemed like an eternity. Her heart beat so loud, she heard nothing else, her breath so heavy it blurred her vision. She knew what would happen if she wasn't able to get everything under control. Holding her hands in prayer position at her chest, she began to slow her breathing. Once she began to hear the birds outside, she opened her eyes, lowered her hands, and slowly got up to walk toward the door and take a look. Only the beautiful sunny day shone from the sliver of the crescent carved into the door. Camile began letting her guard down, thinking the men had given up. She removed the chair from the door and unlatched the lock. The loud CLICK from the lock was the signal her captures waited to hear.

THUD. THUD, THUD.

Several sets of boots hit the wooden slats of the porch. Deep darkness covered the moon. A hard thrust of the door sent Camile flying backward. Three men blocked the doorway.

Camile pleaded, "What do you want from me? What have I done to you?"

A tall man stepped forward, heavy around the center, and missing all his front teeth. He wore a set of torn coveralls coated in what appeared to be dried red clay mud. He had a short, dirty scraggly orange beard. Greasy, long, stringy hair peaked from his backward baseball cap that was stained from sweat and grime. He smelled like spoiled milk and rotten meat.

The man's eyes were dark and beady, exuding a sense of menace as he stared at Camile. The creaking of the wooden floorboards sounded like the slow ticking of a death clock with each step he took toward her. Camile's breath quickened. She was trapped, and the terror in her eyes only seemed to fuel the man's twisted excitement.

Black boots that were busted at the toes displayed hawk-like talons. As he spoke, his voice sounded like he wheezed every word. In his long southern drawl, he said, "Ooohh, you purdy little thang." Drool leaked from the corner of his mouth as his finger pointed down her body. "What don't we want from you? That is the question you need to be askin'. I'm Blazer, 'hind ya' is Tom and Bozy. We got purdy business to handle wit you."

Blazer inched his way closer to Camile with every disgusting word he spat at her. His long, blistered finger reached out for a touch and grazed a strand of her long hair.

213

Camile jerked herself backward from his grasp. She heard her heartbeat in her ears, her breaths coming fast, heavy, and deep. She knew exactly what was about to happen and there was nothing she could do to prevent it.

Blazer got closer to Camile as Tom stood point behind her. Bozy took a quick look outside to make sure there were no interruptions. He locked the door and walked towards Camile and his gang to join the hunt. The room grew colder as Bozy's heavy footsteps approached. Camile's senses sharpened, detecting every creak of the floorboards under his weight. Her mind raced, searching for an escape, but the oppressive presence of the three men blocked every possible route. The atmosphere thickened with their sinister intent, as Blazer's vile grin stretched wider with each step he took toward her. Hope seemed to flicker and dim, but a small spark of resilience still burned within her, fueling her determination to survive this harrowing ordeal.

Tom licked his lips as he pulled some rope from his pocket and tied it around Camile's mouth to gag her. It wouldn't matter much, as there wasn't anyone around for miles. Even if someone were to hear, they knew the girl who lived there consorted with devils so they would never attempt to save her.

Camile slowly lowered her head. The rope tasted like dirt and sweat. She stepped backward towards the wall. She stopped as her back gently reached the wall, and just like that, she was gone. It was as if her soul had left her body.

Camile's body stood as still as a nail on the wall. Her chest stopped rising with her breath. It was as if she'd died standing straight up.

Blazer got excited. "Oh look boys, she decided to stop fighting against us. Purdy and smart."

Tom replied, "Well, that ain't no fun. I like when they fight back."

All three figures laughed and moved in on the terrified girl.

Slowly, Camile's head tilted upward, and her eyes began to open. The closer the men got, the more they noticed her changing. Camile's eyes, once a yellow honey color, were now black as coal. Her hair turned as black as a stallion's mane.

The sunlight disappeared from the cracks in the walls and left them all in complete darkness. The sounds of the birds were gone, replaced by gasping from the confused hunters as they shuffled about in search of a light source. The darkness seemed to seep into their very souls, amplifying the tension and fear that clung to the air. A cold, eerie silence enveloped them, pressing down with an oppressive weight that made it difficult to breathe. Each man felt a primal fear rising within, understanding that they were no longer the hunters, but had now become the hunted. The realization struck them like a physical blow, chilling them to their cores. The balance of power had shifted, and they were caught in the grip of something far more sinister and powerful than they could have ever imagined.

Bozy pulled a lighter from his pocket and struck it bright.

The room was visible once again. Camile was now behind Tom. His eyes widened in shock. He stood shaking with his mouth open. Camile held ropes of human intestines in her hands. She swung them around Tom's neck and wrapped them tighter and tighter. He began grasping at them futilely as they began constricting his throat.

Bozy attempted to shake off the shock and stumbled toward Tom to rescue him. Overcome by a hot rush as he tried to move, Bozy followed the blood trail that led from him to his buddy, then realized the intestines wrapped around Tom's neck were not Tom's, but his. During the panic, he didn't realize Camile had managed to slice him open and pull his insides across the room and around his friend's neck. Bozy fell to the floor, and as he landed, he realized Blazer was already there, knocked unconscious.

Hours later, Blazer came to. With his head pounding and body aching, he tried to reach for his head to examine the pain, but he was restricted. His arms wouldn't budge.

A small candle in the corner of the room gave him enough light to see that he was in a small, dark, concrete room that appeared to be a basement. He screamed for help in hopes his friends would come to the rescue, but something stuck in his throat, killing the cries before he could release them.

Blazer began to sweat, trying to wiggle in his seat, as he suddenly felt even more pain in his rear. His mind raced, trying to comprehend the nightmare unfolding before him. Panic surged through his veins as he attempted to wriggle free from his restraints, but every movement brought excruciating pain. His vision blurred with terror, and his body trembled uncontrollably. Desperation clawed at his sanity, prompting him to muster every ounce of strength he had left. He knew he had to escape, but the odds seemed insurmountable. As he struggled, the room's cold, damp walls seemed to close in on him, suffocating any glimmer of hope.

Tears fell from his eyes. The hunter was unable to move, unable to scream.

A door creaked open from behind. He quieted his sobs and tried to pull himself together, thinking his friends were there to save him.

He saw the small glow of a candle coming from behind him. He heard a tiny giggle coming from whoever held it. With a gust of wind, the candles went out. A large circle of fire surrounded him, and the entire room brightened up like the morning sun.

Able to make out the candle holder, he thought it was Camile, though she now looked different. She was no longer the tiny, delicate, sweet, and innocent young woman he'd chased home. She moved differently, and her energy was much darker and scarier than anything Blazer had ever felt before. As he watched her move closer to him, she began to grow rapidly in height. She grew eight feet tall right before his eyes. Her hair grew longer and darker, now reaching the floor at his feet. The creature pointed its long, scrawny, black bone-sharpened fingers toward him. Its eyes were solid black, with no white in sight, and they began to glow like two black diamonds in the moonlight. Now standing directly in front of him, feeling its breath on his face. The once soft and gentle features contorted into a grotesque visage, her eyes void of any emotion but sheer malevolence.

The creature stood over him and spoke, "Oh, you disgusting little thing, what don't we want from you?" With a loud screeching laugh from the pits of its belly, Blazer realized this creature was, in fact, Camile.

Fear penetrated his soul. His wrists were wrapped in the peeled flesh of his friends, his legs were removed and placed on the floor in front of him. His manhood had also been sliced from his body, but he didn't notice it anywhere on the floor below him.

He went to scream but remembered the object in his throat.

The creature laughed once more and responded. "What's wrong? You're not screaming. I like it when you scream. It appears you may have choked on your manhood. I'm sure if you swallow hard, you should be able to clear it right out. It's small enough."

Blazer's eyes grew wide and he tilted his head back, attempting to take a deep breath with his nose, summoning the courage to swallow hard. Mid-swallow, his head lowered to find that his intestines had also been pulled out and wrapped tightly around the rest of his body. One deep swallow and his penis finally cleared his throat. Midway through Blazer's blood-curdling scream, the creature sliced his head clean off with her knife-sharp fingers.

The once fierce hunter's head rolled across the floor to greet the heads of Tom and Bozy.

Creature-Camile gathered all the victims into a crate and stored them in the cellar room below the basement. Once every drop was accounted for, she made her way back upstairs.

With each step taken on the ascend, her breathing normalized, her body shrank back to its tiny stature, hair shortening and returning to its purple hue. She reached the top step and heard the birds singing outside.

The basement door closed behind her, and the sun was shining beautifully between all the boards of the shack. She closed her eyes, took a deep breath, and smiled.

As she opened her eyes, they returned to their sun-kissed honey color.

Camile walked out onto her porch, happy as she always was, and she began her walk for the day.

Despite the serene exterior, the townspeople whispered about the strange occurrences in the forest. Missing hunters, eerie howls at night, and the unsettling feeling that something sinister lurked just beyond the tree line. None dared venture near the old shack, now a place of dark legend. Yet, Camile remained a beloved figure, her sweet voice and cheerful demeanor masking the horrors she kept hidden so well. For her, the cycle of life continued seamlessly, a delicate balance between light and shadow, innocence and malevolence.

SHAHMARAN
Eva Roslin

Come home, Roya. Your father needs you.

The letter jostles in my shaky grip, each loop of black ink and handwriting a scathing memory of a place I swore to abandon forever. Should I burn it, or open the mullion window next to me and let it descend like a wounded bird, before it fades away? Can I stare instead at the way the sun, brighter for every day I have been in London, filters through the glass's edges and casts shafts of light on the stone floor? This piece of paper—this single leaf, as my colleagues would call it—can be gone in an instant. I can pretend it never arrived and that Ameh Joon is not already making the trek from Manchester to London to see me.

"Roya? Is everything all right?"

Dylan, one of my conservationist colleagues, lowers his spectacles as he regards me with a mixture of confusion and worry. His blue eyes flash, brows furrowing. His hair always reminds me of the yellow foxes in the foothills of my birthplace, Shiraz. I used to pet their fur and dream of the day I could escape. My fists clench once more at the memory of that house that still stands in Vazirabad, refusing to die, just like my father, clinging to the soil that spawned it.

"Yes, fine." I walk near one of the stools in the cramped work area, surrounded by tomes of every kind, from calfskin to Moroccan leather. The smell of old pages in the russet and auburn volumes soothes my temperament. "My aunt is coming to visit."

I place the letter down on the wooden desk in front of me and think back to the first time I encountered that word, *temperament*. A Jane Austen novel. *Pride and Prejudice*, I think. One of my uncles, Soroush Dayi, who moved to Britain years ago, taught my brothers and me how to speak English and lent me his books. I will never forget the feeling of the first bookseller's shop I visited and asked to purchase my own copy of *Sense and Sensibility* that I had saved dearly for, only for the shopkeeper not to sell it to me because he doubted I could read.

Dylan nods. "Is it a happy visit? Your husband will be pleased, no doubt."

I put a hand to my mouth to prevent the loud bark of laughter I want to let out at the mention of Omid. "I have no doubt of his reaction," I say, as if I still see that brute on a daily basis.

Omid, a classmate of my oldest brother, Kayvan, during their apothecary studies. He visited our family home in Shiraz on a semester break. Although he revolted me to the point of nausea with his starchy, cheddar smell and fat belly, he told my parents that he would be glad to make a good wife out of me in England.

"You should be excited to move to a finer country," he'd said.

That had been ten years ago.

"Why do I feel the distinct opposite from you?" Dylan puts a hand on one of my shoulders and for a second, I allow my defenses to drop. I pretend that his home is where I'll be going this evening, that his bed will be the one I share, that his body will be the one keeping me warm.

"It will be fine. I promise." I glance up at him with a small smile before making my way past tables of tomes separated from covers, glues, string, and brushes.

The Reading Room door is across from me. Dylan places a hand on my shoulder again, stroking his fingers over the fabric that covers me. My throat is tight. If Mister Pearce, the Head of our division, catches me like this, I will have to leave this sanctuary that has protected me from my family for so long. That is something I cannot risk.

"I know that tone. You are hiding something from me." Dylan removes his spectacles to clean them with a handkerchief from his coat pocket.

If my aunt discovers I fled Omid's home in West London and now live with a group of older Iranian women in a small apartment above an inn, she will drag me even faster to my father's home in Surrey. She will scream if she finds out I do extra seamstress and laundress work like the rest of the women so that I will have food to eat. "There is much to prepare," I say.

How can I possibly begin to tell Dylan, whose kindness sustains me through each day, that the life I worked so hard to build away from my family is now crashing down on me like a dilapidated building?

He lowers his face to my ear. "Say the word and I can send for a carriage to my family's estate. I can protect you, Roya." The look in his eyes, etched with concern, makes me want to collapse in his arms. Yet, I know better. Someone from my background could never hope to win the affections of a gentleman like Dylan. And if I did? His father, Baron Hastings, who had married both of his daughters to an Earl and a Viscount, would never accept me. Dylan, on the other hand, wants nothing to do with familial obligations and wishes to serve with Her Majesty's Armed Forces in other countries.

He puts his spectacles on again, then takes one of my hands in his own. "If there is anything I can do--"

"What is the meaning of this?" Mister Pearce stands behind us and glowers.

I drop Dylan's hand in an instant.

Pearce's moustache is stiff above his thin lips, his beady eyes squinting. "Young man, you are the son of a Baron. It is unbecoming to sully your family's name with the likes of...this." He does not bother to mask the disgust in his voice as if I am some animal because of my tawny skin.

Dylan nods. "Sir." He stalks off.

"My apologies," I say. Heat spreads up my lower back and to my shoulders, making me tremble.

"As for you, remember your marital duties and vows. I am not aware of what the customs are in whatever barn you grew up in with sheep and cows. Here, a woman's duty is to know her place and to put the needs of her husband first. In the absence of that husband, her superior in the workplace takes precedence. Is that clear?"

I nod. "Perfectly."

For the rest of the day, I busy myself at my workstation but thoughts of my aunt consume me, what she will say if she discovers the truth of my situation, and if she will reveal everything to my father.

Above all else, I pray for her not to ask me to return to the second house of my nightmares, in Surrey.

*****

"This is a quaint little place." Aunt Shari takes a sip from a porcelain tea cup before it clinks down on a small plate. I sit with her in a tea room in Bedford Square. The aroma of steeping leaves and the heat of steam wafts around each table. The damask pattern on the burgundy wallpaper lends the place a refined air as the overhead chandeliers illuminate everything below.

"Did the trip from Surrey take long?" I ask her for politeness' sake but also because I do not know for certain if she has visited Omid's home yet, the place we briefly shared before I could take no more of his physical abuse, and had to flee.

I could not give Omid what he expected—a docile, agreeable wife who stayed at home serving ghormeh sabzi to dinner guests, making faloodeh ice treats in the summer, bearing his children, and minding them—with no life of my own.

"No more than usual," my aunt replies. She adjusts her wide-brimmed hat, which has the same pattern as her floral dress. Her figure is trim, as ever, gloves without a thread out of place. The first time she patted my stomach and told me it had gotten bigger, I'd been sixteen years of age. "No one will want a fat wife," she'd told me without an inkling as to the crippling stomach cramps that plagued me each day. When someone like me constantly looks over her shoulder and worries about her husband's spies finding her, remedies to this stress are difficult to come by.

"What else is—"

"Omid's home is lovely." She cuts me off, her dark eyes glittering.

"It is my home, too, Auntie, and—"

"What a curious thing. When I went to call on you there, the servant said you had not come home for two years." Her jaw tightens into a thin-lipped smile.

Heat rushes to my cheeks and pounds through my ears. "I, well, you see, Omid felt that with my position at the library, it might be best if I took an apartment in the city to be closer."

The server comes by, a young boy with dark hair and eyes. "More?" He angles his teapot in preparation to pour.

My aunt raises her hand and shakes it.

"Very good, ma'am." He walks away, going to other tables.

If I can just explain it to her, if I can persuade her not to tell my father, if only…

"Aunt Shari, please, you must--"

She raises her hand to me now. "The same servant is friends with one of the old ladies in your sewing circle. She told me where to find your apartment. Squalid place." She purses her lips. "Azizam, if you were having such difficulty with your finances, why did you not tell me?"

223

I hate that word, azizam. It makes it sound like Aunt Shari cares. When she utters it, the sound makes my teeth hurt like the lumps of sugar she now stirs into her tea.

"I did not want to trouble you," I say, hoping she will believe it. The room begins to spin where I am sitting as a wave of dizziness overtakes me. *Do not ask me to return to that place. Do not ask me to return to that place.*

"My dear, you are like a daughter to me." She reaches out and takes my hands. "You know that even though I love your cousins Golnesa and David, they broke my heart when they took my money and left." She sinks back into her chair and dusts her dress. "Ungrateful brats. I thought we had raised them better, Hamid and I, may God rest his soul."

Her husband, my uncle, died a few years ago, an apparent suicide, but when the autopsy revealed he had toxins and poison in his bloodstream that killed him before the rope on his throat, it made me question everything.

"My mother loves me," I say to her, as if by pronouncing it aloud I can make it come true, but I have not seen her in years. She moved to my brother Kayvan's estate in Manchester to become a painter, leaving behind my father's abuses and shouting, his drinking—the misery he caused. I thought she would protect me and I was wrong.

My aunt's expression sobers. "Oh, you poor dear. Your mother is so happy with Laleh joon, and her grandchildren. She has always loved your brother's wife more."

Something sharp scrapes against my heart and the strings I imagine connecting it to the rest of my body, threatening to saw them loose. This pain shoves its way toward my throat, which tightens along with my chest. How could she say such a thing—that my own mother loves a girl she did not birth, did not feed milk from her own breast, did not tuck into bed each night, and sometimes put more food on her children's plates, taking less for herself, so that we did not starve instead of her?

224

"You cannot mean that," I stammer out. That sickening feeling overcomes me again. Instead of comfort from her, I will receive a reprimand. Instead of compassion, she will slap my face.

"The truth is difficult. I know, azizam." There is it again, the word that grates on my ears.

"What is the true purpose of your visit, Auntie? Why now?" I say, gathering up every ounce of strength not to let my tears flow in front of her. The pain in my chest amplifies, making it more difficult to breathe.

"Your father is unwell." She looks down at her teacup.

I want to laugh at her, to tell her I do not care what happens to him—not after all the times he beat me for not knowing a correct response to arithmetic, or when he caught me wearing rouge as a child. Not after he told me on my wedding day that I had finally done something right. "What ails him?"

"It is his heart again." She lifts the fan she has brought with her and flaps it open. "He has been asking for you."

"What?" I can scarcely believe my ears. He prefers my brothers who have drunk wine with him, gone on hunting trips, and played card games with their men friends. Every time Omid forced me to make a family visit to the home in Surrey, we had guests each time that I had to serve sweets, holding out a tray, while ensuring the tea and ground coffee and samovar did not overflow.

"A daughter's love is more special, joonam." I hate that word as well. More false terms of endearment. Her grin is wistful. "If only you knew how docile he has become. Like a child in his own universe." She clears her throat. "He is not the man you grew up hating. I can help you with your finances. It will give you a chance not to worry about keeping up with your expenses on that small salary."

"The library is not going to allow me to leave my post," I say. My work must save me. It is all I have.

225

"You needn't worry about that." She picks up the tea saucer and takes a sip. "I've spoken to your superior, Mister Pearce. He agreed to release you from your duties."

"Release... what?" I push the chair away from the table and stand. "How could you do this?" I am shrieking as I bring a hand to my forehead, wanting nothing more than to sweep the tablecloth off, break the plates and cups over my aunt's face, and strangle her for what she has said. She has taken away the only thing that gives my life meaning—the source that breathes life into me each day. "Why are you destroying my life?"

The other patrons are staring as the boy with the teapot comes by. "Please, we must ask you to leave."

"Gladly." I push my way past the other tables and move to exit the tea parlor.

"He is dying," Aunt Shari calls out from behind me. "Only a few days more, perhaps."

With those words, she seals my fate. A daughter cannot refuse a parent who is at death's door. For a fleeting moment, I wish it were me instead of him.

*****

Weeks go by. Each morning as I awaken, my mind forgets that it is back in the family home in Surrey and not in the cramped apartment with the other women.

One morning, as I feed my father with honey and lavash bread, he takes my hands before I grab his plate. His eyes are wider now, and he's smiling as I have never seen before. "Dokhtaram," he says. *My daughter.* "You are a blessing."

I slide my hands out of his grip, pick up the plate from the table, and move toward the kitchen. "What about Aunt Shari? She takes good care of you, does she not?"

As I make my way to the sink and grab a jug of water to rinse off the residue and crumbs, he grabs my wrist. This time his eyes have an alarmed quality. He is shaking.

"Do not leave me alone with her," he says.

I have never once seen my father in this state. My memories of him are always the unsmiling, stalwart head of the household in his military uniform or a pressed suit, a newspaper in his hands, and a pipe at his lips. Angry all the time. Yelling.

Now? He is like a child who tells me that the dark is too frightening in his room and could I sleep with him?

"Farid joon?" My aunt's voice calls from behind. "Come and take a walk with me, aziz."

His expression brightens then as he smiles, then shuffles toward Shari who is standing in a taffeta gown of creamy green, like lime. She guides him toward the French doors that lead to the garden. As the breeze wafts in, the Surrey estate's trees and flowers blow their scent inside, earthy and fragrant. Sunlight glints off the white keys of the piano in the parlor where I would sit and practice for so long.

My father walks with a slow gait, hands behind his back. He goes to a tomato plant and ties twine over the wooden stick adjoining it as Aunt Shari leaves him there and makes her way back inside.

For the first three weeks of my return, I wondered why Dylan had not sent any letters. Before Pearce forced me to clear out my belongings at the library on the last day, I had given Dylan the address to the Surrey estate. Yesterday, I found a group of letters stuffed inside a drawer in my aunt's bedroom. Even if I could get word back to him, would he come? I feared that no one would. I would have to escape on my own, somehow.

Aunt Shari closes the French doors. "Get up." She walks to my father's large table and sits in a chair with a leather backing. "You have papers to sign."

As I stare at the fountain pen on the desk, I wish I could pry it out and stab her between the eyes.

"What about Kayvan?" I ask. "My brothers and their families will want a share of any inheritance."

She lets out a heavy sigh.

I get up and walk to the fireplace, kicking some dried soot.

"Sign the document my barrister has drafted and we can be done with this," Auntie says. "The house will be deeded to you, your brothers and their greedy wives will get nothing, and your father will be safe."

"And you?" I want to ask her why she does not deed the house to herself. The documents mention my father's stipulation that the house must pass to a child of his. Aunt Shari's displeasure with my brothers intensified after they took wives, which left me as the only choice.

She bought all my dresses until the age of ten. My mother complained they made me look like an English doll—apart from my dark hair and ochre skin. My aunt said they were charming. No one cared what I thought, how stifling the gowns were, and the corsets that went with them.

One night, at the home of a family friend, she said "Isn't my little girl precious?"

At which point I shrieked that she was not my mother.

"This deed guarantees you a future, as well, doesn't it?" I say.

Auntie owns her home nearby, but chooses to live in my father's house. She claims it is so that she can help since Madar's passing, but the servants do all the cooking, cleaning, and bathing for him.

I pace around the parlor, the carpet muting my footfalls. "Everything you have done is to your benefit. My cousins fled from you, and I did, too. If you had not sabotaged the life I worked to build, I would still have a chance to escape this prison." I run a hand through my hair. "But no. You had to entrap me—the dutiful daughter who never disappoints her elders." I tremble as the rage builds in me.

She throws the pen down. "I have done no such thing."

"Every time you were unhappy with something I said or did, you told my father. He would bring the hammer of justice on me, my face, my body, my *soul*." I dig nails into my cheeks like claws and wish I could rip off the flesh. "And now you have forced me into this cage to save yourself."

She stands up from the table. The chair behind her scrapes against the floor. "I have always done what is best for you, Roya joon. Who do you think fought your father on the piano lessons and paid for the instrument?" Her voice is agitated.

A loud crash sounds from outside like someone has cut down a tree.

I run to the garden doors and see my father, suspended from bark with a white cloth wrapped around his neck, spinning in a macabre circle, eyes looking up, mouth agape as if he is wondering how this happened, limbs flat.

A scream escapes my lips as I move to open the doors and tears blur my vision.

I never wanted this for him--he had become so tame and meek since his cardiac incident a few years hence, not at all like the shouting abuser who snuffed out my spirit years ago. I must help him.

As I move, I trip over something large and thick. When I turn around, a large, scaly obstruction slides in front of me like another fallen tree branch. I wonder how the appendage has made its way inside, and if it crashed through the window. Then, scales glint in my vision and my eyes take in the sight of a snake-like tail attached to my aunt's torso. The upper half of her body is human, a shock of raven hair covering her breasts. Her face is the same. But she is malformed. A beast.

"How..." Chills of ice run through my veins as I slide back and struggle to understand. "What are you?"

"Do you remember the bedtime stories Madar told you? About the shahmaran and how it will kill you if you cross it?" Aunt Shari says, in a deeper voice. "I cannot let you leave." Her eyes, a jaundiced yellow, have thin stripes for irises.

"But I have to help my father," I say. *What is this monstrosity in front of me and how long has she been like this?*

229

She chuckles. "Remember who you are talking to, Dokhtaram. I know you hate him more than anything. You do not have to lie."

A memory flashes in my mind. The coroner found Uncle Hamid the same way with the cloth tied around his neck, hanging in his bedroom, but he had high amounts of poison in his system.

The venom had come from a reptile found only in the foothills of Shiraz.

"The hanging is your way of covering it up." I stare at her. "You did the same thing to Uncle Hamid."

She moves across the room on her giant serpent's tail, gliding, and I get dizzy from trying to follow her around.

A huge force shoves me from behind, into the table, and spins me around. The serpent's tail is warm as it wraps around me and squeezes. It is a living, breathing thing. I want to vomit, but I can scarcely move. One of my arms feels freer, but barely.

"Sign the document and let the deed go to you," Aunt Shari says. "I will not ask again."

With no choice, I grab the fountain pen and ink my signature on all of the pages, trembling the entire time at this miscreation that could kill me in seconds like it did my uncle, my father, and I dare not ask who else.

"There we are." When the tail loosens its massive grip, I keep the pen in my hands and stab as hard as I can into the scaled flesh.

My aunt screams. The room spins until I am on the ground, my head thudding against the carpet, and I crawl away toward the fireplace, thinking of what else I can use against her.

When she moves, it is like thunder reverberating against the floor. I back up against the wall as much as I can. The iron poker near the fireplace stands within my reach but is still too far.

I inch toward it and my aunt hurtles toward me faster than anything I have ever seen.

Her tail wraps around my throat and squeezes.

Blood drips onto me from her wound.

"The house belongs to you now," she says, uttering it like a threat or a curse.

As I try to wrench her tightening tail from my throat, where it squeezes my windpipe and I struggle to breathe. Her grip holds strong. I do not know how much longer I can last.

Desperate, I bring one of my knees up and kick her in the stomach, but she does not let go. *Cease this suffocation*! I scream in my mind.

"Whether or not you like it, you have always been more like me," Shari says. "Your grandmother also hated me for pursuing music instead of men."

Her grip tightens as the dizziness spreads to my chest and stomach.

"Your father forced me to marry Hamid and to have his children. I wanted to work at the opera, but neither of them cared."

"Stop." My voice comes out in a croak.

Her grip loosens but it could be a trap. I do not move.

"I knew your marriage to Omid would not last." Her tone is wistful. "You were always too clever for your own good. I should know—I spent more time with you than your mother ever did."

Anger surges inside of me in waves as I kick her in the stomach once again. "I have never been and will *never* be your daughter!"

She shrieks at me.

I use all my might to push against her and grab the iron poker.

My hands wrap around the cold weapon and I plunge it backward as hard as I can.

I feel it as it cuts through her flesh. The serpent part of her unfurls from my neck and as I turn behind me, I see the poker sticking out from her chest. Blood splatters onto me, her face a mixture of anger and sorrow.

I rise, put my hands on the poker, shoving it harder through the heart of this fiend who has made my existence unending torture. I scan the room for another weapon and find a letter opener on the desk. I plunge it into her throat and pull it out again, then stab her in the forehead.

She slumps to the ground, the serpent's tail retreating. It turns gray and dust begins to float off it. When I touch it with one of my toes, it crumbles like a sand castle.

Aunt Shari lies there, eyes and mouth agape.

She is dead.

I lose my balance and fall to my knees. It takes some time to steady my breathing as sweat drenches me from head to foot. I look around the room at the bookcases and carpeting, now covered in blood and grime.

Papa. I crawl toward the wooden desk near me and use it to help pull me up.

I have to help, to cut him down. I owe him that much.

He keeps a pair of shears in the garden for when he is cutting excess leaves or weeds. Perhaps if I get to them…

As I walk toward the French doors and turn the gold handles, a searing itch burrows into my skin. When I raise the edge of the dress sleeve, my arm has several shining scales like the ones Aunt Shari had.

She has finally done it.

I am damned and bound to this house forever.

CARLA'S CURIOSITIES
Nora B. Peevy

Carla's hair matched her sign. She loved this smallish town, Milwaukee. Enough to remain anonymous and have enough people–err–victims, to flock to her business, but small enough she still could have relative anonymity. And the fashions of this century, so much more exciting than the 1600s where she originally became reborn. Corsets, fishnets, stacked thigh-high boots, and miniskirts with petticoats underneath them, so short they left nothing to the imagination if a girl bent over to touch her toes. How daring and deliciously naughty! Pigtails and black lipstick and long Egyptian-kohled eyes with necklaces of bones and chain mail and repurposed rosaries with tiny rhinestone skeletons hanging from them. Dresses covered in spiders and stacked Mary Janes. Purses shaped like coffins. Cigarettes called "cloves" that were oh, so dreamy, and reminded her of the opium oils she used to wear centuries ago, musky and intoxicating. And the fake furs, knee-length and cheetah print, or waist length and hairy like a wooly mammoth in solid black, or a fake red hooker's coat with giant matching buttons, so cozy and warm. How could she resist it? And underneath the façade of one of the "east side" girls who owned her own shop, she could go about her business under everyone's nose. Nobody really knew or suspected what she was.

The doorbell chimed and a young mother with her sandy-haired son came rushing into the store on a great gust of wind.

"Can I help you?"

"Oh, we've heard such good things about this place. We'll just have a look around, if you don't mind."

"Well, let me know if you need anything. I'm just going to be right back there powdering my nose." Carla walked to the bathroom. She could hardly contain her glee. Her gift had dropped right into her lap early this morning.

She hummed as she adjusted her curls in the ornate gold gilt mirror, puckering her lips and applying another layer of red lipstick, making her teeth look even whiter.

"Mirror, mirror on the wall–"

"Oh, don't you ever tire of asking me the same question?"

"Why, you're certainly in a mood today." Carla pouted.

"Why can't you ask me how the stock market is doing or if the Brewers will make The World Series this year? Something at least a little exciting," the mirror humphed.

"I have to go tend to a customer. We'll talk about this later. And remember what I did to your last owner."

"Oh, my dear, I do. And you can't kill me because I'm not IN the mirror. I only talk THROUGH it.".

Carla came back out and saw the boy and his mother looking at the tiny push-thumb toys in the case. "Oh, these are delightful. They're my most favorite toys in the store."

"Why?" the boy asked.

"Because they're magic." Carla beamed. "Here, I'll show you." She took a tiny orange striped tiger out of the lit display case and pressed on the bottom of the toy and the tiger collapsed. When she took her thumb off the bottom, it stood straight up again.

The boy smiled.

"Here, you try." Carla gave the toy to the boy.

He took it with an inquisitive look at his mother. "It's okay, the shop lady said you could touch it. Go on."

So, he pressed down on the tiger and screamed. "Ow!"

"What's the matter?" Carla looked concerned.

The little boy put the toy down. "It bit me or something."

"Now that's ridiculous. Toys don't bite people. You probably got a splinter in your finger. Let me see." His mother reached out to inspect his hand and saw a red rivulet of blood running from his thumb down his wrist. "Do you have any medical supplies?"

"In the bathroom. If he comes with me, I can get him all cleaned up."

"I'd rather do it myself. I'm a certified nurse. No offense, but he's my child."

"Oh, of course, I understand. I'll be right back with the supplies." Carla walked off, simpering as she entered the bathroom. She was so close to getting what she needed. So close, yet so far away. Why? Why, oh why, did this happen on Monday morning? If this showed her luck the rest of the week she was going to have to cancel all her weekend plans, and not show her face anywhere except her store. And she'd just have to hope none of her regulars showed up before she remedied the situation.

She marched back into the store area with the gauze, hydrogen peroxide, and bandages. "Here you go."

She watched as the mother cleaned the wound with the gauze and then bandaged it up. Without even thinking about it, she sorted out the mess by putting the gauze and the wrappers into her purse.

Damn it, Carla thought. *She took the bloody gauze. Damn it, Carla. You goofed. You'd spent all that time rigging the toys with razor blades that worked with the push of a button and now look. Nothing.*

The mother and son left the store without making a purchase.

Since the 1500s, she had changed her name so many times it was hard to keep up with them; Elizabeth; Marie, Lucille, Janet, and so many more she could fill an entire diary with them.

Carla sighed and sang along to *Siouxsie and the Banshees* and then *Echo and the Bunnymen* as she dusted her wares with an old-fashioned black feather duster. She strained to reach the top shelf on the third step of her step ladder, always swearing to the Goddess next time she would remember to wear more sensible shoes on cleaning days, but she never did. She loved high-heeled boots. The taller the better because she was a petite 5'2" and the boots made her feel authoritative, or at least on par with her customers.

Her customers ranged from old to young, but most of them were middle-aged. She lit up like a Christmas tree every time a young buyer walked into Carla's Curiosities and hoped they'd ask to see the display of thumb push-up toys in the front display case. They were her pride and joy. A titillating rush of pleasure ran from her lips to her hips as she imagined the nourishment awaiting her.

You didn't need an entire bathtub full of a young maiden's blood to bathe in. Over the centuries, Carla had investigated this theory until she perfected the formula. A simple formula. There wasn't any way the authorities would ever catch on to her. And now in the 21st century, she was just a happy boutique keeper of specialty antique toys and bits and bobs, bringing amusement to everyone. She thought of it as an exchange. They took from her and she took from them. It was fair and they wouldn't miss it. And she brought them such joy. She saw the glee in their eyes as they left with their treasures in brown paper bags.

She read all the pulp novels, and they all claimed she should have superhuman strength and a desire to gorge on human victims every night. She should also be afraid of the sunlight because it would kill her. But frankly, she'd tried walking out in the sunlight to end her boredom and all it did was tan her a nice golden color faster than others. And her cravings were minimal. Why, the older she got, the less blood she needed to satisfy her and keep her youthful appearance. And the more bored she became with her existence.

*****

She opened her tiny boutique toy shop and modified most of the toys so the customers sliced their fingers open. Not serious enough to send them to the hospital for stitches because she was no animal, but just enough blood to keep her youthful appearance alive. She kept gauze and sterilizing supplies for her "donors" because it was more humane.

The first time she rubbed someone else's blood into her aging, liver-spotted cheeks, she'd been skeptical it would work and disgusted by the crimson-soaked gauze she'd used like a powder puff. But with fascination, Carla watched the blood seep into her dry skin like it was drinking in moisturizer. A happy humming sang in her ears like a choir of angels and her lips opened without free will and beckoned in an otherworldly voice through liminal time and space, "You will bring us more next week, for we require it."

What the fuck? Who had taken over her body and made her say those words? Was someone else in her brain? Could she get them out? What if she used a screwdriver and just skewered herself through the ear? Would it stop then?

She turned to Snow White's mirror, which she'd gained for a very hefty price, and said, "Mirror, mirror on the wall, who is the fairest of them all?"

The mirror replied. "Why you are, my dear countess. And then faded to black in silence."

Well, at least she had that going for her, but what about this voice? Countess Bathory, her mother, never had a mirror such as this. She laughed.

*****

At first, Carla thought she could rid herself of the strange voice commanding her to do horrible things. She went to see a priest.

"Father."

"Yes, my child."

"I need help. This is going to seem crazy, but I'm hearing a voice in my head. A demon, I think. And I think I might be a vampire."

The priest laughed. "I'm sorry, my sweet girl. I've been a parishioner for nearly a decade and I have never heard of anyone claiming possession by a demon, let alone a vampire. Let me bless you and I will send you home with some holy water to comfort you. Draw the sign of the cross above each window and door and you shall be protected. I promise you."

And so Carla did as the priest instructed, but the voice still visited her. It taunted her night and day, sleeping and awake. "Did you think visiting a priest was really going to help you, Carla? You are older than the holy water in that font. Older than the church and all the pews built in it."

"Why didn't I burn as soon as I entered?"

"Do you think all stories are true, Anna?"

"Stop calling me by that name! How do I know the blood story is true? You could be lying."

"Ah, Anna. You know this is not a lie. I have been with you since the beginning and whether you choose to admit it, you are what you are. You are your mother's child. Quit denying your lineage and embrace yourself. It will be peaceful. You will be happier if you do. There is nothing you can do to change things now."

Carla shouted at the voice, "Don't call me by my birth name! Shut up! Shutupshutupshutup!"

"You are a Bathory and a Bathory you shall always be," the mirror said.

*****

On Tuesday, the sky was grey, and the wind lashed the trees, bowing their branches, and stealing autumn's leaves remaining before winter. The doorbell chimed above the door and a handsome man in a navy peacoat with brown hair in that "I just got out of bed" style, and the bluest eyes she'd seen since around 1920, walked in casually with his hands in his pocket. His clothes reeked of money–polished black loafers, dark jeans with no label in sight, and a black ribbed turtleneck with not a speck of dandruff or pet fur on it anywhere that she could see. It clung to his tight pecs, and she bet underneath he sported rock-hard biceps as well.

His cologne smelled of smoke, amber, moss, and musk, a heady, intoxicating aroma leaving Carla almost tongue-tied. What was wrong with her? She normally didn't feel like this about any human anymore. Sex was a mechanical blasé pastime. Orgasms were a bodily need, like eating or breathing. She wished she could live without them, but every once in a while she needed to take care of girl business and she detested the "I'll call you later" and "Let's meet up for lunch later this week." Why couldn't men just leave her be in peace?

Carla glanced at the calendar behind her. It was time to collect her weekly blood. She flashed her vixen smile, poofed her hair, and walked over to where the man was looking at a collection of Steiff teddy bears. Some were so threadbare; one could see the cloth underneath where the animal's fur had once been. The Steiff bears Carla carried in the store ranged from one hundred seventy-five to over two thousand dollars.

"Can I help you find something? Maybe you'd like to know more about the history of the Steiff bears?"

The man scratched his wonderfully thick curls. Carla had to resist running her fingers through them. Up close, the scent of musk was even stronger, but not too strong that it would make her sneeze. She watched his pulse in his neck. He cleared his throat.

"Actually, I have absolutely no idea what I'm looking for. A few guys at work mentioned this place. They said it had the most unique selection of antique gifts in town. My fiancé likes antiques, so I thought I'd stop on my lunch break. I'm sorry. I'm babbling. My name is Ryan."

Carla licked her scarlet lips. "How nice to meet you ... Ryan." She paused and stared into his eyes. He was a good soul. His blood would be delicious. She could tell a person's soul by how many tiny black spots swam in their irises. It'd always been a gift of hers. She didn't know what it meant, but she often used it to pick her victims. She didn't want any polluted blood to enter her system. Who knew what would happen then?

"Well, what does your fiancé like? Is she romantic, playful, serious? Silly?"

"I think goofy and silly describes her well, which is one thing I love most about her."

"Well, we have those bears. And we have a collection of other Steiff animals as well."

"No, no. She had her heart set on a Steiff Bear, but I think this is a little expensive for my taste. Do you have anything not so rich?" He laughed, feeling uncomfortable.

"We do have these wonderful toys. I keep them in the front display case because they are so small and easy to steal. They're very popular and so cute. Come with me."

The voice inside her head spoke. "Finally, we will get to eat again. It's been over a week and we were getting worried we would lose our beauty."

"Would you shut up?" hissed Carla.

"I'm sorry?" The man looked puzzled.

"Oh, not you. Just having a running conversation inside my head. I do that sometimes. Have ever since I was a child. Here. Here they are." Carla gestured to the display in the front-lit counter.

"What are they?"

240

"They're push thumb toys or thumb push toys. They come in a variety of sizes, colors, animals, etc. As you can see. Some are older than others. Most of the ones in this collection are vintage."

"What exactly do you do with them?"

"Oh, goodness me! I'm terribly sorry. Here, let me show you." Carla slid open the case and took a worn-painted giraffe on a blue platform from the display. She held it in her left hand, and with her right thumb, pushed the underside. The giraffe collapsed. She let go, and the giraffe stood straight up. She repeated the process a few times. "It's all rather simple, really. Strings connect their pieces. Here, you can even make them sort of do a jig. Look. All you have to do is not press hard enough to make them go all the way." Carla showed the customer.

He smiled. "These are adorable. Do you mind if I look through the case first before deciding?"

"Oh, no problem. Take your time. The more expensive ones are on the left and the further down you go, the more modern and less expensive they become. I'll just be in the back, if you need me." Carla wasn't concerned about this man stealing. She had seen nothing swimming in his eyes. He was a pure soul.

She went back to the mirror hanging in the bathroom.

"Mirror, mirror on the wall. Who is the fairest of them all?"

"Taylor Swift, my dear."

"What? You fucking liar. You mean to tell me all the Swifties have made Taylor so famous she's now the ideal look?"

"I'm sorry, madam, but Taylor Swift is the fairest of them all."

"Fuck. FuckfuckfuckfuckFUCK!" Carla pounded on the porcelain sink. This would not do. She had to convince her customer to examine one of the push thumb toys or she was going to lose her beauty and fade away to ashes floating on the breeze. For that was what would happen after all these centuries. Humanity was an illusion bought with blood.

Walking out of the bathroom, she smiled. "Have you found something you like?"

"I like the spotted dog with the long tail."

"An excellent choice. Shall I bring him out for you to look at?"

"Yes, please."

Carla took the little dog out. Inside, her stomach would have been doing butterflies if she had any stomach left. "See? Just push the bottom." She handed the customer the little wooden dog.

He pushed the push toy with his thumb and cried out in pain. "Something cut me!"

"Oh dear. Let me see. How bad is it?" Carla leaned over the counter with hungry eyes.

"Oh hon, that's pretty deep. Let me see that toy and here, you take this piece of gauze and wrap it around your finger to stop the bleeding."

The customer didn't even question why she had gauze in her pocket. Carla inspected the thumb push toy. She saw nothing. She turned it bottom up and showed it to the man. "See? Nothing there." She pushed it herself and nothing happened. "All good. Why don't you come into the bathroom at the back of the store and I'll bandage that up for you? And for your troubles, I'll give you 20% off the toy for your lady friend. Does that sound okay?"

"I guess." Ryan followed her to the bathroom. The light was rather harsh, but he could swear the store lady looked like she'd aged a decade or two. He shook his head. He just wanted to get his gift and get out of here.

Carla ran the water and washed his cut gently with soap and rinsed it. She scrounged in the medicine cabinet for a bandage big enough to cover the wound, and then she escorted him up front to ring up his purchase.

As soon as he left, she flipped the Open sign to Closed. She ran back to the bathroom to inspect her face,

242

where she saw sagging cheeks and drooping eyes beginning to form with tiny lines around her lips. Hurriedly, she took the gauze with the guy's blood. She ran a bit of water over the thin red fabric to make it wetter and then used it like a cotton ball, rubbing it all over her face and neck. As she did, the gauze became lighter and lighter and the blood seeped into her skin. When she was done with her weekly ritual, she opened her eyes and smiled at her younger self.

She looked into the mirror. "Mirror, mirror on the wall. Who is the fairest of them all?"

"You are the fairest of them all."

Carla smiled and, with a hop and a skip, went back to the front of the store to change back the sign. She was open for business again.

IN THE BLOOD WE LIVE
Nicole M. Wolverton

Clemencia Poole might have been 3,211 years old, but she had the blood of a fifty-year-old human and the skin of one who was, perhaps, just thirty. Had her brood brother Alexander not been killed by a mob a thousand years back, he would have made the obvious joke about keeping the blood and skin in a jar in her boudoir. She would have pretended to laugh while secretly wincing—she had heard the joke over and over again for centuries.

But Alexander was gone, and most of her brood was gone, save one. The ramshackle mansion that had been her home for too many decades to count lurked in a dim corner of West Philadelphia. Quite a city, Philadelphia. Paris had a certain rotting charm, and Buenos Aires was a delight in its own way—but there was something about the women of Philadelphia. Perhaps it was the way they gracefully trounced down the sidewalks as though treasure awaited them at their destination. For as long as Clemencia had called the city her home, nothing much ever changed in the manner that these women moved through life. Their blood held the taste of restlessness, thick and rich with scorn and the slightest afternote of goodness. It was endemic in every one of them, whether born or imported. Philadelphia drew that type like waves to the shore. Clemencia's only regret was not having landed in North America sooner—to see if the Lenape women who came before the city, before the Europeans plundered, had the same wonderful flavor. Some part of her believed the very soil and water itself was imbued with a special feminine quality.

She let the gauzy curtain fall from her hand and turned away from the window. Zahra hipped—a voluptuous sway—into the sitting room and threw herself down on the blue velvet settee. Clemencia had turned the girl herself a year ago. Too many days alone had broken her of the vow to live alone.

"Can you believe the farmer's market was out of that good bread I like?" Zahra threw one arm over her eyes and frowned. Always so dramatic.

"Are you truly that dispirited about the bread?" Clemencia said. "Or are you sad not to have a reason to speak with the baker?"

Zahra grinned, eyes still hidden. "He *is* pretty delicious."

Clemencia could picture the man—dark-skinned, with the finest face she'd seen in many years. Delicate as bone china, but she'd seen him kneading bread. The act belied any belief that he was anything other than powerful. Those hands were strong and capable. She could understand Zahra's yearning.

Still, Clemencia enjoyed teasing the girl. "Delicious in the traditional sense or the vernacular?"

"Both. Definitely both." Zahra's laugh—bold, like the Philadelphia women Clemencia had grown to love—filled the room. "Don't worry—I promised not to bring anyone into the family, and I won't. I'm practicing safe… sex."

245

"It's difficult to blend into this community with too many of us," Clemencia said. "With too many of us *feeding*."

"I really thought you were going to just go with the sex metaphor." Zahra tilted her head to the side. "No, Clemencia. No worries about my intentions. I like it with just the two of us in the house—me and you. It's quiet. But I'm definitely going to keep the baker in pocket."

"How many does that make for you?" Clemencia said it lightly, but there was more to the question. She thought of Alexander, the way he'd attracted attention with his proclivities and needs. She could still feel his blood running down her arms after the townspeople were through with him.

"The baker's the only one nearby. There are a few people in the Mayfair section of the city I see regularly—and an old woman who lives in South Philly, over near Tony Luke's. She barely notices me slip in and out of her house," Zahra said. "I'm not like you—I don't have a type yet. How will I figure out what I like if I don't—"

"Play the field. Yes. I promise I'm not judging."

Zahra stood and fiddled with a stack of books on the side table. She glanced at Clemencia. "You were. I can see it on your face, plain as the fangs in your mouth."

Clemencia's hand fluttered up to her face. Zahra's lips were pretty in the way that all teen girls are pretty—ripe, mysteriously tempting—and the girl's incisors were supple. She would never admit to Zahra that their kind aged, but it was true Clemencia had noticed changes in herself—most notably that when her womanly blood ceased to flow last year, her teeth changed as well.

Zahra was new. She had thousands of years to grow into her abilities and her selfhood. Clemencia wasn't sure how old their kind could get. She'd met a five-millennia-old man once, but men displayed their age so much differently than women—and she hadn't the nerve at the time to ask. That had been hundreds of years ago, before her teeth became sluggish to retract. Before they had yellowed and become smaller.

"Do what you must to flourish," Clemencia said. "I may have made you, but I am certainly not your mother."

"Oh, please—if I went out and turned the baker, you'd be irritated." Zahra crossed her arms over her chest.

"I don't deny that—but what could I do?"

"Kill me. Throw me down a well and let me starve."

"Well, yes, I suppose I could do those things—but I'd like to think there is enough respect between us that you wouldn't put me in that position." The memory of Alexander's lifeless eyes flashed. She shivered. She would never tell Zahra—about Alexander or her doubts about their immortality. "In the meantime, do continue with your safe sex, so to speak."

Zahra grinned. "Yes, Mother."

*****

There were few days more exciting than the first warm day of the year. Philadelphia suffered so in the winter—its skyscrapers hidden in low banks of gray clouds more often than not, and charming cobblestone streets blanketed in sooty snow. A chill wind often barreled down Market Street or across Broad Street, whipping scarves and hats, chapping faces. There would inevitably come that day in March when the temperature crept high enough to shed winter coats, and with it came the baring of necks, so sinuous and pale from months beneath turtlenecks.

When Clemencia rose from her bed in the morning and threw open the window, greeted by a fragile warmth, she planned her wardrobe just so—interesting enough to be admired but not permanently etched into anyone's memory. The art of being just this side of invisible was not lost on her.

She boarded the trolley and averted her eyes when she passed the street on which Zahra had been beaten by human monsters and left bloody. For all that Philadelphia's winters could be terrible, it was a lucky thing it had been so dark and cold that night—not many people from the neighborhood outside their homes in those conditions. No one to see Clemencia gather Zahra in her arms, sink her fangs into the girl's neck. No one to see Clemencia perform the ritual. No one to see Zahra rise and stumble home, Clemencia's strong arms keeping the girl moving until she transformed.

They'd waited for another such night to find the monsters in question. Zahra knew them—or knew who they were, at least. It had been a pleasure to watch Zahra stalk them, to see the fear in their faces with each footfall echoing behind them in the dark.

Zahra was a natural—she took them all to the edge of death, then brought them back. Toyed with them, tortured them. And each one had deserved it.

The police never noticed the men were gone. No one had noticed Zahra was gone, either, though—a blessing and a curse. With no family whatsoever to speak of, and only casual acquaintances to know she even existed in the world, staying on in Philadelphia had been easy. The authorities would continue their blissful ignorance that anything was wrong. And after the blood of monsters made Zahra bloom, no one likely would have recognized her anyway.

The trolley smelled of sunshine and racing blood. A few streets later, a small girl boarded. She was alone, outweighed by an enormous backpack, and dressed in frilly white. Clemencia only noticed because of the girl's sharp blue eyes and the upright way she held herself—so like a doll that Clemencia could do nothing but smile, lips drawn over her diminished fangs. The child briefly returned the smile.

Clemencia went back to thinking of Zahra and what her ward's future would hold, about the aging and what it meant.

By the time Clemencia reached City Hall, the sky was the color of oceans, and the warm spring air was a joy. She strolled up Walnut Street and opted to follow a young couple—two women—hands clasped and swinging between them. Both of them ate the sidewalk with their distinctive Philadelphia stomp, and the charm of it made Clemencia laugh out loud.

"Y'want to get something to eat?" one of them said—she was tall with a wild mane of brown curls.

"What, at DiBruno's? Get a bunch of cheese and meat, have a picnic?" The other woman was of average height, a platinum blonde with long, straight hair.

"You want to cop a squat on grass or concrete? I know some places."

"Maybe grass. That would be nicer."

"Schuylkill Banks—how about that?"

Clemencia followed them into a market. The blonde lingered in the back at the cheese counter, carefully tasting samples before making her choices. Clemencia sniffed the back of the woman's neck while passing behind. The brunette tossed a bag of crostini into the black store basket and added a sleeve of cookies, a large bottle of water.

Yes, they would need the hydration.

Only a block from the park, Clemencia made her move. She only had to smile and think the thought into their heads. "What a pretty thing I have to show you," she crooned.

The blonde smiled vacantly. "Pretty thing?"

Clemencia beckoned, and they followed. When far enough out of sight, Clemencia fed on them both, one after the other. It took longer these days because of her teeth, but it was still a pleasure, just as wonderful as the day. The women mostly tasted of warmth and love, of the very city itself. The brunette's blood came with the memory of an assault. From the flavor of it, it had been years ago, but it would always be fresh in the woman's mind. A broad-shouldered man with meaty fists that broke her bones. The pain made Clemencia's mouth water—if only to find that man and make him pay for what he had done to this woman, who only wanted to be who she was.

Clemencia's fingers curled with the ache to peel off his skin, one layer at a time.

She took just enough blood—these women, they would never know. They would never remember. But she would—she would carry their essence and memories with her for weeks, their blood running through *her* veins, until her body used up the last of it. The depletion period was shorter now that she herself no longer bled. Perhaps Clemencia would run into this man who had hurt the brunette before the recollection faded.

She handed the blonde the bag of food and waved the couple on their way when she was finished. Clemencia watched them go until a small tug on her shirt diverted her attention. The blue-eyed girl from the trolley, the one with the backpack, stared up at her. The hem of her white dress blew lazily in the breeze.

How strange.

"Hello, child," Clemencia said.

"You are the oldest living woman of our kind," the girl said without preamble. Her voice was much too low for that of a child—too low and too confident. "There are things you must know."

The tip of Clemencia's tongue immediately touched one of her own diminished fangs. A kernel of fear ground in her stomach. "Of *our* kind? Do scoot off and stop playing games you know nothing about." Even as she said it, she shivered. Had the child seen Clemencia feeding?

"I would prefer to have this conversation over tea," the girl said.

"I'm afraid that's not possible." Clemencia quickly walked away from the girl, but she could feel her watching. The urge to return, charm her into forgetting, was strong, but she did not feel threatened—after all, what adult would believe a child telling fanciful tales of vampires? But what kind of child would be out alone, demanding tea? It was a coincidence, that was all. Coincidence, and a child playing games that she could not possibly understand.

*****

"Some kid stopped by looking for you," Zahra said when Clemencia arrived home. "Little white girl. Creepy."

"Oh?" A hollow opened beneath Clemencia's skin. The blood wasn't as satisfying as she'd grown to expect, even changed as she was. Hunger clawed up her limbs. A trick of her age, or simply an aberration, she could not say. But the girl's words played back to her. "What did she say?"

"Nothing much. Just that she had to talk to you. Did you add someone else to the brood after all of your lecturing? She . . . I don't know, she felt not human. She felt weird."

"*Felt* weird? You touched her?"

"No, that's not what I mean—she just seemed off. I mean, a little kid dressed for Easter stops at a stranger's house alone to chat? That's weird."

Clemencia's stomach growled. There was a small supply of frozen blood on hand. Or she could take a stroll in the neighborhood, although it wasn't something she preferred to do. She was too familiar here, and she'd given the neighborhood over to Zahra's whims.

Even so, there were those in the community that did notice things about her and Zahra. The two women with several children who lived next door often said hello, mentioned their comings and goings. Clemencia had fed once on the youngest of the daughters before Zahra had come into the house—the women who lived there were best friends, each with a husband who had abandoned them. The daughter's blood Clemencia had spoken of a rough man she didn't remember well, of being hungry, of having too much responsibility for her siblings while her mother worked. The women were better off with each other.

"You look off, too." Zahra studied Clemencia's face. "Your skin looks rough. Wasn't today your feeding day?"

"Maybe I'm just tired."

"Can we *get* tired?" Zahra asked.

"I assure you that anything is possible. We can certainly be killed—so I imagine illnesses can befall us."

"Have you ever met one of us who did—get sick, I mean. Or been killed? You told me we're immortal. Did you just make that up?"

"No, of course not. But we are immortal until the day that we are not. We must be careful—thoughtful—about how we live. How we feed."

"We're immortal until we're not? What kind of garbage is that? Immortal means . . . immortal."

Clemencia forced a smile. "Did you know that bristlecone pines are considered immortal?"

"What does that have to do with anything?" Zahra said.

"At the cellular level, bristlecones don't age. Or corals—the oldest known corals are even older than I am."

"Okay, but what about coral reefs—you hear about them dying all the time."

"Why do they die? If left alone in their perfect atmosphere, they're perfectly fine. What kills them are outside forces—warming ocean waters, pollution, ocean acidification, overfishing . . . or even someone physically damaging them with a boat."

"So we're *not* immortal then."

253

"We are as immortal as corals or bristlecones. We are not outside nature, even as we live outside society in many ways."

The doorbell rang—Clemencia rushed to answer. On the porch stood the little girl from the trolley, the one who spoke to her on the street. Her frilly dress shone in the light. She didn't wait for Clemencia's invitation—she pranced into the house, set her backpack down, and took a seat in the drawing room before smoothing fabric over her tiny knees. "There are things you must know," she said again.

Clemencia frowned. "I'm afraid I was just leaving. Won't your parents be worried about you?"

The girl's sigh was a breath of wind. "You're leaving because you're starving and you must feed, am I correct?"

"Hey, that's the girl who was here earlier," Zahra said. "You should go, kid. This isn't the place for you."

"Your bristlecone and coral analogy isn't a terrible one," the girl said.

Zahra's jaw fell open.

"Who *are* you?" Clemencia asked. And how had she heard their conversation?

"What I mean by that is both bristlecones and corals rarely die of age, but they do change as they age—as do we. You know it for yourself."

"There is no *we*—you are mistaken. You—"

"No, *you* are mistaken," the girl said. "I smell of blood and heartbeats because I was brought into a brood as a child. There are biological truths we must face. That is mine—I will never be like you, or like Zahra. A woman—with biological imperatives. Immortal though we are, you and Zahra both continue your menstrual cycles. Or *did*, as in your case, Clemencia."

"What're you talking about?" Zahra said.

"The woman who made me—she died." The girl stared into Clemencia's eyes. "When I said that you are the oldest living woman of our kind, I meant it. My—her name was Livia—was older, but she is gone."

Clemencia thought again of Alexander. The fire and the pitchforks. "Was it—"

"She died of natural causes. Her body no longer produced the blood and no longer efficiently used the blood she hunted. In the end, she was always hungry. Like you. She knew of you and bid me warn you. Human women call it the change of life. In our kind it is different—it will take a different path for me, but for you—you must recognize and accept what is happening."

"I knew it," Zahra said. "This immortality thing *is* a scam."

Clemencia shushed her. "How long did Livia survive after . . . after the change of life?"

"Another hundred years, but it was difficult. She needed to feed constantly—and there were accidents. We had to move often to avoid detection. She faded away until one day she was nothing but ash and bone."

Zahra said, "I don't want to move, Clemencia."

"And I have no interest in dying." She turned to the girl. "What can be done?"

"Build your brood now. Build a strong collection of those who still produce the blood. Had Livia known what awaited her, she would have created a family that could keep her fed and nourished. As it was, there were just the two of us—much like your own as it currently stands.

And with my limitations, it's too easy to attract notice. Now is the time, Clemencia. Your children will keep you as long as possible—and when you do go, your brood will be prepared."

Clemencia thought again of the Philadelphia women she loved. The couple she had fed from today. The countless others she had watched and taken from. Their blood—their life forces—had sustained her. They were her sisters in so many ways. She *could* make them her kin. Like she had done with Zahra, she could give them strength in return for everything they had given her . . . *would* give her. She would not even have to take them from their families—not really. Her kind were not savages. They did not kill indiscriminately or without cause. She and Zahra could bring the better part of a neighborhood into the brood. All the women. An extended family who gracefully stomped down the sidewalks as though treasure awaited them at their destination.

Clemencia's stomach rumbled. The scent of blood was suddenly everywhere. "Zahra, shall we go next door to visit our neighbors? I shall give birth to a new family—and I'd like to start with them." She smiled—and this time she did not care one whit about who saw her withered fangs.

HOME TO ROOST
Valerie B. Williams

Nancy filled coffee cups, adding cream and sugar according to the orders barked at her by the three men. She balanced the tray from the kitchen to the double oak doors, pausing while Diane scurried over to open them. Entering the lavish office, she placed the tray on the coffee table and carried a cup to each man, making sure to serve her boss first. None of them looked at her or halted their conversation.

"Can I get you anything else, Mr. Harrison?"

Her boss frowned, shook his head, then flapped his hand toward her to shoo her out of the room.

Nancy tucked the tray under her arm and left, quietly closing the doors behind her. She turned, met Diane's eyes, and let out a sigh.

"Is he always this grumpy?" asked the younger secretary, eyes wide. Diane had only been on the job for a week.

Today was Mr. Harrison's first day back in the office after ten days of travel. Ten days of blissful peace.

"He hasn't yelled yet. But the day is young." Nancy gave her a rueful grin and set the tray on the file cabinet before returning to transcribing the latest letter from her shorthand notebook.

She glanced at the page full of squiggles and sighed. Her grandmother pushed her into taking a shorthand course in college—as a 'fallback plan,' she'd said. That stupid course, along with her typing skills, had gotten her this job. No one was interested in her degree.

Four years later, she was still here—an executive secretary. A glorified go-fer. She'd lasted longer than the previous two 'girls' and was looking forward to bringing Diane up to speed. With the menial tasks offloaded, she could put her MBA to use. Mr. Harrison promised her a promotion to administrative assistant, so long as he still had a pretty girl at his beck and call.

The intercom buzzed. "Need more coffee," said a gruff voice.

"Coffee, tea, or me," said another voice in the background, followed by rumblings of laughter.

Nancy's lips tightened and she pressed the intercom button. "Right away, Mr. Harrison."

She grabbed the tray from the file cabinet and reentered the office to collect the empty cups.

"I think you should come in with me this time," said Nancy, nodding to Diane after she closed the double doors.

They filled the cups and loaded the tray. Diane picked it up while Nancy opened the doors and followed her in, waiting as the younger woman served the coffee.

The conversation stopped as the man on the left ran his eyes up and down Diane's body. "Two for the price of one, eh, Stan?" He winked at Mr. Harrison. The men chuckled and watched Diane work, a smile frozen on her face.

Back in the reception area with the office door safely closed, Nancy spoke to Diane in a low voice. "Don't let them get to you. They're harmless. Just do your job."

"I've heard worse," said Diane, "and put up with more for a lot less money." She crossed her arms. "I can handle it."

"Good." Nancy patted her on the shoulder. "I knew you could."

*****

Nancy pulled into her driveway singing along to *Afternoon Delight*. The main radio station in town played all the newest songs, which was good when she'd left her collection of cassette tapes at home. Music never failed to cheer her up at the end of a tough day.

Last year her beloved grandmother, Sophia, died and left her this quaint cottage; 'quaint' being the word used by the lawyer who executed the will. It took months and nearly half of her hard-earned savings to bring the house up to date. But when she unlocked the door and entered, the tension in her shoulders melted away.

A woman's voice suspiciously like Sophia's said, "You're late."

"I know, I know. Sorry."

Nancy went into the living room toward a large cage containing the other part of her inheritance—an African Grey parrot. The bird fluffed its feathers and squawked. She opened the cage. It hopped onto the tall freestanding perch and glared at her.

"Don't look at me like that," she said. "It's only until I get Diane trained."

"Hmmph," said the bird, then climbed the rope ladder hanging from the perch and attacked a small bell.

Aello had been part of her grandmother's life as far back as Nancy could remember. Sophia brought the bird with her when the family emigrated from Greece. The parrot favored women, and she liked Nancy's late mother, Eva, nearly as much as she did Sophia. Nancy's father didn't stand a chance with the bird and wisely kept his distance, which seemed to make both parrot and man happy.

When Nancy was sixteen, her mother drowned in a boating accident while spending the weekend with her best friend at Lake Langston. Pieces of the speedboat were recovered, and eventually the friend's body as well. Eva's body was never found.

Sophia was Nancy's rock after her mother's death, helping her cope with their mutual loss. Unanchored without his wife, her father faded away until he failed to wake up one morning while Nancy was away at college. When the seemingly ageless Sophia died suddenly of a heart attack while gardening, Nancy's world was shaken. Her only surviving family—gone.

Aello took Sophia's death even harder than Nancy. The parrot went into deep mourning, plucking nearly a third of her feathers. Nancy made sure the bird had all the creature comforts and spoke to her constantly. She couldn't be with Aello during the day, so left the television on for company. Caring for the parrot honored her grandmother and Nancy was glad for the distraction.

Slowly, Aello came out of her depression. She left her feathers alone and the two formed a bond. Aello became more talkative until one day, Nancy realized the bird had graduated from echoing words to having a conversation. The parrot listened, responded, and showed reasoning. However, in the presence of anyone but Nancy, Aello reverted to mere mimicry and squawks.

"You're my best friend, aren't you?" She ran her hand gently down the parrot's back.

"And you are my heart," said Aello, fixing her eyes on Nancy.

My heart. The affectionate term Sophia had always used for her granddaughter.

Nancy turned on the oven for her TV dinner and uncorked a bottle of wine, pouring a generous glass. She frowned at the silent phone on the wall, its twisty cord nearly reaching the counter. Paul hadn't called since their date a week ago. She thought it had gone rather well, but then she started doubting herself—had she talked too much, was her laugh too shrill? She sighed and lifted her glass.

"Fuck him." Nancy took a gulp of wine.

"Fuck him," echoed Aello.

Nancy giggled, always amused at hearing salty language in her grandmother's voice.

The oven dinged its readiness and Nancy slid the tin foil tray onto the center rack. She refilled her wine glass and continued the conversation, woman and parrot commiserating about the vagaries of relationships. She sent yet another silent thank you to Sophia for gifting her this amazing bird.

Later that evening, Nancy slipped between the cool sheets and closed her eyes. But she found herself restless, replaying the workday, obsessing over silly things. She punched her pillow, wishing for one of Sophia's enchanting Greek bedtime stories. Whether told by Sophia or by Eva, they always put her right to sleep as a child. Eventually, she fell asleep and dreamed of heroic men and women, warring gods, and magical creatures.

*****

The next two weeks at work flew by, with Diane showing the skills required for the job. Nancy got along well with her and found her to be sharp and funny, as well as unflappable. Diane had now experienced one of Mr. Harrison's full meltdowns and lived to tell the tale. They snickered about it in the kitchen, taking turns mimicking his arm-waving rage. It was going so well that when Mr. Harrison summoned Nancy to his office on Friday afternoon, she went in with a bright smile.

An immaculately dressed young man stood up from the sofa when she entered.

"Nancy, meet Angus," said Mr. Harrison.

Angus stepped toward her with his hand outstretched. Nancy took it, noticing the man's manicured nails. A whiff of expensive aftershave teased her nose.

"Nice to meet you," said Angus, his smile showing perfect teeth. "I look forward to you showing me the ropes."

Nancy's stomach dropped. She turned to her boss with a frown but before she could speak, Mr. Harrison confirmed her fear.

"Angus will be joining us as my assistant starting Monday. Both you and the other girl will report directly to him. Why don't you give him a quick tour before you leave, introduce him to…" He snapped his fingers.

"Diane," said Nancy. She clasped her shaking hands in front of her body.

Mr. Harrison came around the desk and slung his arm around Angus' shoulders. "Nancy will take good care of you. See you bright and early Monday."

Nancy's thoughts whirled while she went through the motions of showing the interloper the office and introducing him to Diane. The other woman was on her way out, just enough time to shake hands with Angus and give Nancy a puzzled look as she left.

"When did you meet Mr. Harrison?" Nancy asked in an even voice. "I usually set up his interviews."

"Stan and Doris came to the graduation party my dad threw for me. Dad and Stan go way back." Angus leaned against the wall of file cabinets, hands in pockets. "I was looking for a job, he had one available, and voila! Here I am."

Nancy's smile wavered. "What did you major in? What school?"

"BA in Business from Virginia Commonwealth," he said, looking smug.

"MBA from Radford," she countered, crossing her arms.

"Good for you," he said, like he was praising a dog for a clever trick.

She gave him a calculating look and retrieved her purse from the desk drawer. "I need to lock up," she said abruptly.

They left the building in a cloud of uncomfortable silence. When they parted at the front door, Angus said, "See you Monday."

Nancy nodded and strode to her car.

*****

During the drive home, Nancy's outrage grew. After parking the car, she stormed up the sidewalk and slammed the door before bursting into tears.

"What's wrong, my heart?" asked Aello from her cage.

"That bastard hired an assistant behind my back! The son of one of his buddies. And this young asshole is going to be my boss. After I train him, of course." Nancy flung her purse onto the kitchen counter. It slid off the other side and thumped to the floor, ejecting its contents.

"He promised me," she wailed, and collapsed onto a chair with her face in her hands.

Nancy heard the cage door unlatch, followed by the flapping of wings. Aello's beak rubbed against her hands, forcing her to look up and into the bird's intense gaze.

"Calm down. Have a drink," said the parrot.

Nancy fetched a half-empty bottle of wine from the counter and grabbed a glass. She filled the glass and took a long swallow.

"Better?" asked Aello.

"A bit. But I've still been screwed. And humiliated."

"What are you going to do?"

Nancy dropped her head into her hands again. "I don't fucking know," she mumbled to the tabletop.

"I can help you," said Aello.

Nancy laughed. "That's very nice of you, but what can you do? Fly to the office and shit on Harrison? Or better yet on his little protégé, Angus."

Aello drew her head back and opened her beak in as close an approximation of shock as Nancy had seen on a parrot. "Nothing so crude." She shuffled closer until her beak was nearly touching Nancy's nose. "Would you like to pay your boss back?"

Nancy emptied the remains of the bottle into her glass, then fetched and uncorked another bottle and topped it off. She spun the glass on the table, turning its stem slowly around and around, watching the deep red liquid sway from side to side while she indulged in fantasies of revenge.

"Of course I would." She shook her head. "But that'll never happen."

Aello fluffed her feathers, then preened a wing. "With my help, you can enjoy the sweetest revenge."

Nancy snorted. "Unlikely, but sure. Why not? I'll take all the help I can get." She raised her glass in a toast.

The bird cocked her head. "Very well. Let's talk more tomorrow." The parrot squawked and flew back into her cage.

Nancy moved to the living room with her glass and the rest of the wine. She pushed a Queen cassette into the player, leaned her head back, and felt vibrations from the music fill her body. Her conversation with Aello tonight went from girl talk to problem-solving. *What was the parrot capable of?* She finished the bottle and stumbled to bed, where she dreamed of the sound of beating wings and unearthly cries.

*****

Saturday morning brought the pounding head and dry mouth of too much wine. Nancy dragged herself into the shower and stood under the steaming water until it began to cool. Oddly, her feet hurt, as though they'd cramped during the night. Once out of the shower, she massaged them and decided to stick with bedroom slippers for today. A couple of aspirins would help both her head and her feet.

Had Aello really talked about revenge? Her memory of the evening was riddled with blank spots, so she couldn't be sure.

After coffee and toast, she felt a bit better. She walked into the living room and unlatched Aello's cage to fill her food dish.

"Good morning, Nancy."

"Good morning, Aello." Nancy cleared her throat and ran her hand through her hair, feeling foolish for even asking. "Did you say something last night about helping me get back at my boss?"

Aello stopped eating and looked up. "Yes."

"I thought I imagined it," said Nancy.

"The process has already begun," the parrot said. "Within a week, you shall have your revenge."

"But how?"

"Be patient, my heart. Much change is in your future."

No matter how many different ways Nancy asked, Aello refused to be more specific. She finally gave up and spent the rest of the day reading and watching television. The definition of a perfect Saturday.

When she awoke on Sunday morning, her feet felt worse. Her toes turned down like her feet were curling in on themselves. Pain shot through her arches when she tried to press them flat. But walking a couple of slow laps around the house seemed to work out the cramps.

The parrot watched her from behind the bars, waiting for her food.

"Anything special I should do at work tomorrow?" asked Nancy with a smile.

The parrot laughed Sophia's hearty guffaw. "Be ready," was all she said.

"You tease!" said Nancy. She fed Aello, then headed into the kitchen for breakfast.

Breakfast turned into quite a meal—eggs, bacon, toast, grits, tomato juice—in portions much larger than usual. All this talk of revenge must be making her hungry.

While she worked her way through the food, she remembered parts of Sophia's stories. Many of the mythical creatures had voracious appetites. Nancy chuckled. Maybe her hunger was a new superpower. *Watch out, Mr. Harrison.* The kitchen cupboards will be bare.

*****

On Monday morning when Nancy entered the reception area, Diane was already at her desk.

"Where's boy wonder?" Nancy asked in a low voice.

"Haven't seen him." Diane frowned. "What's his deal anyway?"

"Nepotism hire. And you and I are going to report to him."

Diane rolled her eyes.

Nancy heard male voices coming down the hall and quickly stepped behind her desk. Mr. Harrison and Angus entered together, laughing at a shared joke.

She pasted on a smile. "Good morning, gentlemen."

"Good morning, girls," said Mr. Harrison. "I'll leave Angus in your good care." He slapped the young man on the back. "See you later, buddy."

Nancy stood. "Let's get started, then."

Angus held up both hands. "Whoa. Can't a guy even get a cup of coffee first?"

"Sure. The kitchen is that way." Nancy pointed.

Angus looked surprised, then shrugged and wandered down the hall, returning with a steaming cup of coffee. He walked past her and opened the door of the small office next to Mr. Harrison, beckoning her to follow. The shiny new sign on the door read, "Angus McLeod, Executive Assistant."

Executive Assistant! That son of a bitch.

"I look forward to working with you ladies," said Angus from behind an oversized desk. Nancy slid onto the hard seat of an armless, straight-backed chair. He

266

looked down on her from his cushioned leather perch as if he were a noble giving alms to a peasant.

"There's plenty of work to be done," said Nancy. Her stomach growled loudly. "Ooh, I'm sorry." She pressed her hand to her belly. "Shouldn't have skipped breakfast."

In actuality, she'd eaten a huge breakfast only an hour ago. Why was she hungry so soon?

She reviewed a typical workday, with Angus asking occasional questions. She told him how the duties were currently divided between herself and Diane, and how the office could operate more efficiently now that there was another person to share the load.

Angus leaned back and laughed. "Your duties won't change. I'll be coordinating special projects, setting up conferences, pulling together data for reports to the Board, probably traveling with him as well. I'm confident you and Diane will keep things running smoothly, but let me know if you have any problems." He showed his teeth in a shark's grin. "I'm here to help."

"Thank you," said Nancy. Her pulse pounded in her ears. "Welcome aboard."

She left his office, closed the door behind her, and walked rapidly past Diane's desk. In the ladies' room stall, she clapped her hand over her mouth to stifle sobs. The arrogance of that little prick! She *hated* that her frustration came out as tears. If she tried to speak to Mr. Harrison today about her promised promotion, she'd lose control for sure and her argument would be discounted as hormonal moodiness. Later in the week she'd put together a rational case and present it in a business-like manner.

*****

By the end of the week, Nancy's feet still hurt, but hadn't gotten any worse. Long days at the office babysitting Angus distracted her from the pain. He questioned every process, certain that it could be done better and more efficiently. Nancy's jaw was sore from biting back sarcastic remarks. To top off the week, she overheard Angus saying he'd see Mr. Harrison Saturday night—at the party Nancy helped plan. She, of course, was not invited.

On Friday she drove straight home, desperate for a peaceful evening with no one vying for her time. Aello greeted her at the door, perched on the coat rack.

"How was your day?" the bird asked.

Nancy groaned. "About as good as the rest of the week." She bent and slipped off her shoes, rubbing her sore arches.

"I'm sorry to hear that. Next week will be much better."

Nancy cocked an eyebrow. "You think?"

"Patience, my heart," Aello said before flying back to her cage.

Nancy fed the parrot, giving her a quick head scratch before going to the kitchen for her own meal. Her strange increase in appetite had not gone away. She grabbed the last can of Campbell's condensed chicken soup from the pantry, heated it, and poured it over leftover rice. The next courses were a handful of pretzels, the lone remaining banana, and a few stale Oreos she found hidden behind a box of Rice Krispies.

"I guess that'll have to do," she muttered, reaching for the open bottle of wine. "Grocery store tomorrow."

She hobbled to the living room and stared sightlessly at the television while sipping wine. Once in bed, she fell instantly to sleep, where dreams of beating wings and the cries of raptors came to haunt her. This time, the wings were hers, carrying her high above the earth. Human figures scattered below when she swooped toward them. She awoke with a start and stumbled to the bathroom.

Sitting on the toilet, her bleary eyes widened when she caught sight of her feet. They had curled inward so much they formed a U. Her toes had doubled in length and the length of the nails had doubled with them.

Another toe had erupted from each heel, complete with its own long nail. The skin on her lower legs looked like scales.

Nancy slid off the toilet and onto the floor where she wrapped her arms around her head, curled into a ball, and screamed.

Aello flew into the room and perched on the edge of the sink.

"It's all right, my heart. The worst is almost over."

Nancy lifted her arms from her head. A fine coating of downy feathers covered them from shoulder to fingertips. She could barely bend her hands. Her whole misshapen body trembled.

"My feet are turning into talons, I'm growing feathers. What have you done to me?" she croaked, her voice shattered from screaming.

"You asked for my help." The parrot bobbed her head.

"I never asked for this! Make it stop. Make me normal again."

"Once your transformation is complete, you'll gladly take your revenge." Aello hopped to the floor and stood beak to nose with Nancy. "Trust me. Go back to sleep."

Nancy stared miserably into the bird's black eyes and hitched in a shaky breath. Her body ached as if she'd been beaten. So tired, she closed her eyes for a moment. The next sensation she had was that of a warm ray of sunshine coming through the small bathroom window. She'd slept all night on the floor.

She stood with a clicking sound. Her talons were now fully formed, long nails curled at the end of each toe. They no longer caused her pain. Nancy moved her arms, spreading them wide. The down that covered them before she slept had matured into shiny black feathers. She shuffled to the sink with her gaze cast downward before slowly lifting her head to look in the mirror. A creature straight out of Sophia's stories stared back at her.

This new being had Nancy's face and her naked upper torso. Wings replaced her arms. Along with talons, she sported a feathered tail. She turned slowly, examining each part of her new form. After a full circle, a terrifying smile spread across her face.

She moved into the living room, where Aello awaited on her perch.

"Thank you," said the newborn harpy. She spread her wings, knocking a row of framed pictures off the built-in shelves. "He can't ignore me now."

*****

For the remainder of Saturday, Nancy alternated between napping and eating whatever she could find in the kitchen. Aello finally told her more. Sophia had known about the bird's power but never had a reason to call on it. Nancy's mother, on the other hand…

"She asked for my help," said the parrot.

"You mean she's not dead? She's like…" Nancy swept her wing down the front of her body, "this?"

Aello nodded.

"Where is she?"

"I don't know, my heart. There are a number of places where your kind are safe. Mountains and thick forests serve as the best nesting areas."

Nancy's head spun at the thought of her mother being alive all these years, no matter her form. She wondered who had earned her mother's fury, prompting such a drastic change.

Talons worked nearly as well as hands for manipulating items, including door handles. At nightfall, Nancy slipped out the back door onto her darkened patio, swept her powerful wings downward, and took off into the sky. The flight she'd dreamed of became reality. She laughed with joy as she turned, rose higher, and swooped lower. She felt as though she'd been flying all her life.

The trip to Mr. Harrison's large estate only took fifteen minutes 'as the harpy flies.' Nancy soared over the house to the back garden, where a large white party tent had been set up. Guests appeared and disappeared from under the awning, carrying drinks and plates of food. Jazz music swelled into the night. The scent of grilled meats filled her extra-sensitive nose and prompted a loud growl from her empty stomach.

She flew a lazy circle over the party, high enough to be unnoticed by the people on the ground but low enough that she could identify them. Finally, she spotted Mr. Harrison at the edge of the party near the woods standing next to Angus. Both men were enjoying cigars.

Nancy folded her wings and plummeted toward her boss, talons outstretched. She hit him hard across the shoulders, throwing him face-first onto the ground. Angus took one look at the giant bird and sprinted back toward the tent. Lucky for him, he wasn't her target tonight. Her talons dug deep into Mr. Harrison's flesh. With a swoop of her wings, she carried him over the woods and away from the party, amazed at her own strength. It felt effortless. His screams of pain and terror mixed with the music, but she and her prey were soon out of earshot.

She flew on, toward the mountains. He stopped struggling and his screams faded to whimpers. By the time they arrived at a clearing in the midst of a thick forest, he had fallen silent. She dropped his limp body face first on the ground. He moaned and rolled over. His eyes widened, scanning her from her bloodied talons up to her wings, her bare breasts, and finally her triumphant face.

"Nancy?" He shook his head, squeezed his eyes shut, then looked at her again. "Who...what are you?"

"I'm the same as I've always been. You just never noticed my strength. You were more interested in helping out your old cronies."

He pushed himself to his feet, looked around wildly, and took a step toward the forest.

"I wouldn't do that if I were you. We're miles from civilization."

He turned his back and broke into a lumbering run. She easily caught him, her talons digging into his legs. She snatched him up and hovered above the ground, dangling him upside down as he screamed for mercy.

"Let you go? Fine," she said. She opened her talons and dropped him twenty feet.

He managed to get his arms down just before he landed. Two loud snaps told her he'd broken a wrist or forearm or both. She landed on him, piercing new holes in his flesh.

"I guess you won't be making any more promises you have no intention of keeping. However, I promise you, this *will* hurt."

Nancy swiped at him again and again with her talons until his back was reduced to bloody ribbons. Finally, she grasped his head and lifted him from the ground, flying from side to side until his neck snapped. She dropped the body to the ground in disgust. *What a pitiful man.* And to think she'd been scared of him for so long.

The sound of beating wings filled the air. Another harpy flew into the clearing and landed opposite Nancy and the mangled body of her ex-boss. She wore a familiar face.

"You've done well," said her mother.

Even though Aello told her of Eva's transformation, Nancy still blinked in disbelief. "You really are like me!"

"Yes." She approached Nancy and leaned in, pressing her forehead to her daughter's. "I'm sorry you've been driven to make this choice but happy to see your strength. Come with me and I'll teach you how to survive." She smiled. "This is not such a bad life once you get used to it. And you will have an advantage I didn't—a guide."

Nancy hesitated. She couldn't go home. She hadn't given any thought to her life beyond getting vengeance. But now she'd been reunited with her mother. Together they could determine her new purpose, *their* new purpose. The coppery tang of blood filled her nostrils. Her stomach growled.

"What about Aello?" Nancy asked.

Eva smiled. "Aello was around long before she joined our family and will be around long after we are gone. She will find another human companion. Whether that person is allowed to see her full powers or take advantage of them, is up to Aello."

The last worry in her old world lifted, Nancy nodded.

With a push of their powerful legs, mother and daughter launched themselves over the treetops and into the night.

VEGETABLE LOVE
Lillie Franks

Every morning, between 10:45 and 11:03, Ms. Allan sets down her gardening tools and takes the same walk into the forest. A subtle, flattened path marks her daily orbit down the hill, along the fence that overlooks the creek, and back up toward the backyard of her humble, off-white house. If it rains she brings a blue polka-dot umbrella; if it snows, she wears her orange parka, but no matter what, when she opens the backdoor again, the clock hanging over the kitchen table reads exactly three minutes past eleven, and that makes her proud.

No one in town knows much about Ms. Allan. According to rumors, she was the CEO of something before she retired to Elmore, but the truth is probably nothing as exciting as that. The kids say she's probably a witch, but the nice kind of witch who fits into the neighborhood and lets you take two pieces of candy on Halloween. Sometimes, when they see her out, people try to engage her in conversation. She smiles back and answers, and at the end of it, they have to think for a second before realizing they've learned nothing they didn't already know.

Between her polite silence and the precise daily walks, Ms. Allan could easily have ended up with a bad reputation in the small town if it weren't for one thing: her garden.

Anyone can putter in a garden, and doing so is a perfectly respectable occupation for old women, but that isn't what Ms. Allan does at all. To her, it's an art, a sculpture coaxed out of living marble. She doesn't just plant her garden and maintain it; she calculates, guides, and nurtures the flowers and bushes of her yard, and each one ends up just where they're meant to go.

The results are undeniable. In spring, when it all blooms, her garden is an assault of beauty. Last year, her theme was spirals and bright blooms of pink, purple, blue, and yellow wound around each other, all perfectly placed and balanced. The smell of the garden wafted to other houses, and they would stand there, on the sidewalk, breathing it in. Butterflies and birds flitted to and fro, as if the flowers themselves had sprouted wings and come to life.

"If she has secrets, let her keep them," the townspeople say amongst themselves. "No one who makes a plot of land so beautiful can be a bad person."

Ms. Allan loves the forest or rather, she loves the things in it. The trees are marvelous in their looming power, but the placement is never harmonious. Some are too close together, while others leave unsightly gaps the bushes and undergrowth simply cannot fill. Subtle colors, like the green of the moss, dulled by brash, blaring ones right next to them. There are no lines to guide the feet or curves to attract the eye. At home, she keeps the blinds down on the windows facing the forest so she doesn't have to think about it.

The sound of the flowing creek rises in the distance. Something she can't see is startled by her and runs away up the hill.

That's when she sees the corpse.

It lies at the very bottom of the slope, next to the creek, eyes open and staring up at the canopy overhead, hands balled into fists that would crack before they opened. Once, it belonged to a young man, a boy who put on heavy blue jeans and a white t-shirt before going out into the world for the last time. That white t-shirt is now stained by four stab wounds. Bruises cover his arms and blend in with his tattoos until she can't tell which is which.

Ms. Allan stands on the top of the hill, looking down at the limp, tragic thing. It rained hard last night, and he had probably been thrown into the creek somewhere upstream and floated down here before getting stuck on a rock or a branch. She ought to hurry home to call the police. The sooner they start the hunt for the murderer, the better the chances of catching him.

She doesn't hurry back. She stands there, looking.

He fits where the river has left him. His clothes and tattoos, the scar down one arm, but most of all the haggard look on his face, the way the skin hangs just a little too much—all just right for the still, quiet scene. He looks like the kind of person to turn up dead in a river. She knows it's a horrible thing to think, but she doesn't *think* it. She sees it.

It's a simple matter of overgrowth. If someone had just been around to prune him where he needed it…

A bird cries somewhere in the distance. She starts and he does nothing.

But he isn't quite as still as he appears, is he? His fingernails are still growing, and so is his hair. Or maybe that isn't quite true; she half remembers reading somewhere that it's more complicated than that. Still, he's certainly changing, and change is just another word for growing.

The right thing to do is to get home and call the police. They won't know that she stood there like this. She can tell them she got started on her walk a little late, or that she was so shocked by what she saw, she couldn't make herself walk back. No, she won't even need to tell them that because they won't ask. Of course, they won't ask, because all they'll care about is finding the man who did this.

Then again, no one else comes this way. If she left him, wouldn't he still be here tonight? And then, she'd have all night for it, and it would be possible, wouldn't it? He doesn't look that heavy, and it isn't such a long way back to the house. There's good, healthy soil there, and water, and most of all her with a sharp set of sheers.

She's nearly ten minutes late when she arrives at the back door of her house again, and she doesn't go to the phone.

*****

She falls asleep quickly when it's all over, but her rest is troubled and fitful. She has the nightmare, the one where she's in her house and she hears the sounds of the forest outside getting louder. At first, she thinks there must be animals in the yard, but the volume keeps growing and growing. Bird calls turn to deafening shrieks and chirping crickets to machine gun rattles. Even putting her fingers into her ears doesn't help. A woodpecker thunders against a trunk that can't be as close as it sounds. She stumbles to the door and opens it, ready to run away, but she can't. The trees have pressed against the door, like poorly spaced bars. The garden is gone and there's nothing but forest and the night stretching out forever.

The next morning, she barely wakes up in time for her walk. When she reaches the creek, she carefully searches it for any remaining traces of her work, but there's only the marks of something being dragged, and when the rain comes that will be gone too. Back in her garden, there's the freshly turned ground in the bed by the window that held the geraniums last year, but no one will have any questions about that. They already know she gardens.

Will there be a search for the missing boy? *Probably,* she decides, *but not much of one.* The police will think the same thing she did, and they won't be so ashamed of it either. They know better than anyone that some people are born to disappear.

Even if they did search, why would they search here? He had nothing to do with her. He was a criminal who got what was coming to him and she is the harmless old woman with the garden. No one thinks of her much at all, and for the first time, that feels like a blessing.

The very next morning, something is already peeking out of the soil. It's little more than a bulge in the ground, with hints of a fleshy color underneath the dirt stains. She's too cautious to touch it now. Instead, she waters it generously and covers it with a green plastic cloche.

*****

On the third page of the newspaper is a small picture of him sitting on his bed and smiling earnestly at a camera next to a terse half-column announcing his unexplained disappearance. The picture is at least a year old but there's no question who it is, and the half smile he gives in it is charming. According to the article, his name is Connor.

"Connor," she repeats, letting the syllables roll off her tongue. "Connor. Connor."

She stands up and walks to the window where, if she cranes her head a little, she can see the cloche sitting in the overturned ground. It wouldn't do any harm to check whether the bud has sprouted yet, would it?

No, she tells herself. Better to give it the full day. If she checks now, she'll only be disappointed.

The newspaper offers a number for anyone who has information about Connor. Her eyes drift to the telephone and she imagines dialing it, waiting for someone at the other end to pick up. But what would she even say if they did?

Your son is safe with me.

She imagines herself saying the words and they feel nice. But what if the telephone company traces the call? What if the police come knocking? Better to wait, she decides.

Waiting is safer.

*****

Ms. Allan lifts the cover and there it is, grown more than two inches in a single night. There's no doubt about what it is now: a finger, probably a ring or an index, its top two joints jutting out of the ground like a stalk of asparagus. She strokes it gently with her glove, and it bends towards her, then straightens again immediately. Unlike Connor's, which were spotted with half-worn black nail polish, these fingernails are clean and well-trimmed, give or take the few clods of dirt caught underneath them.

A brilliant beginning, she decides, and with her trowel, starts to dig up the soil around it. The finger trembles slightly as she does, but stays still and cooperative.

"Hello, Connor," she whispers as she digs. It doesn't respond to that either.

But there is no hand underneath the finger. Instead, there's a fourth joint, a fifth, a sixth. They thicken slightly as they go down, like a taproot. She wraps her hand around the stem of the finger and gives an experimental tug. It doesn't budge.

Tenacious little thing.

The roots go deeper, she thinks, and savors the words as if they mean something. She must have heard that somewhere, but she can't remember where just now. With careless expertise, she gets a better grip, braces herself against the ground and tries again.

"You're a fighter, aren't you?" she says, grunting with effort. "I could tell that the moment I saw you. You're the kind who never backs down from what he wants."

She pauses, wipes the sweat off her brow, and repositions herself.

"Well, look where that got you."

The finger's grip on the ground loosens, holds for a second more, and then gives. Five more joints all come shooting up, and at the bottom, a thick bulb of flesh covered with torn hair. The finger squirms in her hand, but perfunctorily. It's not trying to scratch her or escape; it just wants to register its displeasure.

"Settle down. I'll have you potted again in a moment."

Ignoring her, it continues to twist and writhe.

"It's just we can't keep you out here where everyone can see, now can we? People will ask questions. They'll think I have a body buried out here."

Of course, she does, or at least, she *did*. She dug further unearthing that finger than she had burying the boy, and what did that mean? Again, the phrase returns to her mind.

The roots go deeper.

Unlike the garden surrounding it, the inside of the house is sparse, populated with bare tables and closed drawers. Everything has its own place, out of sight and out of mind. Even the walls are empty, because Ms. Allan never saw the sense of filling them.

"I've never grown houseplants before, you know," she says, as she works. "People buy me pots as gifts because they assume I want them, but I never did. Not until you."

She pats the soil into place around the finger and smiles at it. It looks nice. Beautiful, even.

"I just thought you would want to know you're special. You're the first one I invited in."

She sets Connor's finger near the window and adjusts the blinds so he isn't quite so easy to see from the street. There's an economy of movement to everything she does, as if she's saving her energy for a battle that isn't here yet.

"I love you, Connor," she says. "You may not realize it yet, but you will. You'll understand."

The finger trembles slightly, even though the house is warm.

*****

Her new garden is coming in splendidly. Every morning, she wakes up at 5 o'clock sharp to find out what new appendage is pushing out of the ground. Sometimes she wakes up earlier, from the nightmares, and has to lie there in bed, waiting for the alarm to sound. But for all that, she's never disappointed when she gets there. There's always another finger, a toe, and sometimes better. A whole arm, sunken deep into the ground. A leg. A knee.

They all resist her when she pulls at them, which she doesn't mind so much, but what's stranger is that each day, the fight gets a little tougher. The long dark hair it uses to anchor itself gets thicker every time. Then, she finds it's twined itself together into a single taproot that she has to find with her hand and cut through. Then there are two taproots, and they're thicker than before, and soon enough, she has to go to the general store to get fresh clippers after a particularly exhausting ordeal with a bit of torso.

Even with the new clippers, she finds she has to saw a little, and after, there's something else mixed in with the hair that makes the blades slip off. It might be a tendon, but there's no one she can ask to be sure.

"I tell you, Connor, sometimes I think you don't like me," she says, gasping for breath, a whole foot still stuck firmly in the ground.

It's almost six by the time she finally comes inside again. The house has become something of a mess. Pots everywhere, red stains around some of them, and she's given up on sweeping the floor clear of dirt, so the whole thing looks frightful. At the center of it all is her garden. She's had to sacrifice the dining room table to it, even though she's always thought it crude to eat in the kitchen, but it will all be worth it in the end. In fact, the end isn't that far.

Meanwhile, the nightmares are getting worse. The sounds come from inside the house now, and she doesn't even bother opening the door, because she knows what she'll find. She runs past the windows, which are lined with trees, and looks in every closet, under the bed, and behind the sofa, but she can never tell where it's all coming from. No matter where she runs, the cacophony always seems to be behind her.

When she wakes up, she walks into the dining room and stands over her garden. Its dim quiet, shrouded form calms her. Her breathing stills and her heart fades into the background again.

"You're going to be such a good son, Connor. You're going to be the perfect son."

*****

On the last day, she has the worst nightmare of all. She's in the house and so is the dirt and all the pots, and most of all the noises. There are other animals mixed into the familiar ones now, like a spider monkey or an eagle, and all of them are loud beyond belief. Beyond bearing.

This time, the noise doesn't run from her. It's not coming from behind. It's in the dining room, and as she approaches, it gets louder. Louder, louder, louder. She forces herself to keep walking.

There's nothing on the table in the dining room. All of the pots in which she's grown the pieces of Connor are there, but they're empty. It's all empty. That doesn't matter though, because the noise is right in front of her now. She can feel the shaking in her body, and when she lays her hand on the south wall, *she knows*.

She knocks once on the wall, just to see if it's really hollow, and the whole thing cracks like an egg, paper-thin plaster tumbling into an enormous black emptiness.

That day, she digs further down than ever before, deep enough that the soil becomes dense and clayish, but she knows it's there. She can feel how close he is.

Finally, it happens. Eyes stare up at her from the pit she's dug. She smiles down at the face as she uncovers it, but it doesn't smile back at her. The mouth is pursed tight, the eyes wide, the teeth grinding against each other. Deep, thick roots anchor it into the ground.

"Hello, Connor," she says, and waits for his reply. But of course, it has no lungs attached, no heart to beat blood into it. The eyes hold hers though, full of mute determination.

"Today's the last day. After this, you'll be all grown."

She sets to work on the first of the roots, using an old sickle she stayed up late last night sharpening. There's bone in the roots now too, and if you don't hold them just right, they'll cut your hand.

"You're going to like living with me, you know. I'm usually a quiet old woman, but not with you. I always have something to say to you."

The sickle slips and she slides it back into place.

"It's because I understand you so well. Isn't that funny? The two of us couldn't be more different, but I feel like I know you better than anyone in the whole world. And soon enough, you'll get to know me too."

The first root gives way and the head looks desperate now, all out of tricks.

"We'll talk, of course, all the time. Maybe at first, it will just be me talking, but soon enough you'll join in. It feels good to let the words out when you've been quiet for too long. I'll teach you about gardening and you'll see how exciting it is. Most people say it's relaxing, but that's only at the end, once you've won. It's different in the middle, and you'll see that, soon enough. We can watch movies; not just old, boring black and white ones, but the new ones too. The ones you like."

She smiles as she works and stares off into the distance, her arms pulling mechanically. This is the heat of the battle, and it's her dreams that give her strength.

With one final pull and a loud snap, the head comes out of the ground and into her hands.

"It's finally over, Connor." She laughs. "It's finally over."

She lies there for a minute or so, recovering her strength, then forces herself up. She scans the street for anyone watching, then wraps the head tightly in her arms and hurries to the door.

Inside, her garden is waiting.

The head is aware of it as soon as she enters, but she can't read its expression. She wishes it was joy that Connor finally gets to be a part of this beautiful thing that she has grown, but she can't convince herself of it. It looks more like resignation.

She finds an empty spot on the floor and sets the head down.

"The process of grafting goes back nearly 4,000 years," she explains to Connor. "It involves two plants, the scion and the rootstock, and it's much more common than most people think. Just about every orange you've ever eaten was grafted at some point. Orange branches on the roots of trees that grow better and easier in whatever climate you're getting them from."

She walks over to the table. The saw is waiting next to the limp shoulder which she fused an arm onto.

"It works like this. First, you make a cut in the rootstock. There are a few different methods for this, but I'm making what's called a splice graft, a good, simple technique for plants that knit easily. You just have to make one cut, straight across and at an angle, like.... this."

The neck ends in a rounded, fleshy stump and the saw slices through it like putty. She expects the blood to spray out, but instead, it trickles from the cut in the same lazy, vegetable way as sap from a tree, and only the faintest rhythm even shows there's a heart somewhere in the calm body. Not a finger twitches when the blade slices through. Not a muscle tightens. As the saw bites into the table, she watches the steady up-and-down movement of the chest. She's almost disgusted by its lifelessness.

"Then you make a matching cut in your scion." She picks up the head, turns it upside down, and positions the saw. "It's the plant's own ability to grow that makes this possible. Isn't that lovely? A plant is so desperate to keep expanding, it will literally change what it is. It will nourish another plant's seeds. A powerful tool in the hands of a good gardener."

The mouth on the head opens as she cuts, but it has no vocal chords so nothing comes out but silence.

"Finally, you press the two together and wrap them tight in gauze. From there, the plant will do the work. You'll do it." The head and the neck fit perfectly against each other, and, neither struggles with her as she begins to wind the gauze around, tightly enough to staunch the blood but not so tight as to cut off breath. She keeps the saw next to her hand in case she needs to grab it and fight off the creature she's made, but it simply lies there, lifeless and dead.

She steps back, happily, looking at her creation. No tattoos or scars, and all the old marks of her grafting already faded away. He doesn't even look anything like the picture in the newspaper. With her guidance, he's nobler, better proportioned, like one of those Greek statues. Classical. Perfect.

"Well, Connor?" She beams. "What do you have to say?"

But the body doesn't say anything. It breathes, in and out, up and down, alive but totally passive.

She reaches a hand out, but then hesitates and lets it drop again. There's nothing left for her to do. "It's okay. You can take a few moments if you need."

Still nothing. She steps closer to the table, and grips the slack wrist, tight enough to cut off its circulation. "Connor?"

The nail of her thumb digs into the soft skin on the underside of the arm, almost hard enough to draw blood.

"Please, wake up, Connor. Please."

She lets go of the body and bangs her fist on the table. Still, the chest rises and falls within its cruelly regular rhythm. But it's all there; it's all perfectly fused and bound together. Five toes on each foot, five fingers on each hand. She's done it all just right, so why isn't he here? Why does her garden radiate so much absence?

Because the roots go deeper.

"Connor, I need you," she pleads, but she's not looking at the body on the table. She's scanning the empty pots, hoping against hope that she won't see what she thinks she might.

"Wake up, Connor." But there it is, in the very back, the pot that held the left foot until the leg finally came up. She tucked that one all the way in the corner, and at its furthest point, disguised by a smudge of dirt, is a single strand of hair slipping over the rim and diving down where her eyes can't follow.

A runner. *A weed.*

The house trembles slightly. It doesn't need to hide its presence anymore. She knows and so does he.

"What did you do, Connor?"

As she approaches the corner, she hears from behind her a ghastly croaking sound. At first, she doesn't recognize the wheezing bark as a laugh. The wild peels are interrupted by the hissing gasp of air passing through a wound that isn't yet healed. The body doesn't move but the head shrieks its hoarse derision, coughs, and cackles again.

She can follow the root now. It creeps out, over the pot then hugs the wall tightly, searching for a gap, a space to slip into. About two feet away it finds one, where a floorboard dips down slightly and the wall doesn't answer. Like a magic cave, the hole swallows the strand of hair and welcomes it into darkness.

The wall doesn't crumble when she knocks against it, but it doesn't sound right either. There should be a hollow ring to the plaster wall, but instead, it's dull, like it's been stuffed with something bulbous and soft. Ms. Allan picks up the pot and lifts it above her head. She hesitates for a moment, then closes her eyes and brings its edge down against the wall. A hole appears and she rips at it with her fingers, feeling something warm and fleshy inside. Another tremor.

"No, Connor. No…"

Body spills out of the walls onto the ground, senseless and jumbled together. Tangled. Arms are wrapped around legs. Feet sprout directly out of torsos which twist and bulge into outlandish galls and deformations. The whole wall is full of Connor, endless Connor.

Connor warped and stretched and crammed under the floors and around the pipes and down, down below into the foundation. His eyes peek out from in between electric wires and his nose hangs from a stud.

And it's all laughing.

With one hand, she covers her ear, and with the other, she pulls at the flesh that fills the walls. Desperately, she tries to unwrap it, to undo the chaos and fit the pieces back where they should go. A hand flops onto the ground and she looks for an arm to go with it. She presses a leg against a hip as if the two will fit together, as if order can be restored, but the roots go deeper.

Why is there so much of it? Why is it so beautiful?

The forest runs all through the walls and twists and squirms with laughter. The whole house is laughing. It shakes and cracks and strains at all its joints.

AUTHOR BIOS

CARMEN BACA - As a Chicana, a Norteña native to New Mexico, Carmen Baca keeps her culture's traditions alive through regionalism to prevent them from dying completely. She is the author of seven books and multiple short publications from prose to poetry in a variety of genres, including folk horror and quiet horror. She is a recipient of New Mexico Magazine's 2023 True Hero award for celebrating and preserving her culture through story telling. Two of her short works were nominated to Best of the Net and the Pushcart Prize also in 2023.

CHARLOTTE BROOKINS is a Midwest-based writer who graduated from the University of Iowa with a degree in English and creative writing in 2024 and is currently pursuing her Master's in Library and Information Science. Her work has been published internationally in such magazines as *Haunted Words Press*, *All Existing*, *The Foundationalist*, and more. When she's not reading, writing, or spending time with loved ones, she can be found getting lost in the woods.

BROOKLYN ANN BUTLER - Formerly an auto-mechanic, Brooklyn Ann Butler writes supernatural horror and contributes to the HWA's mental health initiative. She is also the author of the B Mine series, horror romances that follow 80s horror movie plots, but with a Final Couple instead of a Final Girl, as well as urban fantasy and paranormal series under the pen name Brooklyn Ann.

She lives in Coeur d'Alene, Idaho with her family, a few project cars, an extensive book collection, and miscellaneous horror memorabilia.
She can be found online at https://brooklynannauthor.com as well as on most social sites.

ALLISON CELLURA is a longtime special education teacher with over two decades of experience working with neurodiverse learners. She has spent much of her career supporting children with autism and recently transitioned to working with deaf students. This role enables her to reconnect with her early passion for American Sign Language. Once fluent, she is now relearning ASL with renewed purpose and joy.

Allison is a married mother of four sons and the proud caretaker of two cats and a dog. In the rare moments she finds for herself, she enjoys writing science fiction, thrillers, and horror. Her stories often delve into the darker aspects of human nature and the unknown. Remote Control is her debut publication.

EMMA ROSE DARCY is Australian and works in a museum. She is happiest digitising old negatives and snooping through forgotten diaries and records. She writes dark fantasy and horror and blames it all on a lifelong love of folklore and mythology. She stumbled upon horror in her childhood, discovering authors like Joe Donnelly and G M Hague among the Kings and Rices in charity shop books cases. It may be why she has a hunger for reading and writing body horror and transformation horror stories, hauntings and huntings. She can be found on instagram and threads via the handle @ofcoursethehorrors

SALLY DARLING—pen name of Sally Bartolotta—is a writer and aspiring author within the horror and weird fiction genres. She resides in Florida and is a proud member of the Horror Writers Association – Southwest Florida Chapter. Sally is a vocalist and bassist best known for her work with Team Cybergeist, PsyKill and Crossbreed. As a certified yoga teacher, she enjoys teasing the boundaries of her duality, combining chaos and calm. A lover of animals and an eater of plants, Sally is also Vice President of a non-profit Foundation, and co-owner of The Rock Box Music School & Stage. She is currently working on a collection of short stories she hopes will shock and offend the masses.

DAWN DEBRAAL lives in rural Wisconsin and has published over 700 short stories, drabbles, and poems in online ezines and anthologies. She tends to lean toward the horror genre because it makes her life seem so much better! Falling Star Magazine nominated Dawn for the 2019 Pushcart Award; she was Runner-up in the 2022 Horror Story Competition, two-time Author of the Month, nominated 2020,2022,2023 Author of the Year and received Contributor of the Year 2023 for Spillwords Magazine. Her newest novel "The Lord's Prayer, A Series in Horror," won the Literary Global Book Award for Fictional Anthology, 2024.
https://www.facebook.com/All-The-Clever-Names-Were-Taken-114783950248991
https://linktr.ee/dawndebraal

LILLIE E. FRANKS is an author and future eccentric (once she's successful enough) who lives in Chicago, Illinois, but is normal about it. You can read her work at places like Always Crashing, Alice and Atlas, and McSweeneys or follow her on Twitter at @onyxaminedlife. She loves anything that is not the way it should be.

MEG HAFDAHL- Author, screenwriter, producer, speaker, and podcaster, Meg Hafdahl is a fan and creator of horror. Her popular novel series starting with *Her Dark Inheritance* was published by indie press Inklings Publishing, as well as three collections of her short stories. Her work has been produced for audio by *The Wicked Library* and *The Lift*. She is the co-author of the *Science of Horror* book series including the Bram Stoker Award nominated *The Science of Women in Horror*. The most recent installment is the upcoming *The Science of Alfred Hitchcock* coming in 2025. She is also the co-author of *Travels of Terror: Strange and Spooky Spots Across America*, releasing this September. Meg, a mom of two teen boys, is currently a creative writing student at Oxford University.

RUTHANN JAGGE is from Upstate NY, where her favorite month, October, is otherworldly. Folklore, gothic elements, dark fantasy, and mythology inspire her memorable characters and evocative settings. Her work as an author includes a novella, a co-authored novel, reviews, articles, and many short stories featured in successful anthologies.

She's been a guest on compelling interviews and professional panels where she enjoys sharing the creative storytelling process. New work releasing in 2025 includes a highly-anticipated sequel, a Southern Gothic horrormantasy, and several invitational projects.

Extensive travel and backyard superstitions influence her love of writing. Other passions include cooking, sewing, and dancing with her demons. She currently lives on a rural cattle ranch in Texas with her husband and his animals. A large, blended family keeps her sane most of the time. Member HWA/BFS.

CANDY MADONNA - Candice Madonna Eaker, also known as Candy Madonna is an American author from

North Carolina. Traveling the world with her magical husband and constantly expressing ideas with her three incredible children that offer so much life and inspiration to her world. Candy has an Eclectic style of writing. Her first published piece is a spiritual self- help book Gotta Be Shifting Me published by Balboa Press. Now she focuses more on horror genres where she feels her deepest connection and passions. Guided by the spirit world, she writes what is presented to her. Living a life filled with ghosts and now she writes their stories.

JEN MIERISCH - Jen Mierisch's dream job is to write Twilight Zone episodes, but until then, she's a website administrator by day and a writer of odd stories by night. Jen's work can be found in the Arcanist, NoSleep Podcast, Scare Street, and numerous anthologies. Jen can be found haunting her local library near Chicago, USA. She is an active member of the Horror Writers Association.

NORA B. PEEVY is a cat trapped in a human's body. Please send help or tuna. She is an Olympic champion sleeper and toils away for JournalStone/Trepidatio Publishing as a submission reader, a reviewer for Hellnotes, the co-founder and co-editor of Tiny Tales of Terror Quarterly and is reading scripts for The H.P. Lovecraft Film Festival for the second year. Her quirky work is published in Eighth Tower Press, Weird Fiction Quarterly, The Wicked Library Podcast, Sudden Fictions Podcast, and other places. She has stories coming out in five collections this year, her first novel, and her first novelette. As an avid photographer, Nora is also found on Getty Images. Holding a Bachelor of Arts in English with a Concentration in Creative Writing, you can find her on Facebook (as Onyx Brightwing) begging to escape her human body or get tuna. She naps in Milwaukee, Wisconsin.

MOCHA PENNINGTON studied Journalism with a minor in Creative Writing in college. Her short stories have appeared in numerous anthologies, including 2020's *The One That Got Away: Women of Horror Anthology Vol 3* and most recently, *The Encyclopocalypse of Legends and Lore: Volume 1*. When she isn't writing, she is co-hosting Tea Time, a gossip channel on YouTube, which has accumulated over a million views.

EVA ROSLIN is a disabled, neurodivergent, queer writer of fantasy and horror. She is a Canadian author of Armenian and Iranian descent by way of the Great Surgun, Isfahan, and Lori. A previous Mary Wollstonecraft Shelley Scholarship recipient, her work has appeared in "Slay and Slay Again" (Sliced Up Press), "Literally Dead: a Halloween anthology" (Alienhead Press), and "Under Her Skin" (Black Spot Books) among others. She works as a librarian and researcher.

LAUREN LEE SMITH - Born and raised in rural Northern California, Lauren Lee Smith is a novelist and screenwriter whose works confront the darker, more taboo elements of the feminine experience. A mother of three young children, her work explores maternal mental health, trauma, male brutality and the historical intersections of diverse cultures through the lens of feminist horror. Her debut feminist historical horror western '*The Night Pool*' will be published in Fall 2026 with Blackstone Publishing and she is represented by Chad Luibl of Janklow & Nesbit and Matt Berenson for TV/Film.

SONORA TAYLOR (she/her) is the award-winning author of several books and short stories. Her books include *Someone to Share My Nightmares: Stories, Seeing Things, Little Paranoias: Stories, Without Condition, The Crow's Gift and Other Tales*, and *Wither* *and Other Stories*. She also co-edited *Diet Riot: A Fatterpunk Anthology* with Nico Bell. Her short stories have been published by Rooster Republic Press, PseudoPod, Kandisha Press, Camden Park Press, Cemetery Gates Media, Tales to Terrify, Sirens Call Publications, Ghost Orchid Press, and others.

Her short stories and books frequently appear on "Best of the Year" lists. In 2020, she won two Ladies of Horror Fiction Awards: one for Best Novel (*Without Condition*) and one for Best Short Story Collection (*Little Paranoias: Stories*). In 2022, her short story, "Eat Your Colors," was selected by Tenebrous Press to appear in *Brave New Weird: The Best New Weird Horror Vol. 1*. In 2024, her nonfiction essay, "Anything But Cooking, Please," was a Top 15 finalist in Roxane Gay's Audacious Book Club essay contest.

For two years, she co-managed Fright Girl Summer, an online book festival highlighting marginalized authors, with V. Castro. She is an active member of the Horror Writers Association and serves on the board of directors of Scares That Care.

Her latest short story collection, *Recreational Panic*, is now available from Cemetery Gates Media. Her latest novella, *Errant Roots*, is now available from Raw Dog Screaming Press.

She lives in Arlington, Virginia, with her husband and a rescue dog.

Sonora's story in this anthology, *Always In My Ear,* was originally published in her collection, *Little Paranoias: Stories,* in 2019.

ANNE WILKINS is a sleep-deprived primary school teacher in New Zealand. She writes in her spare time (which she has very little of). Her love of writing is fuelled by copious amounts of coffee, reading and hope. Her work can be found in Apex Magazine, Cosmic Horror Monthly, Elegant Literature, All Worlds

Wayfarer, Sci-Fi Shorts and elsewhere. Anne is the winner of the June 2024 "Bad Blood" Elegant Literature Prize, the 2023 "Halloween Frights" Autumn Writers Battle, and the 2023 Cambridge Autumn Festival Short Story Competition.
For more information visit www.annewilkinsauthor.com or facebook.com/annewilkinsauthor

VALERIE B. WILLIAMS - Valerie B. Williams' short fiction has been published by Flame Tree Press, Grendel Press, and Crystal Lake Publishing, among others. Her most recent published story, "Daddy's Girl," appeared in *Bite: A Vampiric Anthology,* from Graveside Press in December 2024. Her debut novel, a story of supernatural suspense titled "The Vanishing Twin," was released by Crossroad Press in October 2024.
Valerie spins twisty tales from her home in central Virginia, which she shares with her very patient husband and equally patient Golden Retriever. When not writing, she can be found reading and drinking either tea or wine, depending on the time of day.
Links: https://linktr.ee/valeriebwilliams

TRISH WILSON writes horror, dark fiction, erotica, romance, and mysteries. She has written using her real name and the pen names Elizabeth Black (for erotica and romance) and E. A. Black (for horror and dark fiction). She grew up in Baltimore, the home of Edgar Allan Poe who inspired her to write. Her short stories have appeared in *Zippered Flesh 2, Zippered Flesh 3, Teeming Terrors, Midnight Movie Creature Feature 2, The Horror Zine's Book of Ghost Stories, Wicked Women, Wicked Tales, Fark in the Time of Covid,* and more. She won a Best Short Story mention on *The Solstice List@ 2017: The Best of Horror* for *Invisible*, which appears in *Zippered Flesh 3*. As Media Director for The Horror Zine, she has interviewed well-known horror writers including Ramsey

Campbell, Kathe Koja, Josh Malerman, Elizabeth Massie, Paul Tremblay, and John Skipp.
Web Site: https://trishwilsonauthor.blogspot.com
Facebook: https://www.facebook.com/elizabethablack

NICOLE M. WOLVERTON is a fear enthusiast and Pushcart-nominated writer of 50-plus works of short fiction, creative nonfiction, and pop culture essays, as well as two novels. Additionally, she served as Editor of BODIES FULL OF BURNING (2021, Sliced Up Press), the first-ever short fiction anthology that centers horror through the lens of menopause.

She lives in the Philadelphia area, where she earned a masters in horror and storytelling from the University of Pennsylvania.

Find her online at www.nicolewolverton.com.

ABOUT THE EDITORS

LYDIA PRIME is a New Jersey born creature of the night. Her dark fiction and emotive poems have been published all over the net. Most notably in the Siren's Call eZine (Sirens Call Publications), The Ladies of Horror Flash Fiction Picture Prompt Challenge (run by the fabulous Nina D'Arcangela and Elaine Pascale), Pen of the Damned, as well as several anthologies from Kandisha Press, Silent House Press, Sinister Smile Press, Pyke Publishing and more. She most recently co-authored the collection, We're Not Ourselves Today, packed with 13 pulp horror tales, with her partner in crimes against fictional beings, Jill Girardi. It includes Prime's story, Sadie, winner of the 2020 Critters Readers poll for best short horror story of the year. When Lydia isn't releasing monstrosities from her mind, she expertly helps others flesh out their brain children through her editing services. Come find her on the socials! She won't bite too much. Link tree - https://linktr.ee/Lydiaprime

JILL GIRARDI is the internationally best-selling, award-nominated author of Hantu Macabre and the founder of Kandisha Press, a company dedicated to women horror authors from around the world. Hantu Macabre has been optioned for film by Siung Films, to be directed by Aaron Cowan, a senior member of the Special FX team that won four Oscars for Lord of The Rings and Avatar. Former MMA fighter Ann Osman is set to star as the lead. Jill loves writing darkly humorous creature features and still believes in twist endings. Find her on Instagram or Twitter @jill_girardi

ABOUT THE FOREWORD AUTHOR

CANDACE NOLA is a multiple award-winning author, editor, and publisher. She writes poetry, horror, dark fantasy, and extreme horror content. She is the creator of Uncomfortably Dark Horror, which focuses primarily on promoting indie horror authors and small presses with weekly book reviews, interviews, and special features. Follow her on all social media and join the Uncomfortably Dark Patreon for free books, merch, and more!

KANDISHA PRESS BOOKS

AVAILABLE NOW ON AMAZON:

UNDER HER BLACK WINGS - Kandisha Press Women of Horror Anthology Vol. 1

GRAVEYARD SMASH - Kandisha Press Women of Horror Anthology Vol. 2

THE ONE THAT GOT AWAY - Kandisha Press Women of Horror Anthology Vol. 3

DON'T BREAK THE OATH - Kandisha Press Women of Horror Anthology Vol. 4

WE'RE NOT OURSELVES TODAY - 13 TALES OF PULP HORROR by Lydia Prime and Jill Girardi

PRETEND YOU DON'T SEE HER - THE INVISIBLE WOMAN Kandisha Press Women of Horror 2025 - Newly Revamped Series!

Printed in Dunstable, United Kingdom